I0658007

A New Breed

#2

THE DAUGHTERS OF DESTINY DIARIES

Cheryl Pryor

Arlington & Amelia Publishing

Copyright © 2020 Cheryl Pryor

Arlington & Amelia Publishing

All rights reserved. No portion of this book may be reproduced or transmitted by any form or by any means, electronic or mechanical, including photocopy, recording, or any information storage and retrieval system without permission in writing from the author or publisher.

This book is a work of fiction. Names, characters, places, and incidents are the product of the author's imagination or are used fictitiously. Any resemblance to actual events, locales, or persons, dead or living is coincidental.

ISBN:1-886541-44-2
ISBN-13:978-1-886541-44-3

First Edition, November 2020

Printed in the United States of America

Books By Cheryl Pryor

Adult

#1 Destiny of The Aliens
#2 A New Breed
Chosen
Children Of The Presidents
Famous Men Throughout History
Women In History Trivia
Where In The U.S. Am I
Where In The World Am I
The Big Book of Presidential Trivia
The Big Book of First Ladies Trivia
Presidents, First Ladies, & First Family Trivia
Presidents Trivia Challenge
First Family Trivia
American Revolution & The Birth Of A Nation
The Big Book of Old Testament Bible Trivia
The Big Book of New Testament Trivia
With Wings Like Eagles
A Humble Spirit
Living the Word of God
Pregnancy Journal
Precious Moments
Treasured Moments Of My Child
My Mother's Life Story
My Father's Life Story
How Much Do You Really Know About The Love Of Your Life
Couples Game Night Challenge
RV Travel & Expense Journal
Wedding Survival Guide

Write Now
Legacy

Children's

My Child's Keepsake Journal
Trivia For Kids: The Presidents
Trivia For Kids: First Ladies
Savannah In The Big Move
Savannah On Stage
Savannah On Horseback
Savannah In Look What Followed Me Home
Savannah & The Grumpy Neighbor
Savannah & The Mad Scientist
Savannah's Disney World Celebration
Savannah Goes To Paris

The Daughters of Destiny Diaries

Destiny Of The Aliens
Book #1

'Destiny Of The Aliens' was the first book in the series of The Daughters of Destiny Diaries.

Elke's life was saved by the aliens when she was but a young girl. The aliens weren't finished with her. She is unaware she has a destiny with the aliens. They are merely biding their time.

Now a young woman in the middle of World War II she is living in Berlin, Germany. She works at a secret location with a scientist who is working on replicating alien technology. The Nazi Party has come into possession of not only flying saucers but aliens.

It is revealed that she has been chosen for a special purpose. Her destiny is revealed and that of her unborn child.

She is to be the carrier, the one chosen to give birth to the first human/alien hybrid...the first of a new breed.

She has no say in the matter. No matter how far she runs they will find her.

Travel with Elke as she escapes Nazi Germany and flees to the Free Zone in France where she joins up with the French Resistance then finally makes her way to America her new home.

Her daughter will become the first of the daughters of destiny.

Her baby's DNA is genetically altered while yet in the womb and becomes the first of the human/alien hybrids.

The daughters of destiny are a new breed whose role is to pave the way for the chosen one. The one who will one day determine the ultimate destiny of the aliens, the humans, and planet Earth.

Elke is given the gift of a diary that came from the aliens. Included is the story of how the aliens first arrived on Earth from the days when the Great Pyramids of Giza were built and the stories of her ancestors throughout many generations whose lives were involved with the aliens.

Her own story will be told in the diary.

The diary will reveal all.

'A New Breed'

#2 Daughters of Destiny Series

A woman who escaped Germany during World War II has now made her home in America. What she brought to America may one day prove to be the biggest threat to not only America but to the entire planet.

She has given birth to a new breed. A child that had been genetically modified by the aliens while yet in her womb.

This new breed known as the Daughters of Destiny will one day determine the fate of planet Earth. Will the aliens one day occupy the planet taking control or will the humans co-exist with the aliens? Neither of these choices are acceptable yet they are a very real possibility.

The head of Project Blue Book has been invited to a private meeting with the president. He is given instructions on meeting a family who he is told will be the most important people he'll ever meet.

As head of Project Blue Book he thought he'd heard of everything. After speaking to the president he learns he's barely begun to scratch the surface of who and what is walking amongst us.

The little girl in the family is the one the president is interested in. She is the first of the Daughters of Destiny.

He has to wonder...what is she? Alien...human...hybrid? Whatever she is...*she is no ordinary girl.*

What is this mission she has been given?

The aliens are there to see to it that her quest is carried out. Even the aliens couldn't foresee how things would turn out.

Follow the life story of the girl from a young child through the days when she becomes a woman, wife, and mother herself. She may appear normal to the untrained eye, but don't be fooled. She is the first of her kind...not quite human...not quite alien. She is the first of a new breed.

Prologue

1970

William stared at the old black and white photograph in his hand. The picture was of two young children building sand castles on the beach.

The picture had been taken on the beach in the same spot where he now looked at through the window of his mother's home.

He walked away from the window and set the photograph on the desk. With a deep sigh he dropped into the seat behind the desk and stared off into space. His eyes occasionally fell on the photograph.

Where are you Nicole? How could you just disappear?

He focused on the photographs his mother had hung on the wall with pride. You could trace the steps of his adult life from the memories on this wall.

His eyes fell on each of the photos, memories of the past. He remembered the day the one was taken of him standing in front of the plane in which he had learned to fly with a huge smile on his face and his thumbs up, the next photo was taken on the day he graduated from the Air Force Academy, and another was taken on the beach exchanging vows with Nicole the day before he left for 'Nam. He knew in each of those occasions in his life Nicole had been sharing those special moments with him.

He knew soon there would be another photo added to the wall. It would be one of his latest achievement. He had fulfilled his dream of becoming an astronaut. His first mission would be a trip to the moon.

He had become the astronaut Nicole had told him he would be before he even knew himself that it was a dream of his.

"You told me the night we met I would marry you one day. I was the happiest man alive the day I became your husband," he spoke to the photo of his bride.

He walked to the window staring out at the ocean waves his mind as turbulent as the sea.

So where is my bride now? And our child?

I imagine by now you've given birth to our baby.

There should be a photo on that wall with our family. Me with my wife and our child. Only my family is missing.

You were there with me when I needed you the most with my child in your belly. You're the very reason I survived and am standing here today.

How could you disappear from my life? Don't you know how badly I need you...how incomplete I am without you?

We belong together. We always did.

Damn it! He banged his fist on the wall.

There's no joy in life without you. You are my life.

He paced the room. He walked out on the back deck and looked at the home Nicole had grown up in as though she would magically appear on her deck waving for him to come over.

But there was no Nicole. No one had lived there for years.

His wife had simply vanished.

1

1952

"The President will see you now, Captain Halloway."

He was startled to hear his name. He had been so deep in his thoughts he had forgotten where he was for a moment.

He'd tuned out all the noise of the typewriters, ringing telephones, and people scurrying in and out of the room seemingly on very important missions, instead concentrating only on this impromptu meeting.

The meeting had seemed very spur of the moment to him. He wasn't sure exactly why he had been called for a private meeting with the president, but he had a pretty good idea of the subject matter they would be discussing.

He stood and walked in the door of the Oval Office which was being held open for him by the president's secretary. Once he entered the president's domain he glanced around seeing for himself a room he had only ever seen on television during presidential interviews.

He had never dreamed as an Iowa farmboy that he would one day wind up in the office of the president for a one-on-one meeting. A meeting the president had requested no less.

The first thing to jump out at him was the president himself. He sat working behind the desk he knew was known as the *Resolute* desk.

The desk had been a gift from Queen Victoria to President Rutherford B. Hayes in the late 1800's. It had been built from the timbers of the British Arctic exploration ship the HMS *Resolute,* hence the name. The desk had quite a history itself and had been used by many presidents.

He glanced down at the Oval Office rug which was a pale green. It wasn't a color he would have chosen, but it was the traditional color of the rug from the last few administrations.

He had been informed by his wife when she learned of his meeting with the president that First Ladies often changed colors in the Oval Office decorating in their own style leaving their mark.

Styles and colors often came and went with changing presidents his wife had told him. That was her forte, not his.

While he wasn't the least bit interested in the color scheme of the Oval Office he knew his wife was so he tried to take it all in so he could tell her all about it later.

The president hadn't looked up when he entered as he was busy scribbling something on a legal pad.

Captain Edward Halloway was a patient man. He was used to waiting on his superiors in the military.

He took a furtive look around him so he could later describe what he saw to his wife and son. They would be anxious to hear about his meeting with the President of the United States.

"Be right with you," the president said without looking up.

While waiting for the president to finish what he was doing he glanced around and admired a painting of Confederate General Robert E. Lee of the Civil War. He couldn't help but wonder to himself why such a man as Eisenhower who had commanded the Allied forces against the Nazis during the Second World War would choose to have a portrait of a man who lost the Civil War hanging in the Oval Office.

He knew that even though General Lee had lost the war he was known to have been an honorable and humble man. Perhaps that alone was enough to deserve a spot hanging on the wall of the Oval Office.

He glanced around trying to take in as much as he could knowing his wife would later drill him like a drill sergeant wanting to know all the details on how the room was decorated and everything he remembered.

He noticed a few landscape paintings which he was too far

away to recognize who the artists were, not that he would probably recognize their names even if he could see them.

What impressed him the most of all of the contents in the room was the statue of Abraham Lincoln. Now this he understood. Lincoln was a president any other honest, upstanding president following in his footsteps would admire and try to emulate.

The statue had captured a contemplative look on the president's face supposedly during the darkest days of our nation during the days of the Civil War. A nation at war with itself.

He heard the president tear the paper off the pad he had been writing on. He seemed preoccupied as he placed his pen in the inkstand and folded the paper in half pushing it to the corner of his desk.

President Eisenhower stood and walked around the desk.

The president had been a military man before becoming president. He was a five star general and had been Supreme Commander of the Allied Forces in the European Theatre during World War Two. Even now he had the bearing and presence of military.

If there was a president that he respected it was this president.

"Sit down Captain," the president said. "I've only a short time before we'll be interrupted for my next meeting so let's get down to business."

The president gestured for the captain to take a seat on the sofa and sat in the chair across from him.

He couldn't help but to notice when the president crossed his legs that he had on golf shoes.

"I imagine you're curious as to why I've called you here," the president said.

Before the captain had a chance to reply the president continued, "Perhaps not. I've heard the news on your assignment as director of Project Blue Book. That's what we're here to talk about."

A tea cart was wheeled in by the same woman who had

ushered him in earlier bringing a pitcher of water and a coffeepot with coffee cups and water glasses.

While she was getting the tray set up the president changed topics and said, "I understand you served in World War Two as a bombardier-navigator."

"Yes sir. I was with the Army Air Corps," he said.

"I was informed that you were highly decorated. Five battle stars, two theater combat ribbons, three Air Medals, and two Distinguished Flying Crosses. Very impressive," the president said.

"Thank you Mr. President," he responded.

"Where were you sta..." the president began before being interrupted.

"Excuse me but shall I serve you before I leave Mr. President," the woman asked standing behind the teacart.

"No, no. This will be a short meeting. If we want anything we'll serve ourselves," the president said.

"Very well then. Your next appointment is in fifteen minutes," she turned to leave the room but before she made it out the door the president called out to her.

"See to it we're not disturbed again regardless if it's past time for my next meeting," the president said firmly.

"Yes Mr. President," she said. "You might want to change your shoes. You won't be golfing anytime soon and those shoes are leaving holes in the floor and rug," she said as she walked out closing the door behind her.

"Damn women," the president said. "Too many women around here always telling me what to do."

Regardless of his grumbling he kicked off his golf shoes and in his socks carried the shoes to the corner putting them next to his golf clubs. He reached under his desk and slipped his shoes on.

The president sat back down and gave the captain his full attention and said, "About your assignment....I'm not here to tell you how to do your job, but I'm curious as to what your thoughts are on Project Blue Book."

"Well Mr. President," the captain said. "It's an interesting assignment. Not anything I expected when I was assigned to the Air Technical Intelligence Center at Wright-Patterson." He appeared to hesitate to say more.

"You don't need to worry about what you say. I've been well informed on what Project Blue Book is all about. Investigating flying saucers and meeting with people who make claims to have seen them isn't your typical assignment."

"No sir it isn't," Captain Halloway said, "though I also worked on Project Grudge so the subject matter isn't entirely new to me."

"I want to assure you that anything said during this meeting stays between you and me. I've made that perfectly clear to your superiors also. You are not to be questioned as to what we discussed or of any information I pass on to you. Understood?"

"Mr. President, I'm really just in the preliminary stages of the interviews. I really don't have anything to report at this time."

The president sat quietly waiting for him to continue.

"This project though on the same subject matter as Project Grudge is different in the fact that I've been interviewing witnesses. Interviewing witnesses who claim they saw something not of this earth is new territory to me. In the past I merely had reports to go by. Working with witnesses, well it's a subject that must be approached with care as you can well imagine."

"Go on," the president encourgaged.

"I'm currently working on interviewing a constantly growing list of the people who have reported sightings to see if it's worth our time to pursue, but I really haven't had time to...."

"I'm sure from what I've heard you're the right man for the position," the president assured him. "I'm really not looking for any information from you at this time. I have to ask though, do you have preconceived ideas going into this?"

As the captain started to answer the president held up his hand and said, "Just a minute, please."

The president cleared his throat before continuing. "What I'm really trying to ask is will you give this your best effort into discovering the truth?"

"Mr. President, I always give any job I'm assigned my best effort," he replied.

"I don't want someone in charge who before even interviewing these people think they're a bunch of crackpots just out seeking attention. Nor do I want someone who doesn't take what they have to say seriously. It's imperative to me to have someone who will really listen to these people and follow up on the evidence *before* coming to any conclusions."

"Understood, Mr. President."

"Both you and I know as military men that there are some strange things witnessed that seem inexplicable. I'd just like to know what you think in all honesty about this subject matter."

"I admit initially I was a bit of a skeptic when I was first made aware of Project Grudge. Since that time I've come across reports from some very credible sources. I've seen and heard too much not to take this seriously."

The president nodded and motioned for him to continue.

"I'm going into this with no preconceived ideas. I'm open-minded and I have no pony in the race either way. I'm out to discover the truth, not sway the facts in any way. The purpose of these interviews is to get to the truth. Like I said, I'm going into this with a completely open mind."

The president stared intently at the captain as though seeing through him, looking to see if he were speaking honestly or just saying what he thought the president wanted to hear.

After a moment he nodded and said, "I believe you. Just know that you may learn some things that will be the complete opposite of what you ever believed possible. What you learn may turn your world upside down. Do you think you can handle the truth?"

"I believe so sir, yes," Captain Halloway said.

The president stood and thinking the meeting was over the captain stood and grabbed his cap. The president motioned for him to sit back down.

"We're not quite through here. Just give me a moment."

The captain eased himself back onto the sofa while the president walked over and reached for the paper he had torn from the pad when he had entered the room.

The president opened the paper that was folded and looked at it again, hesitated for only a moment and said, "There's something I need you to personally attend to. Let me make this *very clear*.... no one else but you and I will ever know about this. And I do mean no one. That includes your superiors."

The president again looked at the paper and seemed to be deep in thought.

"Can I trust you?" the president looked up and asked.

"Yes sir," he answered looking into the president's eyes.

 "Any report you have to make to me on this matter will be done in person. I don't want anything in writing where it could ever fall into the wrong hands. None of your superiors, FBI, CIA, White House personnel, absolutely *no one* other than me is to learn any information you discover in regards to this matter regardless of what they say to you, even if they threaten you, or who they say sent them. Do I make myself very clear?"

"Yes Mr. President," Captain Halloway answered.

"The names on this piece of paper are very important people I want you to meet and interview," he tapped the paper on the armrest of his chair as he spoke.

The president continued, "These people are very knowledgeable on the subject you're now head of. They will be the most important people you'll ever interview on the subject bar none. You can assure them that this information will not be passed on to anyone other than the President of the United States."

"Mr. President, do I understand you correctly in that I am not to include what I learn from them in Project Blue Book?" he asked.

"You understand correctly," the president answered. "You can interview them informing them about your work to let them know you are knowledgeable on the subject, but you are not to report this interview to anyone but me."

"Is there something I should know before I meet them?" he

asked.

"Probably," the president answered in all honesty, "but I think I would prefer it if you went into this meeting with a blank slate, no foreknowledge on the matter or background on them. After you've met them we'll meet again. You'll be given more information at that time."

"When would you like for me to meet with them?" Captain Halloway asked.

"Tomorrow or the next day preferably," the president answered.

The captain's face fell just for a moment but long enough for the president to notice.

"I've been informed you've plans to take your family on vacation this week," the president said. "If it helps I've had my office make arrangements to set you and your family up at a place on the beach in St. Augustine, Florida. Do you think they'd enjoy a trip to the beach?"

"Yes sir," he answered, relieved he wouldn't have to disappoint his family. He knew they'd be thrilled to be spending a week at the beach.

"I'm not much of a host," the president said. "I haven't even offered you a drink."

"I'm fine sir but thank you."

"My secretary will give you your itinerary and flight information on your way out."

The president handed him the paper he had been holding and said, "These are the names and address of the people I want you to interview. Try not to make an enemy out of them or badger them in any way for information. They're not accustomed to opening up to strangers."

He took the paper the president handed him and put it in the briefcase he had brought in with him and stood to go.

The president walked over to his desk and said, "We'll meet here again eight days from today, same time. That should give you plenty of time to meet and interview them. Remember, this is of utmost importance."

"Understood," the captain said.

Before taking a seat behind his desk the president stopped and said, "There's a child. I want you to observe this child very closely. You're a father yourself. You'll know if something is off."

"Off?" he asked.

"You'll know just by observing her. That's all I have to say on the matter at this time. Just be sure you have access to observe the child before you report back to me," the president said as he pulled out the chair from his desk and took a seat.

The president had appeared to bring up the child almost as an afterthought, yet he felt the president meant to broach the subject all along.

By now he knew not to question him any further. The president told him what he wanted him to know and it would do no good to ask any further questions.

"I'll see you in eight days then Mr. President," he said.

Somehow aware their meeting was over the same secretary who had escorted him in now stood in the doorway waiting to show him out.

The president sitting behind his desk merely nodded.

As the captain was leaving he heard the president say under his breath, "This child.... my God, could it even be possible?"

2

"Nicole, don't stick your finger in the icing. Other people are going to eat some too," her mother said.

"Are you making the cake for the visitors who are coming over?" Nicole asked.

"No one is coming over. This is just for the three of us," her mother answered.

"Yes, they are. Visitors are coming over tonight," Nicole insisted. "You'll see."

Nicole dipped her finger in the chocolate icing for one more lick before running out of the room. Just before she went out the doorway she turned to her mother and said, "I know. I'm incorrigible."

Her mother laughed at her precocious daughter. How many little six year old girls even knew what that word meant?

She watched as Nicole ran out of the room.

The thought passed through her mind that her own daughter scared her sometimes knowing things that were going to happen. The scary part was she was never wrong.

So I wonder who's coming over tonight? Elke thought to herself. She was confident that if Nicole said it was so that it would happen.

Klaus came in the house carrying a briefcase and an overnight bag setting them down once he got inside the door just in time to catch his daughter as she ran and jumped into his arms.

Klaus had been one of the German scientists during World

War Two that had been brought to the U.S. during Operation Paperclip and now worked for the U.S. government.

At times Klaus was able to work from home but most weeks he had to be in Alabama where he worked at the U.S. Army Ordnance Guided Missile Project.

"How's my little Schatz?" he asked Nicole hugging her tight.

" Ich habe dich vermisst Papa," Nicole said.

"I missed you too sweetheart," her father said.

"Did you bring me anything?" Nicole asked her father while looking expectantly at his bags.

"Aah, my sweet. Your papa was too busy with work to have time to shop this week. Maybe I have something in here."

He reached in his bag and after rummaging around pulled out a slide rule and handed it to his daughter with a sheepish grin. "Sorry, that's it for toys in my bag."

She looked it over and smiled from ear to ear and said, "Thanks."

She skipped off happy as a lark with her new "toy."

"Now what kind of a toy is that for a six year old?" her mother asked. She walked over and hugged her husband and whispered in his ear, "I missed you too. Did you bring me anything?"

"As a matter of fact I did."

He scooped her up in his arms and carried her towards the bedroom kissing her all over bringing a smile to her face as he carried her to the bedroom kicking the door shut behind him.

"Klaus," Elke laughed while he set her down and reached for her. "It's almost time for dinner and Nicole is...."

"Dinner can wait. I've missed you," he said kissing his wife. "Besides that slide rule will keep Nicole busy."

"A slide rule," Elke laughed. "What six year old knows what to do with a slide rule?"

"We both know she's not your typical six year old. I guarantee you she'll have it figured out in no time," he said.

His wife pulled off his tie, then began unbuttoning his shirt while he kicked off his shoes simultaneously leering at his wife.

Half an hour later Elke was buttoning her blouse as Klaus watched her from the bed.

He asked, "Do you ever regret not going back to work? You're so smart it almost seems a waste to just be a wife and mother."

"I'll do my best not to be insulted by that remark. There's pride in a woman to be a wife and mother and besides Nicole keeps me very busy. She'd be bored to death if all she learned was what she was taught from her teacher at school. She keeps me on my toes trying to teach her myself."

"And you do a great job. I just thought you might get lonely or bored," he said.

While tucking her blouse into her skirt she said. "It would be nice to have an adult friend to spend time with on occasion but apparently Nicole is my destiny. It's been made clear to me that my role in life is to prepare her for hers. By the way, we're expecting guests this evening."

"Oh, and who might that be?" Klaus asked.

"I have no idea but Nicole told me we're having visitors so expect to have company this evening."

"Visitors?" Klaus asked. "Hmm....Would that be the earthly kind or visitors from another planet?" He asked.

Elke groaned and said, "I didn't even think about that. She did say visitors, not people. I guess we'll find out before the evenings over one way or the other."

"Actually, our *visitors* have been unusually quiet and distant for some time. Perhaps they've moved on and forgotten all about us," Klaus said.

"I hardly think that's likely being that Nicole is one of their daughters of destiny," Elke said.

"Yes, I'm not likely to forget that my precious little daughter holds the key to the future of the aliens. I can't quite wrap my head around that," he said.

Elke frowned and said, "If I hadn't read it myself in the daughters of destiny diaries I would laugh it off. Unfortunately it appears my lineage have been chosen for a role we have no choice in. I can't say that I'm happy about it."

"Do you think she knows?" Klaus asked his wife.

"I doubt it," she said sitting back down on the edge of the bed. "I had no clue either when I was growing up. I was familiar with their visits in my younger days. Over time as I grew older I tried to convince myself it never happened until I wasn't able to deny it anymore."

"We try to shut out what we would rather not face," Klaus said. "Perhaps that's what you did."

"I think my father did his best to keep my mother from telling me anything when I was a child. She disappeared from my life before I could ever question her about what it all meant."

"And then you came to work for me..."

"Yes, well that was certainly insightful working firsthand with an alien. I wonder if he ever made it back to his kind," Elke thought back in time to their days in Germany.

"Whether he did or didn't they haven't lost sight of you or our daughter," Klaus said. "One thing I've learned is you can never run far enough. They always find you..."

"Unfortunately," Elke said as she stood and walked towards the door. "Dinner will be ready soon."

She threw him a kiss as she left the room.

3

Bill hung onto the stair rail climbing up the steps to the airplane. There was a lot of activity going on that had him mesmerized. Workers were loading the luggage into the bowels of the plane while others were driving carts and delivering the meals the passengers would be served. It was a beehive of activity on the tarmac.

The engines were so loud he couldn't hear what his mother was saying. He tripped not keeping an eye on where he was going.

His mother reached down catching him and said in his ear, "I told you to watch where you were going. Move along now. You're holding up the line."

The stewardesses greeted him with a smile as he entered the airplane.

One of the stewardesses helped his mother pointing the way to where their seats were but something had caught Bill's eye. The door to the cockpit was open and peering in he could see the pilot and co-pilot. The co-pilot spotted him and waved.

His father with a firm hand on his back said, "Come on. They've work to do. Let's go get our seats."

"I want to be a pilot someday just like them," Bill told his father.

The Halloway family exited the plane on the tarmac. Liz said, "It sure is hot here."

"We are in Florida," Edward said to his wife while wiping his forehead with his handkerchief. "Hot and humid. I don't know how people can live in this kind of heat."

"I can't wait to go to the beach," Bill said.

It had been a long time since the family had a chance to vacation anywhere other than to visit family. With Edward's schedule they didn't get to even do that very often.

While waiting for their luggage a woman walked forward and asked, "Are you Captain Halloway?"

When he shook his head yes she explained, "The hotels were booked solid being that there are a few conventions in town this week. We've rented you a small cottage on the beach. It will be available to you and your family for the entire month."

"We're only going to be here for a week," he told her.

"Funny, that's not what I understood," she said with a frown. "Well maybe your wife and son can stay longer and enjoy it if you have to get back to work. Regardless, it's yours to enjoy until the end of the month."

She handed him a map and pointed out how to get to the house. She gave him the keys to the house and another key ring for a car that had been rented for their use and told him where they could find it in the parking lot. She handed him her business card and said to call if he had any problems or questions.

"Can we Dad?" Bill asked. "Can we stay for the whole month?"

His dad started to answer and his wife spoke up and said, "That would be a lovely vacation and you could come down on the weekends or perhaps even work from the cottage."

"We'll see," he answered.

They were quite impressed with the small cottage they'd been given to stay in. It was small but had three bedrooms so he would be able to set up one bedroom for an office. The best part was they were right on the beach.

His wife walked in the room he had chosen to use for his office and said, "We're going to need some groceries. Would you mind running to the store just to pick up enough things for the next day or so? If you'll go I'll stay here and get the bedding on the beds and unpack."

Thinking he could drive by and see where the family lived the president had sent him to interview he agreed.

His son begged to come along and since he rarely had time to spend with him while working he was happy to have his son's company.

He shouldn't have been surprised to find that the Newhouse family lived just a few doors down. He wondered if the story about the hotels all being booked were true. It seemed a bit too convenient that he was just doors away from the couple he was to visit.

There were some dunes between their house and another house that sat back a ways, but there would be a clear view of their house from the back deck of the cottage where they were staying.

They picked up the groceries from the list his wife had given him along with a few other items Bill insisted were necessary for a proper vacation.

On the way back to the cottage he drove back by the Newhouse's home. This time he saw a car in the driveway that hadn't been there before. Thinking he was lucky to find them all home he thought it might be a good time to go and introduce himself.

"Wait in the car Bill," his dad said pulling off to the side of the road. "I won't be long."

4

He reminded Bill to wait in the car. He quietly closed the car door behind him and looked around to be sure the car was parked in an area that would be safe for his son to sit and wait for him.

It wasn't often he felt awkward of how to go about a job but he felt like he was pretty much in the dark about this assignment. Considering the fact that he had been asked by the President of the United States himself to do this he knew it must be very important.

He walked up to the door and before ringing the doorbell ran a hand through what little hair he had. He'd just wing it he thought. This was just to open the door to introduce himself and hopefully gain their trust before he got down to business.

He noticed as he rang the doorbell that his hand was shaking. He'd fought in a war and faced all types of dangerous situations so what was it about this assignment that left him unsettled he couldn't help but wonder.

The door was flung open by a little girl that appeared to be about the age of his son. She had a big smile on her face that was framed by her hair that was so blonde it was almost white. Even for such a young child he couldn't help but to notice how pretty the little girl was.

"I was wondering when you'd get here," she said while opening the door wide so he could enter.

He looked at her puzzled thinking perhaps she thought he was someone else.

"Nicole, go clean up your mess in the kitchen," her father said as he walked in the room.

She ran off to the kitchen and told her mother that their visitor was here.

Her mother looked at her with a resigned expression on her face. She finished putting the frosting on the cake while wondering why she ever doubted what her daughter said even when she had no way of knowing these things.

Nicole forgetting about her mess as her father had called it ran outside on their back deck where her father had a large telescope set up for them.

She and her father spent many nights out on the deck watching the stars, moon, and planets. He would often tease her when they spotted a shooting star and would say, "There goes an alien spaceship going to visit some unsuspecting human."

Her mother would give his father *the look*, as he called it, when he did this.

So that must be the child Edward thought as he watched her skip off to another room. She seemed perfectly normal to him.

What was it about this little girl that held the interest of the president?

"Excuse me. I'm forgetting my manners," he said as the man of the house stood there watching him watch his little girl.

He held his hand out and said, "I'm Edward Halloway. My family and I have rented the cottage a few doors down from yours for the month. I thought I'd just stop by and introduce myself."

"Nicholas Newhouse," Klaus gave his name and shook the man's hand.

When Klaus had arrived in the United States working for the government with other German scientists he had Americanized his name in hopes that people with long memories wouldn't hold his German citizenship against him. He knew many people had lost loved ones in the war and maybe wouldn't look too kindly on "the enemy" being their neighbors.

He had since become an American citizen as had his wife. People he worked with knew him as Nicholas, however those close to him and everyone else still called him Klaus.

He gave this stranger his Americanized name to test him to see if he reacted to it. Klaus would then know if he already knew his name and had previous information on him and his family.

"Come in and have a seat," Klaus said to their visitor. "Why did you choose to vacation in St. Augustine? And where is home?"

Edward found himself answering a lot of questions and began to feel he was the one being interviewed.

Elke came in the room a few minutes later and introduced herself. When he explained he was there with his family on vacation she said, "You must bring your wife over. If you don't have any plans come over tomorrow evening. We'll have a cook-out."

She ignored the dirty look Klaus was sending her way.

What a lucky break he thought. He was invited back into their home. He wasn't sure how he'd arrange an interview with his wife and son along but if nothing else it was an opportunity he hadn't foreseen.

"I'm sure she'd love that," he answered.

"Good. Tomorrow evening about 6:00 then," she said.

"Does that work for you Nicholas?" Edward asked not wanting to be an unwelcome guest.

"Nicholas?" Elke said shooting her husband a dirty look. "All our friends call him Klaus. Please, call him Klaus since we're going to be friends and neighbors."

"6:00 is fine and yes call me Klaus," he answered a bit stiffly.

Klaus sat quietly watching the man intently. He had noticed immediately that the man was military and doubted that he had just picked their house randomly to come introduce himself.

Klaus wondered about the man. Was he CIA? Were they still being watched? Well, of course they were. He was a German scientist who had worked for the Nazi regime regardless of how he felt about them and their agenda. The Germans would never really be trusted by the American government. And now his wife had invited this CIA agent or whoever he was back into their home for a social visit no less.

"Klaus? You're German then. My grandparents immigrated from Germany. They came from a small town. Perhaps you're familiar with the area. Kallstadt was the name of the town. It's in the southwest of Germany," Edward said.

"I'm familiar with the area. It's not too far from the French border. Have you ever been to visit?" Nicole asked.

"I'm afraid I haven't but perhaps one day," Edward said.

"Come in the kitchen and have a piece of cake," Elke said.

"I really should go," Edward said. "My son is waiting outside in the car."

"No, he's out back on the deck with our daughter. They seem to be having a wonderful time. Come on and sit for awhile and enjoy a piece of cake. I already took them out a slice and a glass of milk," Elke insisted.

Not wanting to turn down any opportunity of hospitality he agreed and followed her and Klaus into the kitchen. He pulled a chair up at the table and glanced down at some papers strewn across the table.

He was confused by what he saw in the few moments he had to look at it before Klaus scooped up the paperwork along with a slide rule and said, "I told Nicole to clean up her mess."

"You know Nicole," his wife said as she was cutting the cake. "Her mind is in other places. Cleaning up behind herself isn't a priority."

Nicole? That young child made those calculations he saw on those papers? There's no way a child of six or seven years of age could make those calculations and know how to use a slide rule no less.

He had noticed the handwriting had been sloppy like a childs, but the mathematical calculations was anything but that of a child. His mind was full of questions with what that could mean.

Elke placed a piece of cake in front of him and a glass of milk.

He heard the laughter of his son and glanced out on the deck. He could see his son looking at the little girl with a quizzical look on his face.

He would most definitely have to question his son later about the little girl. Perhaps he could learn more from him than he could on his own.

"This is a really cool telescope," Bill said in awe.

"Look at how bright the stars are," Nicole said adjusting the magnification.

"When you turn this dial it brings them so close they look like you could reach out and touch them."

"Wow! There goes an airplane," Bill said excitedly. "We flew in one of those today. I'm going to be a pilot when I grow up."

"Of course you are," Nicole said.

He just looked at her and smiled glad she hadn't made fun of him about him saying he wanted to be a pilot.

"Why did you tell me your name is Bill? Your name is William," Nicole said.

Nicole looked through the eyepiece and adjusted the telescope where Bill could see the moon.

"How did you know my name is William?" he asked. "Everyone calls me Bill even though my first name is really William."

She stepped back. "Here, look at the moon William."

He started to correct her but instead just shrugged and looked through the telescope.

"That's the moon?" Bill asked while peering through the eyepiece of the telescope. "It doesn't look like I thought it would. There's craters and everything. That is so cool."

Nicole said, "One day you'll go there."

"What do you mean?" Bill asked while looking through the telescope in amazement.

"You're going to be an astronaut and travel to the moon that you're looking at," she said.

Bill laughed and pulled back from the telescope and looked at her in a strange way. He laughed but could see she was dead serious.

"I don't know about that. I just decided today I want to be a pilot. I'm not sure I want to be an astronaut."

"You will," she said with assurance. "You'll go to the moon and you'll marry me one day."

"I'm only seven. I don't think I want to get married," he said.

"That's O.K. I'll wait for you, but you will marry me one day," she said confidently.

She dropped the subject much to his relief by adjusting the telescope and showing him the planet Venus. She explained that most people believed it was the closest planet to Earth.

"It looks like it is," Bill said looking through the telescope.

"Venus is closest to Earth as it passes by on its orbit but Mercury is closest to Earth the longest," she explained.

Bill looked at her and said, "You're scary smart. How do you know that stuff?"

"I just know," she answered.

"I just finished second grade. After this summer I'll be going into third grade," Bill said.

Nicole said, "I go to school but my mom and dad teach me too. Plus I read a lot of books."

"We might be staying here a whole month," Bill said. "I can't wait to go to the beach and look for shells."

"I'll go with you," she said. "We'll be good friends."

Bill looked at her and smiled. She was awful cute and it would be fun to have a friend to do things with while he was here.

His father poked his head out of the sliding glass door and said, "Bill, we need to go. Your mother will wonder what happened to us."

The adults said their good-byes and confirmed their plans for the following evening.

As they walked out Edward thought to himself that he hadn't learned much but he now had a foot in the door.

It didn't hurt that his son and their daughter were about the same age and seemed to get along.

If nothing else with his son there it had made his story of being there with his family more credible.

For some reason he had the impression Klaus hadn't trusted him but he couldn't figure out why that would be.

He thought his son might come in handy with him learning more about the little girl.

Nicole...yes, that was the little girl's name. He would have to question him later about her .... *the little girl who seemed to be a mathematical genius.*

5

"I thought the two of you had gotten lost you took so long," Liz said as she stood in the doorway waiting for her husband and son to bring in the groceries.

"We went by our neighbors house and we're invited to a cook-out tomorrow," Bill said excitedly.

"You stopped at a neighbor's?" Liz said surprised at this bit of news. Not only was it strange her husband chose to call on strangers but to do so in the evening hours was a strange move on his part.

"They have a kid my age," Bill said. "Too bad it's a dumb girl."

"Dumb she's not," his father muttered under his breath.

He reached over and kissed his wife on the cheek and apologized for their delay.

"I brought you a piece of chocolate cake the neighbor sent home with me though," he said knowing her weakness for anything chocolate. "Will that make up for us being late?"

Smiling at the thought of chocolate she said, "Only if it's a big piece and I don't have to share."

After Bill got in the bathtub Liz turned on her husband and said, "O.K., spill the beans. I know you didn't just happen to stop by a neighbor's house to introduce yourself. That's not like you at all. What's going on?"

He just sat and looked at her and asked her how her chocolate cake was.

"Nice try," she said knowing he was trying to change the subject.

"Is that why we're here in St. Augustine instead of on the family farm in Iowa? Not that I'm complaining, mind you. The beach is quite a nice change of pace, but I doubt it's something you thought up all on your own."

"You know there's some aspects of my work I can't talk about," he said with a sigh knowing his wife would dig until she began to unravel all his secrets. "And this is definitely something I can't talk about."

"Ah-ha, so it is a working vacation," she exclaimed. "I knew I was on the right track. So, who are these neighbors of ours that you just had to stop and introduce yourself to within an hour of arriving in St. Augustine?"

He looked up at her with a pleading look on his face and said, "Liz please, let this go. All I can say is that it was the president who sent me here and that's more than I should say."

"O.K.," she said. "I understand your work isn't meant to be public knowledge but just know that as your wife I can keep a secret. If you need a sounding board I'm here to listen."

"Thanks," he said. "I appreciate your understanding."

"Doesn't mean I promised not to try to figure out a few things on my own," she teased.

"Liz..."

Bill came back in the room wearing his pajamas and asked his dad if they were allowed to read the books in the bookcase.

"I don't see why not as long as you take good care of the book and return it when you're finished with it," his dad answered.

His son turned around and went in the other room to get a book he had spotted.

"Was that my son? Wanting to read a book?" his mother asked.

She picked up the plate now devoid of one very large piece of chocolate cake and put it in the sink to wash.

Bill came back in the room carrying a book on the planets. "Nicole let me look through her telescope. You should see it Mom. It makes the moon look so close and I saw the planet Venus and...

Nicole's funny. She's a little strange but she's nice."

"Strange in what way?" his dad asked.

"When I told her I wanted to be a pilot she told me I was going to be an astronaut."

His mother let out a loud chuckle. "You'd better study hard if you want to be an astronaut."

"I didn't say I *wanted* to be one. I said she told me I would be one. It does sound kinda neat though."

"What else did the two of you talk about?" his dad asked.

His wife looked over Bill's head at her husband with a puzzled look on her face. Since when was he interested in a conversation between two seven year olds she wondered.

"She said she was going to marry me one day," Bill said. "I just might marry her too if she can make chocolate cake as good as her mother."

"That's my boy," his mother laughed.

"I'm going to go look at this book. Then maybe tomorrow if we look through the telescope I'll know what I'm looking at."

After he walked out his mother said softly to her husband, "Seven year olds talking about getting married. I thought I had years yet to start worrying about girls."

"Apparently not," her husband chuckled.

6

"So you didn't find it strange that some random tourist just shows up knocking on our door?" Klaus asked his wife as she handed him another dish to dry.

"We've been in America how many years now and still you don't trust anyone?" she asked. "How sad for you."

"It's obvious he's military," Klaus said. "I ought to know. I've had to deal with enough of them."

"So because he's in the military you don't trust him? You think everyone has an ulterior motive?" his wife asked.

"Not everyone, but no I don't trust the military anymore than they trust us. He may be CIA and coming to spy on us," Klaus insisted.

"Let's give him the benefit of the doubt," his wife said taking the dish towel out of his hands and heading out of the kitchen. "I look forward to meeting his wife tomorrow. It will be nice to have a friend even for the short time they're here."

As she left she turned the light out leaving him standing in the dark.

The Halloways had walked over for the cookout being a short distance and a nice walk on the beach.

The two women hit it off instantly and the kids were inseparable having the time of their lives. The two men however were awkward around each other and carried on little conversation between themselves regardless of how hard Edward tried.

Edward thought of this on their walk home thinking it wasn't like him to feel ill at ease with anyone. He normally had a way to make people feel comfortable around him. It was part of what made him so successful in getting people to open up to him on a topic that other people ridiculed them about. But in this case he couldn't figure out why Klaus didn't seem to trust him.

"It was a lovely time, wasn't it?" Liz said intruding on his thoughts.

She looked up and saw the scorn on his face and said, "Oh dear, didn't go so well with you and Klaus did it?"

"No it didn't," he answered abruptly. "I feel like I've failed. What will I say..." he caught himself and stopped before he said any more.

"What will you say to the president? Is that what you were going to say?" his wife asked.

He gave her a dirty look.

She said, "Bill is far enough away he can't hear. And who am I going to tell? You can trust me Edward."

He remained quiet so she continued, "Perhaps it was that question you asked him if he ever saw any unidentified flying saucers through his telescope? That was a strange thing to ask a complete stranger don't you think?"

"I said it jokingly," he answered gruffly.

"Perhaps you're pushing whatever you're trying to do too fast. Give him time to get to know you a little and trust you."

"I don't have time," he answered. "I have very little time and I really need to get back to my work."

The next day he got a call from the president's office asking if they could move the date up for his next meeting. He knew it wasn't really a question as you didn't turn down a request to meet with the president.

His wife was in the kitchen making a picnic lunch for them all to enjoy on the beach. He chose his words wisely.

"I thought about it and I think it would really be nice for us to stay here for the entire month the cottage is available to us," he said.

She looked at him suspiciously trying to figure out his motive.

"Just last night you were talking about having to get back to work, so what's up? I feel like I'm being buttered up."

"You are," he admitted. "I just got a call that I have to meet with the president tomorrow rather than next week. I thought before the meeting I would fly to the office and pick up some work that I can take care of from here. I may have to fly out for a few interviews if they aren't something I can delegate to someone else, but at least we'd be able to stay here for the remainder of the month. Would you like that?"

She beamed from ear to ear and put the knife down she had been using to make the sandwiches and gave him a big hug.

"Really?" she said pulling back and looking at him. "We can stay for the entire month?"

"I don't see why not. There are a few interviews I can take care of that are closer to this location than if I flew out from the base so it will be easy to justify with the higher-ups."

"Will you have any time to rest and enjoy our time here?" she asked.

"I promise. We'll do some things together as a family. Will you be O.K. here while I'm gone?" he asked.

"We'll be fine," she said. "You take care of what you have to do."

Klaus was also flying out to spend a week working in Alabama which left plenty of time for the children and women to spend together and get to know each other better.

7

The two women were under a large umbrella sitting on beach chairs while the two kids built a sand castle nearby.

Liz sat quietly as her new friend confided in her about how she had come to live in the states. In a matter of days they had become good friends.

She was speechless listening to the life story of this brave woman. She listened in awe as her new friend described how she had escaped Nazi Germany alone while expecting a baby.

Elke described how she had made her way out of Germany through enemy territory in France and saved the life of an American pilot who had been shot down.

Thinking her husband Klaus had been killed in a bombing raid she married the American pilot in order to come to America to start a new life.

She had for a time worked with the French Resistance and just a few weeks before her baby was born sailed across the Atlantic arriving in a strange country to live with a family who were strangers.

"Your life story makes this novel I'm reading boring in comparison," Liz said.

Elke just laughed and said, "It seems so long ago. It almost seems like it happened to someone else."

Liz thought of all this woman had endured. "How was it that you found out that Klaus was still alive?"

"I saw him on the television one day," she answered. "You can imagine how shocked I was since I'd been told he was dead."

"But weren't you married to the American pilot then? How did the two of you get back together?" Liz asked.

"Shannon my American husband's current wife who was his girlfriend before he went to war and I had become friends..."

"My goodness that's a story in itself," Liz interrupted. "You should write a book on your life story, only I'm afraid no one would believe it."

Elke looked at her and said, "You have no idea how right you are. Anyway, you'll meet them soon. They're coming to visit next week."

"You're friends with your ex and his wife?" Liz asked.

"Oh yes, the very best of friends," she answered. "Like I believe our own children will be."

Liz glanced over at the two kids. Having given up on the sand castle they now stood at the water's edge holding hands and jumping over the waves laughing when they got splashed.

Liz couldn't help to smile at the scene and reached for the camera in her beach bag. She shot a few more pictures of the children. She thought the one she had taken of them building a sand castle would be especially cute showing both their faces smiling adoringly at each other.

"According to my son he told me he and Nicole are getting married," Liz told Elke as she put the camera away.

Elke looked over at the children and said, "Is that so?"

Liz explained, "He said the night they met Nicole told him he was going to marry her one day. Isn't that cute?"

"If Nicole told him that then I guess we can assume it'll happen."

Liz looked at her to see if she was kidding but she looked very serious when she said it.

"So he's to be a part of all this," Elke said gazing intently at the children seeming to forget about Liz sitting right beside her. "His destiny has been written then."

Before Liz could ask her what she meant Elke shook her head as if coming out of a stupor and said, "Let's go down and join the kids and cool off."

8

Edward stood by as the president standing on the green judged his distance to the hole. His head and knees bent, his shoulders rounded, he gently swung the golf club back and forth before gently tapping the ball into the cup. It was mesmerizing to watch.

He had previously heard that the president, an avid golfer, had a putting green installed on the White House lawn and that's where the president had revealed the life story of Sophie DuBois aka Elke Newhouse.

The president explained when he met her she went by the name of Sophie DuBois. She had been forced to change her name when she went in hiding from the Germans. She changed back to Elke once she came to America.

While the president concentrated on making his putt he thought about everything the president had revealed to him. It was a remarkable story. He had a feeling the president was saving the best for last, otherwise he couldn't understand what any of it had to do with him as interesting as it was.

It was an impressive story but for what purpose did the president tell him this and set in motion for him to meet her and her family?

It was a hot day for Washington. He wiped the sweat from his brow and wondered how the Secret Service agents who stood at a distance out of earshot but close enough to protect the president in an instant could stand being out in this heat with suits on.

The president made his putt and reaching down for his golf ball he stuck it in his pocket and said, "Let's continue this conversation in my office. We'll have a drink and you can cool off."

"Thank you Mr. President," Edward said. "I grew up in the north. I'm not used to this heat."

"How's the family enjoying the beach?" the president asked

walking beside the captain.

"It's going to be hard to get them to leave," he answered. "I think they're enjoying themselves quite a bit."

"I hear your wife and son have become friends with Elke and her daughter."

"They seem to get along pretty well," he said.

He had noticed the president hadn't said this as a question but more of a statement of something he was already aware of.

They reached the Oval Office and the president pointed out the tea tray and said, "Help yourself. I need to change my shoes before I get chewed out again."

He poured himself a glass of ice cold water grateful for it after being out in the oppressive heat. He sat down thankful to be back in the air conditioning and waited for the president to take a seat.

"I guess you know there's more to this story," the president said leaning forward.

"I assumed so," he answered.

The president then told him the rest of the story. What he was told left him stunned.

He had heard stories of people believing to have been abducted by aliens but this was much more than anything he had been told by others.

His job was to focus on whether or not UFOs were real. Aliens were a whole other topic, though one he had to admit almost every witness wanted to talk about.

He had given the subject of aliens a lot of thought. He didn't have the evidence to say one way or the other if they came to earth and interacted with people as many of the witnesses had claimed. Just the idea that....

"Even though she was very forthcoming in her story at the time I always felt she wasn't quite telling me everything," the president said.

"I can't imagine what else there could possibly be," he said. "She worked with an alien, communicated with him, and had involvement with aliens since she was a child. Do you believe she was credible? Do you believe all of this could possibly be true?"

The president sat and thought about his question wondering just how much he should reveal.

"There's much the public doesn't know about all we learned and what some of our pilots themselves saw during the war over in Germany. I guess that opened the door for me in learning that there could possibly be extraterresterial life. No, not possibly," the president said matter-of-factly. "There really couldn't be any other explanation. I've come to accept it as fact. Yes, I believe it."

"I have to admit," he confided to the president, "since I've been working on Project Blue Book my days of being a doubter are long gone. But aliens involved in humans... I just don't know what their purpose would be in coming here."

"That's the million dollar question isn't it," the president said.

"Why would the aliens come here to study us and our lives when they appear to be so far advanced? It would be like a genius like Albert Einstein going back to first grade. What could they possibly learn that they don't already know?"

"That's what is imperative that we find out," the president said. "I wonder if the aliens are still contacting her in any way."

"I doubt she's going to confide that answer to me," he told the president.

"I guess I sent you in there with your hands tied," the president sighed. "I just thought it would be best if you could get a feel for who they were before you knew about them. I thought it would be too difficult for you to hide that from them or they would sense you knew somehow."

"I can hardly go in there now and tell her I know who you are and that you have worked with an alien. I need you to tell me about them and if they still visit you. I just don't see that happening. Normally people who have seen an unidentified flying object..."

The president interrupted, "I heard you coined the term UFO. I like that."

"I guess I got tired of writing it all out over the years and after abbreviating it a few times it just made sense to call it that," he said.

He hesitated before continuing and said, "Mr. President, normally people who have seen a UFO contact us and *want* to talk about it. They're seeking answers. It sounds to me as though Elke and her husband were trying to leave it behind them."

"No doubt," the president answered. "She was certainly anxious to start a new life. Understandable with the hardships she endured."

The president got up and went to his desk looking over a piece of paper while talking. "She was married to an American pilot at the time I met her."

The president pulled the paper out and glanced at it for a minute and then said, "Bishop. Connor Bishop was the pilot's name she married. I've been informed she and her current husband are still friends with the pilot."

"And you say her second husband the American was shot down by aliens and healed by them," he asked amazed at all he'd learned.

"That was the story I was told. His X-rays were checked and there are no signs of any fracture or of any medical procedure whatsoever," the president answered.

"Then what makes you believe he was healed by the aliens and not just maybe spending a few extra days in hiding with a beautiful woman? I mean Elke is extraordinarily beautiful. I can see where he would have been tempted to do just that," Edward asked. "That seems more credible to me than being taken aboard an alien spaceship and being healed."

"I have good reason to believe his story," the president said leaving it at that.

"Perhaps I should interview him also," Edward thought out loud.

"I think that would be a very good idea," the president agreed. "I really would like to know if the aliens have stayed in contact with her."

Edward was busy scribbling notes to himself to interview Connor Bishop the American pilot.

"Are we as a nation at risk from their visitations? What do they want from us?" the president asked thinking out loud.

"And you think Elke has those answers?"

"No probably not," the president answered. "I believe the aliens would be very secretive about their plans, especially if we are in danger.

Edward sat contemplating all he had learned and what the president was saying about the purpose of the alien's visits.

He himself had wondered why and how many times they had visited Earth and for what period of time this had all taken place. He knew those questions would most likely go unanswered.

Now that he was convinced the aliens and UFOs were indeed real and not a figment of people's imaginations it seemed even more important to find out their purpose in coming here.

He had heard dozens of times now of healing and medical procedures that supposedly went on while taken on board the UFOs. Their powers were way beyond anything the United States was capable of.

"As a pilot it's beyond my comprehension how they travel through space, possibly traveling through a different universe and survive it," Edward said.

"Believe me, men far more intelligent than I have wondered the same thing," the president answered.

The president got up and opened his desk and pulled out a large manila envelope sealed with some type of wax. It had the presidential seal stamped on the outside of the envelope.

Handing it to Captain Halloway he said, "Give this to Klaus and Elke Newhouse and I think perhaps they may then be more willing to open up to you. Elke was willing once before to confide in me. I wasn't the president then. I'm hoping she'll be willing to do so again through you."

"And Klaus?" he asked.

"I never met the man," the president said. "Once I learned he was married to Elke I admit I did have a hand in making arrangements that he was one of the sceintists chosen to be brought to the states during Operation Paperclip. He works for our government now. Even though I understand he has some trust issues with us I believe he'll think it in his best interest to be forthcoming."

The room was filled with silence as both men were lost in their thoughts.

The president spoke first asking, "The child? What are your impressions of the girl?"

He glanced at the president and wondered what was it that he was really asking.

"She seems like a typical seven year old to me other than the fact..."

"Six. She's six years of age but go on..." the president leaned forward to hear what he had to say.

"She has quite a vocabulary. She doesn't speak like a young child but like someone older."

"What else did you notice?" the president probed.

"She's incredibly bright. Way beyond her years from the little I've seen in her math skills," he answered. "I've only seen her for brief moments but from what I saw I was really quite amazed."

He went on to explain what he had seen from the papers she had written and of the few conversations he or his family had with her. He could see the president was disappointed that he didn't have more information to give him.

"May I ask what it is that intrigues you about this little girl? It may help me when I'm searching for more answers for you."

The president gave it some thought and said, "I have to wonder who's child she is."

"You mean is she Klaus' or the American pilot?" he asked.

"No, she couldn't be the pilots. The time doesn't add up, so you can count him out of the equation. What I mean," the president said as he leaned closer towards Edward, "Is she the child of Klaus as her mother claims or could she be the child of the alien? Or something else entirely?"

This wasn't what he expected to hear at all.

The child of an alien? And what did he mean by 'something else entirely'?

Where could the president have gotten such an idea? Everything about Elke's story made it sound credible that the little girl was Klaus' daughter.

"What would give you that idea, if I may ask?" he asked the president knowing he may have crossed the line questioning the president.

"I've had them watched. With the story she told me and that of her pilot husband and both their interactions with aliens I felt I had no choice but to do so. They bore watching is all. We must know if these aliens are a threat to us and if they are using humans in any way that could be a threat to this nation."

"But that doesn't explain your interest in the child," he said hoping to learn more.

"After Elke gave birth there were many reports of UFO's in the area, within just a few miles of their home. Several times in fact. It seemed to me to be far more than just coincidence."

"I seem to recall quite a few reports of sightings in Alabama around that time frame," he said.

"As a matter of fact," the president continued, "one of the men who I had watching her reported seeing a UFO himself. Yet he recalls very little. He seems to have lost track of about an hour or two of his time. And this happened to him twice in a very short time span."

When it seemed the president had no more to say on the matter he pushed for more information. "And you think they... the aliens what? I'm not sure I understand?"

"I have to wonder what their interest is in the child. It seems to me there's no doubt they have somehow tracked them here to the states. They changed countries, names, crossed an ocean, and live on another continent and still the aliens find them. How is that? And why?" the president asked. "What's their interest?"

"It seems to me it's Elke they're interested in and not the child," Edward said after giving it some thought.

"There's something unusual about that child," the president admitted. "There have been reports that her school wanted her tested further. Some of the reports even used the term genius to describe her. This is at six years of age mind you. Then it appears out of the blue she quieted down and has little to say in the classroom. I believe she was told to hide her intelligence perhaps is a good way to say it."

"She does appear to be far above her age level I agree," he said. "I'll keep a closer eye on her and see what else I can learn."

The president said, "It's also her appearance. Did you notice anything different about her looks?"

"She's a beautiful child no doubt about it, but then so is her mother. She certainly doesn't resemble aliens from the descriptions I've been given," he answered.

"Very blonde, blue eyes, pale skin, but a remarkable beauty for such an age," the president said as though under his breath.

"And that concerns you?" he asked thinking the president was way off base on this one topic.

"Have you heard any talk at all about hybrids? A mix of aliens and humans?" the president asked.

Now he really had his interest. "I admit I have but I never gave it any credence. It seemed so far fetched."

"And alien beings from another planet or universe isn't?" the president asked with a chuckle.

"You have a valid point but I don't know...."

"You don't have all the information in Project Blue Book that's out there I'm afraid. My hands are tied and I'm unable to reveal more other than what's been reported," the president said clearly frustrated at not being able to reveal all that he knew in order to get to the bottom of this dilemma.

"I do have Top Secret clearance on this Mr. President," he said. "I can't come up with credible conclusions without knowing all the facts."

The president knew if he were to get the answers he needed he would have to give him a little more information.

The president cleared his throat and said, "I can tell you that I have good reason to believe there are Nordic looking types that appear human that are actually aliens living here on earth. If not aliens then hybrids, from alien and human..."

"My God, is that even possible?" Edward asked astounded.

He stood up and began to pace the room. The thought of the possibilities of what that could mean to life here on Earth made him feel physically sick.

"I'm afraid that's not all. If you find that alarming you better sit down. I have something much more frightening than that to tell you."

Edward took a seat.

"I've been told by a very reliable source who has contact with an alien being that there is a new breed that has arrived on Earth. A breed that the aliens manufactured is the only way I know how to describe it. A breed that has the potential to be very dangerous to us who call Earth home," the president said.

"And you trust this source?"

The president stared at him for several minutes. "Would you believe me if I told you I'm the source?" the president asked.

"I don't doubt you. If you tell me you're the one who is the source who met with this alien then I suppose yes, I would believe it. You're not a man to make something like this up especially considering all that's at stake," he said.

He had grown very uneasy over this entire conversation.

"I wasn't given the full story but only what the alien was willing to reveal to me. It was difficult enough carrying on a conversation with an alien but I tend to believe he wasn't leading me astray," the president said.

"Did he give you any indication of why this new breed was manufactured or what their purpose is?"

"From what I understand this new breed comes from the lineage of one family that had been chosen many centuries ago. Their purpose is to birth new generations of the same breed, only one per generation, until a chosen one will arrive. It appears this chosen one will determine the fate of the world as we know it today. I am told they will blend in and no one will know who or what they are until it's too late to stop them. It appears even the aliens are uncertain as to the fate the chosen one will choose when her time comes. It could mean the end of the world to us as we know it, or to the aliens. It could mean in this future world that we will coexist with aliens."

Edward had remained quiet during the president relating this information. He was stunned to say the least of this revelation, but he had to believe the president was way off course in assuming the child he had seen was of this new breed of which he spoke.

But hybrids...as difficult as even that was to believe it was something he had heard more than once during his research while working on Project Blue Book.

"I have to wonder. No, I don't suppose....I just remain uneasy about the child as to what she is or of her origins," the president said.

"I really think this child you sent me to observe is very bright as are both her parents. I didn't find anything at all to make me think there's anything more to her than that. You really think it can even be remotely possible that she is one of this new breed this alien warned you about?"

"That I am relying on you to find out," the president said pointing his finger at him.

This could change everything. It wasn't just observing us to learn about us if that's what was going on, he thought.

The meeting ended shortly after that.

He had his assignment. Give the letter from the president to the Newhouses and find out what he could about what they knew....*and discover if the little girl his son thought he would one day marry was human or alien.*

9

"Why you're not surprised by anything I've just told you are you?" Liz asked looking perplexed at her husband. "And here I thought you'd be so happy at my sleuthing skills and all I've learned about Elke."

"I am always amazed at your skills," Edward said.

"So why aren't you jumping for joy at all that I've learned?"

Her mouth dropped open as though a flick of a switch had gone off.

"You already know everything I've just told you, is that it?" she asked. "Come on, fess up."

"I admit I didn't know about the first husband."

"Oh, so you didn't know about the doctor who was executed right before her eyes for harboring Jews and helping them find their way out of Nazi Germany?" she asked haughtily. "You mean I actually discovered something you didn't know? Why what a clever wife you have."

He couldn't help himself and laughed. "Yes dear, a very clever wife indeed."

He got up and wrapped her in his arms hugging her and saying, "Thank you my love. I know you were doing what you could to help me, but at this point just enjoy yourself while we're here at the beach and leave the work to me."

"I was only trying to help as you didn't seem to be doing so well on your own," she said pulling back from his embrace.

"True, but from here on out I think you better leave it up to me."

He could only hope and pray she would do just that. If she ever discovered what he'd just learned from the president her world would never be the same.

"Elke and I get along very well and I really do like her. I think she likes me too and considers me a friend."

"I'm sure she does. Coming to America being a German she may not have confided in many people. It's nice she has you for a friend," he said. "But this evening I need to go over..."

Bill banged the door behind him yelling, "I'm home."

"Bill, please don't slam the door," his mother said. "This isn't..."

"William, Mom. I keep telling you not to call me Bill anymore. My name is William. You named me. That shouldn't be so hard to remember," he insisted.

"Yes William," his mom said.

He was excited to see his dad. He gave his father a quick hug and told his parents, "Nicole's mom just took us to the coolest museum in the world. You wouldn't believe what we saw. There was this rug made out of cat hair..."

"Cat hair?" his mother asked appalled.

"It's the oldest rug in the whole world," William went on excitedly. "Thousands and thousands of years old. If you step on it you're cursed."

"Step on the cat?" his mother asked.

"No Mom," William looked at his mom and rolled his eyes. "The cats been dead for thousands of years. The rug is just made out of it's hair, not the cat. The museum is a castle. So cool. I'm meeting Nicole in ten minutes on the beach. Gotta go."

William ran to his room to change into his swimming trunks.

"William?" his dad asked. "Since when did he decide he wanted to be called William?"

"I believe it was when Nicole told him his name was really William," she answered. "If only I had as much influence on him as that little six year old girl."

As their son ran out the back door a few minutes later in his swimming trunks and with a bucket he used to collect shells they just looked at each other and laughed.

"Is he O.K. on the beach unsupervised?" his dad asked.

"I'll go down and watch them in a minute. I'm sure Elke will too. She's a good woman Edward."

"Don't worry," he assured his wife. "I have no intention on messing up your friendship with her. I just have a job I have to do and that does involve your new friend. Hopefully she won't be upset and take it out on you."

His wife just looked at him and said, "Hmmm. I guess I know better than to even ask. Leftovers are in the fridge. Eat a bite before you bury yourself in your office."

That evening leaving his wife and son at home watching a movie and sharing a bowl of popcorn he walked over to the home of his neighbors hoping they would be understanding in the fact that he was only doing his job.

He hoped they wouldn't hold it against his wife who really seemed to enjoy Elke's company and friendship.

Surely they would understand the president's need to learn as much as possible of the alien's intentions and know if our nation was at risk.

Walking back home he took a longer route walking along the beach thinking of the look on Elke's face.

Of course she realized when he was elected President of the United States that he was the same man she had confided in once she arrived in France after escaping from Germany. She had confided everything she knew at the time...or had she? She probably never dreamed that he would remember her and one day look her up expecting answers.

Klaus had read the letter from the president and without a

word handed it to Elke to read while he stood quietly in the doorway and waited for their response.

Elke's face had gone chalk white when she read the letter and handed it back to Klaus without saying a word. Her hand was trembling when she handed the letter to her husband.

Klaus read the letter a second time. Without saying a word he folded the letter and returned it to the envelope.

Klaus looked at him and said, "Give us some time to think about this and talk. We'll talk to you but not tonight."

He turned to leave but before he was out the door Klaus said, "Edward, just to be clear.... Nicole is off limits."

10

The three of them had been talking for hours. Liz had come by and picked up Nicole and taken the two children to the movies and for pizza afterwards so the three adults could talk privately.

Elke watched Edward's body language to see if what she and Klaus had confessed to him would change their relationship. She was pleased to see he didn't appear to be judging them or ready to run out the door to pack his family up and get out of town. He seemed to be taking it well.

He took no notes. He just sat and listened as though they were three friends confiding in one another. He knew notes could be damning and fall in the wrong hands.

He knew there was no way he would ever forget what they confided in him, therefore there would be no need to write anything down. This would go no further than the president.

He had explained from the beginning what his role was in Project Blue Book and that theirs would not be the first story of alien interaction he had heard. He assured them at the same time that their story would not be included in his reports to anybody.

Klaus reminded him, "I have a signed letter here from the president himself that we won't be questioned by anyone other than you. Is that true?"

"I didn't read the letter," Edward said. "From what I understand that's the gist of it. He's a man of his word. You needn't worry about that."

"He wrote in the letter that our story will go no further than to you and his ears only. Do you yourself promise to stand by that?"

"Of course," Edward said.

"You're free to tell Liz anything we tell you. I trust her implicitly," Elke said.

"I appreciate that," Edward said.

"Surely you understand why I was uneasy talking to you about this," Klaus said.

"Not many people are comfortable talking about aliens..."

"No, I mean the threat of us being deported or losing our citizenship," Klaus said.

Edward looked up surprised at what he said. "That's what you were worried about?"

"Of course," Klaus said. "When I was brought over with the other scientists we were let know under no uncertain terms what was to be expected of us. We were told if we didn't fulfill our part that we would be charged as war criminals."

"I didn't know that," Edward said. "That's a terrible thing to do to the lot of you. I understand there may have been a fear on where your loyalties may lie at that time but..."

"Let me be very clear," Klaus said. "My loyalties were *never* with the Nazis, nor were Elke's."

"Klaus, I really don't think the president has any concerns on your loyalties. His concern is with the safety of our nation."

"Why now Edward?" Elke asked softly. "It isn't like visitations from aliens or UFO's are new to your country."

"There's been an upsurge on reported sightings," he answered. "Some of them have been interpreted as threatening, downright hostile."

"If it means anything, it's been quite some time since we've seen any alien spacecraft," Elke said.

"And Nicole?" he asked gently.

Klaus stood up so quickly his chair toppled over behind him. He pointed his finger and said, "I told you to leave Nicole out of this."

Elke gently said, "Klaus, please sit down. I don't believe Edward is here to do our family any harm." She stared at her husband with pleading eyes until he sat back down.

"Why do you ask about Nicole? She's just a child. Surely as a parent you understand a parent will do anything to protect their children. There's no reason to bring her into this," Elke pleaded.

"Isn't there?" he asked.

She held her hand up to stop Klaus from saying anything and asked Edward, "What do you mean?"

"She's exceptionally bright for a six year old," he said.

"Thank you," Elke said proudly. "I take great pride in the fact that both Klaus and I take a great deal of our time in teaching her ourselves. What she learns at school is so far behind her abilities we just took it upon ourselves to challenge her so she isn't bored. "

"In case you haven't noticed both Elke and I are pretty smart ourselves," Klaus said.

"I understand that," Edward said. "I told the president the same thing myself."

Klaus seemed to relax a little.

Edward sat and looked out the window thinking.

He looked back at them and said, "This has really put me in a bad spot. I feel like we've become friends and I don't like putting that friendship in jeopardy. I know my wife treasures your friendship Elke and it appears," Edward smiled before continuing, "it appears my son believes he's going to marry your daughter one day."

"I imagine over time a lot of boys may think that..." Klaus said.

Elke looked at her husband and said, "No, Klaus. Nicole is the one who told William they would marry one day. It appears she has chosen him."

Klaus looked surprised and seemed for a moment to forget Edward was sitting there. "Then he's the destined one?"

Elke nodded her head, "So it seems."

"They're just children," Edward laughed nervously. "I imagine as time goes by they'll change their minds many times about who they'll marry."

"No, not with them," Elke said firmly. "If Nicole said it then it will happen."

Edward seemed at a loss for words. "So you seem to think that because a little six year old girl says something that it will happen? No offense, but if I believed my son everytime he told me what he wanted to be when he grew up he'd be..."

Klaus said, "It's different with Nicole. She has a gift."

"You mean like a psychic or something?"

Klaus said, "I wouldn't have exactly worded it like that myself, but I suppose that's as good an analogy as any."

Elke said to her husband, "It appears they're to be a part of our lives. I think it's only fair they know what they're getting into. Especially because I do think of Liz as a dear friend. I know you respect Edward too. You've just been afraid of what he'd find out. Now you needn't worry about that because you need to tell him yourself."

Edward watched as they discussed this in front of him.

"And what about the president?" Klaus asked.

"Edward can figure out how much he needs to tell him. He has quite a bit at stake in this now too," she said.

Klaus looked at her and took her hand in his and asked, "You're absolutely sure about this?"

"Yes," Elke said. "I am."

"You better put the coffee on then," Klaus told his wife.

"Edward, you may want to call your wife and see if the kids can have a slumber party tonight. I have a feeling this may be a long night," Elke said.

Edward feeling like he was about to discover where Midas kept his gold hopped up and called his wife.

11

Nicole and William ran down the beach hand in hand with Nora, Nicole's best friend and daughter of Shannon and Connor, Elke's ex-husband.

The kids each waved a sparkler watching the lights dance in the night. Every few moments a loud *Boom!* would sound in the distance and they would all look up to see the fireworks above their heads.

The baby sitting on a beach towel next to the three women clapped whenever the fireworks lit up the sky.

Shannon eased herself with her large pregnant belly down into the chair next to Liz.

"You're a braver woman than I am," Liz said. "I can't imagine having three in diapers at once and trying to keep up with them."

"We weren't expecting twins," Shannon admitted while gently rubbing her belly. "That part was a surprise. I can't say I'm not thrilled about it though. We wanted a houseful of kids and we got off to a late start."

Elke reached down and picked up the baby and kissed his little cheeks. She held him up to the sky and he kicked his little legs and squealed in delight.

"You should have had more children Elke," Liz said. "You're so good with them."

"I would have loved to," Elke admitted. "We tried for a long time and couldn't understand why I didn't get pregnant. It happened so quickly the first time. The doctors all said there was no reason we couldn't have more yet it never happened. So I just enjoy Shannon's babies."

"What a shame," Liz said.

"It was later revealed to me that my role in life is to care for

Nicole. She was my destiny and my role in life was to prepare her for hers," she said.

"Revealed to you? What do you mean?" Liz asked.

"By the aliens," Elke said matter-of-factly. "They were the ones who revealed to me that my daughter was to be given my undivided attention and prepared for her future. Apparently my lineage of the chosen ones are allowed one child, the one the aliens choose as the daughter of destiny."

"Daughter of destiny?" Liz asked. "What do you mean? And just because you have one child doesn't mean you couldn't care for another."

Shannon looked at Elke in a questioning way as to ask how much Liz knew.

Elke quietly said, "I thought Edward explained to you about Nicole."

"Yes," she answered still puzzled about the daughter of destiny remark. "He told me about the aliens visiting you and your lineage. I don't recall him saying anything about a daughter of destiny though. What exactly does that mean?"

Nora ran over to where her mother was sitting and grabbed a towel wrapping it around her shoulders. "Nicole and William said they're starving. Me too. When are we going to eat?" she asked.

"It won't be long now," her mom said. "Run along and have fun. We'll call you when it's ready."

Nora ran off again to join the other kids.

"Nicole and William certainly have hit it off haven't they?" Shannon said to Liz.

"I'm having a hard time getting used to calling my son William. He's always been Bill to me," Liz said.

"Oh, I apologize. I thought Nora said his name was William," she said. "She must have gotten his name mixed up."

"No, no. She's right. Actually his name is William. It's just we've called him Bill since he was born. He decided for some reason or another this summer that he was going to go by William from now on. He was quite adamant about the point. I never knew a seven year old boy could be so stubborn," Liz laughed.

"Kids can certainly be stubborn. I ought to know with red headed kids and tempers to match," Shannon said.

Elke laughed. "Sounds like someone else I know."

"O.K.," Shannon said. "I admit they take after their mother in that aspect. It's the Irish in us."

"It's so nice having my friends together and celebrating on such a beautiful evening on the beach," Elke said.

"Are you enjoying your summer here?" Shannon asked Liz.

Liz beamed from ear to ear and said, "It looks like we'll be staying for longer than the summer."

Elke said, "You talked him into it then?"

Liz answered, "He surprised me with the deed to the house for an early birthday present. When the realtor put the For Sale sign up I told him it would be the perfect place to settle down. He's planning on leaving the military in a few years and work in the private sector. Until his retirement we can come stay summers and then we'll live here full time once he does retire."

"I'm so glad we're going to be neighbors," Elke said.

"Elke," Liz said, "Earlier you were saying something about daughters of destiny. What did you..."

The men standing over the bonfire having a beer looked over at the women.

"We're about ready for those burgers and hot dogs," Connor said walking over to the women.

"Good timing. The kids are getting hungry," Shannon said working herself out of her chair.

"Let me get that," Elke said getting up to help.

She hopped up relieved to have been interrupted before she had to answer Liz about the daughters of destiny.

As she began pulling out the hot dogs and buns from the cooler she mulled over in her mind the conversation.

She *thought* Edward had explained everything to his wife... including the fact that her own son now had a role in all this.

Elke knew it was inevitable that one day he too would be visited by the aliens. She knew they would want to check him out for approval of fathering the next generation of daughters of destiny. Not that that time was anywhere in the near future, but still she would have thought Edward would have prepared Liz for what would eventually become their son's future.

Perhaps due to his age the alien visitations with their son wouldn't occur for some time. Or was that hopeful thinking?

The fact that he and Nicole were bound for one another she would place odds that it would be sooner rather than later. She could already feel the bond between the two of them and it was very strong.

She wondered how Liz would respond once she learned of her son's role in all this. She was pretty sure she wouldn't be happy about it. For now Liz was naiive in thinking it was just a childhood friendship. She would learn one day that it was much more than that.

The kids seeing food was being brought out ran over to join in cooking hot dogs over the bonfire.

The women were kept busy putting the dogs on sticks so the kids could hold them over the fire.

From that point on it was too hectic for Liz to question anyone any further about the matter.

With full bellies and the baby sound asleep they all sat and watched as the fireworks reached their finale and then began packing up and heading for home.

12

Sitting on the back deck once William had been tucked into bed Liz finally had a chance to broach the subject with her husband.

Even the sound of the waves crashing on the shore wasn't enough to soothe her at the moment. Apparently she had been deprived of some very important information and she meant to get to the bottom of it before the night was over.

If she had known then what she would later learn she may have wished to have remained ignorant on the matter.

"From your body language I get the feeling that your euphoria of getting the deed to the cottage didn't last very long," her husband said.

"I'm still extremely happy about that," she said.

"I hear a but in there somewhere," Edward said waiting for what she was about to spring on him.

He took a sip of beer and about spit it out from what she said next.

"Don't just sit there. You heard me. What does daughters of destiny mean?" she asked.

Edward walked in the kitchen to buy a little time trying to figure out exactly what to tell his wife. Could this little girl possibly be a danger to the world? If Edward thought so for a minute he would have taken his family and gotten the hell out of Dodge.

He thought perhaps the president had misinterpreted what the alien told him. He felt Elke had been honest in telling him her end of the story. But he wouldn't be naiive either.

Edward walked back out on the deck and handed his wife a drink.

"What is it?" she asked suspiciously.

"A gin and tonic," he answered. "A strong one. Go on. Drink up. You're going to need it."

"I don't like the sound of that," she said.

It was then they saw Elke walking over. "Do you mind if I join you?"

"As long as you both agree the secrets end here," Liz said emphatically. "It seems I've been left out of the loop."

"Yes you have. That's why I came. I apologize for not coming sooner but I had to see to our guests," Elke said.

"You don't have to do this," Edward said to Elke. "I'll explain..."

She shook her head and walked up the steps to the deck and joined them.

"I felt it only fair that I was the one to explain to you, Liz... I heard you asking Edward about the daughters of destiny. I've come to tell you about it. You deserve to know."

"Would you like something to drink?" Edward asked.

"I'll have whatever she's having. Thanks," Elke answered.

Edward went in the house to mix her drink. The women were quiet each deep in their own thoughts while waiting to continue the conversation after he returned.

"The daughters of destiny," Elke said letting out a huge sigh. "I first heard the term from my mother when I was about the age Nicole is now. A bit younger actually. For a time it was wiped from my memory," Elke explained.

"By the aliens?" Liz asked.

"Yes," Elke answered.

Elke gazed out at the ocean waves. "The ocean reminds me of when I came to America."

"Elke," Liz started to say.

"Don't worry. I'm not changing the subject. I'm just trying to figure out the best way to explain it all."

Edward said, "Why don't you start from when Gershom told you about the gift while you were still in Germany."

"Yes, perhaps that's a good place to start," Elke said.

Elke began telling the story without looking at either one of them, almost as if she were reliving it.

"Gershom, he was one of the aliens whose spacecraft or UFO as you call it crashed that we had in our possesion in Germany..."

"I remember Edward telling me about him," Liz said.

"One evening when we were being bombed towards the end of the war I went to check to see if he was all right. It was just the two of us in the room. He placed his hand on my belly. I was pregnant at the time with Nicole. He told me I would be having a girl."

Liz smartly didn't interrupt as Elke closed her eyes and seemed to go back in time describing the event as though it had just occurred.

She placed her hand over her belly as though she were reliving the time she was pregnant with Nicole.

"You must take great care of this child, he said to me. The future will be determined though her lineage. She is a daughter of destiny. I remember at the time I said, She? It's a girl? He continued though as if he were in a trance."

Edward watched her closely as she told her story. She didn't hesitate at all in recalling the events. She spoke as though she were telling the story word-for-word as she had heard it herself.

Remarkable that she could remember so clearly he thought, considering it had been approximately seven years since the conversation had taken place.

"Gershom went on ignoring my question and said, One of the daughters of destiny, the chosen one, will determine whether the lives of the humans and my kind will co-exist."

Liz couldn't help herself. She gasped and put her hand to her heart, "My God, co-exist with aliens..."

Edward placed his hand on her arm and when she glanced over he motioned for her to be quiet and listen.

"Each of the daughters of destiny until the chosen one arrives is of utmost importance in the assurance of the chosen one's future arrival. Their purpose is to pave her way, the chosen one that is, to grow in intelligence and ways of the humans so that co-existence is possible."

Liz forgetting that Edward had motioned for her to be quiet leaned towards her friend and asked, "Elke, are you saying... I'm not sure what I'm asking. You said that Gershom said grow in the ways of the humans...are these daughters of destiny not *human*?"

Elke said, "Please, allow me to tell the story as it happened. I promise it will be self-explanatory."

Liz shook her head and reached for her gin and tonic. Instead of sipping it she took a huge gulp.

"I reacted much as you have," Elke said. "I was revolted by what he was saying. I wasn't so sure I wanted to co-exist with aliens and I knew I didn't want them to have anything to do with my baby."

"I should say not," Liz said indignantly.

"The whole thing was frightening to think about," Elke said. "But please, let me continue with Gershom's words not my thoughts at the time."

She cleared her throat and closed her eyes seeming to have easier recall by doing so. "You will be given a great gift. This gift is something your child will carry within her. Your child will be unique to mankind."

Edward watched his wife carefully not sure she could handle what she was about to hear. He noticed the drink in her hand was shaking violently. He reached over and took it from her before she dropped it.

She wanted to know, he thought to himself. Once you knew this information it was impossible to ever forget it.

"Gershom told me I had no choice in the matter when I told him I didn't want their gift. I wanted them to leave my baby alone.

He told me, You have no say in the matter. You and your lineage have been chosen with great care. It is your child who will be implanted with this gift. It will be passed on through other generations until the arrival of the hope of our kind, the one who holds our future in her hands is born."

"Implanted," Liz mouthed silently to Edward looking horror stricken.

He merely shook his head in acknowledgement.

"Gershom insisted, 'She *will* receive this gift.' He told me I could no more stop it from happening than I could in stopping the sun to rise in the morning. He said my lineage had been chosen long before I was even born. I now know that to be true. It was revealed to me in the daughters of destiny diaries."

Tears ran down Liz's face which went unnoticed by her. Her husband reached over and wiped her tears away. He pulled his chair closer and took her hand in his hoping to offer her comfort in any way he could.

"Gershom told me I had no choice....he was right. He told me my mission in life was to guard the child and protect her and that was my purpose. Nicole's role will be to give birth to the next generation of daughters of destiny."

Elke seemed to come to and opened her eyes and looked at Liz. "I know this is hard to listen to. Do you want me to wait a few moments before I finish?"

"You mean there's more?" Liz asked in a shrill voice.

"I'm afraid so," Elke answered. "The hardest part is yet to come."

13

"Give me a moment," Liz said.

Liz stood a bit wobbly and Edward jumped up to help her.

She pushed his arm away and said, "I just need some air. I'm going to walk for a few minutes on the beach to prepare myself for the rest of this story. I need to be alone."

Edward watched her and knew he had to let her do it her way.

He had known about the aliens and UFO's for years through his work but all this was pretty new to his wife.

He had recently told her about the aliens' involvement with the Newhouse family but hadn't told her everything. She was now about to find out. He wondered how in the world she was going to react when she learned the rest.

Even for him it was no longer far removed, something that happened to someone else that he was merely interviewing. His son was in this....he wished he'd never brought his family here.

"What are you thinking?" Elke asked him.

"That bringing my family here was the worst decision I ever made. If I hadn't brought them here..."

"Your son wouldn't have met Nicole and then he wouldn't be involved. Is that what you're thinking?"

"I'm sorry but yes," he answered her honestly. "I have to wonder if I just packed up my family now and never came back if it would change anything. He's only seven. He would forget about her and she him..."

"It doesn't work that way," Elke said. "Their age has nothing to do with it. They are predestined to be together."

"This is my work. I have to deal with it, but now it appears my son's life is predestined to be involved with aliens with a future wife who isn't quite human..."

"I beg to differ Edward," Elke said. "She's very human. She has a human mother and father. She was conceived through Klaus and my love for one other."

"I apologize. That was a terrible thing to say to you."

"I understand. Truly I do," Elke said. "It's a pretty difficult thing to accept."

"Was it predestined that Klaus become your child's father?" he asked. "Would it have been different if you would have gotten pregnant with your first husband?"

"They would never have allowed that to happen. Klaus had been chosen," Elke said. "I wasn't aware of it at the time."

"But you seem sure of the matter," he said hoping perhaps she was wrong.

"When I learned that the aliens actually caused Connor to be shot down and they led me to him to save his life I started putting two and two together. When I questioned the aliens about whether or not it was through their interference that these events took place they confirmed it."

"My God," Edward said.

"Me coming to America...all of it was of their doing. Like Gershom said, I really had no choice in the matter. I was foolish to ever think I did."

"What you're saying then is regardless of whether I brought my son here or not someway somehow my son and Nicole would have met on their own?"

"Perhaps with a little intervention but yes," she answered. "And now that they've met there will be such a strong bond that absolutely nothing will ever be able to keep them apart once it's their time to fulfill their roles. A child will come from their union that..."

"My son will never be able to choose his own bride or have a normal..."

"I assure you that your son and my daughter will be very much in love with each other. There will be such a magnetism between the two of them that no one, *and I mean no one or nothing*, would be able to keep them apart."

"All I want for my son is for his happiness and well-being," he said. "A normal life....though from what you're saying I presume that's out of the question."

"They were meant to be together. They will be very happy in their love with one another. Perhaps that is the alien's way to assure that the child will be raised and brought up in a way that prepares them for their role."

"That surprises me," Edward said. "From everything I've learned from interviewing people who have had any interaction with aliens they tell me the aliens themselves don't appear to feel emotions of any kind."

"They're right," Elke said. "They never show emotion of any sort whatsoever. Certainly not love or affection in any shape or form. Yet they've studied humans for centuries and they understand that love is an important aspect in our relationship with one another."

"I've often heard from others who have been abducted that they seem to study human's emotions and are quite curious about..."

"Edward, I know all this is hard to face, but our children can lead a fairly normal life. Granted they..."

"You call it a normal life with aliens popping in and out of their life at will and giving birth to a child who isn't quite a normal child..."

"Nicole is a normal child that likes to play and learn and do things other children do," Elke said.

"Yet she is a six year old with the intelligence of...I don't know, but you can't really say she's your normal six year old. You yourself told me she was implanted with alien genes or DNA. I wouldn't call that a "normal child." Her intelligence is way above most adults. Her IQ is off the charts and she's still a young child. No, she is *not* a normal child. She knows things that are going to happen before they do. She can..."

He stopped as he heard his wife returning. She walked up the steps as though she bore a heavy load.

She plopped back in her chair and said, "I'm as ready as I'll ever be. Please tell me the rest before I change my mind."

Elke looked over at Edward. He nodded for her to continue.

"You know the story about how I escaped Germany and met Connor after his plane crashed. What I was unaware of at the time was the aliens set the whole thing up."

"They can do that?" Liz asked with horror etched on her face.

"I'm afraid so," Elke said.

It was Edward's turn to take a big slug of his drink. The thought of what the aliens were capable of was absolutely terrifying.

He still hadn't decided whether or not to inform the president about Nicole and her relationship with the aliens or of his son's role. He contemplated on his choice in the matter.

He feared for the children's safety if he were to reveal what he now knew. He feared they would be taken into government hands and that would be the last they would ever see or hear of them.

No, he must keep his mouth shut. Presidents come and go, but this was his son they were talking about. There was nothing to decide. This would go no further. He would protect the two children with his life if need be.

Elke continued with her story to Liz. "It had been arranged for Connor and I to meet and for me to come to America. It had been predetermined that their chosen one would come from this land."

As Elke told Liz a story he now knew well he realized he had another decision to make.

He was at a loss about what if anything to tell the president about the daughters of destiny. But what more did he have to tell him that he didn't already know? Nothing of any relevance.

Were the daughters of destiny to play a part in a take over of the world? It was a possiblity from what he'd heard. But those words came from the president. From what he understood that was perhaps not going to happen for several generations.

Did the aliens set their sights on a world where humans and aliens co-existed? Or was it a takeover they were secretly plotting?

He felt a heavy burden on his shoulders. If he did nothing and one day the world was in danger because he had kept quiet in order to save his son, how could he live with himself? How could he risk the lives of all Americans, perhaps the world?

As his mind was spinning in turmoil he was barely aware of his wife and Elke sitting by his side.

"I was on the ship sailing for America," he heard Elke explaining to Liz. "As the ship departed from France we were in danger due to mines in the water left over from the war. I sighed with a breath of relief once we were out in deeper waters thinking the danger was past. Little did I know what would happen next..."

Liz sat silently listening.

"Even though we were out in the middle of the ocean I saw a UFO appear. I knew without a doubt the aliens were coming for me."

Sensing this was a difficult memory for Elke to share and go over Liz reached for Elke's hand and held it to give her some comfort as she continued on with her story.

"They found you out in the middle of the ocean?" Liz asked.

"I've since discovered they can find me anywhere. I begged them not to take me when they arrived on the ship. There were two aliens. Each took me by an arm and we rose above the churning waters of the ocean below. We rose into the air and seemed to float into the craft. It was terrifying," Elke said, shivering even now as she recalled the event.

Edward looked over to see how Liz was taking all this. He knew what she was to learn next would open her eyes to the fact that her son would also be involved.

"At the time I wasn't aware of what Gershom had told me about my child," Elke continued. "He had wiped my memory. Once I was on board and one of the aliens looked into my eyes my memory was restored. I've never been able to forget what I've learned since."

Liz sat quietly through the rest of the story. About midway through it hit her that if they were right in predicting a future with Nicole and William then he would be tossed right into the middle of this.

At the end of opening up and telling Liz everything Elke sat back almost relieved that her friend now knew everything.

Liz however was anything but relieved. This now involved her son. Maybe Elke had come to terms with her daughter and her future, but Liz wasn't ready to surrender her son's future to the alien's whim.

As what Elke told her began to sink in she got up rushing to the railing of the deck and leaned over vomiting and emptying all the contents of her stomach.

A few random fireworks went off as Edward reached his wife and wiped her mouth gently with a napkin. He took her in his arms.

Elke quietly walked down the steps to return to her home. She had done what she came to do.

"This is one Fourth of July I'll never forget," Liz said to her husband with a bit of a hysterical laugh.

14

No sooner than the car came to a stop in front of their cottage that William jumped out heading for Nicole's house.

"Wait William," his mother called out. "You need to help me unload the car."

William yelled over his shoulder, "Just leave it Mom. I'll unload it all when I get back."

Liz just breathed a sigh and thought to herself, Why did I think it would be any different this year.

Liz grabbed what she could carry and headed to open up the cottage.

They'd been staying summers at the cottage for ten years now and this time they would be staying permanently. Edward was retiring from the military next month and then they would make the beach cottage their full-time home.

She had to admit she had mixed feelings about the idea. She loved living right on the ocean and it was a time when Edward seemed to leave his work behind and actually relax and enjoy himself. How, she had no idea considering they were living right next door to people whose own daughter was part alien part human.

Lost in her thoughts she hadn't heard William and Nicole come up behind her.

"Hello Mrs. Halloway," Nicole said.

Liz turned around to greet the girl she had just been thinking of and was stunned to see that just since last summer she had grown even more beautiful and very tall.

She was simply stunning. There was no other word for it.

Nicole would have turned heads from both sexes with her long straight hair so blonde it was almost white. She was tanned from spending time on the beach and had legs that were long and shapely.

She imagined the boys were all enthralled with her and the girls would be desperately jealous.

Nicole's eyes were a sapphire blue that when they looked into your own eyes they seemed to look right into your soul. And perhaps they did Liz thought with dismay.

She looked like a model on a magazine cover with those high cheekbones and a ready smile with a mouth that looked like it was just begging to be kissed.

It was no wonder William was so smitten with her.

"We've come to unload the car," Nicole explained.

Nicole gave her a big hug happy to see the Halloways back, this time permanently.

As Liz hugged her she could feel that Nicole had grown quite substantial breasts since they had visited last. Being a teenager she knew her son would probably soon make that discovery on his own. They were growing up much too fast.

Nicole walked over and reached into the car grabbing a handful of items placing them into William's arms. He grinned at her like a little schoolboy with a huge crush.

"Oh boy, are we in for trouble," Liz said under her breath.

Liz sat on the deck chatting with Elke while they both sipped Margaritas and snacked on nachos and salsa.

A bright sunny day and the waves crashing on the beach with a Margarita or two was conducive to taking a nap right here on the deck.

Liz watched as Nicole was showing William how to catch a wave on his new surfboard. It was peaceful here in St. Augustine.

She was more than glad to no longer have to worry about shoveling snow or moving from one military base to another. It was nice to have roots and settle down in one place and have a good friend to spend time with.

Liz noticed Elke had put her sunhat on and appeared to be taking a nap.

Good idea she thought. About to do the same she checked to be sure the kids were all right.

She glanced out at the ocean and saw their surfboards being pushed up on shore by the surf. There was no sign of the kids.

Liz jumped up from her chair and walked to the ledge of the deck. She put a hand up to shield her eyes from the sun and peered out at the ocean scanning in search of her son and Nicole.

Where were they? She knew they were good swimmers so that wasn't a concern. Still, just a moment ago they were surfing.

The sun seemed to have gone in as a few moments ago the sun was bright and now it was overcast.

She glanced up in time to see it was still sunny out. There was a very large UFO hovering over the ocean...right where William and Nicole had been only moments before. Nicole and William appeared to be floating in mid-air heading right it's way.

She jumped up and screamed out William's name waking Elke.

Elke got up and said, "What's the matter?"

"They're gone. The kids are gone," she screamed. "They've been taken."

Liz pointed to the very large UFO hovering over the ocean and looking up Elke too could see Nicole and William disappearing inside the UFO.

Liz was shaking uncontrollably.

The kids appeared to be sucked inside from the bottom of the craft and once they were inside the craft shot off at a terrific speed.

If she hadn't looked just when she did she wouldn't have seen a thing. They would have simply disappeared.

"I'm surprised they allowed you to see that," Elke said calmly.

"What!" Liz spun around and looked at her stunned. "Our kids have just been taken inside a UFO and it disappeared into space and that's all you have to say?"

Elke reached out and hugged her friend who was hysterical. She said, "I know it must be terrifying for you. I'm only surprised it's taken them this long to take William. Being that he's to be the father of a daughter of destiny I would've thought they would have had him checked out long before now."

"Where are they taking them?" Liz asked terrified for her son.

"He'll be back and he may not even recall what happened," Elke explained. "Nicole has been taken more times than I can count. They won't hurt him Liz. He has a destiny with them too. They'll take good care of him and see to it that nothing happens to him."

Liz paced the deck ringing her hands. "I've got to call Edward."

Elke said, "You'll only worry him to death and there's nothing he can do from Ohio. Even if he was here he would be powerless to stop them."

15

"Liz, I'm at work. I'm on an unsecure line. Please be careful in what you say," Edward reminded his wife who clearly wasn't thinking rationally.

"William has been...He's gone. The...you know...they took him."

"Liz, listen carefully. I believe you're trying to tell me William is with our neighbor's visitors? Is that what you're trying to tell me?" he said while looking at his calendar seeing if he could clear his schedule for the next day or two.

"How could you be so calm about..." she almost screamed into the phone.

"We knew this was inevitable. Things will be all right, you'll see. I'll head home right away. I'm sure William will be back before I get there. Please just try to calm down. Everything will be fine."

Edward was packing his briefcase with work to take with him while he was on the phone. He was ready to walk out the door as soon as he could get his wife calmed down and off the phone.

"Elke told me not to call you but I needed to..."

"That's all right. You know you can call me anytime. I'll be home as soon as I can get a flight out. I'll be there in a few hours," he said.

"Edward, I saw it. I saw the.... you know."

"Please don't say anything more on the phone. You can tell me all about it when I get home. I'm leaving now. Just ask Elke to please stay with you until I get there," he said anxious to get off the phone and on his way.

As he was heading to the car he thought to himself, She saw the UFO? She saw him being taken? That was unusual in itself.

And for them to come during the day when other people may have seen them...How would William take all this?

He now knew they should have sat him down long before now and explained to him about Nicole and what that meant for his own future. *I thought I had more time. I guess I was wrong.*

William was sitting on his surfboard with his feet dangling in the water with Nicole by his side on her own surfboard when the day went from being a bright sunny day to dark in a matter of moments.

"I think it's getting ready to rain," William said.

Nicole looked up at the sky and said, "Take my hand. Quick!"

He looked up seeing the UFO hovering over them. He was reaching for Nicole's hand when he felt himself rising up off his board. He reached over and grasped her hand tight.

He looked down and saw his feet dangling over the ocean. Before he had time for another thought he and Nicole seemed to be floating and then entered a room of sorts.

The floor beneath them closed without a sound.

He started to lose his balance as he felt movement until Nicole tightened her hold on him.

"Nicole, what is..."

Two aliens stepped forward. At least he assumed they were aliens. They sure as hell weren't human.

16

The aliens were short, much shorter than both he and Nicole and gray in color. Their large black slanted eyes took up most of their face with only a slit for a mouth and holes where a nose would normally be. If it weren't for the fact that they were the size of children they would be terrifying.

This is what people had been telling his dad about for years. What he had been researching while working on Project Blue Book.

He was somewhat familiar with his dad's work but in the past he had thought those people who claimed to have seen aliens were nuts. His father had tried to convince him otherwise.

Being a know-it-all teenager that he was he had dismissed pretty much what his father said having his own thoughts about the matter. Now he wished he had listened better to what his father had said.

William still held onto her hand as Nicole without even questioning followed the two aliens as though she knew where she was going.

They passed other little gray aliens as they walked down a hall. The hall appeared to be somewhat circular in shape with intermittent windows along the way. There was a faint rhythmic humming sound barely discernable.

William could barely walk he was shaking so badly.

Why was this happening?

One thing passed through his mind that gave him some comfort in this terrifying situation. The people that talked to his dad about seeing aliens were all alive to talk about it so he didn't think they were going to kill them. Those people were all returned home. But what did they want? Why him and Nicole of all people?

William could see by glancing out one of the windows as they walked past that they were not on the ground and they were moving. They appeared to be in the clouds and then rose above the clouds. At that point the UFO appeared to just hover in one area.

William began shaking uncontrollably. Nicole feeling him shaking reached out to put her arm around him to comfort him.

"Everything will be O.K. They just want to see you and check you out," Nicole said.

"Who are *They*?" He asked whispering so they wouldn't hear.

"They're the visitors. They come from another planet. Actually they're from another solar system than ours," she tried to explain.

"What the hell Nicole?" he asked. "You seem to know an awful lot about them. Has this happened to you before?"

He was amazed that she wasn't the least bit terrified or reacting to them at all. She seemed to be very familiar with who they were and where they came from. How could that be?

"Many times," she answered. "There's no need to whisper. They can hear your thoughts."

He stopped dead in his tracks.

"They can what?"

When he stopped short one of the aliens following behind them bumped into him. The alien had reached out to catch himself grabbing William's arm.

William was horrified at the alien's touch. It felt like old, dried out leather.

The aliens motioned for them to enter a room.

The room was entirely white and sterile looking with dozens of steel tables filling the room.

Four aliens surrounded him and he lost sight of Nicole. They motioned for him to remove his swimming trunks.

"Hell no you perverts," he yelled at them. "What right do you think you have to..."

He could hear Nicole nearby but couldn't see her.

"It's O.K., William. They won't hurt you."

When he still refused to take off his swimming trunks the aliens did it for him. He was powerless to stop them. He quickly dropped his hands to hide his nakedness but the aliens seemed unresponsive to his awkwardness.

They led him to a table and motioned for him to lie down.

He looked around for Nicole but could no longer see her.

"Nicole," he yelled looking frantically for her.

A taller alien he hadn't noticed before came forward. The alien reached out placing his hands alongside of William's head.

He found after the alien's touch he was unable to move regardless of how hard he tried.

The alien came within inches of his face and looked deeply into his eyes.

William immediately felt a complete calmness come over him and laid down on the table completely forgetting about Nicole.

Another taller alien came forward and the smaller aliens stepped back as though this was who they had been waiting for.

He was aware that they were doing something to his body but calmed by the alien looking into his eyes he was unconcerned.

The aliens stood around in a semi-circle and looked from one to the other but never uttered a word.

Come to think of it he thought, he hadn't heard a word spoken since he came aboard other than from Nicole.

His mind snapped back and he wondered what had happened to her.

The alien that had held his hands alongside his face and looked into his eyes spoke to William saying, "Nicole is special..."

Wait a minute, he thought. His lips or whatever that slit was on his face never moved. He didn't actually *speak* out loud yet he heard him in his head. How the hell did that happen?

"We are communicating telepathically," the alien explained. "You have been permitted to understand and to communicate in such a manner since you have been chosen..."

"Telepathically? What are you talking about?" William asked becoming anxious. "Or not talking about I should say."

Again the alien looked deeply into his eyes and told him, "There is no reason for you to resist. We are not here to hurt you. We need to know if you indeed are the one chosen for Nicole's purpose. But you must prove yourself. We must know if you are worthy."

He had no idea what the alien was talking about. Nicole's purpose? What was that supposed to mean? Worthy of what? Of Nicole? Shouldn't she be the one to decide that.

The alien stepped back and Nicole was standing at the end of the table.

She held her arms out and said, "Come here, William. Come to me."

It only took him a second to realize it wasn't Nicole at all regardless of the fact that she looked and sounded exactly like her.

"Go to the one you say you love," the alien communicated to him.

"That isn't Nicole," he said firmly. "I don't know who the hell she is, but that is *not* Nicole."

"How can you say that?" the girl who looked just like Nicole asked.

He shook his head vehemently. "That isn't Nicole!"

"Get away from me! Where's Nicole?" he screamed.

He looked around frantically trying to find the real Nicole to prove them wrong.

The one who looked exactly like Nicole shape shifted into a reptilian looking creature.

William repulsed from the creature standing in front of him began hyperventilating. He scooted back trying to get far away from this creature. He broke out into a cold sweat now fearing for both his and Nicole's life regardless of what any of them said.

"What the hell have you done to Nicole?" he cried out. "What the hell are you, monsters?"

"Go to her. Find Nicole," the alien who calmed him and who had stood by him throughout this ordeal said. "If you truly love her you will find her. Prove to us you are indeed the one."

He forgot about the other aliens. He felt an urgent need to obey the alien who had stood by his side and do exactly as he said.

William got off the table compelled to find Nicole forgetting completely that he wasn't wearing any clothes. He now noticed there were dozens of bodies laid out on the tables around the room.

He scanned the room. The lighting was such that you couldn't see the faces of the people lying on the tables. You couldn't see anything to give any clues as to what they looked like or even if they were male or female. They were all covered with some type of shimmering cloth which covered them from head to toe.

He could see the cloth gently rising and falling so he knew they weren't dead. They were breathing, sleeping perhaps.

"Choose wisely," the alien said. "Your destiny relies on it."

Without having to think twice he walked seven tables down and looked down at the body lying there and pointed and said, "That's Nicole."

"You know that yet you can't see her," the alien said. "Are you sure?"

"Positive," he said emphatically.

"How do you know?" one of the aliens asked.

"I feel her. I can tell when she's near. My heart knows. I can't explain it. I just know," he said.

The aliens seemed to approve of his choice and of his answer.

They led him back to the table where they had previously examined him.

The alien who had communicated with him motioned for him to get back on the table and lie down.

As the alien gently pushed him to lie back he noticed the aliens fingers were long as though they had an extra joint in their fingers. They looked like swollen arthiritic joints.

The alien looked into his eyes and said, "Look deeply into my eyes."

It was as though he were watching a movie.

He forgot about where he was and all fear completely left him.

He wasn't aware of anyone around him. It was as though he was experiencing himself what he was visualizing.

He and Nicole walked along the beach hand in hand. She was wearing her new neon green bikini that showed off her tan.

He commented to her on how much he liked it and how good she looked in it.

He could hear a seagull crying out, perhaps searching for food. He could smell the hint of rain in the air. The sea breeze blew Nicole's long blonde hair across her face.

She stopped and looked at him smiling in such a way that made him weak in the knees.

His body responded to her. Just that look. That's all it took.

She wrapped her arms around him pulling him close. He could feel her warm breath on his neck, her breasts pressed against him.

She kissed him while running her hands down his back. Her hands lowered and she gently pressed him against her.

He heard a moan and realized it had come from him. He had become fully aroused.

He knew as close as Nicole held him against her that she had to be fully aware of what her actions were doing to him.

Nicole stepped back and without a word spoken took him by the hand. She led him into the sandy dunes nearby, a secluded spot where they couldn't be seen from the beach. Looking him in the eye she slowly began pulling the strap of her bikini down and then the other, finally unhooking the bikini freeing it.

He couldn't take his eyes off her.

The world around them ceased to exist for him. Nicole had his full attention.

As the bikini top dropped she caught it and held the tiny piece of material across her breasts covering herself.

He longed for her to drop the top so he could see what he'd only imagined in the past. His eyes were glued to her breasts.

He was breathing hard.

He watched as she dropped the tiny top which had barely been covering her. She stood before him with her breasts now fully exposed. He watched as her breasts rose and fell with each breath she took.

"You're so beautiful," he said barely able to speak. He reached out to touch her.

She stepped back just out of reach and paused only a moment before she stepped out of her bikini bottoms never taking her eyes off his.

She stood there naked in front of him watching him look at her with longing.

She looked at him as though she were waiting for him to make the next move.

"Are you just going to stand there?" she asked in a husky voice.

He was beyond thinking rationally. All he knew is he had to have her. He wanted her so bad it hurt. All other thoughts other than to have her then and there fled his mind.

She reached for his hand placing it on one of her breasts.

He cupped her breast in his hand. He ran his hand underneath her breast holding the weight of it in his hand. He stroked the nipple with his thumb making it stand taut in reaction to his touch.

She ran her fingertips ever so lightly just beneath the waistband of his swimming trunks. Her fingertips barely touched his skin making him desire her touch even more.

He quickly pulled down his swimming trunks dropping them at his feet fully exposing himself to her.

He reached for her pressing against her holding her in his

arms. He felt her warm flesh pressed against him with not a shred of clothing between them.

"Nicole," he moaned. "Please... I want to make love to you."

"Yes, make love to me," she whispered in his ear.

He had longed to hear those words for a long time. Up to now he had only imagined how it would be in his daydreams and when he was in bed alone at night.

He was past the point of no return.

Having waited so long for just this moment he lost control and let out a deep groan and ejaculated.

As he did so the alien stepped back and the movie was over.

A different alien stood at his side. He scooped up his semen placing it into a vial.

He realized then it hadn't happened at all.

Somehow the alien had placed those thoughts and visions into his mind which had seemed so real. So real his own body had betrayed him.

He and Nicole as much as they were attracted to each other, no he had to admit he loved her with every fiber of his being, still they had never been intimate.

Not that they didn't desire each other as they definitely did. The desire was there on both their ends he knew without a doubt.

Now he wondered why they hadn't had sex before now. They obviously both loved each other so what were they waiting for?

He knew now after experiencing what he just had that he wanted her more than ever. He wanted to make that vision a reality. He had gone down the rabbit hole and there was no going back. He had to have her.

The alien who had peered into his eyes communicated telepathically to him. "You can have her. The two of you are meant to be together, to become one. There is no reason to wait any longer. The two of you have a destiny to fulfill."

He was still trying to slow his breathing and recover from what had just happened. The vision was still sharp in his mind.

The alien roughly wiped William off after retrieving his semen. This brought him back to awareness of where he was and that none of what he had just envisioned was real.

The alien walked away taking the semen sample with him.

He was humiliated in what had just happened and having the aliens witness it. No, they didn't just witness it. They're the ones who initiated it, who made it happen. He realized now that his reaction was exactly what they had wanted to happen.

He realized while he was experiencing this intimate moment they had stood there watching him. He put his hands over his eyes feeling exploited.

A different alien stepped forward and handed him his swim trunks. The alien motioned towards the door communicating that it was time to leave.

He dressed ashamed that the aliens had witnessed such an intimate scene.

They had deceived him all in order to get something they wanted. They made him believe what he was seeing was real.

It had felt real. So much so that he could even now imagine the touch of her breast and how it felt pressing himself against her.

He was led to a door where Nicole stood waiting for him.

He was embarrased by the whole procedure and couldn't look her in the eye.

At least he didn't have the humiliation of her witnessing what had just happened. He didn't think he could face her if she knew.

They were led down the same hall and that was the last thing he remembered until he found himself lying curled up in the fetal position alone on the beach.

As though from a distance he could hear his mother calling his name. He fully came to as she stood there shaking him frantically asking if he was all right.

17

"Nobody thought it important that I knew that aliens were real? You've been researching them and interviewing people who've seen UFOs for years, Dad. What? You didn't think I should know about this? Not only are they real but it appears that Nicole is....hmm, how do I put this ..." William said while pacing and quite upset, "...a regular visitor of theirs."

His dad let him talk and waited patiently to explain.

"You're absolutely right, William. We thought we had time yet before you needed to know. Apparently we were wrong in waiting to talk to you..."

"That was one hell of a way to find out they're real," William said.

"I'll let the language go this time," his dad said.

"She wasn't scared at all. I was petrified. She seemed to know all about the aliens," William said referring to Nicole.

"You were terrified and rightly so," his father said.

"The aliens and being taken up in the air flying over the ocean was scary enough, but when that alien who looked just like Nicole turned into a huge lizard...Dad, I was so scared," he confided to his father.

"Of course you were, son. Anyone would have been."

"I'm done with her. I want no part of this," he said emphatically.

"When you're ready to listen I'll tell you everything I know," his dad said. "I think you're...."

There was a soft knock on Edward's office door.

"Come in," Edward called out.

Nicole peeked her head around the door. William just turned his head away from her but as she spoke he couldn't help himself and looked back at her.

Who was he fooling, he thought. He'd never in a million years be able to leave her.

"I thought it would help if I was in on the conversation. I think I have some explaining to do," she said.

When she looked at William when she walked in the room and he turned his head away tears filled her eyes.

She thought now that she had been wrong for not telling him before. There was no excuse for it. She had been too scared to tell him in the past.

What guy after hearing that aliens were a part of her life would stick around afterwards? William wasn't just any guy. He was her soul mate. What would she do if he couldn't handle it and left her?

Edward said, "Pull up a seat Nicole. It was a pretty terrifying experience for him. I'm sure you can understand.

The three of them had discussed everything. Well, almost everything he thought. There was one thing he knew he couldn't confide in anybody. No not even Nicole; maybe especially not Nicole.

Nicole had secrets of her own that she had kept from him. Well now he had secrets too.

When William left the room to ask his mother to get them all something to drink at his father's request, Mr. Halloway asked Nicole to keep certain facts of the daughters of destiny to herself for the time being.

William was still completely unaware that she had been genetically modified carrying a part of the aliens within her. Her DNA had become part human part alien.

Nicole had been quick to agree to his father's request. If he was so freaked out about what happened today how would he ever accept the fact of what she carried within her. Not only that, but the fact that they would one day have a child of their own that would be of this new breed...part human, part alien.

She knew she would have to tell him...and soon, just not today. She knew she couldn't wait too long though as the powers that drew them to each other grew stronger every day.

He needed to be told before they ever consummated their love for one another. He needed to be given the chance to back out. She scoffed at that. Like that was even possible. She could never let him go.

They had explained the daughters of destiny to William only as the first daughters of a family being chosen and visited by the aliens. It was explained that the women in her family had been chosen for visitations for a special purpose throughout the generations. The purpose would one day be revealed.

Nicole thought that was true enough that she could live with telling him that much without feeling she was outright lying to him. More of an omission than a lie she tried to convince herself. One day she would reveal the purpose of the daughters of destiny but for now she didn't think he was ready for that information.

He had accepted what they told him and didn't question it further with his mind cluttered with the day's events.

Edward thought his son had been through enough for the time being. He felt he needed time to digest all he had experienced before he was confronted with the fact that Nicole carried part of the aliens within her and their child would one day too.

After Nicole left his father had promised him that his experience wouldn't be written up in any report or discussed with anyone. He had no intentions of doing so but was glad his son wanted to keep this amongst themselves.

"I know we've discussed this pretty thoroughly."

His father drummed his fingers on the desk appearing to be deep in thought. It was a habit he had during times of deep concentration.

"I don't want you to be uncomfortable at what I'm about to say to you, but I have a feeling you haven't told me everything." He waited hoping his son would confide in him.

William immediately became uncomfortable thinking of "the movie" he had been shown of him and Nicole and what had happened as a result.

His father reading his body language knew he was right. "Please don't be uncomfortable about this. I was young once too, believe it or not. I know some things are hard to talk about to your parents."

He looked away not wanting to discuss this any further.

"What I'm trying to say is from all the stories I've been told in the past from people who have claimed to have had encounters with aliens I believe more happened than what you've told me."

His son started to deny this and his father held up his hand.

"Let me just say that there's nothing for you to feel ashamed about. This was forced on you."

"Can we please not talk about this anymore. Can we just let this go," William pleaded.

"Other males that have been taken had sperm samples taken. Did they do anything of that sort to you?" his father asked in a gentle tone.

He hung his head in shame. "Something like that," he said quietly.

"Son, look at me," his father said in a gentle tone. "Don't be afraid to tell me. Please. This was out of your control. There's nothing for you to be ashamed about."

He began crying and spilled the whole story to his dad. How he and Nicole had never touched each other but the alien had made him believe he and Nicole were together and he felt such a strong desire for her he couldn't stop himself.

With shame he told his father about the end result and of how the alien scooped up his semen as though it was nothing and carried it off.

His dad came from around his desk sitting on the arm of his son's chair and putting his arm around him. "It's O.K. son. They put that vision in your head. They work with visions often. It appears that it's a way of putting thoughts into your head in a way to get something they want. In this case it was to obtain a sperm sample from you."

"Why would they want that? That's disgusting."

"Don't concern yourself about why son. Thank you for being honest and telling me."

"Please don't tell Mom," he begged.

"I won't tell her. You have my word," his dad said.

They sat in silence for a few more minutes.

His dad said, "Is there anything else you'd like to talk about?"

"I really do love her you know. I haven't touched her because I do love her if that makes sense, but I don't know how long I can...."

"The two of you are young yet. You have your futures ahead of you. Don't do anything that will jeopardise that," his dad said.

"I want her so bad it hurts sometimes. Did you feel like that with Mom?" he asked.

His Dad smiled and said, "I understand how hard it can be. In your case I imagine it's even more difficult as there's an unearthly draw. I imagine it might have something to do with Nicole and her purpose as the daughter of destiny."

"I don't know what that has to do with me," he said.

"Perhaps it's something similar to the aliens putting that vision in your head about the two of you. Evidently the aliens have accepted you as a mate for their chosen one, their daughter of destiny."

"But the aliens just met me today. I've felt this for awhile now. I don't know how to describe it. It's as though I'm being drawn to her and it's getting harder and harder to resist. I'm not even sure why I am anymore to be honest. Resisting I mean. I want her and I'm pretty sure she feels the same way about me."

"Do you think some of that is coming from the aliens? It could be that the aliens have put those thoughts and desires in your head so you'll act on it," his dad said.

"Maybe that's what the alien was talking about then," William said. "Almost as if he were telling us to go ahead and have sex."

"What exactly did he say to you?" his dad asked not liking what he just heard.

"He didn't say it exactly as they don't talk..."

"Understood," his dad said. "What did he not say then? What was his message?"

"He said, 'The two of you are meant to be together. There's no reason to wait any longer.' It was like he was telling me to go ahead and do what I saw in the vision only for real," he said.

"Please," his father pleaded. "Don't take advice from an alien that you know is not in your best interest. It isn't for him to say..."

"Oh, it's definitely in my best interest," William said smiling. "I wouldn't have to take so many cold showers."

"I do hope you're joking now. I know the two of you have been boyfriend and girlfriend for years. It probably seems like a long time to be together and not be intimate...that and the fact that you're a teenager with raging hormones. I do however encourage you to resist being sexually active at your age. I don't think you and Nicole are quite ready for the responsibilities that go with that."

"I feel such desire for her. It's not just lust. I really do love her and I plan on marrying her one day."

"Let's not rush things. You have a lot to accomplish before then...your education, building a career so you can support a family. That seems far away from where you're at today. Can you just try to enjoy being a kid for a little longer?" his dad said.

"I'm not a kid," he protested.

"You're right, forgive me for being flippant. You're a young man. I do believe you've matured today," his dad said smiling at his son.

"I do plan on going to college. Remember, I'm going to be an astronaut," he said smiling.

"That's right," his dad said. "How could I forget."

They both felt much better after their talk and before he left the room his dad asked him, "I have to fly back to the base and wrap up my work there. Are you going to be all right? I can always delay going back if you need..."

"I'm fine Dad, but I appreciate the offer."

Edward remained at his desk after his son walked out going over in his head all that his son had said.

The handwriting was on the wall and he thought it was only a matter of time before his son and Nicole did give in their feelings and became sexually active.

He knew for now anyway that they were fighting their own natural feelings for one another. How long would that last especially now that they were being encouraged by the aliens to be sexually active?

Why? Why were the aliens pushing it? Were they telling Nicole the same thing? Encouraging her also as they had his son.

Where did the time go? he wondered. He was just a little boy it seemed such a short time ago.

He thought he would have to find something to help keep his son occupied to give him less time to give in to those desires.

He knew his son wanted to be a pilot. Perhaps he could arrange for him to have private lessons and get a head start on his career choice. That would keep him occupied.

He would look into that right away and set it up as a surprise for his son.

18

It was the first of September and normally they would have been preparing for the start of school. Instead they were glued to the television listening to news of the impending storm.

It had just been announced that it was now a tropical storm and expected to become a hurricane in the next few days.

The newscasters gave a list of precautions to take and a list of items to buy to make it through the storm.

Liz was busy writing down the items the newscaster listed, "Batteries. Do we have batteries for the flashlights?"

"I'll go check," William got up and looked through the drawer where they kept their batteries.

By the time he had tested the flashlights his mother had written a large list of items to pick up at the store.

William and Nicole volunteered to go to the store for her. She kept adding items to the list as they waited patiently.

"They said to get plywood to board up windows. Do you think you should go by the hardware store and pick some up?"

Nicole said, "My dad has plenty at the house already pre-cut. He used to be caretaker over this cottage when no one was here and boarded up the windows whenever there was a storm. He'll take care of that for you."

Liz was back to the television switching channels trying to keep up with the latest news on the storm.

The meteorologist was informing the public that St. Augustine was in a high risk hurricane zone and hurricanes should be taken very seriously. There was a threat of high winds, heavy rains, and tidal surges in their area. Many people in the area were evacuating.

Nicole and William traipsed through the streets of St. Augustine taking in the sights. It was the last week before they started back to school and they had decided to do something different even though the weather wasn't cooperating.

The weather forecast had almost kept them indoors. The weather had kept them off the beach but they decided they could take in a few local museums or take in some of the local sights where they would be mostly indoors. Apparently the storm was slow moving and while they may have to deal with rain they would be inside most of the time.

Nicole pointed at a spot on the map they had picked up at the Chamber of Commerce of places they recommended for tourists to visit.

"It's a tourist trap," William argued. "You don't actually believe that if you drink the water from this so called Fountain of Youth that you'll actually stay young forever do you?"

"Of course not," Nicole said pulling him along. "It's a tradition. Everyone does it who comes to St. Augustine. I can't believe you haven't been there yet."

William only pretended to balk. He draped his arm around her and said as though he were giving in, "O.K. Let's go."

"They say Ponce de Leon sailed the seas in search of a way to stay young forever. If he could sail the ocean in search of it surely you can walk a couple blocks to see it," she teased him as they walked down the sidewalk.

"You do know that whole story about Ponce de Leon didn't really happen, don't you?" he said smiling at her.

"Of course, but it makes for a good story," she said laughing.

She reached up and kissed him on the cheek which brought a smile to his face.

The weather had finally let up and it was the first break they'd had from the rain. Nicole folded up her umbrella and tucked it under her arm and reached for his hand.

How can I be so lucky and have the most beautiful, sweetest girl in love with me? I don't deserve her he thought.

"Yes you do but thank you for the compliment," she said.

He stopped in his tracks. "Did I actually say that out loud?" he asked.

I'll have to be more careful she thought or I'll give myself away. My powers are growing. When I'm touching him I can hear his thoughts. I am bound to him so tightly I feel what he feels and there's nothing he can hide from me.

They'd made an entire day of seeing the sights. They drank from the Fountain of Youth teasing each other that they'd stay young and in love forever.

They went through a few of the smaller museums, bought lunch and enjoyed it under the Old Senator tree. As they ate their lunch outdoors they noticed the winds had picked up since they'd left that morning. They knew it would be raining again soon if the weathermen were right in their predictions.

After lunch before heading home they walked to the top of the St. Augustine Light Station enjoying the view from the top.

From the top of the lighthouse they could easily see the skies were growing dark and threatening. The ocean waves below were churning with rough seas. Even the thrill seeking surfers had called it a day at this point.

The sea birds seemed on edge with the sea gulls crying out and other birds flying looking for cover. A pod of pelicans flew in formation through the darkening sky.

"Maybe we better head home. The weather has gotten a lot worse since this morning. It's starting to look pretty bad," he said.

He thought he could actually feel the lighthouse swaying.

"Do you think the hurricane will hit St. Augustine like they're predicting?" Nicole asked.

"It's looking that way," William answered. "I'd better get back and see if Mom needs any help with anything."

They were making their way down to the bottom of the lighthouse. A ranger below was getting ready to close and lock up the lighthouse saying it was too dangerous to go to the top in these high winds.

They passed few people as they walked. They had noticed earlier that there were few tourists out today with the prediction of a hurricane coming on shore. Most of them had cut their vacations short and fled the area ahead of the storm.

"I guess this weather will delay your first flying lesson," she said.

He smiled, "I couldn't believe it when my dad surprised me with flying lessons."

"You'll have to fly over my house and tip your wings at me when you fly by," she said.

"I'll do better than that. I'll take you up in the plane with me once I get my license."

As they headed through the downtown area they noticed restaurants bringing in their outside furniture and boarding up windows.

"It looks like they're taking this storm pretty seriously," he said. "I've never been through a hurricane. What's it like?"

"It can be pretty scary," she said. "Winds can be pretty strong at over one hundred miles per hour. They're predicting these winds will be even stronger than that. One of the biggest concerns is roofs being blown off and flying debris."

"Let's hope the weathermen are wrong about it hitting St. Augustine," William said.

"Whether it comes ashore here or not it looks like we're definitely going to be feeling the fury of this storm," Nicole said tucking her head down to avoid the stinging wind.

19

Within the next few days the threat had become reality and instead of heading out to sea as the hurricane forecasters had hoped it might do it was headed right towards Florida's coast line.

No longer a tropical storm it was a named hurricane and reaching peak winds of 130 miles per hour. It was aimed right at northeast Florida with the bullseye being around Daytona Beach or St. Augustine. Either one would be devastating.

The entire first week of school had already been called off due to the hurricane.

William helped his mother bring in the furniture off the deck and bring anything in that could be blown away. Elke had warned her that anything left outside could be picked up by the winds and would be a flying projectile.

"I wish your dad was coming home," Liz said. "This storm scares me. I've been through tornadoes but never a hurricane."

"I'll be here. I'll help you with whatever you need," he said.

"Elke said for us to go stay over there until it passes. She's making up food in case we lose our electricity. Do you think we should stay with them?" she asked her son.

"Yeah, I definitely think we should. That sounds like a great idea," he said glad to hear he'd be riding the storm out with Nicole.

"Well of course you would say that," she said. "I don't know why I even asked."

The phone rang and he went inside to answer it. His dad explained how he was unable to get a flight home as all the flights that flew into the area had been canceled due to the hurricane.

He went to call his mom to the phone.

Klaus had arrived with supplies and was nailing up plywood to cover the windows that would be facing the high winds.

"Give me a hand," Klaus said to William.

While they worked Klaus said, "Look, I didn't want to scare your mom but they predict this is going to be a pretty strong hurricane. By tomorrow the weather should be pretty bad. I think it best if the two of you come stay with us for the duration. Why don't the two of you pack your bags and come over this afternoon."

"Mom told me that Mrs. Newhouse invited us to stay. We're planning to come stay with you. I think that would give my mom some relief since my dad isn't able to be here."

Once the house was secured William and his mother packed a bag to take with them to the Newhouse's. They thought they would leave the following morning before the weather got much worse. They should have listened to Klaus and gone the day before. The winds had intensified by morning.

His mother opened the door as they were leaving. The door was whipped out of her hand by the strong winds and thrown back slamming against the wall. The wind was whistling so loud they couldn't hear each other even though they were standing side by side.

Sand was blowing along the street while the palm trees were blowing with their fronds dancing wildly in the wind. The rain had begun coming down relentlessly sometime during the night and was now coming down in sheets.

"This is much worse than I expected it to be," Liz said.

"Hold onto the back of my shirt and I'll block the wind and lead us to the car. Hold on tight," William said.

She nodded and he told hold of both their bags. He had to bend his body almost in two to fight against the wind just to get the few feet they had to travel to get to their car. The sand was being blown up from the beach stinging their faces.

"Close your eyes and hang on," he yelled back to his mother. His words were lost in the wind.

As they made their way towards the car his mother's raincoat was ripped backwards and a few seconds later was ripped right off her and blown away before she had time to grab for it. Her clothing was soaked through within a matter of seconds.

William struggled to get the car door open while at the same time stepping on the bags so they weren't blown away.

He got his mother into the passenger side as he could see she was far too nervous to drive.

He tossed their bags in the back seat and made his way to the other side. He finally made it to the driver's side and let himself in.

"Oh my," his mother said with her hand to her heart. "Perhaps we should have evacuated like they suggested. This is really bad. And with your dad...."

"We'll be fine Mom. Try not to worry. We'll be safe with the Newhouses," he tried to assure her.

She nodded and said, "Please, just be very careful."

He was anxious to get them safely to the Newhouses' and though it was only a few doors down he drove slowly avoiding any flying debris as much as possible.

He could feel the strong winds rocking the car. At times he feared they were going to be blown off the road. His knuckles on the steering wheel were white.

They were both tremendously relieved by the time they arrived.

Klaus had been watching for them and spotted them as soon as they drove up. He came out and helped Liz into the house. He pointed to a spot where he thought the car would be safe from flying debris from the hurricane for William to park.

Nicole was in the kitchen with her mother. Elke and Nicole were busy making food that would last a few days that they could eat in case they lost electricity which Nicole informed him was almost sure to happen.

He could hear the wind getting stronger outside. It was dark inside as most of the windows had been boarded up. He heard something hit the side of the house obviously blown by the wind.

He walked to the front of the house which wasn't an area that had the windows covered and looked outside. As he watched he saw a beach umbrella that had been ripped inside out being blown down the street.

Nicole had quietly come up behind him and put her arms around him with her chin on his shoulder.

"I can't believe the storm got so strong so quick," he said. "I had no idea the storm would develop this fast. For days it seemed to hardly move but this has really gotten a lot stronger just since yesterday."

"We'll be fine. The first one you go through is pretty scary. Well, actually they're all pretty scary. I will say they're reporting that this is going to be a bad one. I'm glad you're here."

"Me too," he said turning around and taking her into his arms.

Klaus came into the room and cleared his throat.

20

Nicole was getting ready to serve everyone dessert when the lights went out. She reached for the flashlight she had near by and switched it on. They had pretty much assumed that eventually they would lose their electricity and kept flashlights and candles in each room.

"Can you light this candle for me William," she said pointing at it with the flashlight. "We can all have our dessert by candlelight."

They all sat around talking by the flickering candlelight long after they finished dessert.

Klaus had been eyeing the last piece of pie sitting in the pie plate and tapping his fork on his plate.

He said, "There's no sense in saving this last piece of pie. If no one else is going to claim it I think I'll finish it off. Maybe a big scoop of ice cream on top too since we don't have electricity and it'll just melt anyway."

"Now that's the best excuse I've ever heard for having ice cream," Liz said.

"Go ahead honey. You've been eyeing it for the last ten minutes. I can tell the temptation is too much for you," Elke said as she pushed the pie plate towards him.

"I can't believe you made that pie," William said to Nicole. "I'll be a lucky man when you marry me. Not only will I have the most beautiful wife but a great cook too."

Nicole blew him a kiss across the table.

"I think the least you could do is finish high school before you start worrying about marrying my daughter," Klaus said.

He looked sheepishly at the man who he knew would one day

be his father-in-law.

"Not worried about it," he said. "Just stating a fact. She is beautiful. She sure can cook. And I *will* make her my wife one day...but I promise I'll wait until I finish high school and have a career so I can offer her a good future."

Nicole smiled at him from across the table.

"Very well then," Klaus said. "Sounds reaonable enough."

Klaus put the last bite of pie in his mouth and pushed his plate away and said, "Why didn't someone stop me from making a glutton of myself? I'm so stuffed now I can hardly move."

William laid in his sleeping bag tossing and turning. He couldn't sleep knowing Nicole was so close yet out of his reach.

He got up quietly and listened at the door where her parents slept. He could hear Klaus snoring and heard no other sound so knew they were alseep.

He went to the door of the guest room and checked to see if his mother was asleep. He could hear her tossing and turning but then he could tell from her breathing that she too was asleep.

He knew the Margaritas the adults had shared to "take the edge off" had helped put them soundly to sleep.

He decided to sneak in Nicole's room and see if she was awake. What he'd really like to do is crawl into bed with her, but out of respect for her and her parents he knew he would have to resist that temptation.

One day soon though, he was telling himself. One day soon....

He was feeling such a strong urge to be with her. He knew it wasn't just that he was a horny teenager like his father had indicated. He loved her and wanted to be with her. The feeling had become so much stronger ever since he had the vision in the UFO.

He stood outside her door and quietly turned the knob to go in. He was thankful the door wasn't locked. He softly closed the door behind him.

"Nicole," he whispered in the dark standing just inside her room.

He got no response. Something didn't feel right but he wasn't sure what it was.

He walked quietly to her bed and pulled the covers back to surprise her and climb in beside her. He just wanted to hold her and cuddle for a few minutes he tried to convince himself.

As he eased himself in the bed he reached out for her but found only a pillow. He sat up and felt along the bed as it was too dark to see anything. Her bedroom window was one of the windows boarded up against the hurricane and it was so dark you couldn't see your hand in front of your face.

She wasn't here. Where was she?

Did she sneak out to see him while he was checking on whether their parents were asleep. Could she have had the same idea as he had and was planning on crawling in his sleeping bag with him to surprise him?

He got up and quietly went back to the living room but there was no Nicole. He searched the house but couldn't find her anywhere.

Where could she possibly go during a major hurricane?

21

Nicole felt their presence even before they showed themselves. She sat up and put her bedside light on. The aliens had come for her. She watched as soundlessly three aliens stepped out of her closet.

"How could you travel here during a major hurricane?" she asked sitting up in her bed.

"It is important. Come with us," the aliens communicated.

"I'm not going out there in this weather," she said firmly. "Are you crazy? We're liable to be blown out of the sky."

"It is imperative that you come. We will see to your safety. There is a message which you need to hear and obey."

"Not saying I'm going to *obey*," she said sarcastically, "but what's your message? What's so important that you risked coming out here during a major hurricane? Just give me the message and leave. Go back wherever it is you come from."

She turned the light off and plopped back down on her bed. She pulled the covers up to her chin determined to ignore them and go back to sleep.

The alien looked deeply into her eyes, dark or not it didn't seem to make a difference. It was as though he were looking into her mind.

She didn't recall being taken or how they traveled through a hurricane but they must have as now she was on a UFO. She could feel it's movements. They were none too reassuring. She felt like the UFO was being tossed around like a frisbee.

She was soaking wet as were her pajamas. Her teeth began chattering from the cold.

One of the aliens placed a hand on her back and at his touch her teeth stopped chattering. She felt a warmth flow through her, as warm as if she sat before a fire bundled up in a blanket.

A group of five or six aliens stepped into the room and explained that they would be traveling to get out of the harm of the storm.

They all heard a large bolt of lightening strike very close to the UFO.

The UFO began to spin out of control. They seemed to be falling out of the sky, plummeting towards the ocean.

Nicole screamed and fell. She slid across the floor having lost her balance. As she was sliding she reached out to grab hold of a table leg to stop her momentum. Grabbing the table leg was a smart move as it was bolted to the floor but the stop was so abrupt she felt her shoulder had been pulled from it's socket.

She stayed put after she quit sliding feeling that she was safer on the floor rather than taking the chance of falling again.

She noticed all the aliens were leaning up against the wall with their bodies and arms planted firmly against the wall.

Seeing them all lined up like that it reminded her of the Gravitron, a ride she had gone on once at an amusement park. You would get on the ride and lean against the wall. The ride would spin around at a high rate of speed. The floor dropped out from under you but you didn't fall because you were pinned to the wall by the force.

After about ten or fifteen seconds which had seemed terribly long the UFO regained control and sped to a higher location.

"Fine time you picked to come," she said getting up off the floor and brushing herself off. She winced at the pain in her shoulder.

"I thought you guys were so smart. Everyone, even us humans know enough to stay out of harm's way when you're in the path of a hurricane," she told them.

She heard the communications between the aliens saying perhaps they should have waited as they were having a rough time keeping steady and making it to safety.

"I can not believe you brought me out in this and put my life in danger," she screamed at them.

One of the aliens communicated to the others that perhaps she was right and they should have waited.

She understood the one that seemed to be in charge communicate to the others. "We had our orders. We couldn't wait."

Two new aliens in addition to the original bunch arrived and joined them. When they stepped forward the other aliens stepped back out of the way.

She was angry and she lashed out at the new arrivals feeling it was due to them that she had been brought here.

She shook her finger at the one closest to her and said, "You need to take me back home right now."

One of the aliens that had recently joined them leaned forward and looked deeply into her eyes.

At first she snapped her eyes shut knowing the powers they had when they did this but she felt compelled to open her eyes and couldn't fight it.

He transferred his thoughts to her. "You yourself have chosen the one who is to father the next daughter of destiny. So why is it you have not mated with him? You have a mission. You are to provide us with a daughter."

"I'm not *providing* you with a child of mine," she said. "Are you completely insane?"

"You misunderstand," the alien communicated. "The child will remain in your custody for you and the one you love to raise. It is your destiny to raise her for our purpose. Our fate and the fate of humans rest in your hands and in the hands of the future daughters of destiny. Until the chosen one arrives it is important that the daughters...."

"I'm practically a kid myself," she said. "I'm too young to be..."

"The feelings you have for him are anything but that of a child. We feel your desire for him. We have waited patiently but now it is our desire for you to..."

"*Your* desire for me?" she laughed at him. "Sorry, but it doesn't work that way."

Another alien stepped closer and picked up where they had left off before.

"There is no time to waste. This weather puts us at risk. We need an answer and then you will be returned to your home. Why do you not mate with your chosen one? You desire him, that is clear."

"Look," she said, "love him or not it's not up to any of you to tell me when to "mate" with him as you call it. Here on Earth we call it making love when it's someone you care deeply for and love."

"Then why do you not making love?" he asked.

"Make love, not making love," she said exasperated.

"I feel your desires and his too," the alien continued. "You both desire one another. Why do you deny yourselves this pleasure?"

"It's really none of your business," she said.

"You are our business. You are *our* mission. Everything you do is our business. Your future and your mission we rely on for our future well-being and for our very existence. The new breed cannot continue without your compliance in this matter."

"I'm not having a baby so you can say I've fulfilled my mission," she said. "I'm only seventeen. What's your rush?"

"Sixteen," he corrected her.

She let out an exasperated breath. "Fine, *almost* seventeen."

She winced again at the pain in her shoulder and reached back to rub it hoping to ease the pain.

One of the aliens placed his hand on her shoulder and after a few seconds the pain was gone.

She rotated her shoulder around to check and everything was back to normal.

The alien then took her hands in his. He motioned for her to hold her hands still. He then placed his fingertips against her fingertips, the palms of his hands against hers.

She was confused as to what he was doing. Then she felt an electrical jolt and heat transferring from his hands to hers. She started to pull away but he shook his head.

She kept her hands in place and she could literally feel the heat flowing through every part of her body. It felt as though it were an actual physical thing flowing through her veins. It was a burning sensation but comforting all the same. After a few minutes she began to feel the heat subside and when it was completely gone only then did he allow her to drop her hands from his.

The alien then removed his hands and communicated to her, "Use this gift sparingly and wisely and only when you deem absolutely necessary. Use it in the same manner I have just showed you."

"What gift?" she asked. "What did you do?"

"You have been given the gift of healing. I foresee that you will have need of this gift in the future. But choose wisely as to when to use it. It is limited to be used only a few times and then the gift will no longer be in your power."

She contemplated on this gift she had been given until her thoughts were interrupted.

"I ask you again," the alien who had been communicating with her asked, "Why do you wait? This is your entire purpose for being on this earth. You were selected and inputted with our..."

"I'm well aware of what you did to me," she snapped. "You seem to forget that I was conceived in love by my parents because they loved each other and wanted a child. So no, that's not my only purpose for being here. Maybe it's my only purpose as far as you're concerned. I don't know why you all had to come along and mess things up."

Nicole began to cry. "How do I even explain to him what you've done to me?"

The alien not understanding her tears continued with no compassion. "Your parents too were chosen for the purpose of delivering you to us. Their love for one another was a gift from us. They didn't fight their desires for one another like you are doing. We do not understand why you do so."

This was shocking news to her. She had no idea the aliens had intervened in her parent's relationship with each other.

She shook her head as though to shake away what thoughts he had put into her head. She would not let him get to her. She knew her parents loved her. The aliens would not lessen that.

"You are indeed loved by your parents as your child will be loved by you and your chosen mate. You are blessed to be one of the new breed. You are the first of this breed. That makes you very special. Your child too will be special and carry a part of us. It is you and your future generations that will bring about a new world. A new way of life for humans and us. This far outweighs the importance of the life you describe."

"Not to me or to the ones I love," she argued. "I refuse to be told by you and your kind on how to live my life. What you're wanting me to do is a personal choice. A decision that should be made between me and William."

"Do you not understand the power you carry, how you and your lineage will change the world?"

The alien who had given her the gift of healing transferred his thoughts to her. "Even now your powers far outweigh the capabilities of other humans and hybrids. Though you are strong, each daughter of destiny following you will each grow stronger."

She stood silently contemplating all they had told her.

"What do you mean hybrids? Is that what I am?" she asked.

"No, you are different. You are a breed of your own. The first of your kind. That is not the hybrid he is speaking of but that is of no concern of yours. We only need to know why you delay in fulfilling your destiny."

The aliens looked at one another and communicated with each other. They thought they had put a barrier up so she couldn't hear their thoughts but her powers had grown stronger and she was able to break through their thoughts with little effort.

"Perhaps we have made her too strong. Her powers are too great. She is the first to ever be able to not obey without question."

"She is powerful this one," one of the other aliens agreed.

"She may be powerful but I sense it is painful for her to defy what she is feeling. It is taking great strength to deny herself what she desires. She wants him. She desires to become one with the chosen male human, the one she loves. When that happens...."

"Her powers will be even stronger. The two of them will be as one and the next generation will soon arrive."

"How we long for that," all the aliens thought in unison.

The other aliens nodded in agreement while another alien said to the others, "Even now she has such strong powers. I wasn't aware the powers would grow so strong so quickly."

"Imagine what it will be like when the chosen one arrives. She will be master over us all. Humans will bow to her and do her bidding. She will hold the key to a new life for us and our kind. The earth..."

"Let us not concern ourselves with that for now. Leave that for the future. Get back to our immediate concern. If the mating doesn't take place there will be no chosen one."

"What do we do? It is time for her to breed. We need...."

"I can understand you. You do understand that, right?" she asked them.

They actually looked shocked that she had been able to read their thoughts.

"Yes, this one's powers are strong. She is mighty this one. They chose wisely in choosing from her lineage. It is more imperative than ever that she provides us with the gift of life."

"A life that will provide us with hope. A future."

"Can you take me back now?" she asked. "We are in the middle of a hurricane and if anyone discovers me gone they'll be worried sick."

"Please," one of the aliens asked, "Explain to us why you deny yourselves the pleasure of breeding. We have learned this is something you humans enjoy. We feel your desire to do so. Why do you wait?"

At first she refused to respond but after thinking about it a moment she thought maybe if they knew the reason they would give her the time she needed. For what they were asking of her she didn't think it was asking much of them to grant her some extra time.

"He needs to know," she said despondently. "I won't give myself to him until he knows what you've done to me. Not only to me but what it will mean for our future children. The children we will have together one day."

She looked into their faces to see if she could tell if they understood what she was telling them. Their faces showed no expression whatsoever.

She continued with her explanation, "Either he accepts it or rejects me. He must know what he's getting into. I'm giving him a choice, unlike what you've given me...no choice. It's his future too."

"And if he wants no part?" the alien asked.

"I'll have to accept that. In that case I'll do my duty as a daughter of destiny. I'll still have the child who is to be the next generation daughter of destiny regardless of his decision. Even if he doesn't want to be a part of our lives, but I won't make him beholden to me."

The alien nodded approving of her answer. "You need not fear on that part. He will not turn you away. His love is too deep. He will always want you and only you. There could never be another for him. His life will never be complete without you."

"I hope you're right," she said softly.

"Then once you speak to him of this matter then you will carry out your mission."

"A child should never be looked at as a mission," she said. "When we humans have a child together it's...why do I try to explain feelings to you. You don't have feelings or emotions of any kind so how could I ever expect you to understand."

"We eagerly await for the arrival of the next generation of daughters of destiny," one of the aliens explained. "Perhaps that is as close to these feelings that you describe that we will ever feel."

"William and I have things to accomplish before that happens. He needs to further his education and have a career."

"But he can do that with you and the child. There is no need to wait."

"As I said, I have foreseen certain things. My vision for him is such. One of your gifts to me was foresight and what I have seen for him...he needs to experience certain things before we are at that point. He won't be allowed to do that if he has a wife and child. Then and only then I will do as you desire and give birth to the next daughter of destiny, but *not* before then. I will not bend on this. I will do this for him."

"That is your desire then, to give him this future?"

"Yes. In order for our future to be what I have foreseen there are things we both need to do *before* I fulfill my destiny," Nicole explained.

"You feel that strongly to give him this future?" the alien asked.

"Yes I do. I too have a destiny other than giving birth to the next generation of daughters of destiny. There is a role I must fulfill in order for him to be able to see his to fruition. If I don't, the vision is muddled at this point, but from what I foresee he won't be able to complete what he needs to do. Everything I do will be for him, for the two of us. That is what love is all about. It's a shame you are deprived of those feelings. Since I met him I can't imagine life without love."

The alien looked at her intently. "You are stronger than they realize."

The alien was silent for a few moments deep in thought. When one of the other aliens began to communicate his thoughts he held up his hand for them to be quiet.

This alien that appeared to be in charge looked at Nicole. "I accept your wish for more time to gift us with the next generation.

I feel that this new route you wish to take in your life will make the next generation even stronger. Your strengths will be passed on to her. Yes, I submit. You will be given this additional time."

"Thank you for understanding. I know there are things that have to happen first before William and I can be together as a family. It has been seen in my vision for our future."

"Not all has been revealed to you through these visions, you must understand that. There is much you do not know. Not all is meant to be known beforehand. The choice is yours to make. I will abide by your wishes.... this time."

"It's the only way I see possible for him to meet his destiny. All this must take place before I have the daughter you so deeply desire for me to have," she said.

"You have made your choice then," the alien asked.

"Yes," she responded firmly. "This decision I am making is for what is in his best interest."

"Your desire for him is stronger than for this child you are to bear?" the alien asked.

"Nothing compares with the love we have for one another," she answered. "That is why our child will be deeply loved. You needn't fear on that account."

"You speak of this strong love you have yet you have doubts about telling him about yourself. Surely he must feel you are different from others. Surely he knows this without being told."

"Maybe he wonders at times, but he doesn't really know for sure what it is. There's no way he could... what you've done to me is beyond the imagination of humans, of my kind. What it means for our future and our future child...he needs to be told," she said.

"You speak of humans as being of your kind, but do not forget you are also a part of us," one of the aliens said.

"Like I need to be reminded of what you've done to me. But no, I am *not* of your kind. I have human parents. I may carry a small part of you but...," she said.

"What you carry is much more than a small part of us. It will grow with each new generation. Some future generations may even be unaware of what they will carry within, but it doesn't make it any less so. Your kind is an entirely new breed," he said.

The alien in charge was watching her reaction as the other alien was imparting this information. She seemed horrified by what the alien was saying. He felt it imperative to step in and put a stop to this banter and get back to the subject of why they had brought her here in the first place.

"Your request for more time has been granted," the alien in charge said. "Use your time wisely. We will wait patiently for this time you feel you need."

"We will return you now," one of the other aliens said as the alien in charge walked off and left the room.

"This was indeed a bad time to come," he informed her as they prepared for their departure. "The winds whip us in the sky relentlessly. The lightening threatens our craft. We will see you safely home now."

After the aliens left she knew what she had to do. She convinced herself it was her decision and not due to the persuasion of the aliens. She knew there was no better time than the present. She had put it off long enough.

She was drenched and cold from being brought through the storm. How did they survive traveling through a hurricane of this intensity?

She grabbed a new pair of pajamas and took a long, hot shower. She noticed she was shaking and she knew it wasn't from the cold. She feared William's response to what she was going to tell him.

She tried not to dwell too much on what the alien had said about future generations. She was mostly concerned with getting through this night and letting William know that the girl he had fallen in love with was no ordinary girl.

22

Still cold after taking a hot shower she wrapped herself in a blanket and came out in the living room where William had a sleeping bag laid out to sleep in.

"Is there room in there for me?" she whispered.

William lifted the top for her to slide in beside him. "There's always room for you. Where were you? I went to see you..."

"I'm here now," she said. She dropped her blanket and cuddled up in the sleeping bag next to him. He rolled over on his side and kissed her.

With his arm around her he could feel her breasts pressed up against him. He moved his hand to caress her breast through her pajamas and stroke it ever so gently.

This was probably a bad idea she thought.

She shifted positions and he pressed up against her. He reached down and stroked her thigh rising his hand just a little higher.

He could feel her breathing quicken.

"Nicole, I want you so bad. I love you. Please..."

"We have to talk," she said while moving his hand off her thigh.

He moaned and flopped back on his back.

"Why Nicole? I know you want me as much as I want you. I feel it. We love each other. What's the..."

"There's something I need to talk to you about first. Only after you know everything, only then. "

"Tell me quick then before I die of frustration," he said.

"I wouldn't want you to die of frustration. Just think of what you have to look forward to," she said trying to lighten the tension.

She sat up and wrapped the blanket around her thinking it would be easier for him to concentrate if she wasn't sitting practically naked in front of him.

"You're the best thing that ever happened to me," he told her.

"We'll see if you still feel that way after our talk."

"Nothing could change how I feel about you. My feelings for you grow everyday. Nothing you tell me will ever come between us," he said.

He felt closer to her than ever and knew there was no way he'd ever let anything come between them. Whatever it was that was bothering her that she felt she needed to tell him he would assure her didn't matter...as long as they were together nothing else was important.

"I don't even know how to begin..." she said.

She dreaded telling him but she knew she had to. He had to know everything about her before he made that final commitment to her.

She had to know now if he would stay with her after he knew what the aliens had done to her. How would he feel about her when he knew she carried alien DNA within her? As would any child they may have together in the future.

He'd seen the aliens. How would he feel knowing that a part of them flowed through her own veins? How would he feel knowing she had certain alien powers? And how would he feel knowing that she was partially responsible for the determination of the future of the aliens and humans on earth? Even she wasn't sure what all that was all about but even to her ears it sounded foreboding.

Love her or not she knew it would be a lot to accept. Was it too much to ask of him?

His answer was something she was unable to foresee.

23

Nicole asked him to move into the kitchen so they could sit at the table while they talked.

"It's a long story," she explained.

He had a feeling of trepidation of what she was about to tell him.

He started to light the candle on the table.

Nicole said, "I'd rather you didn't. I prefer to tell you in the dark. I don't want you to look at me when I tell you what I have to say."

William took her hand in his and said in a soothing tone, "You know you can tell me anything. Whatever you have to tell me isn't going to change things between us."

"I don't know how it couldn't," she said. "But it has to be told. You need to know. Only then can you make your final decision."

"Decision about us? I made that decision the first time I laid my eyes on you," he said smiling at her while holding her hand.

"Go ahead, light the candle."

He lit the candle and sat back. He waited patiently letting her begin on her own time.

She stared at the flickering candle as though lost in her thoughts.

He knew whatever it was she had to tell him must be something hard for her to face. He'd never known her to be frightened of anything. He hated the thought that it was hard for her to talk to him about anything.

"You know my mother escaped Germany during World War Two," Nicole began.

He nodded. He had heard the story of her mother's escape.

What that had to do with them he couldn't imagine.

"What you don't know is previous to leaving Germany she worked for the German government..."

He appeared surprised by this revelation.

"Don't get the wrong impression. She wasn't a Nazi. Far from it. However both her and my dad worked for the government and they had an alien in their possession that had crashed over Germany. She worked with that alien," Nicole explained.

"Wow. That must have been strange. Is that how the aliens knew about you?" he asked.

"I guess I'm skipping part of the story," she said. "She actually first had an encounter with aliens at the age of five or maybe it was six. I don't remember for sure. Anyway, she drowned and they saved her life."

"Seriously?" William said stunned by this bit of news.

"My mother wasn't the first in her family to have a relationship with the aliens. Her mother went crazy due to aliens being involved in her life."

"Your grandmother?" he asked.

"Yes, she would have been my grandmother. I never met her and my mom has no idea what happened to her. After my mom drowned my mother's father blamed her mother for the accident and my mom never saw her again."

"That must have been hard for a little girl," he said.

"I suppose. Anyway, my mom had forgotten about the aliens while growing up. It all came back to her when she began working with the alien that was in custody of the government. When she was pregnant this alien told her it was a little girl and he told her a premonition, prediction...whatever you call it."

"A prediction about you?" he asked.

"Yes," she answered in a subdued tone of voice. "They told her of a gift the aliens were going to give her baby daughter. It's a long story but anyway she met with them again....."

She told William in great detail about her mother and

Connor's encounter with the aliens during their escape from the Germans.

He was amazed at the story but now she sat back and when she brushed her hair out of her face he could see her hand was trembling.

"Nicole, you don't have to tell me anymore if this is upsetting you. Really. I appreciate you wanting me to know..."

"No," she said emphatically. "You need to know. You *have* to know. You see your future too will be impacted on the rest of the story. What I've yet to tell you."

He got up and poured her a glass of water and set it in front of her.

Nicole took a long drink and then told him how her mother was on the ship sailing for America. She told him how the aliens came and took her mother from the ship. It was at this point that Nicole started crying.

He came around the table and helped her up and took her into his arms and sat her on his lap. "It's O.K. Whatever it is you're trying to tell me won't change how I feel about you. I love you. I always will no matter what."

She nodded and got up and sat back down in the chair across from him while he went to get a kleenex for her.

"My mother inside the spacecraft, UFO whatever you want to call it, anyway she was led to a table. My mother told me she watched as one of the aliens picked up an instrument. She knew immediately it was meant to be used on her. Other aliens had entered the room carrying something on a tray with a syringe."

Nicole took a sip of the water and then looked at him deeply to see how he was accepting what she was telling him. She knew what she said next was going to make him realize the importance of what she was telling him.

"Go on. Tell me the rest," he said prompting her.

He didn't know why but he feared what she was going to tell him. He had a bad feeling deep in his gut.

She nodded and said, "First just let me tell you I love you very much."

"I love you too," he said. "Go on. Tell me the rest."

She sighed and picked up where she had left off. "The alien explained to my mother, 'Your daughter will be a daughter of destiny. The first of her kind. She will be the first of a new breed. The future will be determined through her lineage. Each of the daughters of destiny following your daughter until the chosen one arrives is of utmost importance in the assurance of the chosen one's future arrival."

He wanted to ask her to explain about the daughters of destiny and about this chosen one she mentioned. As many questions as he had he thought it best to let her tell it in her own way.

Here she hesitated and a fresh set of tears ran down her face. "Their purpose... *our purpose* as I am one of them... is to pave her way, this chosen one."

With that he couldn't stop himself, "What do you mean you're one of them?"

She held her hand up signaling him to wait. She picked up where she left off. "Our purpose is to, honestly I'm not exactly sure what it is other than to also give birth to a daughter who will be the next generation of the daughters of destiny. Our purpose has something to do with making it possible for co-existence between the aliens and humans."

"Are you saying that the aliens plan to live here on Earth with humans? To live together on this planet? Is that..." he asked shocked by this revelation.

"I need to tell my father about this," he said getting up and pacing. "I'm sorry Nicole. This isn't something I can keep to myself. This could mean they have something treacherous planned for the future. He needs to know about this. Then he can decide who or if he needs to share it with the higher-ups."

"He already knows," Nicole said quietly.

"What did you say?" William shouted. "My father knows about this?"

24

William was about to knock on his father's office door when his mother came around the corner and said, "Oh William, don't bother your father right now. He's working on his book. He told me he needs some peace and quiet so he can concentrate."

The door opened and his father stood there in the doorway and said, "It's fine Liz."

"Did you want to talk to me son?" he asked.

"If you're not too busy," William said.

"Come on in."

He ushered his son into his office.

His father had retired from the military and had started working on a book of all he had discovered about UFOs.

His father believed the public had a right to know and who better to tell the story than the man who had worked relentlessly on the project for years.

"I'm sorry if I'm bothering you."

"Not at all. You're far more important than anything else. What's on your mind?"

He opened up to his father at the astounding revelation Nicole had told him on the night of the hurricane.

"Dad, I don't know what to think. She's not even human. Well what I mean is she's part human part alien. What does it mean to be genetically modified? She said she wasn't really a hybrid, but a new breed is how she described it. What does that even mean?"

"Actually William she has two human parents. The other part is a bit harder to explain. I don't know how much you've studied about DNA in your science classes but from what I understand the aliens took certain alien cells inserting it into her while she was still in her mother's womb."

"I understand some about DNA but it's not a subject I know much about," William said.

"What is it that concerns you?" his dad asked.

"Uhh, the whole thing. She told me the aliens inserted a part of them, harvested cells into her while her mom was pregnant. That their cells would intertwine until the human cells and alien cells co-mingled and became one. So am I in love with an alien or human? I'm not even sure what she is."

His dad sat back and let out a deep sigh, "I certainly hope you didn't express those thoughts to her."

"Of course not," he answered. "I told her I still loved her..."

"Can you imagine how she must feel? She had nothing to do with this, no choice in the matter. It's not as though she did something wrong. They did this to her without anyone's consent. I can't even imagine how such a young girl could be brave enough to reveal to you what she did. That must have been a heart wrenching decision on her part knowing you could as easily shun her and walk away. Frankly I admire her that she was able to tell you."

"I know," William said. "I got the impression I let her down from my reaction to what she said."

"You know..."

"Dad, I know. I messed up bad. I told her I needed some time to think about it."

"I can only imagine how hurt she must feel right now," his dad said. "If nothing else admire the fact that she was honest and opened up to you in such a personal matter. That was amazing for such a young girl to realize she needed to do that and to give you a choice in the matter. That's quite admirable."

"It's just that it shocked me. That was the last thing I expected to hear. I thought maybe she was going to tell me she wanted to go out with someone else or something trivial. Well, that seems trivial now anyway. The last thing I expected..."

"Have you talked to her about this since that night?" his dad asked.

"No," he answered. "I really did need some time to think

about everything."

"Understood," his dad said. "You don't think she needs a little reassurance about your feelings towards her?"

"Yeah, probably...yes," he said.

"Especially after you told her you'd love her regardless of what she told you. You told her it wouldn't change your feelings for her. I think the least you can do is..."

"I know, Dad. I know. You don't have to remind me about what a jerk I was...am," he said.

"I don't know how I myself would have handled it to be honest," his dad said. "It's unprecedented."

"That's why she's so dang smart," William said. "She remembers everything."

"It's called a photographic memory," his dad explained. "It appears to be one of her gifts. A gift is how the aliens described it anyway. Myself, I'd rather do without their gifts as they come with quite a price."

"She said she sometimes hears my thoughts. That's scary," William said. "She told me each new generation of these daughters of destiny would have different gifts."

"And you do understand the next generation would be your own child," his dad said. "Your daughter too will be a daughter of destiny if the two of you marry and have children."

"Maybe we'll have boys," he said.

"I doubt it from what I understand," his dad said. "It's destined for the daughters of destiny to each give birth to the next generation until the chosen one arrives. I don't believe anyone knows when that is supposed to occur. Evidently even the aliens have been left in the dark on that."

"When they did what they did to Nicole the alien actually said to her mother that she was lucky they let her keep the child, that it was theirs too. They told her that her baby had a purpose in the future of humanity and alien life. To think that the girl I love is part alien and if we have a baby it will be too. I don't know if I can handle that."

25

William came home from school and walked into his dad's office where he found him organizing his papers.

"What're you doing?" William asked.

"Writing the book is the easy part," his dad explained. "It's the organizing of all these papers from years of research, notes, and interviews that take up so much time."

"I'll help. How are you organizing them?" he asked.

"Right now I'm just trying to put them in order by date. See up here in the corner. Just look for the date and put them in piles according to the dates. Thanks. I can really use your help," his dad said.

William worked quietly for over an hour and a half and then told his dad, "Done. They're all in order."

His dad looked amazed that he had finished so quickly a task that had seemed to take him all morning and afternoon.

"You wouldn't want a job would you? I could use your help after school."

"Would I get paid?" William asked.

"What the flying lessons aren't payment enough?" his dad joked. "Of course I'll pay you. What do you think you're worth?"

"How long would it take me to make $300.00?" he asked.

His dad looked up surprised he had a certain figure in mind. "What do you need the money for?"

"I picked out a ring I want to buy for Nicole's birthday," he said.

"What kind of ring?" his dad asked. "That sounds like a lot of money."

"It's just a promise ring, don't worry. We've talked it all out and we plan on going to college and working towards our careers before we get married. I just want to give her something now to let her know I'm serious about her."

"I think she knows that already," his father said.

"I was a real jerk when she told me about... you know. I'm ashamed I treated her like I did. I'm glad she forgave me as I really do love her. I can't imagine life without her."

"It was a lot to take in," his dad said. "You just needed some time."

"I'll tell you just between you and me Dad. I am worried about any kids we have. I don't want aliens to be a part of my baby's life."

"That's certainly understandable. I think you have to accept it as inevitable if you and Nicole do marry one day. Nicole has seemed to manage and she lives a pretty normal life....other than that anyway."

"Yeah, other than that," William laughed.

"How soon do you need to make this money?" his dad asked.

"Her birthday is in three weeks," he said. "I put the ring on hold. I'm making payments on it but at the rate I'm going it will be the end of the school year before I have it paid for."

"I think we can work something out," his dad said.

"So put me to work. I'm on the clock," he said.

26

Nicole and William walked home from school talking about college and making future plans.

Just the day before he had received a letter from the Air Force Academy in Colorado accepting his application. He was elated. This was the first goal he could check off towards his ultimate goal of becoming an astronaut.

Nicole even though still a junior had applied to a few colleges of her choice and also planned to apply at the Air Force Academy once she graduated the following year. There was little doubt that she would be accepted anywhere she applied with her high IQ and grades.

William reflected on the moment he had handed his father the letter of acceptance to the Academy.

His father read it and looked at his son and said, "The United States Air Force Academy is one of the most competitive schools in the nation. You have to meet high standards to be eligible. This is something to be proud of," his father said with tears in his eyes.

"I know," William said. "That will set me on the right track of becoming an astronaut."

His father had stood and hugged him. "I can't tell you how proud you've made me. You're an amazing son."

Nicole brought him out of his daydream of that special moment with his father by asking, "Do you have to work for your dad today?"

"No, he went with your father to Orlando for an interview for a job at Martin Marietta. Your dad is introducing him to someone so he can hopefully get a job there once he gets his book published."

"So our fathers would work together. That's pretty neat," she said.

"From what he told me it's a pretty big place so I'm not sure if they'd actually work together. They both work in the field of aerospace engineering so maybe they will."

"Your dad has a pretty extensive history in the field. He shouldn't have any problem getting a job there," Nicole said.

"I hope you're right. He was offered a job at Northrop in California and I know my mom would be a lot happier if she could stay here in St. Augustine. She and your mom have become good friends and I'll be off to the Academy so it would be pretty lonely for her in California."

"Speaking of the Academy and the good news of your being accepted," Nicole said. "I thought we should celebrate."

"Sounds good," he said. "Did you have anything in mind?"

"Go home and put on your swimming trunks and meet me on the beach in fifteen minutes. Not a minute before," she said.

"Should I bring my board? It's the last day of summer but I imagine the water is getting cold," he said.

"No, just wear your swimming trunks," she said.

No one was home when he got there so he changed into his swimming trunks, looked at his watch and seeing that he still had seven minutes before he was supposed to meet Nicole he grabbed a snack.

William walked out his back door and from their back deck could see Nicole walking up from the opposite direction of her house. She motioned for him to come down.

He walked down the steps of his deck admiring her in her bikini. It was the one he liked the most, the neon green one. He knew it was probably the last time he'd see her in it with the summer ending.

"Let's take a walk down the beach," she said taking his hand in hers.

Seagulls flew overhead crying out.

The day was warm but a bit breezy with fall right around the corner.

Nicole's long blonde hair blew across her face. She stopped, turning her face out of the wind and pulled the hair out of her eyes.

She smiled at him in that way that made him weak. His body always responded with a will of it's own when she smiled at him like that.

She wrapped her arms around him. She held him so tightly her breasts were pressed against him.

She reached up and kissed him.

She stepped back and without a word spoken took him by the hand. They walked a ways down the beach and then she veered off and led him into the sandy dunes nearby. They were in a secluded spot where they couldn't be seen from the beach.

He wondered where she was going. Something about this seemed oddly familiar.

He noticed that Nicole had been here earlier and left a few things behind. Her beach blanket was laid out on the sand nestled between the dunes.

Looking him in the eye she slowly began pulling the strap of her bikini down and then the other, finally unhooking the bikini freeing it. She held the tiny piece of material across her breasts covering herself.

"Are you just going to stand there?" she asked in a husky voice.

That's when it hit him.

He'd experienced this before. This was *exactly* what he'd seen the day he'd been taken aboard the alien spacecraft.

Had they shown him something that would happen in the future?

Could this possibly be the day their love would be

consummated? He could only hope.

If so, please let it end differently this time he thought.

"Do you want to make love to me?" she asked.

He was breathing heavily when he answered, "More than I've ever wanted anything."

At those words she dropped the tiny top which had barely been covering her. She stood before him with her breasts now fully exposed.

He watched as her breasts rose and fell with each quickened breath she took.

"You're so beautiful," he said barely able to speak.

She never took her eyes from him as she stepped out of her bikini bottoms. Not a bit shy in front of him she stood there letting him devour her with his eyes.

He was beyond thinking rationally. All he knew is he had to have her. He wanted her so bad it hurt.

He began to pull his swimming trunks down when she stopped him.

She wasn't going to torment him like this was she?

He felt her fingertips ever so lightly just beneath the waistband of his swimming trunks. Her fingertips barely touched his skin making him desire her touch even more. Where she touched him he felt like he was on fire.

This time it was Nicole who pulled down his swimming trunks fully exposing him.

She watched as he stepped out of his trunks kicking them aside.

She took him by the hand and without saying a word led him to the blanket she had spread out in anticipation of just this moment.

They laid down next to each other. He took her in his arms kissing her and pulling her body up against his own.

His breathing was quick and erratic. Her breathing matched his own.

"Nicole," he moaned as he stroked her breast. "I love you so much. I want to make love to you."

He felt her warm flesh pressed against him, not a shred of clothing between them.

"Make love to me William," she whispered in his ear.

Remembering how it had ended last time he wanted to be sure this time it had a different ending. It most definitely did, a very satisfying ending. Better than anything he had ever imagined it would be like.

Afterwards they lay back content in each other's arms.

Finally they had become one.

27

"Congratulations honey. I'm thrilled you got the job and I'm so happy we'll be able to stay here in St. Augustine," Liz said.

"We won't have to move to Orlando will we?" William asked his dad.

"No, Klaus and I plan to carpool. We'll rent a small apartment there for the days we have to work long hours and come home weekends. Otherwise it's not that far that we can't drive back and forth," he answered.

"Good. I wouldn't want William to have to move the end of his senior year of high school," his mother said.

"I wouldn't do that to him. He's had to make enough moves during my days in the military," his dad answered.

"I imagine I'll be facing that myself once I'm in the Air Force," William said with pride.

"You'll be in one place for the first few years you're studying at the academy. It shouldn't be too bad. With your future pretty much planned out it's evident you'll either end up in Houston or Cape Canaveral where the space industry is," Edward said.

"I think that's pretty amazing you'll be working in the aerospace industry with a company that works under contract with NASA and their space program. Just think one day you may be doing work on the very spacecraft that'll be taking me to the moon," he said.

"You're pretty sure of yourself aren't you," his mom said with pride.

"I am," he said.

"You're not there yet. You have quite a few years of hard work ahead of you before you get there," his dad reminded him.

28

His parents and Nicole were at the airfield to witness him take his solo flight to get his pilot's license. His instructor stood by only to witness this time not to instruct as William went through his pre-flight checklist.

William knowing the procedure by heart still preferred to have a written checklist to go by for added security that nothing was overlooked.

For the purpose of his flight instructor to know he was going through all the proper steps he called each step out as he went through them.

"Auxiliary fuel pump off. Flight controls free and correct. Instruments and radios checked and set," he called out.

"Why isn't he taking off?" Nicole asked his father.

The three of them stood out of the way of any aircraft but where they could watch.

"He's going through his pre-flight checklist," Mr. Halloway answered. "That's the last thing a pilot does before letting the tower know he's ready for take-off."

"I'm so nervous," Mrs. Halloway said. She physically flinched when a small plane buzzed overhead coming in for a landing.

Mr. Halloway put his arm around his wife and patted her shoulder. "The instructor wouldn't allow him to go up if he wasn't sure that he was ready."

"I don't understand why his instructor can't go with him," Mrs. Halloway said.

"That's why it's called a solo flight," her husband reminded her yet again. "Now try not to look nervous. You don't want him to see you looking scared."

Nicole too was nervous for him but she knew everything would go well. He had studied hard and flown many hours with his instructor. She felt confident in his abilities.

She knew he would in the future be flying much bigger planes and even pilot a spacecraft. This was something she had foreseen in his future and today was the beginning of making those dreams come true.

William had completed his pre-flight checklist. The chocks were removed from behind the wheels and he climbed in the cockpit. He buckled his seat belt and slammed his door ready for takeoff.

They could barely hear themselves over the sounds of planes coming in and taking off.

His parents and Nicole watched with their own thoughts as he got word from the control tower and taxiied down the runway.

His father was so proud a tear escaped that he quickly wiped away. He couldn't be prouder at the son he'd raised. He had become a young man he was extremely proud of.

He knew he had a great future ahead of him. He had studied hard and had great promise. He knew he had some great hurdles to meet with aliens being a part of his life which would be inevitable once he was married to Nicole.

He still wasn't exacly sure what it meant to have their child, which would be his own grandchild, become a daughter of destiny.

He promised himself he would be there to help his son through any difficult times he might have to face.

"There he is!" Nicole pointed.

He'd been up in the air for about fifteen or twenty minutes. They'd lost sight of him long ago but they could see his instructor was staying in radio contact with him and all seemed to be going well.

They watched as his plane circled around getting ready to come in for a landing.

They saw his plane land on the runway and immediately take to the air again.

"What happened? Is something wrong?" his mother asked her husband.

"That's called a touch and go. That's part of his test. Everything's fine. He'll be landing shortly."

No sooner had he finished explaining and they saw his plane circling around aiming for the runway to land again.

He made a perfect smooth landing.

When William exited from his plane he shut everything down and put the chocks underneath the wheels.

They watched as his instructor came forward and shook his hand. He patted him on the back and when William turned to where Nicole and his parents were standing he was wearing a huge smile.

William held his thumbs up letting them know he had passed his test.

A photographer stepped forward and took a photo just at that moment.

29

William was given free access to his father's papers and notes from Project Blue Book while he helped his dad work on the book. There were times when he stopped to read some of the reports. He had taken an interest considering the fact that aliens were now a part of his own life.

He read out loud from the notes in his hand, "In 1952 at the Mitchel Air Force Base in New York it says here 'there was an incident where a UFO drew away from their pursuers with increasing speed performing extraordinary maneuvers beyond the technology of the present day.' I'm assuming the pursuers were military."

"Your presumptions are correct," his dad said.

He pulled another paper from the pile in front of him, "Here's another one where it mentions the UFO activity in July of 1952 with the invasion over the White House Capitol in Washington."

He reached for another report from the pile he was working from. "And then there's this encounter which was reported by military personnel where their aircraft was circled by a cluster of glowing objects."

His father just listened to see where his son was going with this.

He set the papers aside and looked at his dad, "How were these incidents explained?"

"The July 1952 invasion was officially explained as metrological, which is heat inversion which are layers of hot air pressing against cold air with mirroring lights from the city. Of course that theory is absurd. Absolute fiction," his dad explained.

"UFOs over the Capitol building. I'm surprised they didn't try to shoot them down," William said.

"I imagine it came close to that," his dad said.

"These with the military I would think would be hard to explain with some cockamamie explanation. Pilots in the military are a little more educated about what's flying in the air to accept some ridiculous story," William said.

"Some of the theories given were more credible than others. Some have never been explained in a way that they were able to pass off to anyone with even a bit of common sense," his dad said.

"In your notes here it says the years you worked on this there were over twelve thousand sightings of UFOs reported. That's a lot of people seeing something. How is it that the government continues to hide this from people and why? What's their point?"

His father sighed. "I know. It's ridiculous that they continue to try to deny the existence of UFOs and hide this information from the public. I think everyone has the right to know what may be at stake here," his father said.

"You think they're a threat to our nation don't you?" William asked.

"Not just our nation, but yes. I do believe that they have their own best interests in mind not ours for whatever they have planned," his father said. "And now that I'm more aware of their capabilities it's terrifying to say the least. If only I knew then what I know now some of my theories and reports may have been a bit more persuasive with the government to dig into this subject more deeply."

His father went through some of his papers and pulled out some reports with notes written on the sides.

"This one in particular is about what they called the Lubbock Lights. And this one is about two jets radar-visual with jet-intercept cases which occurred over Washington D.C. There were times when the UFOs interferred at military bases shutting down our systems."

"Whoo... that sounds bad," William said.

"Potentially *extremely* bad, you're right," his father replied. "The government kept this all hush-hush in order to not start a public panic. Nothing's ever changed. They would rather write it off making witnesses feel ridiculed. Witnesses in the military more "in the know" they make sign agreements of confidentiality threatening them if they ever reveal what they've seen."

"What do you mean?"

"If ridicule doesn't work making people afraid to come forward for fear of being made to look the fool then the government would reply by giving false explanations when anyone asks them about reports of sightings. They tell them they were weather balloons or meteors. They'd tell them anything but the truth," his dad said.

"I can't imagine they're very happy about you writing this book then. You'll be exposing this information to anyone who's interested enough to read your book," William said with a worried expression.

"No they aren't happy about it," his dad said.

He was quiet wondering if this would be a problem for his father.

"They can't stop you from publishing your book can they?" he asked.

"It's pretty much a done deal. I have a publisher and they've already received the first few chapters," his dad answered. "I made sure some of the information with verification was out there before the government got wind of what I was doing."

His dad looked at his son making a decision to confide in him.

"I've made arrangements that if anything happened to me that the publisher would receive all my notes and someone else could finish the book. I let those interested know it so it would do them no good if any harm came to me."

"Are you serious? Do you think your life may be in danger?"

"I think you've grown up enough for me to be open with you about this. Your mother doesn't know. She'd only worry," he said.

"What?"

"I've received a few phone calls from people I worked with in the past on this project and some higher-ups," his dad said.

"What did they want?" he asked setting the papers aside and giving his father his full attention.

"They tried to persuade me not to publish the book."

"What did you tell them?"

"I told them I gave it a lot of thought and I was going ahead with it. I told them I thought the public has a right to know," his dad said.

"What did they say?"

"When the phone calls didn't work they sent some visitors. They threatened me telling me that the information was classified."

"They threatened you?"

"They did. I guess they thought that would scare me off," his dad answered.

"I guess they don't know you very well," his son said with pride.

His father smiled. "They seem to have forgotten or hoped I was unaware of the fact that it was the following year after I was no longer head of Project Blue Book when it became a crime for military personnel to discuss classified UFO reports with the public. If I had still been working on it at that time I wouldn't be able to write this book or I would be breaking the law and could face imprisionment," his dad said. "But the law changed after I was off the project."

"Dad, they couldn't put you in prison for writing a book could they? That's crazy."

"No William. I guess they weren't aware that I was up to speed on when that all changed. They thought they could scare me off until I reminded them that it came out after I worked on the project and I hadn't signed anything. They know they can't really stop me. I have to be honest. I'm worried all the same."

"You're still going to finish the book?" he asked.

"I am," his father said. "There comes a time when you have to take a stand and do what you believe is right."

"Good for you," William said.

"I'm worried about you and your mother," he said.

"Why?"

"They know the two of you are what means the most to me. If they can't convince me they may try another tactic."

"Like what?" he asked.

"I believe our phone lines are being tapped. Whatever you do, *do not* speak about the aliens or anything of the sort while you're on the telephone or even when you're out in public with Nicole."

"I won't," William said astonished at what his father had confided in him.

His father sat back looking worried. "I just need to get the book completed and in the hands of the publisher. After that I believe any threat will be over. There would be no point in them threatening me once the book comes out."

"This is the same government you fought a war for. You worked blood, sweat, and tears for them. They would do this to you?"

"I did it for my country not for any government entity."

William shook his head. He pondered all his father had told him. He hadn't seen this side of the government before. He didn't like what he was hearing.

"I believe when it comes to the government they justify whatever is necessary to get what they want. I just want you and your mother to be aware of what's going on around you and don't let any strangers in. If someone says they're here to fix something and need to get in, do not let them in."

"O.K. You better warn mom too," William said.

"I will. I just didn't want to scare her."

"Mom's tougher than you think. I don't think you have to worry about scaring her. If anything she'll just get mad. I think she needs to know though so she'll be careful," he said.

"You're probably right. I'll talk to her," his dad said. "Just be aware of your surroundings and who's around you at all times. If you think you're being followed or you begin to see strange faces that seem to be hanging around you need to let me know right away. Whatever you do, don't make light of this and don't try to confront them yourself. That would be a big mistake. Once the book is out I think the threat will be over, but until then...please be very careful and aware of your surroundings."

He shook his head letting his father know he understood.

30

"When is Dad getting home?" William asked for the third time.

"I'm not sure honey. He told me he may have to work late and if so he and Klaus will probably just stay overnight in Orlando," his mother said.

"Mom, tomorrow is Nicole's birthday," he said sounding anxious.

"I know dear," his mom said. "They'll be back in plenty of time. I'm sure Klaus will want to be here for his daughter's birthday. Did the two of you have plans?"

"Dad was supposed to give me my last paycheck today so I can pick up her ring," he said. "What am I going to do if he doesn't come home till tomorrow? It will be too late then."

"I'm sorry honey. I completely forgot. Your dad said he left an envelope on his desk for you. It's probably the rest of the money he owes you for working for him."

Before she had the last word out of her mouth he ran to look on his father's desk for the envelope. I sure hope it's enough to pay off the ring, he thought. He barely had time to get to the bank to cash the check and then to the jewelers before they closed.

He found the envelope and sat in his dad's chair behind his desk and tore it open. He was distressed not to find a check but a letter addressed to him.

When he pulled the letter out of the envelope a key dropped onto the desk. He picked it up and looked at it but had no idea what it was for. He set the key aside and began reading the letter.

William, the letter began. *I want to thank you for your invaluable help in aiding me in completing the book. You'll be relieved to know I mailed off the final manuscript to the publishers today. I think we can all rest easier now.*

"Come on Dad," he said impatiently. "My money you promised so I can get Nicole's ring.... please mention that and maybe that you have some money hidden away for me."

He continued reading the letter and his dad told him what the key was for.

"O.K., O.K.," William said, "but please let the money for the ring be there."

He unlocked the drawer. Inside was a ring box. He picked it up and quickly looked inside.

"Yes!" he said with joy when he discovered the ring he had placed on layaway for Nicole inside. He took the ring out of the box and looked at it from all angles.

The jeweler had polished the ring. It caught the light making a rainbow on the wall.

The ring had two hearts intertwined with a diamond in the middle of the hearts. He had it engraved saying *'To the moon and back.'*

"Thank you Dad," he said. "You're the greatest."

He kissed the ring returning it to the box. He picked up the letter to continue reading it.

I wasn't sure if I'd make it back in time, he read from the letter, *so went ahead and paid the rest of your bill and picked up the ring for you. In addition there's a bonus check in the drawer. Have a wonderful birthday celebration. All my love, Dad.*

"I love you Dad," he said and meant every word of it.

He and his dad had grown really close through all they had experienced and with his discovering that aliens were real and a very real part of his life.

He had found himself often confiding in his dad even things he had thought in the past he would never be able to talk to him about. His father was always understanding and never lectured him, though at times gave his opinion and the reasoning behind his thoughts. He enjoyed those moments with his dad.

He looked in the drawer and picked up a check. It was in the amount of $300.00. Wow! he said. This in addition to the flight lessons *and* paying off my ring.

"William, did you find the envelope from your dad?" his mother asked poking her head in the doorway.

"Yeah, I found it. Thanks. I've got to go meet Nicole. We have to make plans for her birthday tomorrow."

He locked the ring back in the drawer and started thinking of when and how to give it to her. He knew he wouldn't be here for her next birthday so he wanted it to be a memorable birthday for her.

31

"It's too cold. We'll freeze," Nicole said as he pulled her towards the dunes where they had first made love.

It was just after midnight so officially it was her birthday. He couldn't wait any longer and wanted to give her the ring while it was just the two of them.

He had sent her the message they used when they could sneak away and meet.

Their code was to flash a flashlight once, then four times, then three times. Once would have been sufficient but this way they were assured the other one wouldn't miss it. Their secret code of the flashing lights was once for each letter for the words I love you.

"Don't worry. I don't plan on freezing your butt off in the middle of the night. I just wanted to be the first one to wish you a Happy Birthday," he explained.

"That's really sweet," she said. She let him lead her into the dunes where he had set up a beach blanket with some little twinkly lights around the blanket. On the blanket was a bouquet of yellow tea cup roses.

She stepped on the blanket and picked up the flowers. She held them to her nose and inhaled deeply. "They're so beautiful. Thank you. I have the sweetest boyfriend in the world."

"Sit down for just a minute," he said grinning at her.

She brushed the sand away and sat and looked at him waiting to see what he had up his sleeve.

He pulled a box out of his pocket and bent on one knee. "Nicole, I think you have an idea of how much you mean to me. I love you more than I could ever put into words. One day we'll be together forever and I can't wait for that day. Until then so you'll always have a reminder of the future we'll have together and so you'll always know who owns my heart I hope you'll wear this ring and think of how much I love you everytime you look at it."

Tears were running down Nicole's cheeks as he opened the box and showed her the ring.

"It's beautiful. I will think of you everytime I look at it and I'll wear it always."

Before he placed the ring on her finger he showed her the engraving inside the ring which made her cry even more.

He slipped the ring on her finger and she said, "I'll never take it off."

32

They had just seen the new year in when the Halloway family was delivered a large box.

"I believe that's something I've been waiting for," Edward said.

"It's your book isn't it," his wife said.

William got up and went in the kitchen and brought his father a steak knife. "Here. Open it with this."

He and his mother eagerly awaited the opening of the box. When Edward pulled back the flaps of the box they all peered in to see.

Edward reached in and handed them each a book to look at.

They all became very quiet as they looked through the book his father had spent quite some time writing and even more years researching.

"Well it's out there now," William said. He looked through the book recognizing some of the information that he had read previously while working with his father.

"Honey, I'm so proud of you," Liz said.

"It's a done deal now and it's out there for all who are interested to see. Hopefully this will put an end to the government trying to bully me," Edward said.

"I don't think you should let your guard down. The government is a big bully. They don't like losing," his wife said.

A few weeks had passed since the book had been published when Edward and Klaus began to notice they were being followed.

It was unnerving considering that there were quite a few lonely stretches of road that were pretty deserted between St. Augustine and Orlando where they worked.

"It's not the first time I've seen them. I don't believe they're even attempting to be discreet," Edward said.

He watched through the side mirror of the car and noticed that whenever Klaus changed lanes they did the same as though they wanted them to be aware they were being followed.

"That makes them all the more dangerous," Klaus said while checking his rearview mirror.

In the past they had followed them from the time they left the house until they arrived at the gate to enter Martin. Without a pass they wouldn't have been able to enter.... or so they thought.

Before Klaus pulled down the long stretch of road that led to the Martin building the car following them made a U-turn and drove off.

Edward thought it was because they knew exactly where they were going. They had made their point.

"Did you get their tag number?" Klaus asked.

"What would be the point? I know where they're coming from and believe me if I ever tried to get information on the car or plates it would turn up as non-existing. They cover their tracks well," Edward said.

"You think all this is because you wrote that book?" Klaus asked as he pulled in to park.

They got out of the car and as they walked towards the building Edward answered, "That's exactly what it's about. Now that the book is published I can't figure out what their point is. It's past the point of trying to convince me to change my mind."

"They must have a reason," Klaus said as he stepped inside.

They were both quiet while their I.D.'s were checked.

As the two friends walked down the hall Klaus said, "Be very careful Edward. I don't like it. I have a bad feeling about this."

33

William saw the flash of the light on his bedroom wall. He sat up in bed and looked out his window. Thankfully it was a hot night and he had left his window and curtains open.

He saw the flash again. Four flashes and then three. Love you too he thought as he got up and quietly checked the door to his parent's bedroom to make sure no one was awake.

Not hearing a sound coming from his parent's bedroom he tiptoed back to his room and quickly pulled on some shorts and went out the back sliding door. He left the door unlocked and open just enough so he wouldn't get locked out.

Nicole was already on the beach waiting for him.

Edward scooped her up in his arms and said, "How did you know I couldn't make it through the night without you?"

Nicole laughed as he set her back on her feet. "Perhaps because I couldn't make it through the night without you."

They walked down the beach hand in hand. They arrived at a spot where the beach was somewhat lit up from a hotel further up on the beach.

Nicole said, "Let's go for a swim."

"I don't dare chance going back in to get my trunks on and then sneak out again. My dad's a pretty light sleeper," William answered her.

"Who needs a suit?" Nicole began lifting her pajama top over her head dropping it in the sand and quickly kicked off her bottoms.

William said, "You're crazy you know that." But while he said it he too was stepping out of his shorts.

"Last one in is a rotten egg," she called out as she took off

144

towards the water.

They splashed each other and swam out just far enough where they could touch the bottom but be up to their waist in the water.

He reached over and pulled her into his arms.

She wrapped her legs around him holding on.

They made love there in the water with the waves knocking them off balance.

Afterwards they walked up to ankle deep water where they could sit in the water and talk.

"I can't believe I'm heading to the academy in less than two months," he said. "How can I make it through a day without you let alone six months?"

"I feel the same way," she said.

"I mean it Nicole. I can't do this without you. Let's get married. Why do we have to wait?"

"I still have a year of school to finish," she reminded him.

"What about right after you graduate?" he said. "Please, Nicole. Then we can be together. We can still get our education even if we're married," he pleaded.

"It sounds wonderful. To be with you every night," she said dreamily. "Let's think about it. See how it goes with you at the Academy first. They may keep you too busy to have time for a wife."

"Just promise me you'll think about it," he said.

They shook their clothes out trying to get all the sand out. They were wet from being in the ocean but there was nothing to be done about that. They hadn't come prepared for a swim.

He walked her back to her back deck and he waited to be sure she made it back in safely.

Before she went in the door she turned around and threw him a kiss.

His mind was on the evening with Nicole and thinking about them getting married, not waiting like they had originally planned. He thought it was a good plan. He honestly didn't see a reason why they should wait. He was determined to talk her into it before he left for the Academy.

He noticed when he got to the door that the curtains were blowing outside. The door was open more than the way he usually left it. He must have been careless, anxious to see Nicole.

I better be careful next time he thought. If mom or dad get up to get a drink or go to the bathroom during the night they would notice the door being open with the ocean breeze blowing in.

As he was tiptoeing past his father's office heading towards his bedroom he heard a noise.

The next thing he remembered his mother and father were standing over him with worried looks on their faces.

"Don't try to sit up," his father said. "The police and ambulance are on their way."

"Police? Ambulance? For what?" he asked realizing he had a terrific headache.

"Liz, go check and see if the police or ambulance are coming yet," his father said.

After his mother walked out of earshot his father asked, "Where were you son? You were wet when I found you."

He remembered meeting Nicole on the beach and smiled.

"There's nothing to smile about. Did you leave the door open? Someone was in the house and knocked you out. They could have as easily killed you."

They heard the sirens of the police and ambulance arriving.

This time he didn't obey his father and sat up and said, "What? Someone was in here?"

"Yes, and if I hadn't heard you hit the floor and cry out there's no telling what might have happened to you," his dad said. "I saw one of them standing over you. They saw me and they ran out the back door."

The police had arrived simultaneously with the medics. While the medics were checking him out Nicole came flying in the back door.

"I saw the police and ambulance. Is everyone O.K.?"

Edward noticed that Nicole's hair was wet and she didn't look like she'd been asleep.

Liz took her aside and explained they had a break-in and William had walked in on them and the prowlers had knocked him out.

Before the night was over the police dusted for fingerprints and assumed it was merely a break-in and nothing would come of it.

Edward knew better. He saw his office was the only place they had been and they had ransacked the room.

When he mentioned that fact to the police they brushed it off as they were probably interrupted by William before they had a chance to go through the rest of the house.

Did I put my family in danger over writing this book? he wondered.

34

"I don't know how you can tell me he'll be safe and not to worry. Look what happened to him the other night," Edward argued.

"I think the only reason that happened is he walked in on them and spooked them," Klaus tried to reassure his friend. "Seriously though, the aliens under no circumstances will allow anything serious to happen to him."

"You sound awfully confident," Edward said unconvinced.

Klaus looked intently at his friend. "You heard the story of Elke escaping from Germany during the war, but there's something else that happened too that may give you some reassurance. The only reason I'm going to bore you with my story is so you'll be reassured your son will be safe."

"No offense but what does your story have to do with my son?" Edward asked.

"It will give you an inclination of how seriously the aliens take their role in protecting those whose lives are intertwined with their own. I don't care who these men are who you feel are a threat to you and your family but they are no match for the aliens."

"I'm glad you feel confident but it's *my* son I'm concerned about," Edward reminded him.

"Perhaps it's for their own selfish reasons but all the same they will protect those who they deem a necessity in fulfilling their final outcome."

"And that's supposed to reassure me?" Edward asked. "That they look at my son as a...."

"Edward just listen," Klaus said. "Perhaps you'll feel a little more reassured once you hear what I have to tell you."

"Go on. Tell me your story," Edward said.

Klaus waited till he knew he had Edward's attention before beginning.

"It was nearing what appeared to be the last days of the war. Not knowing what would happen to us who had worked for the German government Elke's godfather made preparations for her to leave the country. We didn't know at that point whether our own government would shoot us all to keep any information we had from getting into enemy hands or what the victors of the war would do to us. Our futures looked pretty bleak. We really doubted we would survive the outcome."

"I can't even imagine," Edward said.

"Just as you now want nothing more than to protect your own family that's what Elke's godfather and I wanted to do...protect Elke and our unborn child."

"Understandable," Edward said.

"Just days after Elke and her godfather left Berlin the Kaiser Wilhelm Institute where we worked was bombed relentlessly. The area where we worked was a total shambles. Nobody could have survived it....yet I did. Everyone assumed I had died."

"Were you hurt?" Edward asked.

"Not a hair on my head," he answered. "The building was complete rubble, totally demolished in the area where I worked. Yet I had landed in an air pocket without a scratch anywhere on my body. The only survivors were those who had gone to the north end of the building for a meeting. Everyone else was killed instantly....except me."

"And what? You think it was the aliens that protected you?" Edward asked doubtfully.

"I know it was," Klaus answered.

"What makes you think so?" Edward asked.

"Gershom, the alien we had in custody had forewarned me without giving me specific details. He told me where to go at a certain time and told me to stay there until the following morning. He was emphatic about it. Thank God I listened to him."

"The alien you were keeping prisoner saved your life?" Edward asked.

"Don't be mistaken. He wasn't our prisoner by any stretch of the imagination. We might have believed so at the time but he could have walked through those walls and disappeared any time he chose to."

"Why would he have stayed if he could have left?" Edward asked.

"He too served a purpose in being there," Klaus said.

"And because of what he told you he saved your life? How could he have known?" Edward asked.

"He most definitely is the reason I survived. He saved my life. There's no doubt about it. If I had been at my work station there's no way I would have survived and at that time of day that's exactly where I would have been if he hadn't forewarned me."

"Is that why Elke thought you were dead?" Edward asked.

"Yes and though it may sound extremely cruel of me to allow her to believe I was dead, I knew it was most likely the only way she would ever leave Germany willingly and save herself and our baby."

"But she was already pregnant with Nicole when she left," Edward said. "Not to sound crass but as far as the aliens were concerned hadn't you already served your purpose? Elke was already carrying the child that was to be the daughter of destiny."

Klaus laughed, "Yeah, what a tough job I had. To impregnate the woman I loved more than life itself. The most enjoyable job I ever had."

Edward hung his head and said, "Sorry. I'm not thinking very clearly for worrying about my family."

"I didn't mean to make light of it. Yes, I guess you could say I had served my purpose. My job didn't end there though. They want their daughters of destiny to be raised by both the mother and father that love the child. It seems important to them for some reason. They aren't capable themselves of giving a child the affection and love the child needs to grow normally."

"Or to have children themselves from my understanding," Edward said.

"I'm not familiar with any of that," Klaus said. "Only the fact that they had our lives set out like a road map and there was no deviating from their plan."

"How so?" Edward asked.

"They set Elke and I up to meet. Initially we were colleagues but then something happened that forced our hands. It was at that time I realized that I was in love with her...madly in love. After that there isn't anything that could have kept me from being with her. I thought it was all one-sided while she was thinking the same about me. After that we were....well, I don't want to get graphic," Klaus said.

"Are you talking about sexual attraction?" Edward asked.

"There is that and it is intense but it's so much more than that, much much more," Klaus tried to explain. "It's a love so intense that you can't stand to be apart from one another. There's definitely a deep sexual attraction too that becomes almost painful when you don't allow nature to take it's course."

"I believe that's what my son is feeling towards Nicole," Edward said. "When he described those feelings to me I attributed it to teenage hormones."

"No, that may intensify it but what he's feeling.... I can't really explain it but I understand it. I felt the same way towards Elke so I know exactly what he's feeling."

"That will give me something else to worry about," Edward said.

Klaus sighed. "I didn't really like the idea of my teenage daughter having sex at such a young age either..."

Edward jerked his head up at this revelation.

"You didn't know our kids were having sex?" Klaus asked.

"I guess I suspected," Edward said thinking of the night William had been knocked out.

"Don't lecture your son or try to stop them," Klaus said. "I'm telling you in all truthfulness that they couldn't stop themselves if they wanted to. It's that powerful."

"Perhaps it's a good thing he's leaving for the academy shortly," Edward said. "The last thing they need right now is to have Nicole get pregnant."

"It's going to be very difficult for them to be apart," Klaus said. "I'm speaking from experience. This isn't a normal yearning to be with a loved one."

Edward was thinking perhaps it would be easier once William was at the academy and kept busy with his studies.

"I didn't finish telling you my story. I got sidetracked but I wanted you to understand that William and Nicole belong together. It's useless in trying to stop them."

"Perhaps I'd better see to it then that they have some sort of protection," Edward said.

"You mean like condoms?" Klaus asked then laughed heartily.

"Save your money. When the aliens deem it's time for a child to come of their union nothing will prevent it. Like you I'm hoping it won't be too soon as they're both so young, but if it does we'll be here to help them."

Edward sat and thought for a time. "Even though I've worked on the subject of aliens and UFOs for years and have been informed more than most, it's still hard to imagine they have that sort of control over human lives."

"You'd best believe it because they most certainly do," Klaus said.

"They'll be apart soon and we'll have less to worry about for awhile," Edward said.

"If that doesn't suit the aliens' timeframe don't forget they have a sperm sample from William," Klaus reminded his friend.

Edward looked shocked at what Klaus said.

"Nothing, I assure you absolutely nothing will stand in their way. When the time comes for Nicole to give birth to the next generation of daughters of destiny they will make it happen with intervention if need be. Nothing will get between them and their plan or stop them."

"Let's hope they're not in any rush then. They're both so young and have their education to get."

"I doubt the aliens care what any of us have planned out for our lives if it doesn't suit their purpose," Klaus said. "I realize as her father that this can happen at any time and there's no reason to worry about it. It's out of my hands. It doesn't mean I'm a bad father in turning my head knowing my teenage daughter is having sex, it's just that I realize a higher power than me has complete control of the situation and there isn't a damn thing I can do about it. I'm just thankful it's William and they love each other."

"Thank you for telling me this. Perhaps I can understand what he's going through a little better now too."

Klaus said, "But back to what I was saying about why I have faith that William will be safe...."

"I'm sorry. We keep getting off track. Please finish telling me your story," Edward said.

"Elke learned of the bombing and believed I was dead I think is where we left off. When she met the American pilot she believed herself to be a widow. Connor who you met on the fourth of July, was the pilot. He also had his life altered. The aliens were the ones who caused his plane to be shot down. They arranged for Elke to find him and nurse him back to health. In the time Elke and Connor were together they planned to marry so she could start a new life in America. Little did they know this idea was implanted in their heads by the aliens."

"How?" Edward asked.

Klaus just shrugged. "I guess as a gift for his role in bringing her to America they healed Connor's leg. Perhaps his broken leg kept them together long enough to get to know one another enough to plan for a future."

"The president mentioned something to me about a medical procedure had been performed on him," Edward said.

"I probably shouldn't tell you this part as it's rather personal, but I think at this point the more you know the better understanding you'll have in this whole situation. Connor was sterile due to having chicken pox as an adult. When they healed his leg they also fixed that problem. As you saw when they were here they're now expecting twins and have two other children besides the ones they're expecting. He most definitely isn't sterile any longer."

"This is hard to believe," Edward said. "They have that kind of power that they can completely manipulate people's lives and even heal them?"

"If it suits their purpose yes," Klaus said.

"It's a fascinating story but I'm not sure this gives me any reassurance about William and his safety."

"If you think about it you'll understand. Let me just finish and hopefully you'll see why that is."

Klaus looked out the window thinking, trying to find a way to assure Edward that his son would be watched over and protected. Edward may not like the thought of aliens being a part of his son's life and future but he would be protected.

"You could say I had performed my duty in getting Elke pregnant," Klaus continued. "Yet even so they kept me alive and led us back together over time. I fought my own feelings for a time believing she was in love with Connor and that I was doing right by staying out of their lives. I couldn't stay away from her. Once we found each other again it was inevitable for us to get back together. We were both miserable until we did. We've been together ever since and believe me nothing could come between us ever again. And as far as love and sexual desire, it's as strong today as it was when we first got together."

"I don't believe anything could keep Nicole and William apart either. It's pretty intense from what I've seen," Edward said.

"They'll be fine. They found each other at a pretty young age but their love has always been strong," Klaus said.

"It's what's happening right now I'm concerned about. With the threats I'm receiving and implied that my family could be at risk isn't something I can take lightly," Edward said.

"You needn't worry about your son. He'll be well protected.

He's very important to the aliens considering his role as the father of the next generation of daughters of destiny. That role affects their entire future or if they'll even have one. I assure you they won't allow your son to be irreparably harmed."

Edward looked at Klaus who had become a dear friend, "Thank you for that."

"It's you I'm concerned about," Klaus said. "You serve the aliens no purpose so you won't be protected. I believe these men that have been following you and threatening you mean business."

"I thought once the book was published things would go back to normal."

"Apparently not," Klaus said as he walked his friend to the door. "Maybe because you stood up to them and wouldn't back down they feel they have an ax to grind. You'd best watch your back. I'm here for you if there's anything I can do, but you have made some pretty powerful enemies."

35

"Have you given any thought to our getting married after you graduate?" William pressed Nicole.

"Will you promise if we get married then that you'll study hard, just as hard as if I weren't there?" she asked.

Encouraged by her response he answered, "If you're with me as my wife I promise I'll study harder. I won't be worrying about you. I'll be at the head of my class. With you by my side I can accomplish anything. Does this mean yes?"

"Promise?" she asked.

"Yes, I promise I will work hard and become the astronaut you told me I would be when I was seven years old. I won't let you down I promise." He looked at her eagerly waiting for her answer.

"Yes, I'll marry you the day after I graduate," she said.

He picked her up and spun her around and around making her laugh.

"My wife, my beautiful, beautiful wife...*you're going to be my wife!* You've just made me the happiest guy in the world," he said.

"That's still fourteen months away," she reminded him.

He whispered in her ear, "We can practice being husband and wife until then."

"I don't think we need to practice. I think we're pretty good at it already," she answered.

36

"My goodness you're both so young," his mom said when William and Nicole came to tell his parents of their decision to get married the following year.

His father stood up and took his son in his arms and said, "I'm happy for you son. I know the two of you are meant to be together. I know it would be tough for most young kids your age but I think you and Nicole will do just fine. You have our blessing. Isn't that right Liz?" he said looking at his wife.

"Yes, yes... of course," she answered hesitantly. "It's just so much so fast. You're graduating from high school, moving across the country, going to the Air Force Academy and now planning to be married. And you're both so young..."

"They may seem young to us old folks," Edward interrupted, "but if you remember we weren't much older than they are when we got married ourselves."

"I hardly think we're old folks," she said. "You're right though and we turned out just fine."

"We did indeed," he smiled at his wife.

"I am happy for the two of you," she said. "You just caught me off guard."

William laughed and gave his mom a big hug. "Maybe you can help Nicole and her mom plan the wedding while I'm away. We want to get married as soon as she graduates. Then I'm taking her back to the academy with me as my wife."

William and Nicole smiled at each other obviously very much in love.

Something hit a nerve at what William had just said.

His father was quiet and said, "You did check the academy

rules, didn't you? I seem to remember something…"

"What?" William asked growing concerned.

"Just a minute. Let me check the paperwork the academy sent."

Edward went into his office and found the literature the academy had sent along with a list of their rules. He looked through the pamphlets and found what he was looking for. He knew William wouldn't be happy about this.

Edward walked back into the living room where the kids were talking about planning to get married on the beach.

"I honestly hate to be the one to break this to the two of you. The rules of the academy is that the students must be single. You can't get married during the entire time you're attending the academy."

William looked like he'd been hit in the gut with a 2 x 4.

He looked crestfallen at Nicole.

"It's all right. We can go back to our original plans. It's more important you get your education at the academy behind you and do the best you can. I would just be a distraction to you anyway," Nicole said.

Edward was amazed at what a mature girl Nicole was. She had accepted this news well even though he knew she must be as disappointed as William.

"There's no way for us to…" William started to ask.

"You heard your father. He read it directly from the rules of the academy. It will be all right. This way you can concentrate on your studies. While you're away I can get started on my own college education. By the time you get your degree at the academy perhaps by then we can finish our education together at the same university as a married couple," Nicole said.

William looked like he would break down in tears.

"That's a long time for us to have to wait," he aruged.

"We'll be married in our hearts. Nothing can take that from us," Nicole said.

She reached over and gave William a big hug.

"Nicole's right. There's nothing to be done about it. The academy isn't going to change their rules for you. There's a reason they have that stipulation. The academy is going to be tough and they assume a married man or one with a family would be torn with his work at the academy and his home life," his father said.

"Nicole can get started on her college classes while you're at the academy. The two of you will be married before you know it. You've been together all these years. It's just a few more and then you'll have a good start to a future," his mother said knowing how devastated the kids must be with this news.

Nicole wanted more than anything to spend the rest of her life with William. She didn't want to spend a day apart from him.

Disappointed, yes. She had thought their plans to move their plans to marry early had been a good one. Apparently not.

William was her life and her soul mate. She certainly wasn't going to make this roadblock harder on him than it already was. She knew she would have to be the strong one through this.

Later that evening they agreed that they would have their own secret ceremony just between the two of them. While they still wouldn't be able to be together and live as man and wife and the marriage wouldn't be legally binding, their hearts would be bound together as though it were.

37

William balanced the packages in his arms so he could unlock the trunk of the car.

He and Nicole had spent the morning shopping getting everything he needed before heading to the academy. He knew he had a couple months yet but didn't want to leave everything until the last minute.

Nicole unloaded the bags she was carrying and reached around to help William put his packages in the trunk.

"I believe you're going to need another duffel bag to carry all your things in by the time you leave for the academy," she said.

"It does seem like a lot of stuff," William frowned looking at all the packages. "Just remember all that isn't just for me."

"I know. That was really thoughtful of you to buy going away gifts for your parents and for my parents," Nicole said.

"That's the last of my spending spree. From here on out I'm saving to buy you a proper engagement ring and save for our future."

William slammed the trunk closed.

Nicole got in the car and looked at her ring. "I love the ring you gave me. This is all I need. You don't have to buy me another ring. Besides I already told you I'm never taking this one off."

"That was just to let you know I love you and so you could see it on your finger while I'm away. I wanted to make sure you didn't forget you're loved while I'm gone," he said.

"How could I ever," she said. "Besides we'll be secretly bound together, legal or not, by the vows we take."

"Yes we will," he said smiling at her. "Though I feel as though I've been bound to you since the day we met."

"It will be our secret and our own special ceremony," she said.

William double checked his rear view mirrors before pulling out. He was a careful driver always wearing his seat belt and double checking before pulling out into traffic.

Nicole was chatting away nonstop when she suddenly realized she'd been the only one talking.

"Are you even listening to me?" she asked.

William was looking in his rear view mirror. "Sorry. What were you saying?"

She could tell he was preoccupied and that something was bothering him. When he made a turn different from the normal route they took she looked at him with a confused expression on her face.

"Did you forget your way home?"

"We're being followed," he explained.

He realized he'd made a mistake in the turn he made trying to lose the tail. The road they were on was a seldom used road with lots of twists and turns.

Nicole whipped her head around to see who was following them and how close they were.

"It's those same two men that were following us last week," she said.

The two men were getting closer gaining on them as they approached a sharp turn.

"Can't we turn off somewhere? I'm getting scared. They're on our bumper," Nicole said.

They were so close she could see the passenger leering at her.

William didn't answer her putting all his concentration on keeping them safe.

He didn't dare slow down as he made the turn or the other car would run into the back of them.

No sooner had they made it around the curve when the car was on them.

Their heads flew forward as they were bumped from the rear.

They braced themselves as they saw the other car drop back and then speed up again even faster ramming into them again.

The car swerved. William regained control turning the car into the oncoming lane with a white knuckle grip on the steering wheel.

"Brace yourself," he said.

He sped up hoping to avoid being hit again. If only we would get to the end of this road and back to the main road, he thought. He knew it couldn't be much farther ahead. He felt at that point it would be too dangerous for the men to try anything drawing attention to themselves.

The other car pulled back a little ways and then sped up and drew up alongside them.

"Hold on," William said as he braked hard just as the other car swerved into their lane to try to knock them off the road.

The car with the two men not expecting William to brake lost control and started to run off the road themselves.

William sped by while Nicole watched them recover and get back on the road heading for them again.

"They're coming again even faster," she said nervously. "They look angry."

"I won't be able to trick them with the same maneuver again," he said.

"There's nowhere to pull off. What are you going to do?" she asked frantically.

William sped by trying to stay ahead of them.

The other car had dropped back about two car lengths but as they reached a sign to slow down 25 MPH Dangerous Curve Ahead the other car sped up.

As they reached the curve the other car rapidly pulled into the lane for traffic heading the other direction to try to force them off the road at the curve.

Nicole looked up and screamed.

There was a large truck coming from the other direction that the other car wasn't able to see yet due to the curve in the road.

William increased his speed as much as he dared before rounding the curve. He wanted to be out of the way as he was sure there was about to be a collision.

The sound of brakes and the air horn on the truck gave out a large blast but it was too late. The next thing they heard was the horrific sound of impact.

The car with the two men ran into the truck head on at a pretty high rate of speed. The car crumbled like an accordion. It was dragged for several hundred feet locked onto the truck before the truck was able to come to a stop.

William made it safely around the curve. It was quite a ways before he reached an area where it was safe for him to pull off.

Nicole was crying hysterically.

William put the car in park and pulled her into his arms to comfort her. He too was shaken up thinking of what almost happened.

"Nicole...I've got to go check and see if everyone is O.K.," he said. He pulled Nicole to arms length and looked her in the eyes. "You stay here. I'll be right back."

"No please," she said shaking her head back and forth. "They could go after you."

"I don't think so. I doubt either one of them survived that crash. I have to go see to be sure. The truck driver may be hurt too. I have to go check on them."

After a minute she shook her head that she understood.

"I'll be back as soon as I can," he said checking to see if she was going to hold it together.

By the time William arrived at the scene of the accident the truck driver was outside of his truck walking back from the direction of the passenger's side of the car.

William could see that he was limping.

"Are you all right? I witnessed the accident. Is everyone O.K.?"

The truck driver shook his head. "The driver's dead and the other guy doesn't look much better. He's unconscious and he needs medical help," he answered.

Another car that drove by a few minutes later stopped and told them he would drive ahead and stop and notify the police and call for an ambulance.

William was thankful for his help as they hadn't passed any other traffic since they had turned onto this road.

The truck driver walked around to the side of his truck away from traffic.

He shook his head and said, "What the hell was he doing? Was he trying to pass you on a curve?"

"He was trying to crash into us and run us off the road. It wasn't his first attempt in doing so," William answered.

"Not friends of yours I take it," the driver said.

"I don't know who they are," William answered honestly.

"I never come this direction. I don't know what made me use this road today. If I hadn't..." the truck driver said.

"If you hadn't me and my girlfriend would most likely be dead. I wouldn't mourn too much over these guys. They were looking for trouble. If anything, consider the fact that you most likely saved the lives of two innocent people."

"Thanks," the truck driver said. "I've been feeling pretty bad about what happened, but honestly I don't see how I could have avoided them."

They heard sirens heading their way after about ten minutes.

"I better go check on my girlfriend. She was pretty shaken up," William said.

"Thanks for stopping and coming back to check on us," the truck driver said. "I imagine the police will want to take a statement from you on what happened."

"I'll do that."

William walked back to his car and could see Nicole walking

back from the other direction.

"I called your dad," she said once she got back to the car. "I thought he needed to know. He's on his way."

His father arrived a short time after the police arrived and took his son in his arms holding him tight. "Thank God you and Nicole are all right."

38

"I have to go get measured for my cap and gown after school. Want to go with me?" William asked as he met Nicole at her locker.

"I have an appointment to meet with my counselor after my last class," she said.

She took the books she needed out of her locker and slammed it shut and leaned back against the locker.

Other students walked by on their way to classes. A couple of girls walked by and waved at Nicole.

"Let me at least walk you to class then," he said.

William was proud to be walking with the prettiest girl in school. He knew he was a lucky guy.

What's the meeting about?" William asked.

"Probably something to do with my schedule for next year," she answered as they came to the door of her classroom.

"I'll call you when I get home then and see if you're back yet," he said.

He looked around him and quickly gave her a kiss before she headed into the classroom.

"I've been going over your school records and you're only lacking two credits before you can graduate," the counselor said.

"It seems like a waste to spend a whole year just for two credits," Nicole said. "Could I take the classes over the summer and graduate early?"

The counselor looked over the top of her glasses at Nicole.

"You could," she said. "Wouldn't you want to graduate with your friends and the other students?"

"I would hate to lose a whole year just so I could wear a cap and gown and accept a diploma. I really don't care about that," she answered.

"Well then, let's see what we can do," the counselor said.

Nicole sat quietly with her mind going a mile a minute on what this could mean for her and William. She was snapped out of her daydreaming when the counselor began speaking to her again.

"It looks to me like we could do a couple things here. You could go to summer school like you mentioned to get your last few credits, you could get a GED, or I think the best choice would be is for you to take these last few classes at college. It would get you in early and give you a head start on your college credits."

"If I can do that then that's what I'd rather do," she said.

"I see from your file that you've already been accepted at a couple different colleges. They must be pretty interested in you considering you're still technically a junior. Did you have a preference in one or the other or have you given it much thought yet?"

Nicole had received a perfect score on her SATs and the counselor agreed that she'd really be wasting her time at high school.

She knew Nicole had set her goals pretty high with wanting to work towards becoming a doctor. These were goals Nicole had pretty much kept to herself and only confided to her counselor and to the colleges she had applied to.

Nicole wasn't too sure how William would like the idea of her having to go to college for the amount of time it would take her to become a doctor.

He would also be studying for his future for about the same amount of time so if they could attend the same college after he finished at the Air Force Academy things would work out nicely.

The best-laid plans of mice and men oft go awry, she thought.

She sighed as she thought about how their plans to get married had gone. No sense in borrowing trouble and worrying about years down the road now. Once he's out of the academy there's no reason why we can't get married then and finish our studies together.

She could never confide in him that it was due to what she foresaw in his future as the reason she chose the aerospace medical field. She had made up her mind that information she would keep entirely to herself.

Every goal Nicole had set had to do with William's future. The future she had foreseen for him swayed her in her own thinking and planning for what she too would do with her own future.

If it were up to her she would be content to just be his wife and spend her life by his side.

She missed the last bit the counselor said to her lost in her thoughts but she got up too as she saw the counselor walking towards the door.

The counselor held the door open for Nicole and said, "I'll get in touch with a few colleges and see if they'll work with us on this. There are a few I have in mind that are suited for the classes that would be most beneficial for you. I'll start there. I don't see why they wouldn't agree to this with your grades. I'll get back with you sometime next week with their answer."

The counselor smiled at her and said, "I wish all my students were as studious and hard working as you."

Before leaving Nicole reminded her, "Don't forget. I want to surprise my parents so please don't call and leave a message."

"I understand. I know they'll both be very proud of you," the counselor said.

"So if the colleges agree then does that mean I could attend as early as this fall?"

"That's only a few months away. It doesn't give you much time but I believe this fall you will be a college student and on your way to a bright future," the counselor said.

At the same time that William was picking up his cap and gown and Nicole was meeting her counselor William's father sat in the back pew of the Cathedral Basilica of St. Augustine deep in thought.

The cathedral was the oldest Christian congregation in the contiguous United States. While Edward wasn't a Catholic he always found great comfort and peace in the old historic church building.

Over time he had met and often confided in the priest. They had formed a friendship of sorts and he knew his confidences and advice were something he took to heart.

When the priest saw Edward sitting in a pew in the back he could tell he was troubled. The priest came and sat next to him.

"What's troubling you my friend?" the priest asked.

"Is it that obvious?" Edward asked.

"Only to those who know you well. Do you want to talk about it?"

"My son and his girlfriend could have been killed all due to something foolish I've done," Edward said.

"Foolish, you? No my friend...you are anything but a foolish man. This I know for a fact. Do you perhaps take on this weight and burden needlessly?" the priest asked.

"No, it's all because of me. The burden is rightfully mine to bear," Edward said.

The priest sat quietly knowing he would talk if he wanted to and if not he would still know there was someone who cared.

"After I retired I wrote a book..."

"I've read it," the priest said. "It's very enlightening."

"Perhaps too much so," Edward said.

"How so?"

"Perhaps those in the government would have preferred that information not to be revealed. They blame me for bringing it to the public's attention."

"And they thought the public wasn't already aware of UFOs and aliens." The priest scoffed. "There's been talk for many years..."

"Yes but that was merely talk. Now they have a so-called expert in the field writing facts and admitting that they do indeed exist," Edward said.

"And this has brought danger to your family?"

"I was threatened before I published the book but I didn't listen. I felt the public had a right to know. I put my family in danger by doing so. My son and his girlfriend were recently confronted by these thugs and could have been killed if events hadn't turned out differently. I believe those were their intentions."

"Are you positive the events of your son and girlfriend are related to this?" the priest asked.

"Men have come to me again since I wrote the book. They strongly suggested a re-write, a so called new revelation."

"I see," the priest said.

"When I refused they've been tapping my phone, following me and my wife and son. They sit outside places where they know my family members are trying to scare them, and now..." He shook his head. "They've gone too far. This is beyond anything..."

"Have you reported this to the police?" the priest asked. "They sound like dangerous men."

"The police are skeptical," he said. "I guess when you hear it put into words that the government is out to get me because I wrote a book it does sound far fetched. Believe me though, it's the truth."

"I believe you my friend," the priest said. "There's a dark side to the government. There's the government the public is aware of then there's a deeper hidden group who are the true power, the puppeteers who are really running the show. I realize it can be extremely dangerous to cross them. They hold a lot of power and many of their actions they wouldn't want brought to the light of day. Have you decided on what you are going to do?"

"I'm going to do the damn re-write. Anything I have to do to keep my family safe..."

"Is this the right choice? I know you're concerned about your family but is caving in to the bad guys the right decision?"

"What else could I do?"

"Have you considered putting this into the Lord's hands? Who better to take this burden from you?" the priest asked.

Edward sat back and looked at his friend without saying a word.

"This building we sit in is built of coquina. Coquina was chosen, not just because it was widely available but due to the fact that it's strong when exposed to the elements yet soft enough to work with. That's you my friend. You are much stronger than you think, yet you are soft and giving where it matters. You're a good man Edward. You will do what your heart tells you is best."

Edward stood to leave. "Thank you for listening."

As Edward turned to leave the priest said, "I will pray for you my friend. I fear you are at battle with Satan. He doesn't give up easily."

39

William arrived home from school and came in to get his surfboard. He was going to meet Nicole on the beach and they were going to spend the first day of spring surfing even though the water would still probably be pretty cold.

He had planned on getting a job after school until the time he left for the Air Force Academy. His father talked him out of it and told him to enjoy his last few months. He told him that he had a check to give him for graduation that would help him out.

He thought about the days when he had worked with his dad on his book and how close they had become.

Life was good. He didn't think things could get any better....unless of course the academy would relax their rules and he and Nicole could get married right away.

He knew the first year at the academy would be a tough one. He couldn't even see or get in touch with friends or family for the first few months. It would be Christmas before he could even contact Nicole.

As he walked towards his room to change he could see the door in his father's office was partially open. He could hear his father on the phone so he walked quietly by so as not to disturb him.

As he changed into his swimming trunks he heard his father raise his voice. Whoever he was talking to on the phone it wasn't a pleasant conversation.

He was dressed but decided to wait to ask his dad who he was talking to and what the conversation was all about.

He heard his father hang up the phone with a bang.

William put his head in the doorway of his father's office.

"Everything O.K.? I heard you on the phone," he said.

"What did you hear?" his father asked brusquely.

William was taken aback. It wasn't like his father to snap or be impatient with him.

"I'm sorry William," he said. "I've got a lot on my mind." He stood and grabbed his keys off his desk.

"Anything you want to talk about?"

"No, son. I have to meet up with.... I have a meeting I have to get to. Do you happen to know if Klaus is home. I thought I'd see if he wanted to go into town with me," his dad said.

"His car wasn't there just now when I dropped Nicole off so I don't think so," he answered. "Do you want me to go with you?"

"No. It looks like you're heading out to the beach. Go and have a good time. I'll see you when I get back," he said.

William didn't know why he did it but he walked around and gave his father a hug. "I love you dad. Be careful."

"I love you too," his father said and patted him on the back. "I'd better get going. I'll see you this evening."

He didn't know why but William felt uneasy as he watched his father leave.

The water was cold and they didn't stay in long. They decided to go in to town instead and get a burger.

Sitting in the diner William told Nicole, "You know what I want. Go ahead and order for me. I'm going to play a couple songs on the jukebox."

He could hear Nicole giving the waitress their order as he selected a few songs.

William having made his song selections looked up and before he turned to head back to his seat he saw his dad across the street talking to another man.

He didn't recognize who he was meeting but his father

certainly didn't look happy. He appeared to be angry and the man stepped forward and whispered something in his ear.

"Our foods here," Nicole called out.

"Just a minute," he called out without taking his eyes off his father or the other man.

His father looked around and shook his head yes but he didn't look happy about it. The man clapped him on the back but his father stepped back out of his reach. The man with his father handed him what looked like some folded papers.

His father without saying another word snatched the papers from his hand. He turned around and walked off at a rapid pace as though he couldn't get away fast enough.

Nicole was putting ketchup on her burger when he sat down. She saw his face and asked, "What's wrong?"

"Nothing," he answered. He tried to get through the meal but the burger was sticking in his throat.

He didn't know what that meeting was all about but he could tell his father wasn't happy about the outcome of the meeting.

40

William came in the door throwing his books on the dining room table.

He'd been busy looking at his schedule for his first semester at the academy and had skipped lunch.

He went in the kitchen looking for something to eat. He lost his appetite when he saw his mother standing over the sink crying.

"Mom, what's wrong?" William put his arm around his mother. He couldn't ever recall seeing his mother cry before.

"Nothing, it's nothing. I didn't expect you home so soon," she answered him while wiping her tears.

William pulled her by the hand over to the kitchen table and sat her down. "Talk to me. What's the matter?"

She just shook her head and remained quiet. She picked at a crumb at the table that she'd missed when she wiped the table off. All her focus seemed to be on that one little crumb.

"Did you and dad have a fight or something?" he asked.

He couldn't really remember ever hearing his parents argue before but he couldn't imagine what it could be.

His mother just started crying harder.

"Are grandma and grandpa all right?"

"Everyone is fine," she answered. "I'm sorry. I don't mean to worry you."

"Then tell me what's wrong. Please," he begged his mom.

"It's those men that have been threatening your father."

She had his interest now.

Had they been threatening his father again? One of them had died in the accident and from what he understood the other one had been hurt pretty badly. Since the accident he thought any threat was over.

"What about them? Has someone been threatening him again?" William asked.

"I guess they won't be anymore now that he's agreed to their demands," she said.

"What demands?"

"He thinks if he does this they'll leave us alone. You and me I should say. He says he can take care of himself but evidently he doesn't think we can," she said in a huff.

"Mom, you're talking in riddles. Please...tell me what demands he's agreed to."

"He's agreed to rewrite the ending of his book," she said.

"What's that going to do?" he asked.

"He's agreed to rewrite it saying that after all his years of research in the matter he has been unable to prove that aliens or UFOs are real. That everything the government has researched after witnesses reported sightings has all been logically explained away by either weather or government experiments or whatever. Anything *but* aliens or UFOs."

"Why would he do that? All his years of hard work. This will discredit him in the field. He put years of his life into this..."

"That's what I tried to tell him," she said.

"And what did he say? Did you tell him we wouldn't want him to do this? He doesn't need to protect us," he said.

"Well good luck in convincing him of that," she said. "His mind is made up. He's made an agreement with the devil as far as I'm concerned."

With that she got up, threw her dish cloth on the table and angrily swatted the crumb to the floor and walked out of the room.

William walked into his father's office without knocking. His father reached for some papers and slid them into a drawer in his desk.

"Is that the papers the man handed you the other day when you went to town for a meeting?" he asked.

His father looked up stunned that his son knew about that.

"I saw you. I was going to ask you about it but I respected your privacy," he said.

"I'm glad someone does," his father said.

"What I don't respect is a man, my father, a man of integrity who would agree to back down and do the bidding of those who threatened him and his family. Why would you allow them to win?" he asked.

"That's exactly why," his father answered. "My family means more to me than a damn book."

"Or your reputation?" William asked.

"More than anything yes," his father answered.

"A lot of people have received hope after reading your book. They've been given respectability after being ridiculed for years after telling people of seeing UFOs. You gave them confirmation that they weren't crazy. A man of respect who had researched the subject for years, why would you do that to them?" he asked.

"To keep you and your mother alive," his father said.

"After awhile that book will be off the front shelves and out of bookstore windows and another book will replace it. You don't think if you just give it some time things will calm down? Be reasonable. It won't be a best-seller forever," William said.

"But it's my name and the fact that I was head of the Blue Book Project that make people realize I'm not just a nut case and that I do indeed believe in what I wrote," his father said.

"Dad, you can't do this. Please don't..."

"It's done. I've only agreed to changing the last three chapters. The rest of the book and information will still be out there for people to see. With the information given in the book they can do research on their own and decide for themselves. The only changes I'm making is saying after further thought and research I have come to a different conclusion," his dad said. "I've already agreed to it. It's a done deal."

"And after that you think they're going to just say 'Sayonara' and leave you alone?" his son asked.

"They agreed that they will never again bother you or your mother or endanger your lives," his father said.

"And you believe them? Wait a minute. What about *your* life?" William asked.

"All I asked is that they leave the two of you alone. Once I've caved to their wishes and go on with my work at Martin and no longer have anything to do with aliens or UFOs they would have no reason to bother me anymore," his dad said.

"That's what you thought before the book was published too. Evidently that didn't work out if they're still threatening you. What about the book signings and the public speaking events you have scheduled?"

"I've cancelled them all. I'm done. That work is behind me," his dad said.

"And you're O.K. with letting the bad guys tromp all over truth and integrity and rewrite history and the facts?" his son asked.

"You seem to forget the fact that you and Nicole are very much forefront in the lives of aliens. Your own daughter one day will certainly be wrapped up in their lives. I can't risk that they'll stick around and see something they shouldn't or put you, Nicole, or any future children you may have at risk. It's not worth the risk."

"I didn't even think that far ahead," William said.

"Well, I have. The government has a long memory. It isn't just us to consider. One day your wife and child would be very much in their sights and I won't allow that to be because of me. This is not only to keep you and your mother protected but your future family. This could put them at a terrible risk."

William finally sat down and calmed down considering what his father had just said.

"If they ever got wind of daughters of destiny and put two and two together that Nicole or your child were connected in any way with the aliens there's no telling what would happen to them."

"I see your point," William said.

"If they ever discovered what the daughters of destiny were and that they were connected in any way of the alien's future and whatever that might entail I'm afraid rather than taking a risk they would eliminate Nicole and your child."

"Eliminate? You mean..." William asked. He had turned white as a sheet.

"They wouldn't think twice about it if they thought this nation was at risk. It wouldn't bother them anymore than swatting a fly."

"Our own government would do this?" William asked.

"Their agenda and interests don't lie in looking out for the individual citizen. They do what they deem necessary for the good of the country and justify their actions to themselves. They don't have to account to anybody for their actions."

Edward looked to see if this was getting through to his son before continuing, " If they even had an inkling about Nicole and her origins or her DNA they would most likely kidnap her and experiment on her like she was some type of a guinea pig. But if they heard so much of a whisper of the role of the daughters of destiny and how it may one day determine whether aliens themselves will live on our planet, well you're smart enough to know they would eliminate any such potential risk. If you're not concerned about yourself think about your future wife and child," his father said.

William was deep in thought and he didn't like what he was hearing. For the first time he thought his father's decision was based on a valid point and not that he had caved in to pressure from the other side.

"You're right Dad," he said in a subdued tone of voice.

"I was hoping you were mature enough to understand," his father said.

"I feel bad that you put so much work into writing your book and now to have to do this."

"It's only the end chapters. Those who bought the book who are seeking the truth will have information in their hands that they can pursue on their own."

"I feel bad that you had to do this for us," William said.

"I'm protecting those I love and a little one I hope to meet one day. My future granddaughter," his dad said with a smile.

William got up and came around the desk. His father stood and took him in his arms and they embraced.

"Dad, I love you. I hope one day to be half the man you are and an exceptional father like you've been to me."

"Thank you for that son," his father said. "I love you too. More than you could possibly understand. But perhaps you will one day when you have a child of your own."

William remained standing in his father's office thinking about all his father had confided in him.

"Now let me get this finished so we can put all this behind us."

William saw his father was already back to work on making the changes to his book as he quietly walked out and closed the door behind him.

41

William's father had been quiet since he had made the changes for the book. He never was one to back down from something he strongly believed in but this time he knew the risks were just too great.

William was appreciative for all his father had done. He knew it had been a heart wrenching decision on his father's behalf. It was his family and William's future wife and child that had made his father agree to change the end of his book regardless of what it would do to his reputation.

William went in to the local book store after school and picked up a copy and sat on one of the benches they had set out for readers.

When he skimmed through the book it appeared at a glance that everything was as it had been previously published.

Was this the original copy then that they were still selling?

He flipped to the copyright page and saw that it was listed as a first edition. He noticed the date of publication was missing entirely. To anyone who didn't know better they would assume this was the original copy. They sure did get this edition out fast, he thought.

He closed the book and looked at the front cover and realized that the dust jacket had also been changed ever so slightly. How had he missed that when he first picked up the book? It was only a slight difference and if he hadn't noticed he doubted others would either.

The store clerk came by and smiled and said, "The author of that book is a local man. That's a new edition you have. It just came out two days ago. I think you'll really enjoy the book," she said and smiled and pushed her cart of books down another aisle.

William flipped to the back of the book and sure enough there were the changes his father had been forced to make.

He read the last few chapters.

In these re-written chapters his father claimed he now after much soul searching and studying no longer believed that UFOs or aliens from another planet or solar system other than ours existed. He called the belief in them a "space age myth."

Those three words alone put the topic of aliens and UFOs on a list for conspiracy theories.

In William's eyes those words would discredit anyone who tried to claim UFOs were real and that the government was covering up the information they had. Yet that's exactly what damage would be done by including this addition to the book.

Due to those words written by his father who knew for a fact that they were indeed *very real* would set back the clock for those in the UFO communities trying to gain respect for witnesses who had the courage to come forward and discuss what they'd seen and experienced.

He felt terrible for those people. This was a huge setback for them.

If his father hadn't changed his words he would have been in high demand for speaking engagements and interviews on the very topic that could expose his future wife and child putting their lives at risk.

He still would be in demand but only by those trying to discredit people who believed or had witnessed UFOs or had alien encounters. His father wouldn't add salt to the wound. He would close the door on the topic and refuse any further interviews.

William continued reading.

His father had written arguments for what unexplained sightings were. He wrote that regardless of how much people wanted to believe UFOs and aliens were real it just wasn't true in his opinion. He stated that he had years to have studied the subject and access to all information and he had science and logic to back up his belief.

William closed the book not wanting to read any more. He felt literally sick to his stomach.

Walking home he was oblivious to the traffic and activity around him. He knew if he was this depressed about it that his father must be even more so.

"Do you have any plans for the day?" William asked his father on his next day off.

His father looked up from his newspaper and said, "No, did you need me to do something?"

Just with that answer William realized what a selfless man his father was. Always doing for others. This time he was going to turn things around. He was going to do something for him.

"You're not going to tell me where we're going?" his dad asked while he was fastening his seatbelt.

"Nope. Just enjoy the ride," William answered with a smile on his face.

About forty-five minutes later they drove in the gates of a private airstrip where William had made arrangements to take his father for a plane ride with him as the pilot.

"What are we doing here?" his father asked.

"I'm taking you up in the air. I'm going to be your pilot," he said. "Scared?"

"Scared? Never. I'm excited as hell," his dad said.

"Good. You can be my navigator," William said.

"I'd be honored to be your navigator anyday," his dad said with pride.

William saw a smile on his father's face for the first time in weeks.

Up in the air they had headsets on where they could speak to each other over the engine noise as they flew over St. Augustine picking out familiar sights.

"See if you can figure out where you are navigator," William said.

His father pointed out the ocean and the drive towards their house.

"We're going to fly by and give mom a thrill," William said.

When they flew over his house they could see Liz, Elke, and Nicole standing outside on the deck shading their eyes from the sun.

Nicole was the first to spot them and pointed. She jumped up and down and waved her arms wildly at them.

William flew as low as safely possible and tipped the plane's wings as they flew by. They circled around and did it again before heading back to the airport.

His dad was all smiles when they landed.

"That's the best time I've had in a very long time," he said. "Thank you for that. I'll never forget this day."

William put his arm around his father's shoulders as they walked back towards the car and said, "Thank you. If it weren't for you I wouldn't be a pilot."

His dad said, "I look forward to the day when you can take me for a ride on that spacecraft you keep telling me you're going to fly to the moon."

Both of them laughed heartily at that.

They went out to eat afterwards at a seafood bar right on the beach and had a plateful of raw oysters and all you can eat shrimp.

"Thank you for this wonderful day. I'll treasure this memory," his dad said. "I'm so proud of you. I couldn't have raised a better son."

"Thanks Dad. You're a hard act to follow. I love you too."

$$42$$

Edward had been hard at work all morning on a special project at Martin. Feeling a headache coming on from concentrating so hard for hours he decided to get some coffee. He finished writing his notes and got up to take a coffee break.

When he walked in to the employee's lounge a heavy set red headed woman walked in right behind him.

She was friendly though he didn't recall ever having seen her before.

"Are you here for coffee?" she asked.

"Yes, I've got a terrific headache. I needed a break," he replied.

"I'm sorry to hear that. Have a seat. I'm fixing a coffee for myself. I'll fix one for you too," she said.

"You don't need to do that but I appreciate it," he said.

"I'm going to fix one for myself anyway so it's no trouble to pour an extra cup. Take a rest for a few minutes. Close your eyes and give yourself a chance to get rid of your headache," she said.

"Cream and sugar?" she asked.

He was grateful for a few moments to relax and said, "Cream and two sugars. Thank you."

He sat down and leaned his head back against the wall and closed his eyes.

As she poured the coffee she looked over her shoulder and saw that he had closed his eyes.

She poured his coffee and gave it a quick stir.

He could smell the coffee she had placed in front of him.

"I got you a couple aspirin too," she said. "This project has really been stressful. I've been eating aspirin like candy lately."

He accepted the aspirin from her and took them with a sip of the hot coffee to help wash it down.

"I'm heading back to work. Drink your coffee. Between that and the aspirin you should feel all better in a short time," she said.

"Thanks again," he said.

She left the room and he sat quietly and drank about half of his coffee. He was so tired. He thought he'd just rest a few more minutes before heading back to work. He quickly drank the rest of the coffee and put his head back to rest for just a few moments.

He'd be glad when they finished this project was his last thought before he fell asleep...a sleep he would never wake up from.

Klaus heard his name being called. He looked up and saw his boss motioning for him to follow him.

"Have a seat, Mr. Newhouse."

Klaus sat wondering what this was about. He hoped it was important as he had a pile of work waiting for him on his desk.

"Do you know if your friend Mr. Halloway had a heart condition?" he asked.

"Had....What do you mean? He's pretty healthy as far as I know. I've never known him to be sick in all the years I've known him. Why?" Klaus said growing concerned with this conversation.

His boss didn't answer right away.

Klaus stood up. "Is he all right?"

"Please sit down."

Once Klaus sat back down his boss said, "I'm sorry to be the one to tell you but Mr. Halloway passed away. Someone found him in the lounge. He was already dead when they found him. The medics assumed he had a heart attack."

"Dead? Edward is dead? Are you sure it's Edward?" Klaus asked.

Klaus was distraught. He had grown very close to Edward and

186

his family.

"I'm afraid so," his boss said.

"He was fine this morning. We carpool together. He's never complained about a heart condition. I don't understand..."

"I'm sorry. I know the two of you are close friends. Do you know the family?" his boss asked.

"Yes, of course. They're my neighbors and good friends. We're very close," Klaus said.

His boss sat quietly for a few moments letting Klaus have a few moments to come to terms with the announcement of his friend's death.

"Would you prefer to be the one to inform the family of his death? I thought a telephone call from someone they didn't know would be harder on them," his boss said.

"You're sure about this? They've pronounced him dead?" Klaus asked.

"Yes, he's been taken to the morgue. I'm sure they'll run some tests to see the exact cause of death but they believe he suffered a heart attack."

Klaus sat stunned. How could this be? Just this morning they were talking about their plans for their kids' futures.

How would Liz and William take the news? Not good, that's for certain.

"Can I leave? I have a long drive ahead of me and I want to be sure I'm the one to inform the family. I need to be there for them."

"Go ahead. Take some time off if you need to help them make arrangements," his boss said.

43

The family was in shock over Edward's death.

Liz had decided against an autopsy. She couldn't bear the thought of them cutting her husband's body.

There had been a small announcement of Edward's death in the local paper but no details were given.

The priest from the Cathedral Basilica of St. Augustine who had befriended Edward came to the house to pay his respects to the family and see if there was anything he could do.

Liz was barely coherent. She told the priest she didn't want to have a funeral and possibly have the people who had threatened the family or made her husband's last days miserable to show up pretending to mourn his death. She told him she wanted for those closest to him to be able to mourn in private.

The priest and Klaus made the arrangements.

Klaus walked the priest out.

Once out of earshot of the others he asked the priest, "Do you think she's being irrational? She seems so sure that these men who have been harrassing him about his book had something to do with his death. She swears he's never had heart trouble in the past."

"Edward has mentioned you many times. I understand the two of you were very close so I'm going to assume he would understand my confiding in you," the priest said.

Klaus nodded his head for him to continue.

"I'm inclined to think she may be onto something in her assumptions. However, she refuses to have an autopsy performed so I guess we'll never know. I have to tell you though, in my opinion I'm not so sure Edward died of a heart attack," the priest said.

Klaus started to speak but the priest kept talking.

"Now before you ask if I have any evidence to believe this I have to say no. I'm only going on my gut feeling and on what Edward confided in me about the government harrassing him and threatening his family over his book. So no, I don't think she's being irrational."

"I'm glad to see someone else has their doubts about all this that's a bit removed from the situation. I too had my doubts about the heart attack story but I didn't share that thought with Liz. I thought it would only make it harder on her."

"She said he's always been the picture of health. If I'm wrong in my assumptions then may God forgive me for thinking the worst of our own damn government."

The following day the priest performed a personal memorial with only the two families in attendance.

William had taken his father's death very hard. He and his mother had flown out with his father's casket to bury him in his hometown where he had grown up. William was preparing to fly back home arriving just days before he had to leave for the academy. His heart wasn't in it.

He had wanted to postpone his leaving for the academy but his mother insisted that he go as planned.

"Your father was so very proud that you were joining the Air Force and that you were accepted at the academy. He would want you to go and work hard towards that future you've had planned since you were a young boy."

"But Mom..." William said.

"No buts," she said as she wiped his tears. "Do this for him. You're the man of the house now. You go show them what a Halloway is capable of. Your dad and I already know. Now you go show the world."

He shook his head in agreement that he would do just that.

44

"So young lady, I've received several responses to the letter of reference and applications I've sent out. There are some pretty impressive colleges that are very interested in you becoming a student at their university," Nicole's counselor said.

"I'll be able to start this fall then?" Nicole asked.

"Yes ma'am," Mrs. Brackett said. "Your perfect SAT score and your academic record speak for themselves. They were most impressed with your essay and your lofty goals. Would you like to hear which colleges have accepted you?"

"Yes please," Nicole said.

"I took it upon myself to apply to a few other colleges other than the ones you mentioned keeping your ultimate goal in mind. I think some of these colleges may be more suited for you with getting you into the aerospace medical field."

"O.K. I appreciate that," Nicole said. "Is there one in Colorado or close by?"

The counselor looked at her with a puzzled look. "I don't recall you mentioning you wanted to go out west. There isn't anything in that area that offers what you'll need for a medical degree in the aerospace field."

"I was just hoping to be able to attend a college near William," Nicole said.

"If that's really important you can get your bachelor degree somewhere out west and then go to one of these colleges for your graduate work. Considering how difficult they are to get into and that they're willing to accept you on such short notice I really think it's in your best interest to at least consider one of these that I've heard back from," Mrs. Brackett said.

"Go ahead and tell me which ones are on your list and your

opinion on which is the best choice," Nicole said.

"I've heard back from these colleges all saying they would accept you for this fall."

The counselor picked up the stack of letters and started naming them, "University of Michigan, Georgia Institute of Technology, Duke University, and John Hopkins. These are some very respected names in the medical field."

"I'm surprised. That's quite a few," Nicole said.

"There is one university out west that may be suitable for what you're looking for. Stanford University in California but even so that's over a thousand miles from the Air Force Academy where William will be. I wouldn't want you to make such an important decision based on just being closer to your boyfriend," Mrs. Brackett said.

"He's much more than my boyfriend," Nicole said.

"Even so at your young age once you get to college both of you may lose interest in each other and find someone else so I..."

"No. That won't happen," Nicole said.

The counselor was a bit exasperated not expecting this response from a girl who she had considered wise beyond her years. At the moment she thought she was acting like the young teenager she was.

"I hope you'll make your decision based on what's best for you and for your future. If you and William are meant to be together then down the road..."

"Let's not discuss that," Nicole said. "Which of these colleges do you think would be best suited for someone interested in working with NASA in the future. My goal is to eventually work with astronauts in training. My desire is to work with those training to go into space," Nicole said.

"I see. I have to admit that's a new one for me. I'm not very informed in the aerospace medical field I have to admit. I know your father works in that field, not in the medical aspect but in aerospace engineering. Is that what made you decide to go in this direction?" Mrs. Brackett asked.

"Not exactly. What's your recommendation?" Nicole asked changing the subject.

"Honestly I would go with the Georgia Institute of Technology. Before you came in this morning I was leaning more towards John Hopkins as the best pick for you, but now that I understand the direction you desire to go I really do think Georgia is your best choice."

"Can you make the arrangements in whatever I have to do then? I definitely want to start this fall. I want to take as many courses as they'll allow and get started."

"In a hurry?" Mrs. Brackett asked.

"Very much so," Nicole said.

"If you're planning on achieving your goal of getting into aerospace medicine as a doctor you're facing at the very least twelve years of education. Are you up for that?"

"If that's what it takes," Nicole answered. "I doubt it will take me that long. Let's just say I have great motivation to reach the end goal sooner rather than later."

"You may be in for a surprise then. I don't think anyone can rush through this."

"We'll see about that," Nicole said as she went out the door.

After Nicole left Mrs. Brackett said out loud, "If anyone can do it she can. I wish her the best of luck."

"We're so proud of you. We thought we'd have you home for another year though. This is so sudden," her father said.

"You're not going to tell William? I don't understand," her mother said.

"Mom, he just lost his father and he's leaving a few days after he gets back from burying his dad. He's got a lot on his mind. I don't want him worrying about me being away and how I'm doing in college. It would just worry him needlessly," Nicole said.

"But Liz will find out once you're gone," her mother said.

"I don't think so. Even if she did she couldn't tell him since he can't receive any contact from outside the academy for the first two semesters. Besides, William just called and he said his mother decided to stay with her family in Iowa until William is coming home for the holidays," Nicole said.

"Poor Liz," Elke said. "I feel so bad for her."

"You know what's best as far as William is concerned. You're probably right. He has a lot on his plate right now," her father said.

"I can't write him or contact him at all his first two semesters. When he comes home for Christmas I'll explain everything to him then. By then I'll have half a year behind me," she said.

"It's all happening so fast. You'll be leaving so soon," her mother said.

"I'll see how things work out these first few semesters. I want to take a heavy work load and get my degree as soon as I can. Maybe when it's time to go for my masters we'll be able to attend the same university since we're both going in the field of aerospace. I really want to be with him as soon as possible."

"Just do what you have to do. It's inevitable you and William will be together. Right now just be concerned with what's best for your future," her dad said.

"William is my future," Nicole said. "We'll work it out somehow. William has to get through the academy first then perhaps we can make arrangements to be together. I can do both...study and be his wife," Nicole said.

"By the time you come home for Christmas you'll have a better idea of how that will work. We won't say anything to William. I don't like the idea of keeping it from him but I see your point. I know you're right in the fact that he would worry about you," her dad said.

"When is he coming back?" her mom asked.

"I'm picking him up at the airport in about three hours. He'll only be home for two days before he has to leave for the academy. I hope you'll understand but I'd like to stay with him until he leaves," Nicole said.

"We understand," her father spoke up before her mother had a chance to get in her opinion on Nicole's plan.

"I certainly hope we'll have a chance to see him to tell him good-bye before he leaves," her mother said.

"We'll definitely plan on seeing you before he leaves. Thanks Dad and Mom."

45

Nicole rushed in the door and headed for her room. She rummaged through her closet until she found what she was looking for. The dress still had the price tag hanging from it. She had saved it for a special occasion and nothing would ever be as special as her wedding.

Her mother stood in the doorway and saw the dress in Nicole's hand. "What a beautiful dress. I don't think I've ever seen you wear that before."

"I haven't. I've been saving it," Nicole answered her mother.

"It looks like you and William are going out tonight. Anywhere special?" her mother asked oblivious to their plans.

"We're just going to make our last evening together extra special," she answered her mom.

"Well have fun dear," her mother turned to head back to what she was doing then stopped in her tracks and said, "I have a beautiful necklace that would be gorgeous with that dress. Would you like to wear it?"

Nicole looked through her closet for a pair of shoes to go with the dress when her mother came back in the room.

"I found it."

Nicole got up and looked at the necklace and said, "Mom, that's beautiful. Are you sure you don't mind if I borrow it?"

"No, go ahead. Keep it. I don't think I've worn it since your dad and I got married. I wore that for our wedding. I was saving it to give you one day for your wedding but go ahead and take it now," her mom said.

Nicole wrapped her items carefully and gave her mother a hug on the way out.

Without her mother being aware she had just given her daughter the 'something old, something borrowed,' she had the 'something new and blue' in her dress. All the tokens of good luck a bride is required for her wedding day.

Her mother watched her daughter go knowing her little girl had grown up.

That evening Nicole and William went out for a fancy dinner by candlelight.

"It looks like a big night for the two of you. Are you celebrating something special?" the waitress asked.

"The best night of our life," William answered never taking his eyes off Nicole.

The waitress smiled dreamily walking away wishing someone special would look at her like that.

That night under a full moon in their bare feet and fancy dress clothes they stood on the beach and exchanged their wedding vows they had written to each other.

Nicole began:

"Once upon a time I chose you to be my forever.

Together and even in the days we are apart I will wake every morning with you as the first thought wondering what I can do to make each day special for you letting you know how very much you are loved. I will end the night the same way, never letting the sun go down without telling you and showing you how very much you are loved.

I will be your navigator through life. The times when you're ready to give up I will be there to lift you up and show you that you are stronger than you think. I rely on your strength and your courage to face life.

The days ahead when we are physically apart know that however many miles there are separating us that our hearts will be forever joined. Our love will always bring us back full circle joining us together once again and forever...for our forever days are ahead.

I know there will be times when our love will be tested but I have faith we will endure. A love like ours is lasting.

I devote myself to you and to making your life a better one than you ever imagined. I will celebrate your successes as they are my successes also. I mourn your losses as they too are mine.

I will love you, my husband, and rejoice in your love for me for all of the years of our lives.

I believe in you. I believe in us. Our love will remain forever strong.

I am honored to consider you my husband. One day I will be honored to take your name and become your lawful wife, but even now with God as our witness I consider myself your wife as we exchange our vows. Until then know that I, Nicole Newhouse, most definitely do take you William Halloway as my beloved husband. My love for you is eternal."

Tears were flowing freely down both the bride's and the groom's faces. They were tears of love and joy.

William cleared his throat and said his vows:

"Nicole, my precious one. The greatest joy and gift of my life... I promise to be your pilot and guide you on a safe journey through life.

You make me a better man than I could ever be without you.

Your smile brightens the day like a ray of sunshine. Your laughter lightens my heart. Your love is something I will forever cherish and never abuse or take for granted.

When I am with you everything else fades away to the background. You are everything I could ever dream for. My dreams and accomplishments are nothing without you.

Together we will go through life and support one another through the best of times and the worst of times.

My life became entangled with yours from the day I first laid *eyes on you.*

Even the time we will be apart my love will remain forever strong and faithful.

You are my life...my greatest gift.

I am blessed on this day to call you my wife. To the moon and back, I will love you forever.

I, William Halloway, do take you Nicole Newhouse as my beloved wife...forever and ever...until death do us part."

William looked at Nicole with such a deep love in his eyes, "My wife. Boy, I love the sound of that."

"I do too. My husband."

William said, "You may now kiss the bride."

And he did. He then swept her up in his arms and carried her inside to consummate their marriage.

46

William unwrapped himself from his wife's arms to board his plane. The stewardess had announced last call for boarding.

He knew once he walked away it would be six months before he'd see her or even be able to talk to her again.

Their parting was emotionally and physically painful for the two of them. They felt as though a part of them were being ripped in two.

The half a year they would be apart sounded like an eternity to the two of them.

Nicole had made him promise that he would focus on his studies and his future, their future.

This was a hurdle and a time they must get through. Since they must be apart she convinced him they make good use of the time and study hard knowing their separation was temporary.

She advised him to use this time to put all his energies into meeting his end goal...to become the astronaut he had dreamed of since he was a young boy.

Not taking her own advice after watching his plane depart she went home and cried for hours.

She too would be leaving in just a few days headed for her own future.

She knew she had to accept their separation and use the time wisely. She was determined to pursue her studies with a furvor that would insure her that she would lessen the time frame demanded of her to become a doctor.

How can such a deep love hurt so bad? she asked herself.

Whoever said 'Absence makes the heart grow fonder' was crazy she thought pounding her fist in her pillow. My heart did just fine when we were together. How will we ever get through four years apart from one another?

47

Nicole knew this should be an exciting time for her. She had been accepted at a prestigious university with a great future ahead of her. The problem was that the only future she was interested in was the one with William.

The dean had tried to discourage her from taking such a heavy load but she knew she could handle it. With a photographic memory all she had to do was hear it or read it once and it was imbedded in her memory forever.

She made a deal with the dean to give her the classes she requested and if by the middle of the semester she showed she couldn't handle it she would drop some of the classes. She knew that wouldn't be necessary but it seemed to satisfy the dean enough for him to relent and give her the additional classes.

She walked the campus learning where the buildings were where her classes were and planning her route out. As she walked she wondered how William was doing at the academy.

Opening the door to her dorm room the first thing she noticed was it looked like a cyclone had hit since she last left and had set her things up.

A girl stuck her head out of the closet with a handful of hangers in her hand. A pile of clothes a foot high laid at her feet.

"Hi, I'm Rhiannon. You must be my roommate. Don't mind the mess. I'll have things set up in no time."

Nicole introduced herself and said she was going to take a walk around campus and give her roommate the time and space she needed to set her things up.

She returned two hours later and didn't notice much of a difference from the time she had left except the room was now devoid of her roommate.

She took the pile of clothing and shoes that had been thrown across her own bed and laid them on her roommate's bed and then laid down.

She turned around and sobbed into her pillow. She missed William something terrible.

Her roommate Rhiannon popped back in just long enough to change her clothes and talked the entire time about some guys she and a girl down the hall had met and were meeting for pizza.

She tossed the clothes she had been wearing on the floor and said, "I'm off. See you later."

Nicole groaned and covered her head with her pillow.

Ten minutes hadn't passed and annoyed by the mess she got up and hung up the girl's clothes and set the room back up in an orderly manner.

At least keeping busy will keep my mind off William for a bit she thought. Like that's going to happen, she thought as she hung up one of her roommate's tops.

William thought about Nicole the entire plane trip to Colorado. He wished they were married now legally and she was able to go with him.

He couldn't help but to smile thinking of the secret wedding ceremony and vows they had taken on the beach the evening before he left. In his heart he considered her his wife already. He didn't know how he was going to make it without her.

The academy was demanding and their time was filled every minute. They had everything scheduled from when they slept, showered, studied, ate, a schedule for everything except when he would have time to go to the bathroom. He thought perhaps this was a good thing. The busier he was kept the time would go faster and the less time he would have to dwell on missing Nicole.

He had originally promised himself he would write to Nicole everyday and though he couldn't even mail the letters to her he would give them to her when he saw her for Christmas.

Ten days went by before he had time to write the first word to her. He had barely written two paragraphs when he fell asleep at his desk pen in hand utterly exhausted from the grueling schedule he was keeping.

48

The first semester was coming to an end and Nicole was making great strides.

"I'll admit it. I was wrong," the dean said. "I never thought you'd be able to take on such a work load and keep up. I've checked with all of your professors and looked at your grades and you're at the top of every class. I don't know how you do it."

"I have no life. That's how I do it," Nicole said.

"We want you to enjoy your time here with us," the dean said frowning. "Perhaps if you lighten your load next semester you can enjoy some extra curricular activities.

"I'm here to study and to get my degree. I'm not here to have fun," Nicole said.

The dean stared at her. Such a beautiful girl and no social life.

She was the most memorable student in the university one of her professors had said. Not only was she at the top of her class but she was no studious nerd. She didn't brag or try to show off.

He told the dean every guy in the class wished she would go out with them but she kept to herself. She didn't really mingle with the guys or the other girls.

He thought that probably suited the girls just fine as they would see her as serious competition for the guys' attention.

The dean wondered what her story was but he was well aware she had lofty goals and she as much said that nothing would stand in her way of reaching them.

He believed her. She had more than proven that her first semester.

49

Nicole waited impatiently as the people unboarded from the flight her parents and William's mom flew in on. The first one she spotted was her father looking around trying to locate his daughter.

She wasn't hard to find standing at six feet and her long blonde hair, so blonde you could describe it as white. She was breath taking and turned many heads that walked by.

Nicole ran up and threw her arms around him. "It's so good to see you. I've missed you all so much."

Her dad was equally enthusiastic to see his daughter. While they were hugging and catching up her mother and Liz caught up with them and hugs were passed all around.

They walked leisurely to the gate where they would catch their connecting flight catching up on the news as they walked.

"Thank you all so much for flying into Atlanta so I could fly with you to Denver," Nicole said.

"We were happy to. It gives us a little time to catch up," her mother said.

"Goodness Nicole. We don't live that far from the university. Why don't we ever see you anymore?" Liz asked.

"I've been swamped with my classes and studies," Nicole answered. "I'm doing my best to get my degrees ahead of time so I can be with William."

"You do understand Liz that we've become second rate," Nicole's father teased. "Any time she does have off she flies out to Denver to see your son."

Liz smiled and said, "That's understandable."

William had spent the last four years at the Air Force Academy working harder than he'd ever worked in his life – both physically and mentally.

He had no social life per se, which was fine with him. The only social life he was interested in was with his wife. Now that he was about to graduate he was committed to making that title legal and make Nicole his lawful wife.

A grin broke out on his face as he recalled the night four years earlier when he and Nicole had exchanged their vows, just the two of them on the beach with only a full moon and a sky full of stars to witness the event.

They hadn't been allowed to marry legally at the time due to academy rules and regulations but he thought there shouldn't be anything to stop them now.

In the years he had been at the academy he had earned a science degree following in the footsteps of his father and studying aerospace engineering. Now about to finally graduate from the academy his training as a pilot was about to begin. He was on course of becoming an astronaut, a lifelong dream.

The Air Force didn't allow time to sit back and dwell on your laurels. No grass would grow under the feet of these cadets. They would all be flying off the following day towards the next step in meeting their goals.

The following day he would fly to the base where he would earn his pilot's wings. While in the academy he had been promoted and was now an officer about to begin pilot training.

He knew there were many of his fellow graduates who would be doing the same thing. The Vietnam War had been going on for more years than anyone dreamed it would ever last.

The current president had made promises he hadn't kept in bringing home the American troops. Instead it seemed the numbers being sent over were increasing and there was a heavy demand for pilots.

Many of the cadets if not most of them eventually would wind up fighting in the war. It seemed inevitable with what was going on in the world that it would be sooner rather than later that he would be called up to serve.

The four years he and Nicole had to spend apart other than holidays and a few long week-ends had been the longest in his life. He never knew loving someone could be so painful. The times they were separated he felt incomplete without her.

He knew chances were strong that they would be separated yet again if he was called to serve in the war and there seemed little chance that he wouldn't be.

Nicole herself had graduated receiving her bachelor's degree in biology and was well on her way towards completing her masters degree specializing in aerospace physiology. She was also working towards a space psychiatric degree believing it would help immensely in getting her foot in the door at NASA.

William knew she had set high goals but believed if anyone could do it she could. He thought it would be great if they could work together at NASA one day and supported her endeavors.

He would have been just as happy if she just became his wife and she stayed home and raised their children but he supported her in whatever decision she made.

He had requested to be transferred to Florida's Eglin Air Force Base or MacDill, both located in Florida where he would be closer to Nicole and to his mother who was now widowed and living alone. Fortunately his request had been granted and he would be going to Eglin Air Force Base which was about a four or five hour drive from where Nicole was attending the university.

He knew realistically that even though they would be a lot closer geographically that with both their heavy schedules they would probably have little time to actually see each other.

He hadn't spoken to Nicole about it yet but he had hopes that when they married she would be able to transfer to Florida State University near where he would be stationed if they offered the courses she needed to earn her medical degree.

He knew even if, no he thought realistically *when* I'm sent to

Vietnam Nicole would be able to use the time he was overseas to complete her degrees and get her residency. He hoped by the time he returned home she would have the letters M.D. following her name and they could start a family without any further delays.

He was much closer to realizing his dreams with becoming a pilot and one day he hoped to become the astronaut he had dreamed of since he was a young boy. Or were they Nicole's dreams? He couldn't even remember anymore, not that it mattered. One's dreams were shared by the other.

He checked his watch and smiled knowing that the plane with Nicole, her parents, and his mother should be landing in less than an hour. He wished he had been able to greet them at the airport but then so did all the other cadets who were waiting for their families.

He admired himself in the mirror as he dressed in his parade dress uniform. He had worked hard these last years to see this day come to fruition. His only regret was that his father wouldn't be here to see him graduate from the academy. He knew his father would have been proud.

Daniel his best friend from the academy poked his head in the door and said, "Time to stop gawking at yourself in the mirror pretty boy and get a move on. Besides, that girl of yours won't be able to recognize you in this sea of cadets."

William grabbed his cap and closed the door behind him.

"She'll spot me. I guarantee you. She'll know where I am."

"Sure buddy, sure." Daniel said slapping his friend on the back. "You'll be just another handsome face in a sea of many."

"I'll bet you twenty bucks if you ask her after the ceremony where I was seated she'll be able to tell you exactly where I was," William said with a smile.

"An easy twenty in my pocket. You're on," Daniel said.

When they stepped out onto the field Daniel asked him, "Still think she'll be able to spot you."

William had to admit the field was packed with cadets who in their dress uniforms all looked alike. The stands were filled to capacity with family and friends eager to see their sons, brothers, or grandsons graduate and take the next step in life.

Nicole sat in the stands sitting between William's mother and her parents watching the men out on the field in their parade dress uniforms at Falcon Stadium.

"Can you spot him, Nicole? They all look alike in those uniforms," William's mother said while searching the sea of cadets trying to spot her son.

"He's right over there," Nicole said pointing at the eleventh row and near the end way on the other side of the field.

"Where? Where did you say? I can't tell which one he is," his mom said looking frantically about trying to spot her son.

"Just look for the most handsome man out there," Nicole said with pride.

"I don't know how you can tell that's him from here," her father said.

"I feel him. My heart is pulled towards his. He couldn't hide from me in a crowd of ten thousand," she said with pride.

The graduation was a lengthy process but Nicole and William's mother and her parents all had tears flowing at the moving ceremony.

The patriotic music boomed from the loud speakers and the Thunderbirds did a flyover at which point the cadets all tossed their hats in the air cheering the end of their long years of hard work at the academy.

After the graduation ceremony William posed for photo after photo appeasing his mother and then he said he was going to steal Nicole away for awhile to introduce her to his friends. They made plans afterwards to meet up with their parents for a celebratory dinner.

William looked around for Daniel. They had become close friends during their years at the academy and he was anxious to introduce Nicole to him. He saw him and waved him over to join the two of them.

Daniel too had dreams of becoming an astronaut which is one reason he and William had hit it off so well. William had been thrilled to learn they would both be stationed at Eglin.

"Damn William," Daniel said after being introduced to Nicole. "You told me she was beautiful but that doesn't even do her justice. No wonder you kept her to yourself whenever she visited you."

William smiled to himself later as he was talking to one of his fellow cadets when he spotted Nicole talking to Daniel and pointing to where he had been sitting during the ceremony.

He walked up and joined them and heard Daniel say to her, "He told you, right? He told you to tell me that. There's no way you could have known where he was sitting."

"He didn't tell me. There's no way I could *not* have known," she said with a smile.

"You can pay me later," William said laughing. "I won't even rub it in with an I told you so."

A few other of William's friends came up and joined them and he introduced his girl to each and every one of them.

Nicole was embarrased from his friends fawning over her but was glad to be arm candy for William for a short time before she was determined to steal him away and spend some alone time with him.

This was his moment. He had worked hard for it and he deserved to celebrate with his friends. She knew many of them would be going off in different directions to further their careers in the Air Force and may never see each other again.

It was a bittersweet moment for them knowing they had accomplished something to be proud of and yet many of them would be facing a fate of being sent off to fight in a war few people believed in or thought worth dying for.

Nicole shuddered at the morbid thought and was determined to make this a memorable day for William and not focus too far ahead in the future.

50

When William arrived at the base it was a matter of hit the deck running. There had been no time to lounge about and learn your way around. *Relax...* the Air Force had taken that word out of their dictionary.

From day one he had academic instruction which was extremely challenging but rewarding.

It was drilled into you that you trained as if it is certain you would be on the front lines. He knew for a fact that it was a certainty that he and all the other men he was training with would indeed be fighting in the war.

He was aware that every day of studies was one day closer to being shipped off to fight in a war halfway around the world.

He had completed his studies in Aerospace Physiology. These classes he was well aware could possibly one day save his life.

The classes covered emergency situations where you would be required to escape from your aircraft during an emergency by ejecting. The studies covered aircraft pressurization, learning to use night vision, fly both by instruments and by the stars, and discovering the physiological effects of altitude.

William's day consisted of twelve hour training between academics and flight training. His day started at 0600 and he didn't have a moment's rest until 1800, a long twelve hour day.

With his full day that left practically zero time to fit in any time with Nicole. When he did have half a day off or anytime at all it was inevitable her hours were filled with her studies at the university or the hospital. They had been able to meet half way between the university and the base just a handful of times to spend a measly few hours together.

In today's classes they were covering the science of

aerodynamics. They covered the capabilities of the planes in which they would be flying, the best angles of attack, and how to pull out of an impending crash.

There wasn't much horseplay as they all knew that these classes and what they learned could mean the difference of coming home to hug your family again or be brought home in a body bag.

As for him he had every incentive to come home to Nicole. He had waited for years for her, now that she was within reach of becoming his wife he wasn't playing around. He would do everything in his power to return home to her whole.

He grinned to himself thinking of how the UFOs defied all the odds in flying through different solar systems. He thought the Air Force could learn a thing or two from them in their flying skills.

He wondered what his instructor and fellow students would have to say if he volunteered the information he had actually flown in a UFO. Kicked out of the Air Force and put in a straight jacket would most likely be the result he thought.

The thought crossed his mind that if he was ever taken aboard a UFO again he'd ask to see the cockpit, if they even had one. Maybe they'd even let him try his hand at flying the thing. He knew Nicole's father had a chance to do that himself from the UFO the Germans had in their possession during World War II.

Wouldn't that be something to put on my resume when I apply at NASA. William caught himself chuckling and when his instructor turned to look at him he quickly turned it into a fake cough.

Quick recovery Halloway, he thought.

William had completed his courses with flying colors in aircraft systems, flight regulations, instrument flying, navigation, flight planning, and aviation weather.

His next step up was time in the flight simulator and aircraft training.

During basic flight training was the time he recognized his classes had thinned out quite a bit. Many men who had volunteered and even a few who had graduated at the academy dropped out during this time.

This was the time when men learned who couldn't cut it. It was a humbling experience after all the time they'd already put into the studies to have to admit at this point that they couldn't measure up.

He knew flying as glamorous as it sounded was stressful in peaceful times and here they had to learn what it would be like to fly during combat when you were dodging enemy planes shooting at you.

In the flight simulator he had been tested for his heart rate during stressful times and learned to land and take off. He had yet to master evading the enemy which was crucial if he planned to survive, which he most certainly did.

They experienced night flights using night vision and even learned when and how to eject from an inoperable plane. His first experience being shot out of an ejection seat was one he hoped he wouldn't have to repeat in real time.

Classes covered every eventuality. In case the worst did occur classes covered reading maps, terrain, and how to survive in the wilderness until you could be rescued. There were even classes on what to do if taken prisioner, how to survive captivity, and ways to possibly escape. It was a comforting thought that at least the Air Force made sure their men were well prepared for any eventuality.

Each day of training was a constant reminder of what was happening on the other side of the world. It was obvious in their training that they were being prepared for war.

His previous experience in flying and becoming a pilot helped him move up quickly. He had spent less time in the flight simulator than most before he graduated to flight time in an actual aircraft.

William was volunteering as much as possible racking up his flight time. He knew he wanted to be as prepared as possible for when he was called up to be shipped out to Vietnam. Even more important to him was he knew NASA had a certain quota to meet both education and air time for their pilots. He was determined to keep his mind focused on his end goal.

Between the academy and his current studies he would easily

meet the education requirements. He was still lacking in flight time if he wanted to apply as a pilot at NASA to fly the spacecraft. He was looking to close that gap so was getting in as much air time as possible. He knew once he returned from the war he didn't want any further delays and planned to apply as an astronaut as soon as he returned.

The only disappointment in life at the moment was being so close to Nicole and still rarely having any time to spend with her.

He knew she was working feverishly to meet all her requirements to become a doctor and she was getting close to meeting her goal. He knew this constant requirement of their time would pass and they would have the rest of their lives together but in the meantime it was hard as hell.

William walked into the dorm he shared with Daniel still wearing his flight suit.

Daniel was sitting on the side of his bunk his hair still wet from his shower sewing his flight patch on his flight suit.

"Hey Moonstruck, you best think twice about all that time you're volunteering to be up in the air," Daniel said.

"Why? That's what we're here for," William said stepping out of his flight suit.

William had been given the name Moonstruck for his call sign as he talked about his goals to go to the moon one day. His friend Daniel often teased that it had a double meaning. He said he was also over the moon over his girlfriend.

"With all that flight time you're racking up you may not be around long enough to marry that gorgeous girl of yours. If you're not around it may just be up to me to console her and keep her company," Daniel said.

William snorted, "She wouldn't give you the time of day Cheese. Besides, you'll be shipping out with me."

"I don't know. It seems like you're on a fast track on your way out of here. I have a thing for doctors in white lab coats. I may just forget about what a good friend you are and have to step in and take over for you."

"As close as you'll get to that is being my best man in our wedding," William said while rummaging through his clothes looking for some clean clothes.

Daniel's head shot up. "I'm going to be your best man? Did you guys finally set a date?"

"Of course you're going to be my best man. No best man even thinks about stealing another guy's girl so get that out of your head," William said.

"Aah, you know I was just joking with you. So when is the big day?" Daniel asked following William.

William stopped in his tracks. "I'm heading to the shower. Alone."

"Oh yeah, sorry." Daniel stopped in his tracks.

William closed the door to the bathroom and Daniel went to the door and yelled through the door. "So when is the wedding day?"

All he heard in response was the shower running.

A few minutes later when William came out of the bathroom he answered, "The first day we can both get off together. I'm going to pin her down so we can set a date. We've waited long enough."

"I should say. Together since you were seven years old. That's crazy. So what do you guys have left to fight about? You must have covered everything by now," Daniel said.

William looked at him strangely and said, "You know I don't think we've ever had a fight. We might soon though if she can't manage to get a day off to get married."

51

Nicole was grinning from ear to ear as she drove away from the university. She finally had a day and a half off and she was going to enjoy the time. No studies, no rounds at the hospital; nope, she wasn't even going to think about anything academic at all.

After an hour and a half on the road she came to a sign that said 32 miles to Montgomery. She checked her gas gauge and thought she ought to gas up once she reached Montgomery. From there she had another two and a half hours before she'd reach Mobile.

She hadn't been to Alabama in years. She and her family used to visit quite often as she was born here and this is where her best friend Nora and her family lived.

She felt guilty for a minute or two thinking she was this close to the Bishop's house and wasn't stopping to visit. Best friends or not with a choice between spending a few hours with William or the day with Nora and her family...well, there was really no contest.

It was a rare occurrence for her and William to both have time off at the same time and they made plans to meet in Mobile. He had less time off than she did so she agreed to drive a little further in order to give them more time together.

She drove into the front entrance of the Battle House Hotel. It was a beautiful historic hotel where William had made reservations for the two of them.

A valet had her car door open almost before she came to a stop and gave her a hand out of the car.

She grabbed her suitcase out of the backseat and was met by a bell hop who offered to take her bag. She told him she could manage as the bag was light.

He smiled and held the lobby door open for her to enter.

She was immediately struck by the grandeur of the place when she walked in. She gazed up at the vaulted ceiling and gazed on a beautiful archway. It was beautifully done while still keeping the ambience of the historical aspect of the place.

The second floor balcony overlooked the lobby. She could only imagine herself in the past standing on the second floor looking down on the lobby watching presidents and famous people walk through the doors of the spectacular lobby.

The carpets were so plush you just wanted to kick off your shoes and walk barefoot on them.

But all the grandeur and marvelous interior architecture that had caught her eye was forgotten the moment she spotted William watching her from the desk where he was checking in.

He walked across the lobby and caught her up in his arms and spun her around. Her suitcase dropped at her feet as she wrapped her arms around him.

The bell hop came up behind them with William's suitcase in one hand and picked up Nicole's that she had dropped.

"Would you like me to show you to your room?" he asked.

"You'll have to forgive us. We've missed each other terribly," William said never taking his eyes off Nicole. "Fate keeps us apart for one reason or another."

The bell hop smiled and said, "I'm sure if I had a girl as beautiful as her I'd lose my head too. This way," he said as he ushered them towards the stairs.

They had a beautiful room, old but with character that had a balcony that overlooked downtown Mobile.

"I hope you brought your schedule like I asked," William said later as she was soaking in the claw-foot bathtub.

"I did but you're not going to like it. I don't have any more time off for weeks other than one or two weekdays. At the end of the semester I have five luxurious days off but until then not much," she said frowning.

"That's what I was afraid of," William said frowning.

"What about you? What's your schedule look like?" she asked.

"Not much better than yours," he admitted.

"Regardless, I'm determined that we find a date that will work for us and make you my legal wife. I've been a patient man but my patience has run out," he said.

"Our vows on the beach mean as much or more to me than standing in front of a stranger and him saying we're married. You know in our hearts we're already married," she said.

"I want to make it legal all the same. We want to have a family and I want you to not only carry my child but my name. We have to do this right, Nicole. If something were to happen to me while I'm in Vietnam I need to know you're..."

"William, are you worried about that?" she got out of the tub and he handed her a luxurious thick towel to dry off with.

She dried off and wrapped the towel around her.

He ignored her question because yes he was worried as hell. At the same time he didn't want her to worry. He did want to be assured she would be cared for if anything happened to him.

Being that she was about to become a doctor he knew financially she would be fine, but all the same he wanted to know he had done right by her.

"You are one gorgeous woman," he said.

She dropped the towel at her feet and said, "I'm not really hungry. Are you? Why don't we just stay in?"

She held her arms out for him.

"I'm hungry for you," he said picking her up and carrying her to the bed.

An hour later they laid across the bed planning a day when they could make it legal. They already figured out they wouldn't have a chance to have anything elaborate nor was it what either of them wanted.

"I just want to wear a pretty dress and have you say what a beautiful bride I am. Have our parents there and your best man and Nora as my maid of honor. That's all I want," she said.

"You could wear an old rag and I'd still think you were beautiful," he said.

They looked at the schedule and picked the second day she had off at the end of the semester. He circled the date in red in her appointment book.

They were both startled when there was a knock on the door.

"Room service," William said.

Nicole not wearing a thing jumped up, grabbed her towel and ran for the bathroom.

William slipped on a bathrobe and opened the door.

Room service wheeled a cart in and set the table up for the two of them. After the waiter left with a hefty tip in hand Nicole came out of the bathroom wearing a matching robe the hotel had provided them with.

Now that the wedding date was set it was a load off both of their minds. A day they had both looked forward to for years they now believed was finally going to happen.

52

It was sometime before midnight when the aliens paid Nicole and William a visit.

The room lit up as though someone had turned on the lights at a football stadium. The lights had penetrated into the bedroom waking them up.

"We're about to have a visit," Nicole said when William asked where the lights were coming from.

He jumped up and looked out the window. The lights went out but still he could see the dark silhouette of the UFO against the evening sky.

"Surely we're not the only ones who saw that," William said. "I bet those lights lit up the entire city. Geez, it woke me up."

"Ummm, William. Turn around," Nicole said.

When he turned around to see what she wanted he saw two aliens standing there behind him.

William looked startled.

"How did you get in here?" he asked.

"Much time has passed since you have chosen him for your mate," the alien communicated to Nicole. "You have chosen well. It is a good match."

William walked over and sat on the side of the bed and took Nicole's hand in his own.

"We are a good match," William said. "Not that we need your approval."

"The two of you will deliver us the next generation of daughters of destiny."

Nicole interruped the alien, "Yes one day but not now. We spoke of this before and you agreed...."

"We have come to see if that time has come," the alien directed towards Nicole. "And we are here to open the gateway."

"Gateway, what are you talking about? Changed her mind? About what?" William asked.

"They seem anxious for us to have a daughter sooner rather than later," Nicole said.

She directed her next words to the aliens, "You agreed to my terms. I told you there are things we need to do first."

"Can someone clue me in to what this is all about?" William asked.

Nicole ignored William's question determined to get her point across to the aliens.

"You agreed. You gave your word. I explained before there are things we have to accomplish before...before..."

Nicole argued. Suddenly she wondered why she was even arguing about this subject. It was something she had thought of a lot lately herself. She herself was anxious to have William's baby. She thought perhaps it would be a good idea if she became pregnant before he left for Vietnam. But she wanted it to be their decision and they hadn't even discussed it.

"Yes, we agreed to give you time. We will honor that if that is still what you wish. Considering the circumstances with his inevitable departure we thought you may have reconsidered. We anxiously await the arrival of this child and we have felt those same thoughts cross your own mind," the alien communicated telepathically.

"I agreed that we will have a child. We look forward to one day having children..."

"A child. A daughter," the alien corrected her. "That is all we ask of you."

"Demand of me is more like it," she said.

"We have given you much in return for what we ask of you. You have received many gifts beyond that of other humans and your life is protected, as is his. We don't ask much of you but this is something we *require* of you. This is not a request. It is your destiny. It is your duty as the first of the new breed... as a daughter of destiny," the alien said firmly.

"Hah," Nicole snorted. "You don't ask much of me? Only my firstborn child."

"All we ask is you give birth to a daughter. It is a child you and your chosen one will cherish. There's no reason to be upset about it."

"And what if we agree and it's a boy," William said.

"This will not happen," the alien said with confidence.

He leaned in close to her and looked intently into her eyes and said softly for her ears only, "You know as well as I do that you long for a child with him."

"We'd like to maybe have more than one child in the future. Yes, we will have the next generation of daughters of destiny. Just...not...quite...yet," she said as though she were questioning herself about waiting. She couldn't seem to remember why she wanted to wait. Her thoughts felt muddled, confused.

"You are fertile and your body is ready to receive life. We wish at this time to open the gateway to allow conception to take place. In the past we have kept the gateway locked and sealed in respect of your demand for more time. We have come at this time to open it."

At this point the alien spoke only to Nicole putting these thoughts in her head as he stared intently into her eyes, "*You know you want us to. You desire this child as much as we do. Tell me now...open the gateway. Say, I am ready to receive life. To allow life to form.*"

At this point he dropped eye contact with Nicole, but not before she transferred her own thoughts to him, thoughts he had implanted in her head. "*Open the gateway. I am ready. I too desire this life.*"

This conversation would not be one she would remember.

As if nothing had transpired between the two of them he continued the conversation between the two of them as though there had been no interruption.

"This life we speak of will be revered. Each new daughter of destiny that arrives brings us closer to the arrival of the chosen one and our final destiny," the alien explained.

"Wait! What gateway are you talking about?" William asked confused by what the alien was saying.

"The barrier to her fertility," the alien answered. "Have you not wondered why she has never conceived in all the times you have been together? It is time for it to be removed...past time."

"I have wondered, worried really," William said. "I was concerned perhaps we couldn't have children. We have certainly been sexually active over the years so yeah it was a concern I had pushed to the back of my mind. I would have gladly welcomed a child of ours at any time, but now I would love to welcome a child of ours into this world," William said looking lovingly at Nicole.

Now the alien blocked his thoughts from Nicole and spoke only to William, *"You agree then. You wish for this to happen. You are ready to welcome this child."*

William looked into the eyes of the alien and nodded his head. He spoke telepathically for the alien's ears only, *"I too long for this as you do. Let us wait no more. I am ready to fulfill my duty."*

"As we too would love to welcome your daughter into the world," the alien responded happily to William.

"You put some kind of barrier in me? That's why I've never become pregnant?" Nicole asked completely unaware of the private conversations that had taken place.

"It was as you wished. You demanded time and it was given."

"You never told me," she said angrily. "When did you do this? How? I don't remember. Whatever it is, get it out of me."

"It is dissolving as we speak," the alien said. "The door to the gate has been thrown open never to be locked again. Our kind rejoice in this throughout all the universe. The heavens tremble at the loud cry of their rejoicing."

"My God. I never asked for any of this. I wish you would just get out of my life. Leave us alone," Nicole said furious at this revelation of the alien.

"The final destiny waits for no one. Even if you have personal desires there are many who await this great event with eagerness. You and your child are of utmost importance to our kind," the alien said.

"We plan to marry very soon. Perhaps we will have children sooner than I originally said due to the circumstances but we haven't discussed it. William and I. It needs to be our decision, not yours."

"Be aware the gate has been opened and I am unable to close it again. That will be on you this time," the alien said.

"Nicole, please. What they're asking I've thought of myself many times. I would love more than anything to have a child with you now. Why wait? We don't know what lies in the days ahead. Please my love, let's make a baby. I don't want to wait. It seems with us we're always waiting for everything we really want and desire. I desire more than anything, other than to make you my wife, to have a child with you. Please. I'm tired of waiting. How about you?" William pleaded with Nicole.

Nicole looked at him and appeared to be looking into his heart. Without responding to him she turned to the alien.

Nicole spoke up, "I don't want to waste the little bit of time I have left to spend with William. When William and I agree the time is right we will happily bring a daughter into this world. Now please leave."

"We look forward with great longing for that day," the alien said.

He bowed towards Nicole and looked intently into William's eyes.

William stared transfixed into the alien's large dark eyes. After a few seconds William dropped his gaze.

After a moment the alien communicated solely to William, *"Proceed."*

And just like that they were gone.

William looked out the window. He was waiting to see the UFO disappear but it remained hovering over the hotel.

As he turned and looked at the woman he loved he seemed to forget about the visitation.

"Nicole..." he said. He joined her on the bed and took her into his arms.

"I know you wanted to wait till after you became a doctor and I was an astronaut before we started a family but..." he said.

"That doesn't seem so important anymore, does it? Let's not wait. Like you said, it seems like all we've done the last few years is wait for everything we want so badly."

"Have my baby Nicole," he said. "Make me a husband and a father. I can't think of anything I want more."

"Our wedding is only a few weeks away. I can't even remember why we wanted to wait. I want to have your baby William. Maybe by the time you come home from the war ...."

"Hush. Quit talking. Let's make love..." he said.

"And perhaps a baby..." she said.

"Yes, let's make a baby. Let's not waste this night sleeping," he said.

He was suddenly very desirious to be with Nicole. He could see from her response that she too wanted him as much as he wanted her.

They made love throughout the night knowing it would be the last chance they would have to be together for quite some time. Their love making was intense and sexually heightened. The aliens had seen to that.

As they made love they were unaware that they were being observed by the aliens.

When William rolled over exhausted from a night of lovemaking he was unaware that the one alien nodded and communicated to the other, "It is done."

Only then did the aliens depart.

53

The following morning William had to leave bright and early to get back to the base. Nicole was going to leave shortly and stop by and visit the Bishops on her way back to the university.

"I may not have a chance to see you for awhile," William said as he held her before he left.

"I know. Our schedules have been crazy. The end is in sight though," she said.

"Maybe for you but it's definite now that we're being called to serve in the war. It will probably be just a short time after we finish with our pilot's training."

"So soon?" Nicole said looking distressed.

"That's why I really want us to get married as soon as possible. We don't dare put it off much longer. I doubt I'll have much warning before I have to leave," William said.

"I really didn't see this in our future," she said.

"Me neither. I thought this war would have been over long before now. Hopefully it won't last much longer," he said.

She had a look of despair on her face.

"Nicole..."

She looked at him.

"I know you wanted to wait till after you became a doctor and I was an astronaut before we started a family but I hope last night was fruitful and we...." he said.

"That isn't important anymore. It seems like all we've done the last few years is wait. I want it too William. I want to have your baby."

"Really?" William asked. "I hope you mean that. I hope so too. I want so badly for us to have a child together."

"I've been thinking of it for awhile now, but I didn't know how you'd feel about it since we haven't even had time to get married yet. I didn't want you to feel pressured about anything important before you had to leave to go to Vietnam. I want you to..."

"Yes, I definitely want us to be married and I want us to have a baby. It doesn't matter what the aliens want. That has nothing to do with it except maybe to make us face up to it. What better time than now, Nicole? I'll be leaving soon. I'll have something to fight for besides a career. I don't know why we've waited this long to be honest," he said.

"Who knows? Maybe I'll have a nice wedding gift to give you. News that I'm carrying your child," she said smiling at the man she loved with all her heart.

"A baby..." he said. "You are a dream come true my love. Please let it be true. I'll leave with a much lighter heart knowing I have a wife waiting for me and a child on the way."

"Well, let's not get our hopes up. If not now perhaps it will happen soon," she said.

"I certainly hope so," he said. "That's all the time we have left I'm afraid."

He wrapped his arms around her and held her tight. "I love you so much. I long to make you my wife and for you to have our child. A little girl that looks like her mother."

"I hate to let you go, but you don't dare be late getting back to the base. They'll never give you time off again if you are," she said.

They said their final good byes and he rushed out the door with one final look back.

54

Nicole had an entire day off. She knew being in the middle of the week there was little chance William would be able to get any time off but she thought she'd give him a call just in case.

Daniel came to the phone and told her William was in class and he was scheduled to fly later that afternoon.

Nicole had an idea and asked Daniel about it. He thought the plan was a good one though a long drive for Nicole for only being able to see William from a distance.

Daniel said he had the day off and to call him when she arrived and he would take her to where she could see William.

When she hung up Rhiannon was standing close enough to have overheard the conversation.

"Are you really driving all the way to north Florida?" Rhiannon asked.

"I am," Nicole answered. "I may not get to be with William but I'll be able to watch him fly."

Nicole turned around to leave when Rhiannon called after her. "Do you want some company? I'll help you drive if you let me go with you."

"Are you sure? Wouldn't you be bored?" Nicole asked.

"No, even as a kid my dad would take us and park near the airport and we'd watch the planes take off. I'd love to go with you."

"His roommate is meeting me to take me to where I can see him but I doubt he'll want to stick around. Sure come on if you're serious. I'd love to have the company," Nicole said.

Rhiannon ran into her room to change her clothes while Nicole grabbed a few things to take. They were out the door in less than ten minutes.

Nicole got to rest in the car since Rhiannon offered to drive. She was a little chatterbox but once she saw how tired Nicole was she got quiet and let her rest.

"I hate to wake you but we're almost there and I don't know where to go," Rhiannon said.

"Pull over at the Texaco station. I'll call Daniel from there," Nicole said pointing at the station ahead.

Nicole called Daniel and he told her where he'd meet her.

While they were waiting for him to arrive Rhiannon said, "So tell me about this Daniel guy. Is he cute?"

Nicole gave her a look. "I guess. I never really thought about it. Come to think of it, I think the two of you would get along great."

"So tell me about him. Quick, before he gets here," Rhiannon said.

"He's an officer and went to the academy which is where he and William met. He wants to be an astronaut too..."

"Ooh, that sounds exciting," Rhiannon said.

Nicole laughed as Rhiannon rummaged through her bag and pulled out a tube of lipstick and put it on and ran a brush through her hair.

"There he is now. Call him Cheese. That's his call sign," Nicole said.

"Cheese? Why, Cheese? Is he from Wisconsin or something?"

"No, his last name is Kraft. Get it...Kraft cheese?"

"I think I'd come up with something better than that," Rhiannon said. "Maybe Stud. Yeah, he looks like a Stud to me."

Nicole laughed. "Stud. He'd like that."

Daniel got out of a Jeep and started walking over to the car.

"He's really cute," Rhiannon said.

Nicole looked at her with a funny look on her face but didn't say anything.

Daniel walked over to the driver's side before he noticed Nicole wasn't the driver.

"Oh, who are you? I was expecting Nicole but you're a nice surprise."

"I'm Rhiannon. Nice to meet you," she said.

"Rhiannon, what a beautiful name. A beautiful name for a beautiful girl," he said flirting with Nicole's friend.

"All right you two. Make lovey dovey on your own time. I'm anxious to see William," Nicole said.

Daniel climbed back in his Jeep and motioned for them to follow him.

They followed him to a city called Crestview about five miles from the base. Daniel said they would have the best view at this spot.

Nicole pulled out two lawn chairs to sit on so she could watch William go through his maneuvers.

She put a sun hat on and rubbed some sunscreen on her face while she watched from a distance as her roommate and William's roommate were getting to know each other. Interesting she thought wondering why she'd never thought to introduce the two of them before.

Daniel told her William had completed his stint in Flight Test Operations and had just begun flying the F-4 Phantom II. He didn't tell her this was in preparation for his tour in Vietnam. That's what he would be flying today Daniel told her. He described to her what to look for so she could easily recognize the plane William would be in.

"I got a message to Moonstruck that you were going to be here watching. He said he'd tip his wings at you," Daniel said.

"I'm so glad I got to come watch him," Nicole said.

"He just completed his requisite hours for basic and intermediate training so now he's in the cockpit. He's on a fast track to Nam," Daniel said.

Nicole gave him a dirty look and said, "Not too fast I hope."

Once the planes started flying overhead Daniel pointed out how to spot Daniel's plane. Nicole was occupied watching for him and wasn't paying any attention to Rhiannon and Daniel.

"Do you mind if I take Rhiannon for awhile and show her around?" Daniel asked.

Nicole never took her eyes off the sky and said, "Sure, go ahead."

She had been watching for several hours and was glad she had thought to bring sunscreen and a cooler with water. She looked at her watch and realized Daniel and Rhiannon had been gone for quite awhile. Several hours in fact.

She had seen William fly over a total of about eight or nine times. Once he flew over low and circled back and tipped his wings verifying that it was indeed him. At the speed he was traveling she might have missed it if Daniel hadn't told her ahead of time what he intended to do. It wasn't like when he flew the twin engine plane he had learned to fly in. It had been well worth the day driving to see him.

By the time she got the car packed back up she realized it was late in the day. Where in the world have Daniel and Rhiannon disappeared to she wondered. She'd have to head back home soon.

She sat in her car waiting for them to return and about ten minutes later Daniel's Jeep came flying up.

"Hurry up. Follow me," Daniel said.

Rhiannon jumped out of the Jeep and got back in Nicole's car.

Nicole pulled out trying to keep up with Daniel.

"Where are we going?" she asked.

"Cheese talked to Moonstruck. He's going to take you to see him. He'll only be able to see you for a minute or two," Rhiannon said.

This was an unexpected surprise Nicole thought.

Daniel pointed to an area by the fence. He held back some bushes and said, "Go through there. Try not to make any noise. He'll be here in a few minutes. He can only stay a minute though or he'll be busted," Daniel warned.

"Thanks," Nicole whispered.

William ducked behind some bushes on the other side of the

fence a few minutes later.

"I can't believe you're here," he said.

"I had the day off and I had to see you. I didn't know we'd have a chance to see each other face to face," she said holding her hands up to the fence so she could touch his fingers.

He looked around. "I'll be missed if I'm not back in a minute but I wanted to thank you for coming. You certainly made my day."

"Mine too," she said. "I saw you tip your wings. Reminded me of when you first learned to fly."

"Are you...you know, are you pregnant?"

She looked surprised at his question. "No, I don't think so. It's really too early to tell but I think I'd feel something if I was."

He looked disappointed and said, "Next time. We'll have to work harder at it."

He reached through the fence to touch her fingertips and they tried to kiss each other through the fence.

"I have to go. I love you...to the moon and back," he said.

"Love you too," she said.

And he was gone.

Rhiannon talked nonstop about Cheese the entire drive back. Finally Nicole pulled over and said, "Do you mind driving the rest of the way? I have a big day tomorrow and you seem wide awake."

Once they changed seats Nicole put her head back and thought how exciting the day had been watching William fly.

He had asked her if she was pregnant. She was disappointed that she didn't have good news to share with him. Maybe next time like he said.

55

Nicole was making the rounds when she saw one of the doctors down the hall point her way. She automatically thought she was being given a patient and waited for the woman to walk up. When she got closer she realized it was one of the women from the dean's office at the university.

"Nicole Newhouse?"

"Yes I'm Nicole," she answered.

"We received an urgent message at the office. We've been trying to locate you," the woman said handing her an envelope with her name on it.

Nicole assuming the worst ripped it open.

The woman said, "I'm glad I found you. It sounded pretty important."

Nicole didn't even think to thank the woman before she walked off.

William had called trying to locate her. His time was up. He was being shipped out to Vietnam.

Her hand went to her throat and a gasp escaped. Tears welled up in her eyes.

The doctor who had pointed her out walked up and kindly asked, "Is everything all right? I heard you received an urgent message."

"No, everything's not all right. I have a family emergency. I need to leave right away," she said.

"I'm sorry if it's bad news. I'll let scheduling know you'll be off for a few days. Go on then."

Nicole practically ran down the hall.

William was going off to fight in a war. They had talked about it but it always seemed in the future as a possibility. She had just been slapped in the face with reality.

He was leaving the day after tomorrow. He had off the rest of the day and the next day. He said please come right away and bring her wedding dress. No time to delay.

It would be a sad wedding day. They would say I do in one breath and good bye in the next.

When she reached her car she bent over and threw up her entire lunch. The stress of his leaving to go off and fight in a war halfway around the world had just hit her hard. The tears came at the same time.

He was leaving. It was really happening. What if something happened to him over there? For the first time she realized that she could lose him in this war. They'd wasted so much time apart.

56

The sun was going down by the time she arrived. He had given an address where to meet him so she followed the directions from the map.

When she arrived at the address she saw it was a new hotel. They would be staying their last two days together at The Island in Fort Walton Beach.

It was a beautiful hotel that had opened just a few years previously on the beach front. He had gone all out on making their time together special.

It could have been a tent in the woods and it would have suited her just fine as long as they were together.

As soon as her car pulled up William walked out from the lobby to greet her.

"I've arranged for the chaplain from the base to marry us. It isn't going to be a memorable wedding with your father walking you down the aisle but it will be legal. We can do it over again when I get back if you want to wear a gorgeous dress and do it the way you probably always dreamed of."

"I don't care about any of that. I just want to share your name with you and share your life," she said.

He took her in his arms and she sobbed.

After a few minutes she pulled away and said, "I didn't mean to do that. I've been so emotional. I guess it's just that this all happened sooner than we expected."

"Wars are like that," he answered running his hand gently through her hair doing his best to soothe her.

He reached in and took her overnight bag and she reached back in for a garment bag which held the dress she planned to wear for their wedding.

"It's too late to get married tonight but the chaplain said he'd be available tomorrow," William said.

"I'm sorry. They had a hard time finding me. I was making my rounds at the hospital," she said.

"We're together now. That's what matters," he said in a subdued tone.

"What about your mother? Are you going to get a chance to say good-bye to her?" Nicole asked.

"She came up about a week and a half ago when I had a few hours off and we said our good-byes then," he answered.

When they went to check in to the hotel the person at the desk asked them to wait a moment as there was a message for him. He made a call and the concierge came out of his office with a written message.

"I received a call from the chaplain at the base. He asked me to make arrangements and to call him when you checked in. He said if it suits the two of you he can perform your wedding ceremony this evening," the concierge said.

William looked at Nicole, "You ready to become my bride?"

She shook her head eagerly. They were both suddenly all smiles.

The concierge said, "One moment and I'll have my staff give him a call."

After the concierge gave the number and information to his staff to make the call he guided them over to some seats in the lobby.

"We can perform the ceremony either in our ball room or if you prefer we can have the ceremony by the poolside or on the beach. Which would the two of you prefer?"

"They both said in unison, "The beach."

The front desk clerk walked over and said the chaplain would arrive in about two hours that he had one more ceremony to perform before theirs and then he would make the drive over.

William shook hands with the concierge and thanked him. As the bellhop was taking the bags and speaking to Nicole William asked him if there was any way he could arrange to have a bouquet or some type of flowers made up for the bride.

"I know it's short notice but we didn't have much notice ourselves," William said.

The concierge said the floral department was closed but he would see to it that she had something.

William and Nicole's step was lighter just knowing they would finally realize their dreams of becoming man and wife.

An hour later Nicole called out from the bathroom. "I know you're not supposed to see the bride before the wedding but under the circumstances..."

William opened the door and said, "Forget those old wives tales. Let me feast my eyes on my bride."

Tears came to his eyes when he saw how beautiful Nicole was. Her hair was swept up and she had on a white lacey dress that appeared vintage but not out dated.

"I'm speechless. You take my breath away," he said.

Nicole spun around so he could admire the woman who was to become his bride.

"This was my mother's wedding dress. My sentimental father saved it. When he left Germany to come to America he brought it with him. My mom sent it to me. It just arrived a few days ago and was a perfect fit."

The phone rang and the concierge said the chaplain had arrived and he was waiting in the lobby.

William in his Air Force dress uniform and Nicole in her bridal dress turned every head that passed them. They were truly a handsome couple.

The concierge walked up to William and handed him a box. William opened it and was very pleased with the magic the concierge had been able to perform.

He gently pushed back the tissue paper and lifted a beautiful bouquet, small but perfect for their ceremony.

Nicole looked at him and said, "You thought of everything."

The chaplain arrived, a large black man with a slow drawl and a comforting way about him. He greeted the two of them and remarked what a beautiful bride Nicole was.

The chaplain said to William, "I heard you graduated number one in your pilot class. Congratulations."

William merely said, "Thank you, sir."

Nicole looked stunned at this bit of news and said, "Why William, you never told me that."

"No, I wouldn't imagine he would. He's a humble man this man you're about to marry," the chaplain said.

As they walked outside the chaplain asked if they'd known each other long.

"Yes sir. Since I was seven years old and Nicole was six," William responded.

The chaplain smiled. "I guess you've had plenty of time to get to know one another then. Earlier this evening I married a couple who'd only known each other for two weeks."

Nicole kicked off her high heels and left them on the pool deck and they walked down on the beach. Earlier they had found the perfect spot with the help of the concierge. The hotel kept the area lit up with little fairy lights and it was a picturesque spot perfect for a wedding.

They repeated their vows almost word for word that they had said to each other years ago at another beach ceremony...the difference this time is it was legal and binding.

When it came time to exchange rings William surprised her

yet again by pulling a matching set of rings from his pocket.

He whispered that when he returned he was going to buy her a ring with a big sparkly diamond to go with the wedding band.

The chaplain pronounced them man and wife and announced her as Mrs. Halloway as the bride and groom exchanged rings and kissed to seal the deal.

The chaplain said he had performed seven weddings since the announcement had been made that their platoon was leaving sooner than expected. He said he was trying to accommodate everyone but admitted to them that theirs had been the most moving ceremony he had performed.

He wished them luck and said he was off to perform yet another ceremony and had appointments up to midnight and then four more the following day.

He chuckled and said, "I imagine there will be a few Air Force babies delivered in about nine months."

After he left William said, "Speaking of babies..."

"Yes let's," Nicole said.

When they arrived in their hotel room they had been left a cheese platter, a few sandwiches, and a bottle of champagne courtesy of the hotel. The bed had been turned down and chocolates were laid on the pillows. Scattered red rose buds lay across the sheets.

William popped the cork as Nicole wrapped her mother's dress back up carefully thinking maybe one day their own daughter would wear it to her wedding.

They drank to Mr. and Mrs. Halloway and said the ceremony had been wonderful after all and had been worth waiting for. They looked forward to a lifetime ahead.

That night William and Nicole "worked hard" at making sure he left a little surprise package behind.

57

MATS, or the Military Transport Service, would be flying the troops in a stretch DC-8 from Eglin the following morning. William had been notified that the plane had just landed at Hurlburt Field.

William had strongly suggested to Nicole that they say their good-byes at the hotel. He knew watching him get on the plane and watching the plane take off would be traumatic for her. He didn't want her to go through that alone.

Of course she wouldn't listen to reason and made no promises.

They got up early the following morning after a sleepless night with heavy hearts.

William sat on the side of the bed where Nicole was and stroked her hair and her face. He wiped away her tears. "I may be leaving but my heart remains here with you. You're on your final lap now with the end of your residency in sight. You'll make a wonderful doctor. I'll picture you here caring for others and eagerly await the day when we'll be reunited."

Nicole sat up and wrapped William in her arms sobbing wrenching sobs.

"Why is love so hard and so painful?" she asked.

"We've just hit a bit of a detour before we're back together forever," he said.

She felt his own tears mingling with hers on her cheek.

"Take care of yourself while I'm away," he whispered. "And our baby if there is one."

"Don't worry about me. You watch your back and come home to me as soon as you can. Promise me you'll come home to me," she said.

"I will. I promise. I have a lot to live for. Hopefully you'll write to me soon and tell me you're expecting and I'm going to be a father."

"I'll write to you as soon as I know if I'm pregnant. I won't tell a soul before I tell you. You'll be the first to know. I promise," she said.

"Nicole, pray for me. Pray I return to you whole and in one piece," he said soberly.

"You will, sweetheart. And yes, I will pray for you everyday...fervently. I love you so much. William, I'm lost without you. I don't know how I'll bear being without you," she cried.

"I feel the same way, my love. I'll carry a part of you with me..."

She pulled back and wrenched off the ring he had given her over a decade ago before he left for the Academy. At the time she swore she'd never take it off, but now she wanted him to carry it with him so he'd have a piece of her with him at all times.

"He held the ring in his hand and looked at it. He kissed it and put it in a safe place. "I'll carry this with me on everyone of my missions. Having this part of you with me will keep me safe and sane. I love you," he said.

"To the moon and back," they said in unison.

"I need to go my love," he said. "Please don't come see me off. It would be too hard on you. We'll say our good-byes now...remember this is temporary," he said.

They held each other and dragged out their good-bye till the last possible moment and then he pulled away. He took one last long look at the woman he loved more than life itself before he quietly closed the door behind him.

He almost turned around and went back when he heard her heartbreaking sobs through the door, but he knew he had no time to waste. He had waited as it was until the very last moment possible. He turned and with a heavy heart made fast time down to his car and sped off to the base.

Nicole waited till she was assured he was gone and wouldn't be coming back before she rapidly dressed while wiping away her tears. She closed up her bags and quickly checked to be sure they hadn't left anything behind. He had already let the front desk know they would be checking out this morning so she left the room key on the desk and took off down the hall.

She threw her bag and carefully placed her wedding dress in the backseat of her car and headed in the same direction he had just traveled.

She may not be able to speak to him or hug and kiss him good-bye again but she was determined she would be there to see him off.

She wasn't alone when she arrived. There were many family members there to watch their loved ones fly off to southeast Asia.

She spotted him almost immediately and almost as though he could sense her presence he turned and his eyes found hers.

He smiled and threw her a kiss and she reached up as though to catch it before he had to turn and board the plane.

The mobile stairway was pushed to the door of the plane and the men began to board. He stepped back and let another take his place and took one last long look back at his wife and placed his hand over his heart. She did the same. Then he too boarded the plane.

She watched as the plane went down the runway and took off feeling as though her heart had just gone with it.

She stood there with the tears flowing. She knew she wasn't alone. Others standing around her had also watched their loved ones depart wondering when or if they would return.

She heard someone speaking behind her but didn't realize they were speaking to her. Then someone tapped her on the shoulder and she turned to see the last person she expected to see here.

"Rhiannon, what are you doing here?"

Rhiannon held up her left hand and showed her a wedding band.

Rhiannon wore a huge smile on her face and said, "Daniel and I got married yesterday, can you believe it?"

"Wow! That's a surprise. Daniel, Daniel Kraft? Cheese? The two of you got married?" she asked to be sure she had understood correctly.

"Yep, me and Cheese we tied the knot. I know we've only known each other about two weeks but we've talked on the phone for hours everyday since we met and I snuck up here and met up with him twice. We're in love. You were right. We're just right for each other," Rhiannon said with a big smile.

If nothing else Rhiannon's news and enthusiasm made her heart a little lighter.

When Rhiannon asked if she could ride back with Nicole since she had come on the bus Nicole was glad for the company. Suddenly she didn't want to be alone and she welcomed Rhiannon's nonstop chatter and bright outlook in life.

58

When the men arrived in South Vietnam they departed the plane and were immediately hit with a blast of heat that surely measured over 100 degrees F on the thermometer. It wasn't just the heat though. The humidity had you drenched with sweat in a matter of minutes.

William and Daniel had both been assigned to a Tactical Fighter Squadron at Danang Air Base located in South Vietnam.

The days ran into each other with the men seeming to spend as much time in the air as on the ground.

They had flown what he believed to have been about forty to fifty combat missions since he'd arrived but he'd lost count. He just knew it seemed as though he was strapped into his plane and in the air more hours than he could keep track of.

When he had a few moments at the end of the day he would write a letter to Nicole. Sometimes it would only be a line or two if he had little time or was exhausted from the day, but he made an effort to write often so she would receive a letter from him every few days assuring her he was all right.

She wrote often too, or as often as she could as a resident doctor. There were times when her letters wouldn't arrive until weeks after she'd written them. He always looked forward to mail call and for a word or two from her.

The only disappointment was she hadn't mentioned news of a pregnancy so he had to assume it hadn't happened.

He had really hoped when he left the States that he would soon hear she was expecting, but evidently it wasn't meant to be at this time. You couldn't say they hadn't tried.

Rhiannon was packing her bags. Now that she was a married woman she was quitting the university and moving home to get a job to save money to buy a house once Daniel returned from Nam.

She told Nicole she had come to college to get a husband, the heck with a degree. She said she had sat through half a semester of classes after Daniel left and that was it. She was over it. She was going home to spend time with her family and get a job until Daniel came home.

She would be sorely missed. She had a great personality and kept Nicole's spirits up.

She had proven to be a good friend when after William left Nicole had been terribly sick for a time from the stress of seeing her husband go off to war.

Rhiannon had spoon fed her chicken soup, her grandmother's recipe which she said was guaranteed to make anyone feel better. She had held her hair back for her while Nicole heaved all the chicken soup into the toilet.

She hated to see Rhiannon leave. It seemed like she was saying good-bye to everyone she was close to.

Rhiannon carrying out a load of her clothes took one of her tops and threw it towards Nicole. "I guess you should just keep this now that you've stretched it all out. It doesn't fit me anymore."

Nicole's jaw dropped, "What are you talking about? *I* stretched it out? We've been sharing clothes for years and you never complained about me ruining your clothes before."

"In case you haven't noticed since William left you've been obviously drowning your sorrows in junk food and you've put on weight," Rhiannon said.

"I'm a doctor. I don't eat junk food. I know better," Nicole said with her hands on her hips.

"Maybe not junk food but you're eating something that's putting on the weight. My guess would be the hospital food. When is the last time you actually cooked a meal?" Rhiannon asked.

"I can't remember. My pots and pans probably have dust on

them. I don't have time to cook...or eat. I just grab a bite at the hospital when I can."

"Well, hello...it's caught up with you. Have you looked in the mirror lately?" Rhiannon said.

"O.K. I admit I have put on a few pounds but I've always been too skinny," Nicole argued.

"You're right about that. Anyway, the top is stretched out now. You might as well keep it," she said.

"I'm sorry. I'll buy you another one," Nicole said.

"No need. Appreciate the offer though. Just help me carry these boxes out to the car, would you?"

They carried the rest of the boxes out to the car and jammed the last two boxes in. They barely got the back door closed the car was so loaded down.

"I'm going to miss you, ya know?" Nicole said hugging her friend.

"We'll be together again. When our guys come back they're going to be astronauts and maybe they'll get to fly on the same spacecraft," Rhiannon said.

"Let's call and order a pizza for your last night, shall we?" Nicole said grabbing the neighborhood Italian restaurant's menu off the refrigerator.

"And you say you don't eat junk food," Rhiannon laughed.

While they were waiting for the pizza to be delivered Nicole saw she had started her period. She wanted to cry.

She had been hoping she was pregnant. She had been afraid to take a pregnancy test earlier thinking if it was negative she would be devastated. She had a light period the two months previous but it was more like spotting than a period and this month she was late. She had hoped this month would prove her prayers had been answered. Obviously not.

59

Nicole was finishing her rounds when one of the visiting doctors that came to give the residents specialized training walked up and said, "Good call on that patient. A lot of residents and even seasoned doctors would have missed those symptoms. You're going to be a great doctor."

"Thank you. I appreciate that," Nicole said stunned.

It was a rare day when a specialist gave a resident a compliment though she admitted she had really liked working with this doctor. She didn't seem to carry around a huge ego like so many of the doctors did.

"Have you got a few minutes. I'd like to talk to you about something," Dr. Archer said.

"Sure. I'm through with my rounds," Nicole said.

Dr. Archer pointed her towards a waiting area. She looked in and saw it was vacant and they took a seat.

"Where are you from?" the doctor asked her.

"My home is in Florida. I grew up in St. Augustine," Nicole said.

"I thought someone had said you were from Florida, but I wasn't sure. I work in Gainesville not that far from St. Augustine."

"I didn't know you were from Florida," Nicole said.

"Like I said before I think you're going to be a great doctor. I have to admit I came down here for two reasons. One I come to train the residents in my field every year and also because I'm looking for someone to come work with me temporarily. I have an opening I need to fill and I think you'd be a perfect fit. Think you'd be interested?"

They discussed the details further and Nicole had promised to give it some thought but she was already pretty sure she'd accept the offer. It was a temporary job which was perfect to fit her needs.

"I'm just curious as to what your future plans are," Dr. Archer asked as they were standing up to leave.

"I really have my heart set on working at NASA. My desire is to work with the astronauts in the field of aerospace physiology," Nicole answered.

Dr. Archer laughed, "I knew there was some reason I was drawn to you. I think today is your lucky day."

"Why is that?" Nicole asked.

"I happen to have a very close relationship with the director at NASA in exactly the field you're looking to get into. I'll definitely put in a good word for you. I also happen to know they're going to be looking in the near future to fill a spot that you would be perfect for," Dr. Archer said.

Nicole looked surprised at this serendipity.

"I'll accept your offer to put in a good word for me and I guess there's really nothing to think about as far as the job offer goes either then. I just didn't want to start something new and then have to leave if I had an opportunity to get into NASA. When do you want me to start?"

Dr. Archer smiled and said, "I really need you right now but how about anytime between now and the next three or four weeks? Will that time frame work for you?"

"That works out great. I'll look forward to it. Thank you Dr. Archer," Nicole said.

"One other thing. Call me Mariah. We're going to be colleagues Dr. Newhouse," the doctor said.

"Mariah it is then. Call me Nicole, but I'm not Dr. Newhouse. It's Dr. Halloway now," she said.

"A newlywed? How will your husband feel about the move to Florida?"

"He's in Vietnam at the moment. When he comes home I'll be that much closer to home. He'll have no problem with it. Hopefully by the time he comes home I'll be working for NASA," Nicole said.

"I'll send you the information you'll need. Welcome to our doctor's group. I think you'll be very happy working with me at Shands Hospital," the doctor said.

While Nicole was making future plans back home William was about to go into combat.

During the early morning the U.S. troops were preparing for their first air strike of the day against the North Vietnamese.

The men were subdued as they suited up and climbed into the cockpits of their planes. Normally these pilots were cocky and arrogant Type A personalities but when you're about to go on a mission the thought of the possibility of not coming back whispers in the back of your mind.

Anyone who ever fought in a war and said they weren't scared were either stupid or liars, William thought.

He said a short prayer and kissed his finger and touched the photo he had taped up of Nicole and placed within his line of sight in his cockpit. He touched the outside of his pocket to feel for the ring she had taken off and given him before he left to assure it was there. He put his helmet on and waited for his go signal.

The day had begun before daybreak with the first strike launched by aircraft carriers *USS Constellation* and the *USS Kitty Hawk*.

With no time for the North Vietnamese to recover from the initial attack the planes took off one immediately after the other blackening the skies with Phantoms and F-105Gs Thunderchiefs our military's flight bombers. The aircraft was on a course across North Vietnam heading towards their targets. Just the sight of them would have initiated fear.

They were armed and ready for air-to-air combat. Their mission that day was to bomb North Vietnamese airfields and intercept any MiGs which managed to take to the air and were a threat to the men in the skies.

That day William would win a victory in shooting down two MiGs.

"Moonstruck, multiple bandits in your area," he heard repeatedly through his headset.

William spotted the MiGs. The hostile aircraft was within range and he locked on the radar.

A direct hit. Score one for the good guys!

The MiG fell out of the sky trailing smoke and missing it's left wing.

He didn't have time to celebrate his victory before he was notified another hostile was headed his way.

By the time he set foot back on the ground that day he had scored two kills. He didn't look at it as a personal victory but as a few less threats to the American troops.

He never wrote of these missions in his letters to Nicole. He didn't want to bring the harsh realities of the war to her doorstep. Instead he preferred to write of his love or describe the countryside or of the antics of the other men doing his best to keep it light hearted.

In return she wrote of the news back home and of how she was counting the days until he returned home.

60

Nicole was looking in the bathroom cabinet when she came across a box of Tampons with one missing.

She picked up the box and it hit her that she bought this box the month before William left, or was it two months before? She remembered the night Rhiannon moved she thought she had started her period but it was basically that one evening.

"My God, could I be pregnant and missed it all this time? I'm a doctor for crying out loud. How could I have missed the symptoms?"

As she stripped her clothes off she remembered the days Rhiannon had been there when she thought the stress had gotten to her and was throwing up everything she ate and sleeping all the time. She had attributed it to working long hours and stress.

She didn't want to get her hopes up as she looked in the mirror. There was a bulge where she normally had a flat stomach. There was no denying it.

She ran her hand over her stomach and realized there was a most definite bulge. In fact, it was a quite obvious bulge.

No wonder her clothes were feeling so tight. She stood sideways admiring what Rhiannon had referred to as her "junk food revenge."

She didn't want to get her hopes up only to be disappointed but....she looked again. Yep, a definite bulge. My goodness, not only was she pregnant but she was already showing.

She remembered her breasts being tender and thought at the time it was because her period was about to start but it never did. She took a good look at her breasts and was stunned that she hadn't noticed that they too had filled out.

No wonder she'd stretched out Rhiannon's top she thought

while looking at herself in the mirror.

"My goodness they're quite voluptuous," she said out loud and laughed. I've never had big boobs before. Wouldn't William love to get his hands on these, she thought laughing.

She had to sit down. Reality was setting in. She was stunned.

How had she missed all the signs? This was something she and William had wanted so badly. It had happened.

She went into her bedroom and grabbed the calendar counting back to the time when William left. She knew this happened either the night of their marriage or possibly even earlier when they had met at the hotel in Mobile.

When they had been in Mobile they had a visitation from the aliens who spoke of opening a gate. Something to do with opening the gate or something to that effect so she could conceive she thought was how they had described it.

Counting back she realized she was either four or five months along. She was already half way through her pregnancy.

"How could I have been so stupid?" she asked herself. "How did I miss all the signs? Now that I look back, they were so obvious."

She thought back and knew the signs had all been there: being overly emotional, sick to her stomach, dizzy, tender breasts, tired all the time, missed periods. She had written them all off as signs of stress or working too hard.

She got dressed and drove to the drug store and picked up not one but three pregnancy test kits. She wanted to be sure she got the correct results before she wrote William and told him.

When she went to the register to ring her purchase up the woman asked her, "Are these for you?"

"Yes," she answered even though she thought it was a very personal question to ask a customer.

The woman looked at her and said, "Save your money, honey. I can tell by just looking at you that you're definitely pregnant. Do you still want to buy these?"

Nicole just shook her head yes not wanting to carry on this

conversation with a complete stranger.

"Suit yourself," the woman took her money and bagged up her purchase.

As Nicole turned to leave the woman said, "Congratulations."

Nicole went in the bathroom and tore open the first kit and quickly read the directions. She followed the directions exactly and then paced the floor waiting for the time to pass before she'd get the results.

"Please, please, please...let me be pregnant. Please be positive," she kept saying over and over.

She ran her hand over her belly and laughed and thought, of course it's positive.

She checked the clock and walked over to look to see if the results were positive or negative.

Positive!

She and William were having a baby. She was going to be a mother, William a father. She was so happy she cried. If only he was here to share this moment with her. Instead he would learn of it from a letter.

Thinking of how long it sometimes took for him to receive letters from home she realized she would already be feeling life before he even knew.

She tore off the wrapper from the second pregnancy kit and got the same results. She did a little happy dance right then and there. They were having a baby.

She went in the room and wrote to him immediately. She had promised him before he left that if she found out she was pregnant she would tell him before she told anyone else.

She better hurry. She wouldn't be able to hide it for long.

She stroked her belly knowing she had a child growing inside her. Hers and Williams.

She already knew it would be a little girl. That was inevitable as this child was to be the next daughter of destiny.

She knew the aliens would be rejoicing once they discovered she was expecting.

Before the evening was over she took the third test too, just to be sure she told herself.

It too was positive just as she knew it would be.

61

Nora's mother had heard from Elke that Nicole had accepted a job and would be moving to Florida. Nora decided to drive up and see her before she left and see if she needed any help moving.

When she arrived at Nicole's no one was home. She peeked in the window and saw empty boxes and packing tape and decided she had made a good call.

She didn't know when Nicole would get off work so she decided to drive to the hospital and see if she could get the key to her apartment from her. She'd start packing her things for her while she was at work.

Nora walked in the emergency room and saw Nicole sitting behind a desk filling out paperwork.

Nora walked up to the desk and said, "Miss, I need help..."

Nicole looked up and smiled. She stood up to come around to hug her best friend.

Nora gasped and her jaw dropped when she saw her.

"You're pregnant!" she said.

Nicole steered her out of ear shot of everyone and said, "What makes you say that?"

Nora looked at her like she had lost her mind and said, "First of all you have enormous boobs which you never did and second your belly is poking out of those scrubs. So unless you've had a boob job and swallowed a melon you've got some explaining to do. Remember I've known you all my life. How could I not know?"

Nicole walked outside the emergency doors with her and said, "I can't believe you knew that immediately. I just found out two weeks ago."

"Two weeks ago? What have you had your head in the sand all

this time? How could you have just learned two weeks ago? What did you do, close your eyes every time you walked by a mirror. You must be what about six or seven months?"

"Four or five," she said.

"When's your due date?" Nora asked.

"I don't know. I have my first doctor appointment later this afternoon. What are you doing here by the way?"

"Your mom told my mom that you were moving to Florida in a few days. I thought you might need some help moving and I wanted to see you before you left. I can't believe your mom didn't tell us about the baby," Nora said indignantly.

"She doesn't know."

"What! You haven't told her she's going to be a grandmother?"

"No, and you have to promise not to tell anyone either. I promised William he'd be the first to know. I told him I wouldn't tell anyone until I told him. So, please promise you won't say anything," Nicole asked of her friend.

"That will be tough. O.K. You have my word. Why don't you give me the key to your place and I'll go start packing your things," Nora said.

"I have a better idea. I have to finish up but I'll be done in about ten minutes. If you'll wait for me we can go grab a bite to eat and you can go with me to my doctor's appointment. You know moral support from my daughter's godmother."

"I'm going to be her godmother? Oh, yeah. I guess it will be a girl. The next daughter of destiny...the next generation of alien..."

"Please," Nicole started to tear up. "Please don't remind me that my daughter will be part alien. I can't bear to think of that."

Nora hugged her best friend and said, "I'm sorry. I didn't mean to make you cry. Don't worry about it. You're part alien, this new breed whatever they call it, and you're perfect. Your baby will be too."

Nora went in with her for her examination. The doctor confimed that she was a little over five months along. She said she was in great physical shape and didn't foresee any problems.

"Let's listen for that heartbeat, shall we?" the doctor said.

Nicole's face lit up. She would actually hear the heartbeat of her baby.

The doctor ran a wand over her belly. Almost the minute she put the sensor on her belly the room filled with the sound of a thudding heartbeat.

Nicole looked at Nora and smiled.

The doctor took the monitor off her belly and said, "Everything sounds as it should."

"Could I listen just one more time?" Nicole asked.

The doctor wanting to accommodate a first time mother placed the monitor back on Nicole's belly. She ran it over Nicole's belly and picked up the heartbeat in a different area this time and again the room filled with the sounds of the baby's heartbeat.

"The baby seems pretty active. He must be doing flips in there. Have you felt life yet?" the doctor asked.

"No, should I?" Nicole asked. She had to hold her tongue when the doctor called her baby "him." She didn't want to be questioned as to how she knew it was a girl. That would have to be her secret.

"It won't be long before you feel movement. You're far enough in your pregnancy where you'll start feeling life at any time. You may not recognize it for what it is at first. It may feel like a butterfly's wings fluttering or just a light sensation. It will be a little later when you'll feel hard kicks," the doctor explained.

Nicole was all smiles as they left the doctor's office. She was glad since William wasn't there to share this special moment with her that she had Nora with her.

62

Nicole had talked Nora into going with her to Gainesville where she would be working.

Nora thought that was a great idea and said maybe she could look for a job while she was there.

Nicole found a small two bedroom apartment close enough where she could walk to the hospital. She convinced Nora to become her roommate at least till the baby came.

Nora herself brought up the subject of what she would do with the baby once she had to return to work after the birth.

"I guess things have happened so fast I hadn't thought that far ahead," Nicole admitted.

"You'll need someone to help you with the baby while you're working," Nora said.

"I hate the thought of having a stranger take care of my baby," Nicole said.

"Then don't. What do you think about me being the baby's nanny?" Nora asked.

Nicole's eyes lit up. "Are you sure? You would be willing to stay and do that?"

"I would absolutely love to," Nora said.

"That would be perfect. You certainly have experience with all your brothers and sisters and I know she'll be in good hands with you."

Nora hugged her as hard as that was getting to be with her belly that seemed to be growing daily and said, "I've thought about it a lot and I was kinda hoping you'd ask me."

"That's a load off my mind. Thank you so much, Nora."

"Have you heard back from William yet since you wrote and

told him about the baby?" Nora asked.

"No. I'm not really surprised. Sometimes my letters take weeks for him to get. I imagine any day now though he'll be getting my letter. Boy, won't he be surprised. He'd probably given up on thinking I was pregnant after all this time. I hope he'll be able to get some time off and come home after the birth," Nicole said.

Nicole looked around the apartment and said, "I need to do some shopping pretty soon. I haven't got the first thing for the baby yet."

"You're off for the rest of the day. Let's go shopping," Nora suggested.

They came home utterly exhausted but elated at their purchases.

"It's a good thing I just got paid," Nicole laughed. "I think we got everything we'll need in one trip."

"It's a good thing the store delivers. We never would have fit all that in your little car," Nora said.

Nicole picked up a little onesie with pink ruffles on it's bottom and decorated with little rosebuds. "These are so adorable."

She set the outfit down next to a pile of diapers.

"Where are we going to find room for all this? Goodness but babies need a lot of things."

"Just figure out where you want everything and I'll help get everything set up while you're working. Once it's closer to the time of the birth I'll wash all her new little clothes and sheets," Nora said.

"I'll set up the bassinette in my room but I don't think I can fit another dresser in there. Maybe I should look for a bigger place," Nicole said becoming overwhelmed just thinking about it.

"She'll be little for months. We can make do here for awhile. By the time you're ready to move to Cape Canaveral to go to work for NASA then you can look for a bigger place," Nora said.

"Don't jinx me," Nicole said. "The interview went well but they haven't committed to hiring me yet. I hope my huge belly didn't scare them off."

Nicole heard the mailman put some mail in her mailbox. Hoping to find a letter from William she got up and checked the box.

A huge smile crossed her face when she saw there was indeed a letter from her husband. The letter had been sent to her old address and been forwarded so had been written weeks earlier.

I need to add that to my 'To Do' list and send a forwarding address to the university and hospital. I forgot to do that before I moved, she thought as she rapidly looked through her mail.

I didn't even think to mention that I'd moved when I wrote William about the baby. He still thinks I'm in Georgia, she thought. Won't he be surprised to hear I'm working in Florida and had an interview with NASA.

Speaking of NASA, she thought as she flipped through the mail. She saw she also had a letter from them. She supposed it was either a letter saying she'd been hired or not.

She set that letter aside wanting to read her husband's letter first.

Nicole excitedly tore open William's letter. She scanned it quickly to see if he mentioned the baby but there wasn't anything in the letter to make her think he had received her letter yet.

She thought as she held his letter he may be at the same time reading the letter she had sent him. She was anxious for him to receive news that he was going to be a father.

She ran her hand gently stroking her belly and said, "It's a letter from your daddy."

As she ran her hand over her belly she felt a kick. She'd been feeling life now for a week or so. The baby definitely made her presence known. It seemed night and day she was doing acrobatics.

The letter he wrote was a short one as many of them were. She was just thankful to hear from him.

She read his letter, *Nicole, my love. I hope this letter finds you well. You are in my thoughts always, day and night, 24 hours a day. I miss you more than you can possibly know. I know you are probably thinking you miss me the same. I guarantee you I miss you more. I hate being so far away from you. I'm counting down till the end of my tour until I can be back home with you.*

We had a USO troop brought in to entertain the troops. Daniel talked me into going. It was quite a drive from our base but it was a nice change of pace. It's moments like these that lift the men's spirits and give them something to look forward to, he continued in his letter.

Her heart was heavy reading between the lines. He sounded down and discouraged. It sounded to her that the men's spirits needed lifting including William's, that things weren't going so well on the war front.

She cursed President Johnson who had made empty promises of bringing the men home. No one put much faith in his empty words anymore. She knew both of the president's daughters also had husbands fighting in the war but still he didn't seem to do anything but make promises he didn't keep in bringing the troops home.

She continued reading William's letter. He wrote of the entertainment he and Daniel had gone to telling her over 10,000 men had been at the show to see Sammy Davis Jr.

She read her husband's words trying to imagine they were having a conversation about their day.

I was surprised to hear that Sammy Davis, Jr. was going to be part of the show as he had initially declined due to his anti-war sentiments. The men are hearing a lot of rumors that folks back home feel the same way as Sammy Davis, Jr. It's really affecting the morale of the men. Please keep us in your prayers my precious wife.

His letter seemed a little more cheerful as he told her how he had met John Wayne who was a supporter of the war who visited many of the air bases and took the time to stop and talk to the troops posing with them for photos, signing autographs, and trying to lift the morale of the troops.

We face another enemy here which is the heat. The thermometer always seems to register over 100 degrees. The heat and humidity sap our energy. And on top of that we're now in monsoon season which leaves our navigational equipment nonexistent. We now have to rely on visual only due to the weather. We've lost several aircraft due to weather and mechanical problems. More than once it has put us in a dangerous situation, as if things weren't dangerous enough over here.

I'm just anxious to finish my tour and come home to my loving wife. I miss you more than you can possibly know.

I keep your photo by my bedside and another in my cockpit so you're with me always, but how I long to hold you in my arms again.

I love you so much. Know you are in my heart and thoughts always. I keep your ring in my pocket during every mission. It's a great comfort to me.

I'm sorry, my love. I'll do my best to write a more light-hearted letter next time. I guess between the weather, missing you, and no sight of the end of this damn war it's worn me down a bit.

I hope and pray you're doing well.

Your loving husband who loves you to the moon and back,

"Moonstruck."

She kissed his letter and said, "I love you to the moon and back too my dear husband. And so does your daughter who you don't even know about yet. Don't you sweetheart?" she said rubbing her belly.

It made her sad to think that her husband sounded depressed. It wasn't like him. Who's to blame him gone off halfway around the world fighting a war that...Don't even go there, she told herself.

She set his letter aside knowing she would read it several more times before the evening was over.

She picked up the letter from NASA and said, "Well, I hope this one has some good news. I worked awful hard to get there."

A big smile crossed her face as she read the glowing letter of how much they looked forward to working with her.

They wrote that they would like her to come in about a month to get acclimated and to go through training. Her actual work with the astronauts wouldn't begin for another six to nine months but there was a lot of preparation for her that was necessary before she began working with the astronauts.

The letter said when it came time for her to give birth that they would give her twelve weeks off after the birth before she would need to return to work or longer if needed.

63

Moonstruck and Cheese walked out to the tarmac discussing the mission. It was a dangerous mission they were being sent out on no doubt about it. Cash, Moonstruck's GIB walked up and joined them.

The leader of the squadron led their flight of F-4 Phantoms across the countryside of Vietnam.

Moonstruck at one point happened to glance down at some workers in a rice paddy and saw them run for cover. He could hear Cash saying something in his headset about the same time that he heard over his headset, "Multiple bandits in your area."

They were given the coordinates and told there were four MiGs heading their way.

Barely having received word two of the MiGs attacked two Phantoms separating them from the formation. The Phantoms had speed to their advantage.

Moonstruck saw that one of the Phantoms being stalked by the MiG was the one Cheese, his best friend, was flying. He saw Cheese instinctively pull hard and did a barrel roll and before the MiG had a chance to catch on to what Cheese was doing he made a half loop bringing him behind the MiG with the enemy fighter losing his advantage.

With an evasive maneuver of its own the MiG had turned his plane. Cheese pulled a quick manuever and was heading directly towards the hostile to meet the MiG head on.

It was like watching a game of cat and mouse but Moonstruck was far too busy himself to keep an eye on Cheese for long. He seemed to have things under control on his end.

The MiG lost the game of chicken seeing Cheese headed straight for him and fell away. As the MiG made his evasive maneuver Cheese was able to lock on and sent a missile with his name on it. It was a direct hit and there was one less hostile in the air to worry about.

Moonstruck had his own ass to be concerned about. Two more hostiles seemed to appear out of nowhere hidden from sight by low flying J-6s. Moonstruck realized he was within their sights and had become a target.

He launched his first Sparrow missile at the leading MiG. After a short lived classic dog fight he scored a victory. He had just become an "ace" having shot down his fifth enemy aircraft.

That's when he saw it.

One of the other MiGs flew up and took the place of the one he had just shot down. Not only was he facing a MiG but wasting no time the J-6s came to join him in battle. The tables had suddenly turned and not to his advantage.

The MiG had opened the space between them enough for him to fire a missile at him but he too had been hit.

He was losing speed and initially thought he could limp back to base as the other Phantoms in his formation had come up and taken care of the hostiles taking that threat from him.

One of the other MiGs had gotten off another shot at Moonstruck's plane. This time the MiG scored a direct hit. His left engine had taken the hit and he lost all his hydraulics.

As he fought to control his plane he saw Cheese pull out to protect his wing, to keep any other hostiles from attacking when there was no possibility of fighting back.

His engine exploded. Cheese pulled away to stay out of harm's way of flying debris.

Moonstruck's training and education from the pilot training class rushed through his mind enabling him to keep his aircraft under control. Hopefully he would be able to keep it that way until he was away from enemy territory. He looked below and knew the hostile jungle below wasn't a place he would want to have to traverse.

He didn't dare announce his position over the air waves as he knew the Vietnamese constantly monitored their frequency. He would fly as far as he dared before ejecting, but he knew his plane would never make it back to base.

He had faith that his friend Cheese would give his coordinates for a quick recovery. He headed for the gulf but his plane was falling out of the sky too fast. He knew he was going down and fast.

Cheese swung his plane within sight and frantically motioned for his friend to eject, saluted him, and then pulled away.

Cash, his GIB or guy in back, had a limited view and Moonstruck wasn't sure he was aware of how bad of shape they were in. He contacted him and told him they were going to have to eject but he was going to try to get them out of hostile territory first. He let him know their time was limited and when he called out to eject to do so immediately.

The hydraulics gone and bleeding fuel and not knowing what other damage had been done the plane suddenly took a nosedive and began spinning fast and furious towards the ground. He lost his equilibruim and couldn't tell up from down.

"Eject! Eject!" he hollered through his headset to Cash.

He waited till the last possible moment to be assured the GIB had made it out. His equilibrium gone the spinning was making him nauseous and hard to find the lever to eject.

The ground was rapidly approaching when he took a quick last look at the photo of Nicole and whispered, "I'm sorry." He believed in that moment that he was about to meet his Maker.

He pulled the lever to eject knowing there was a chance his parachute wouldn't have a chance to open as fast as the plane was spiraling downward.

The booster rockets under his seat fired and blew him and his entire seat out of the cockpit with such force he immediately blacked out. Within seconds he was floating with his parachute automatically deployed over his spiraling aircraft.

His parachute barely had time to deploy before he hit the ground. Thrown by the booster rockets out of the range of where his plane would crash was a saving grace.

The aircraft crashed below in the jungle. The heat was intense and left scorched earth.

Cheese nearby was close enough to get a pretty good reading of where to send rescue. With tears and prayers flowing for his friend he prayed his friend would survive.

After landing back at the base Cheese wasn't even out of his cockpit before he started shouting orders for rescue to go pick up his buddy and Cash.

Moonstruck had passed out and was unaware he was deep in enemy territory who even as he lay unconscious was being sought on ground by hostiles who were closing in on him.

As four Huey helicopters prepared for take off to try and recover the downed airmen Cheese jumped aboard and said he was going along. No one argued.

They took off immediately. The faster they made a recovery the better the men's chances were on surviving.

They would be flying directly into enemy fire to rescue the downed men but the recovery crew was good at what they did. They left no men behind and wouldn't give up until the men were rescued.

Cheese directed the men towards where he had seen his friend go down. When they came near to the area where they suspected he had gone down they began taking on fire from North Vietnamese on the ground.

The gunners in the helicopters did what they had to do. The door gunner in the Huey in which Cheese was flying was relentless in his firing towards the enemy to keep them back from the men they were there to rescue.

One of the helicopters had a damaged fuel tank and even so didn't turn back. These men were determined to come home with two of their men recovered and out of the enemy's hands.

Ground fire kept them at bay until they had to retreat for a time. It was a little too close for comfort when a rocket shot through the skin of the helicopter but failed to explode.

The enemy fire was relentless and the helicopters were debating on whether to turn back. Then the strangest thing happened.

There was silence. Complete and utter silence where a moment before the air was filled with the sounds of machine guns and the Viet Congs opening fire with everything they had.

All the firing had come to a complete halt. Even the birds were quiet with not a sound coming from the jungle.

"What the hell? Is this a trap?" one of the crew asked over the headset.

"I'm going in," the lead helicopter announced.

"We're following you in," the other helicopter reported back.

It was then the lead helicopter noticed a large shadow that circled the area of the jungle where they believed the downed crewmen to be.

The pilot glanced up thinking he had a MiG or something over top of him. He about crashed when he saw a UFO above him that had somehow set up some type of protective barrier around the men they were attempting to recover.

Cheese too saw it as he was sitting on his haunches watching out the windshield looking for smoke or any sign of the men.

"Do you see that?" the pilot asked Cheese.

"Yeah, I see it but I don't believe it. Is that what I think it is?" he asked.

"I don't know what else it could possibly be. Are they going to shoot us?" the co-pilot asked craning his neck to get a good view of the UFO.

"They aren't acting in a hostile manner towards us," the pilot answered. "If I didn't know better I'd say they're protecting our men. Hell, I'm going in."

He made a large circle and searched for the men all while keeping a leery eye on the UFO to see what it's intentions were.

The UFO seemed to back off giving them free rein to get to the area where the downed airmen were while still somehow holding off the Vietnamese.

"Is this some kind of secret weapon of ours?" the co-pilot

asked in disbelief.

"I believe this is some kind of gift and I'm not asking any questions. I'm just thankful they appear to be on our side," the pilot said as he frantically searched for the men they were attempting to rescue.

When they flew over an area that was somewhat clear they saw smoke.

Cheese was elated. That meant that either Moonstruck or Cash at least was alive and signaling them where they were.

"There. Smoke. That's our men," Cheese pointed the way.

The pilot radioed the other Hueys in the air that he spotted smoke and he was going in for a recovery.

Two of the helicopters hovered above ground, one to fire at any hostiles and to cover the men as they were out in the open, and the other Huey was there as support to help rescue the men.

Cheese jumped out of the copter when he saw Moonstruck crawling across the ground dragging his crew member behind who obviously hadn't made it.

If the UFO was going to strike him dead, so be it. He was going after his buddy.

Cheese and one of the other crew from the helicopter scooped Moonstruck up in their arms. Moonstruck screamed in agony. The men ran with him to the first helicopter.

The men from the other helicopter retrieved the dead soldier. Seconds after the men were on board they were airborne.

As the Hueys took off and were out of harm's way the UFO streaked across the sky and disappeared.

Medics in the back began working on Moonstruck while Cheese hovered over his friend telling him he had to make it back to Nicole.

Hearing his wife's name Moonstruck responded to his friend.

"Call her. You tell her. Don't let her find out from strangers," Moonstruck said barely over a whisper.

"I'll tell her you need a little patch job and she's just the doctor to do it. Then you'll be as good as new."

Moonstruck passed out and remained unconscious for the remainder of the trip. It was just as well as this way he felt no additional pain as the medics worked to stabilize him.

As they landed at the base emergency crew were on hand to rush Moonstruck for medical care.

The pilot pulled the crew aside from both his helicopter and the one that had followed him in. He asked his crew and those from the other helicopter if they had seen anything. They had not.

The pilot pulled his co-pilot and Cheese aside, the only men to have seen the UFO.

"You men didn't see anything, right? Do not and I repeat *do not* say a word about what was out there. We'd spend the rest of our lives filling out paperwork and being interrogated. Do we all agree?"

The three men all agreed to keep it to themselves.

Moonstruck had been taken for medical care to stabilize him. His friend Cheese himself donated blood and stood by while a surgical team worked on him so he would be stable enough to transport for further medical attention in which they weren't able to do out in the field.

Moonstruck was medevaced out to a hospital in Germany who was taking in the injured that were in serious and life-threatening condition. He would remain there until he had recovered enough to return to the States. His stint in Nam was done.

The tears ran unchecked down Cheese's cheeks as he stood and saluted the plane that took off carrying his best friend. He wasn't sure if he'd ever see his friend again. He was in bad shape.

"Please God. Let him recover."

With a heavy heart he turned to go make the hardest call he'd ever have to make. He needed to let Nicole know her husband had been shot down and was on his way to a hospital in Germany.

64

"You've really popped out these last few weeks," Mariah said looking at Nicole's belly. "It doesn't look like you'll be working with us for long."

"I'm sorry about that. I didn't even realize I was pregnant when I accepted your job offer," Nicole said.

Mariah just brushed it off and told her she was glad to have her for any amount of time she could spare.

"I heard back from NASA and I accepted their offer. Thank you so much for putting in a good word for me," Nicole said. "I wanted to let you know right away."

"Your new boss called me just yesterday. He said he didn't even get my letter until after they'd already interviewed you. He said they had already determined they wanted to hire you and my letter just confirmed their thoughts, so really I didn't do much," Mariah said.

That evening when Nicole got home she decided to give Rhiannon a call and see how she was doing.

As soon as Rhiannon heard Nicole's voice she said, "Nicole, where have you been? Everyone has been trying to reach you."

Nicole's heart sank at these words. She knew this had to do with William.

"Sit down, Nicole. I'm afraid I have some bad news," Rhiannon said.

Nora stood nearby listening as she could tell from the look on Nicole's face that something had happened.

272

"What, Rhiannon? Who's trying to reach me? Is William all right?"

"No, he's been in a terrible crash. Daniel called me to get your number. Everyone's been looking for you. They had to medevac William out. They flew him to a hospital in Germany but..."

"He's alive then?" Nicole asked fearing the worst.

"Yes, he's alive but he's in really bad shape. Let me give you the name and number of the hospital where they took him. You can call them and get the details."

Rhiannon gave her the contact information for the hospital where William had been taken.

Her hand was shaking so badly she couldn't write the information down and repeated it so Nora could write it down for her.

She realized after she hung up she hadn't told Rhiannon where she was or given her the information of where she was now living.

She looked at Nora and burst out crying. "I thought he was dead when she told me. How could I not feel he'd been hurt? I used to feel everything he felt."

Nora held her in her arms and let her cry. "Maybe it's because he's so far away. Don't think the worst. Why don't you give the hospital a call and see what you can find out."

"Thank you for being here. Your coming to the hospital that day was a Godsend," Nicole said hugging her best friend.

As Nicole was waiting to be put through to the floor where William was she asked Nora, "Do you mind packing me a bag? I'm flying over there."

"Do you think you should....being so far along in your pregnancy?"

"I have to. I have to be there for him."

A nurse came on who spoke broken English and after Nicole verified who she was the nurse gave her as much information as she had. The news was better than she expected but he was in bad shape facing a very long recovery time. The good news is he wouldn't be returning to Vietnam. The war was over for William.

"Can you get a message to him?" she asked the nurse.

"I'd be glad to. He's done nothing but call for you even when he was unconscious, so I know he'll be happy to receive word from you."

"Tell him I'm on my way. I'm going to get a flight out as soon as I can and I'll be there as soon as possible," Nicole said.

"I'm sorry but you can't do that. There are no visitors allowed here. The hospital is overwhelmed with patients. This is where they bring the patients that need the most care and until they're stabilized and moved to another hospital they can't receive any visitors. I'm really sorry," the nurse said.

"But I'm his wife," Nicole insisted.

"I'm sorry. The policy at this time is no visitors. We're just too busy and too full of patients right now. We barely have space for our patients let alone visitors. Once he's moved though you'll be notified and you can see him then."

"When will that be?" Nicole asked.

"I really can't say at this point. They'll let you know. I'm sorry, but I really need to go tend to my patients. I'll give him the message you called."

"Thank you," Nicole said to dead air.

The nurse had already hung up.

Nora was in the bedroom rapidly packing her a bag but had overheard. "You aren't going then? They won't let you in to see him?"

"Yes, I'm going. I'd like to see them try to stop me from seeing my husband," Nicole said.

"But didn't she say..."

"Do you think they could possibly stop me? I'll just have to figure something out," Nicole said.

While Nora called the airlines and made arrangements for a direct flight to Germany Nicole's wheels were spinning. She jumped up and added a few more items to her suitcase.

"Your flight leaves in an hour and a half. That doesn't leave much time," Nora said.

"The sooner the better," Nicole said.

On the drive to the airport Nicole left instructions for her to call Mariah to let her know she wouldn't be able to work for a few days and let her know what happened. She then told Nora of her plan on how she was going to get in to see William.

"And if that doesn't work I'm going to call on the aliens to come and make it happen."

"You can do that? Just call them out of the blue?" Nora asked in amazement.

"I haven't ever in the past but they always seem to appear at times when I think about doing just that. Somehow they seem to know."

"That's creepy," Nora said.

"Yes it is but this time it may work to my advantage," Nicole agreed.

At the gate to her flight Nora begged Nicole to take it easy and keep the baby in mind.

Nicole said she wouldn't jeopardise the baby's health but above all else she had to be there for William.

65

Nicole sat outside the Landstuhl Regional Medical Center which she had discovered was the largest American hospital outside the United States located in the German state of Rheinland-Pfalz.

She sat outside the hospital long enough to get the answers she needed. She watched as doctors and nurses came and went. Seeing how they dressed was what she needed to know in order to gain entrance and blend in so she could see her husband.

Nicole had learned that in order not to be questioned you had to look the part and be assertive. If you acted like you knew what you were doing you were less likely to raise suspicion.

One thing she knew was to her advantage was the hospital staff were overworked and overwhelmed.

It's a good thing I learned fluent German from Mom and Dad when I was growing up too. That is certainly going to come in handy now she thought. Though she hadn't spoken the language in quite sometime with her photographic memory it came back to her as clearly as English.

She learned from Information where her husband was. He was on the 4th floor, room 418. Her heart started beating fast as she rode up the elevator excited to be seeing her husband and at the same time uneasy about the condition she'd find him in.

If need be I'll nurse him back to health if it takes the rest of my life she thought. Isn't this why I became a doctor after all?

She walked by the nurse's station not wanting at this time to engage in conversation with any of the staff. She just wanted to see her husband right now.

She walked by room 408 and felt such a strong feeling that he was in that room that she found she couldn't take another step.

But she'd been told he was in room 418.

No, there was no question about it. She hadn't lost her touch after all. Her husband was in room 408 right behind this door.

She listened a moment to see if she heard any activity in the room. She didn't want to walk in when he was being examined and have William give her away as being his wife. She had to portray herself as a visiting doctor from another hospital if she was going to gain entrance to see him.

There was no sound other than someone crying out in terrible pain. It came from her husband she knew and it about broke her heart.

She gently pushed open the door and softly closed it behind her.

"Nurse?" He called out. "Is there any word from my wife?"

"Darling it's me," she said going to his bedside.

She gasped as she saw him. His eyes were covered in bandages as was his right arm and hand and he had a cast on one leg and foot.

"Nicole? You're here? I'm not dreaming?" he said holding out his good arm towards his wife's voice.

"I'm here. I came as soon as I heard. I'm so sorry it took me this long," she said.

She took his hand gently in hers not knowing the extent of his damages yet and not wanting to cause him any more pain.

"Please...come closer. Let me feel you. They have my eyes bandaged and I can't see you," he cried.

She stepped forward and pulled her mask off along with the scrub cap covering her hair and placed his hand on her face. He caressed her cheek and ran his hand down her hair.

They kissed, their tears intermingling. Tears of joy.

"Nicole...love of my life. I thought I'd never see you again," he cried. "I still can't see you but it's you...it's really you."

He tried to reach out to hug her but cried out in pain.

"Darling you're going to be coming home to me soon. Once

277

you recover enough they told me you'd be sent back to the states to recover. We'll be together every day then," she said.

A nurse peeked her head in and apologized for interrupting thinking a doctor was in to examine the patient.

Nicole quickly explained to her husband that no visitors were allowed and to not let on that she was his wife but was there as a visiting doctor from another hospital volunteering to help.

She wasn't sure if what she said got through to him as she could tell he was heavily medicated. He kept falling asleep but she could see he was fighting to stay awake to visit with his wife regardless of how much pain he was in.

She adjusted the pain meds in his IV so they weren't strong enough to knock him out but would still give him some relief.

Once when he fell asleep for a few minutes she took a look at his chart at the end of the bed. She felt like someone had punched her when she saw the extent of the damages he'd suffered and knew his recovery wouldn't be quick or easy.

He'd have many months if not a year or more of physical therapy plus he had suffered burns on his right arm and hand that were pretty severe.

When he came to again he called out for her.

"I thought I was dreaming," he said.

She leaned over the bed and gently took his good arm and said, "I have a surprise for you."

"Your being here is all the surprise I need," he said.

She placed his hand on her belly and with perfect timing he got a swift kick from the baby.

"Nicole? Is that....are you expecting?"

"Yes sweetheart. We're having a baby. I wrote and told you but I think my letter has been late in arriving," she said.

"We did it? We made a baby?" he asked.

"That big belly isn't from eating too much," she laughed. "I was surprised myself. I didn't figure it out until I was about five months along. And me being a doctor."

He gently rubbed her belly. I want to see you. I want to see..."
he began reaching to pull off his bandages.

"No sweetheart," she said placing her hand gently on his and
moving them from his eyes. "You'll need to keep those on just a
little longer."

"I want to see my beautiful wife and see my baby growing in
her belly," he begged. "Please...all I've dreamed of for months is
seeing you again."

She thought hard. She wasn't sure this was in her power to do
but she said, "With your good hand place it on my face and think
hard of what it looked like when you looked into my eyes.
Concentrate now."

She gazed at him intently.

"My God, you're so beautiful. I don't know how, but I can see
you. Stand back a little. Let me see your pregnant belly."

She placed his hand on her belly and thought intently of how
she looked when she gazed at her pregnant belly in the mirror
projecting those thoughts into his head. It took great effort on her
part but it appeared to be working.

"I see it. My goodness you're huge," he said. "Huge but
beautiful. I'm going to be a father?"

"Yes, William. You're going to be a father. We're having a
baby," she said laughing with joy. She was thankful to have this
opportunity to share this with him and tell him in person.

"Let me feel it again," he said.

"Her. She's not an it," Nicole said. "We're having a little girl."

It was like something woke up in him, "Aah yes, the next
daughter of destiny."

"We'll soon have a baby to love and take care of. That's why
you have to work real hard on getting better," she said.

"When is the baby due?" he asked enjoying feeling the baby
moving and kicking. "She sure is active."

"She's excited to meet her daddy," Nicole said. "She's due in
about three months, perhaps a little sooner."

He was quiet counting back trying to figure out when she got pregnant. "My guess is then it was the night the aliens paid us a visit. They said something about opening the floodgates or something..."

Nicole laughed. "I don't think they said floodgates. I think they said something about opening a gate and allowing conception to happen. Yes, I believe that's the night our daughter was conceived."

"We did work at it pretty hard that night, didn't we?"

"If you can call that work. Yes we did," she said smiling.

This visit was exactly what he needed. He had been despondent and depressed when he had been admitted up till the time his wife arrived.

They heard voices out in the hall and Nicole whispered in his ear, "Remember, don't give it away that I'm your wife. They'll make me leave if they find out."

A nurse and doctor came in and surprised to see her she introduced herself with authority. "I'm Dr. Neuhaus, a visiting physician from Charité. I was specifically given this patient as a case study."

Nicole had researched well. She looked up the largest hospital in Berlin thinking if they actually took the time to try to look into her credentials it would take them some time to get an answer and she'd be long gone by then. She also used her German maiden name Neuhaus, the form before her father Americanized it.

The doctor looked at her and said, "We can certainly use any extra hands and appreciate you volunteering to give us a hand. Have you looked over his chart?"

She spouted back enough medical jargon that he was convinced she was indeed a doctor with extensive medical knowledge and would be an asset in the patient's care.

"I'll leave him in your care then. He needs to have his bandages changed. Would you like the nurse to assist you?"

"No, I'm sure they've plenty to keep them busy. I'll take care of it," she answered.

The doctor looked at Nicole's belly and said, "It doesn't look like we'll have you around for long by the looks of things. We can certainly use the help around here."

The doctor and nurse left and both William and Nicole gave a sigh of relief.

The nurse returned a few minutes later with fresh bandages and salve for Nicole to take care of her patient.

Nicole was glad his eyes were bandaged when she uncovered his bandages and saw how badly he was burned. She called the nurse back and asked her to give him a shot for pain before she worked on the burns as she knew it would be terribly painful.

He fought crying out as she tended to the burns but she could tell that even with the pain meds he was still in excruciating pain.

After awhile Nicole said, "I better leave for now. They'll grow suspicious if I stay here in your room for hours on end and don't see any other patients."

"You'll come back tomorrow?" William begged.

"I'll be here bright and early," she assured him.

She bent to kiss him good-bye and he kissed her in return and said.

"Thank you Nicole for coming. Seeing you and hearing the news about our baby girl changes everything. I'm going to fight hard to get well enough to come home to the two of you as soon as possible."

Before she walked out the door she heard him quietly say, "I'm going to be a father."

Before she left she talked to the head nurse and was surprised to learn they didn't expect him to leave the hospital for several months. She said they estimated it would be at least four to five months and possibly even longer before he would be sent to a hospital in the states to complete his recovery.

As Nicole walked down the hall she said to herself, "We'll just see about that. He needs his wife and his daughter."

66

Nicole was visiting William on her third and final day in Germany. She sat by his bedside as he thrashed in his sleep crying out in pain.

How could she leave him like this in so much pain, she asked herself. Isn't this why she had become a doctor? She had foreseen that he would have need of her medical help one day but she had been unclear as to what that would be.

She had known back while still in her teens that one day he would need her medical attention. That's why she had studied for years to be a doctor. But she felt what she was doing any caring nurse or doctor could do in her stead.

She knew she was missing something. But what was it?

While he slept she thought and thought. What am I missing? I feel as though something is tickling the back of my mind, but I can't grasp what it is.

When he awoke he called out, "Nicole, help me. I'm in so much pain. Please make it go away. I know you have the ability to help me."

It came to her.

His words may have had a complete different meaning but she realized she had the power to heal him. She thought back hard to the day when the alien had given her the gift of healing. He had told her to use it wisely.

There was no better time to use this gift than to heal the one she loved. But how? She had been given no instructions on how to heal someone, just that she could.

She thought back to that day and recalled the alien had taken her hands in his and she had felt a warmth flow through her. It had been almost painful but she could feel it working from within.

She had tried to remove her hands once and he said no, it wasn't complete.

Once that warmth had reached every corner of her body from head to toe he had removed his hands and she had been healed.

Is that all she had to do? Would it work? Even if it helped a little it was better than him remaining in so much pain. She had to find out. She would do anything to take this pain from her husband.

She spoke gently to her husband explaining to him what she was going to do. She was gently unwrapping his bandaged hand as she did so.

"You may feel a tremendous amount of pain for a few minutes, but please trust me. Whatever you do...don't let go of my hands until I say it's done. I'll be as gentle as I can."

He nodded his head that he understood.

Before beginning she gave him something for the pain hoping it would make it easier for him to get through this.

As she gently took his burned hand in her own she saw him bite his lip stopping himself from crying out.

"Trust me, darling."

"I do," he said through gritted teeth.

After a few moments she asked, "Do you feel anything?"

"I feel a burning running through my veins. It's as though an intense heat is running through my body lighting every part of me on fire," he answered.

His forehead was breaking out in a sweat which she knew was brought on by the pain.

"It's working then. Don't let go. I need to concentrate," she said.

She felt as though energy was escaping her and flowing from her into him. She was feeling the same thing he was only in reverse. To her it felt as though ice water was running through her veins.

She knew when it reached her toes and then the cold

diminished and left her that the healing was complete. She could only hope and pray that it had worked. To what extent she had no idea.

She gently lowered his hands back on the bed. "How do you feel?"

He was quiet for a moment and then smiled, "The pain is gone. Is this temporary?"

"I hope not. I've never used the gift of healing before so I guess we'll just have to wait and see."

He reached up and pulled his bandage off his eyes. At first his eyes were blurry and the light hurt his eyes but in a few moments his eyes cleared up and he was feasting his eyes on his wife and unborn child.

After a few moments she convinced him she had to put his bandages back on as his miraculous healing would be hard to explain.

She told him to let the doctors discover after she left that he was healed. She said also not to rush it as it may be temporary and he may still have some recovery ahead of him.

They knew their time together here was coming to an end.

"I hope I'll be home in time for our baby's birth," he said.

"Me too but if not we'll be there waiting for you when you do come home," she said.

It was hard for her to have to leave him but she knew she had to leave before the staff at the hospital caught on to them. Besides, as big as she was getting she wouldn't be allowed to fly much longer. She had to get home and prepare for the birth.

On the flight home she was much more at peace than she had been when she flew to Germany. It occurred to her that she hadn't thought to ask him what he'd like to name their baby.

She still had a few months to go. She'd write and ask him.

67

"Are you sure you have the date right?" the doctor asked her as she measured her belly.

"Absolutely," Nicole answered. "There's only the possibility of two dates. I'm positive of that."

"Just checking," the doctor said.

"Is something wrong?" Nicole asked. Doctor or not, she was a typical nervous first time expectant mother.

"No, you're just large for being a little over six months along. I just thought maybe your dates were off."

"I am pretty big. I love my big belly though," Nicole said. "I look at my belly and I can't imagine that it could possibly get any bigger."

The doctor laughed and said, "Just wait until the last month if you think you're big now."

Nicole laughed as she could visibly see a foot kicking on her left side. Immediately after there was a big lump that pushed up just below her ribs.

The doctor was watching herself and said, "Either that baby is stretching or he's really tall."

"She. It's a girl," Nicole said forgetting to keep that to herself.

"You and your husband are hoping for a girl?" the doctor asked.

"We just want a healthy baby," Nicole answered. "It's just that girls run in my family. We always seem to have girls."

"Perhaps boys run in your husband's family," the doctor said.

The baby was very active and it looked like she had just turned from one side to the other.

"It will be one or the other. If it's a girl it appears she's doing pirouettes in there," the doctor said.

Nicole sat up.

"Everything looks fine. You do need to slow down a bit these last few months. Sit down and put your feet up more often."

She patted Nicole's arm and said, "I'll see you next month."

Once Nicole had returned home from Germany she longed for her husband to come home and be there for the birth of their baby.

She insisted to Nora that they must start getting things ready for the baby. She didn't want to wait until the last minute. She wanted to be able to relax at the end knowing everything was prepared.

"You better start coming up with a list of names or that poor baby will be leaving the hospital called Little Miss No-Name Halloway," Nora said while setting up the bassinette.

"I've been working on a list. I wish I would have thought to ask William about what he wanted to name the baby when I was there. I'll write him right away and tell him to send me a list of girl names he likes," Nicole said.

"In the meantime work on a list of your own," Nora insisted.

By the time she left for work that day she had a list of five girl names she liked.

Now that William knew about the baby she was enjoying this pregnancy even more. She only wished he were here to share these moments with her.

She wondered if he had any word on when he would be shipped to a hospital in the states. She'd give the hospital a call in the next day or two and see if there were any updates.

68

That evening she was tossing and turning trying to get comfortable when she felt the presence of the aliens.

She looked up and saw two of them standing there watching her.

"I'm tired. I don't want to go with you," she moaned putting her pillow over her head.

"No need. We are here to see you and the child," the first alien communicated to her.

"You used your healing power," the other alien spoke telepathically to her.

"Yes," Nicole said. "If you are the one who gave me that gift I thank you for it."

"He is doing well. It was a close call in the jungle. He was close to being taken as prisoner of war," the second alien said to her. "He would not have survived that ordeal. We couldn't let that happen."

Nicole sat up. "How do you know that?"

"You don't need to speak out loud. We can read your thoughts and you may wake your friend," the first alien said.

In answer to her question the other alien let her know they were there watching over him until he could be rescued. They said it was impossible to intervene earlier but they assured his safety by giving the rescuers a safe perimeter in order to reach and rescue him.

"Thank you for that. For that I am indebted to you," she said meaning every word of it.

"We are here to check on the child," the alien said.

"What do you mean?" Nicole asked.

"We only wish to see that all is well," the alien assured her.

"May I?" He asked as he stepped forward.

"What are you going to do?" she asked fearful for the safety of her child. She remembered what her mother had told her that they had done to her while she was yet in her mother's womb and feared they were here to do something similar to her own baby.

"I am only going to place my hand on your belly. It won't hurt. I just need to feel the life of the child."

Nicole didn't like the idea of being touched but after them letting her know they had protected William and knowing they had given her the ability to heal him she didn't feel as though she had the right to decline their request.

She lay back and reached for the alien's hand. She placed it on her belly and immediately was rewarded with a hard kick.

The alien drew his hand back startled. Then he looked to the other alien and said, "I felt the life flow."

As the alien moved his hand away Nicole felt a movement within her like she hadn't felt before. It felt as though the baby within her had made a complete flip. She thought perhaps the baby had turned head down as the doctor had told her would soon be happening.

The other alien stepped forward wanting to feel the baby. She took his hand and placed it on her belly. This time the baby didn't kick and he ran his hand around feeling for the child.

"This life is not strong," the second alien said to the other.

"What? I felt it and got a strong feel of life flowing from the child," the other alien responded.

"No, you are wrong. That is not what I felt at all," the second alien insisted.

"What do you mean her life is not strong?" Nicole asked. "I just went to the doctor and she said everything was fine."

The aliens put a barrier to their thoughts so Nicole couldn't pick up on their communicating with one another.

"Please, once again," the first alien requested of Nicole.

She nodded for him to go ahead.

This time he placed both hands on her belly and stared intently. The alien felt movement but it wasn't strong.

The aliens appeared to be communicating back and forth with each other but this time she couldn't break through and "hear" their thoughts.

"This is a man-child. How can that be?"

"How did this happen?"

"What of our next generation? Our daughter of destiny?"

"A man-child. Oh, this is not good."

"We have waited so long....and now this....and the life force of this child is weak. He may not survive."

69

"A man child? Do you mean it's a boy?" Nicole practically shouted. "Are you sure?"

The alien paced back and forth and the other one stared at the other.

"A man-child. What do we do?"

The one alien walked to her and communicated, "Something has gone terribly wrong. A man-child flowed through the open gateway taking the place of the next daughter of destiny."

"A boy?" Nicole said rubbing her belly. "All this time we thought it was a girl. It's a little boy."

"But we saw it when it happened," the one alien argued with the other. "We were so confident the life force was that of a girl." The alien was confused and disheartened by this unexpected revelation. "How could we have been so wrong?"

"Obviously this man-child defeated the other. Perhaps it is just as well. If she could be replaced so easily she wasn't strong or capable of being the next daughter of destiny. Again we will have to wait for her arrival."

"Wait. But for how long? We've waited so long all ready. We all anxiously await for the hope of the next generation. We feel we are getting closer to the long awaited one."

"Evidently the time was not right. She will arrive when she is meant to. Even we did not foresee this. She will be worth waiting for."

The alien looked at her and asked. "You are soon to give life to this child. Do you wish to keep this child? It is not the girl child we all have waited for. We can take this problem from you if you decide you don't want it."

"What? Are you crazy? Of course I want this child! He isn't a problem. He's a baby. It's my son...mine and William's. We want this child more than anything."

"Then you must start anew as soon as he breathes life. It is time for the daughter of destiny to make her presence known...it is past time for her arrival."

"How could this have happened?" The other alien was still fretting over this unexpected news.

She thought of how the aliens had protected William while he was in Vietnam and how they had given her the gift of healing which she had used on him. She felt she had taken and it was time to give back. This time she would agree to their request.

"William and I want more children. As soon as William is healed and returns I promise you we'll have another child. As soon as it's possible, we'll have another. I won't ask you to wait this time. I promised you years ago and I will hold to my promise, but I want this child very much. Your daughter of destiny will be forthcoming soon, I promise."

"There is nothing to be done. It is too late to change things now," the alien said.

He looked intently at Nicole.

"I will hold you to your promise. There will be no more delays," he said firmly.

"I give you my word," Nicole said.

And just like they had arrived, they were now gone.

70

Nicole couldn't get William off her mind all day. It had been heart wrenching seeing him in so much pain. She hoped the healing had taken affect and would be lasting. She was at a loss as to how it worked since she'd never used it before.

She hoped he wasn't suffering. The thought crossed her mind that if the healing helped to what extent it would help him she had no idea, but if it helped even a little she hoped he would be released from the hospital in Germany soon and sent back stateside to continue his recovery.

"I'm glad to see you're back," Mariah said catching up to her in the hospital's cafeteria.

"I wish I could say I was glad to be back but I really feel that my place is by my husband's side," Nicole said.

"With your pregnancy so far advanced it's good you came back when you did," Mariah said.

"I still have over two and a half months before I'm due," Nicole said.

"I keep forgetting that. You look like you're ready to give birth any day."

"Should I be offended by that remark?" Nicole said pushing her plate of food aside.

Mariah pushed her plate back towards her. "You're eating for two. Eat up. No, you shouldn't be offended. It just looks like you're going to have a large baby which is no surprise considering how tall you are."

Nicole stabbed another forkful of food and said, "Tall is one thing, huge is another. I know everyone looks at me like I'm some kind of balloon from Macy's Thanksgiving Day parade. I've always been thin. I'm not used to carrying around all this weight."

"It's only for a few more months....weeks," she quickly changed her words when Nicole gave her a look.

Nicole sat back and propped her feet up on the chair beside her. "I'm exhausted. I don't sleep good. I can't get comfortable. My ankles are swollen and my back is killing me. Then when I complain I feel so ashamed as William and I wanted this baby so much. To think of what he's going through I know I have no right to complain."

Mariah said, "Why don't you just finish the week out and take a few days off."

"I want to work as much as I can to help you since I'm only going to be here a short while. NASA is giving me a couple months off after the baby is born so I'll have plenty of time to rest then."

"Hah," Mariah laughed. "That just proves you're a first time mother."

Mariah finished eating and stood up and said, "Just sit here and relax a bit. I'll finish the rounds on the 4th floor. After that we just have four more patients and then we can call it a day. You can go home and take a bubble bath."

Nicole put her feet down and said, "I don't want you to have to carry my load. I'll go with you."

Mariah saw Nicole catch herself and wince a bit as she stood up. "Nora went with me the other night for my first Lamaze class. I think I'm having those Braxton Hicks contractions they told us about. If this is preparing me for labor I cringe to think what that's going to be like."

They walked down the hall talking and like Nora Mariah told her she needed to start considering names. She said the time would be here before she knew it.

Nicole thought to herself that she'd have to start all over on that list of names now that she had learned it was a boy she was carrying.

They finished the 4th floor and were going up to check on their last few patients when Nicole leaned back against the elevator bent over.

"Everything O.K.?" Mariah asked.

"Maybe the baby turned or something and is pressing on my back. My lower back has really been bothering me all day."

When Mariah came out of the last patient's room she saw Nicole up ahead filling out her patient's chart. Mariah decided to wait on her.

When Nicole walked up she was moving pretty slowly.

"I think I'm going to call the doctor and have her check me out. These Braxton Hicks are getting stronger and they seem to be coming one right after the other."

"Are you sure you're not in labor?" Mariah asked in a concerned voice.

Nicole bent over with another contraction and Mariah could see her stomach tighten up hard as a rock. She reached over and placed her hand on Nicole's stomach throughout the contraction.

When the contraction passed Nicole said, "Maybe I'm paying for that trip to Germany and all the hours I've been on my feet lately. I couldn't be in labor. I'm not due for ten more weeks."

Another contraction came on and Nicole held tightly onto Mariah's arm until it passed.

"We're going to Labor and Delivery. We need to at least have you checked out. Braxton Hicks aren't painful like that and they shouldn't be coming two minutes apart," Mariah said.

She walked Nicole to a seat nearby and went in search of a wheelchair. When she came back she helped Nicole up and as she stood up her water broke.

Nicole looked at her co-worker and said, "I think my water just broke. What am I going to do?"

"Have a baby I would imagine," Mariah answered.

"But it's too early," Nicole said concerned for her baby.

"Yeah, well tell that to your baby," Mariah said.

Mariah rushed her to an employee's elevator and practically

ran with the wheelchair to Labor and Delivery.

Mariah explained to the nurse that Nicole wasn't due for another two and a half months but had been having contractions all day without realizing it. She explained that she was having back labor and her water broke.

The nurse watched Nicole as another strong contraction came on. When another followed less than two minutes later she said, "I need to get you to a room."

The nurse quickly whisked her down the hall after seeing how strong her contractions were.

Nicole called out to Mariah to please call Nora and tell her to come.

The nurse helped Nicole change into a gown and helped her lay on the bed and examined her.

"Is this your first baby?" the nurse asked.

"The first and last if this is what labor feels like." She grabbed the bed rail as another strong contraction came on.

"Honey, this baby is ready to be delivered," the nurse said after examining her. "You're already dilated eight centimeters."

"But my baby's not ready. He won't survive this early," Nicole cried.

"We have a great team of specialists who'll be right there for the birth. They'll take good care of the baby. Now let me run have someone call your doctor and the medical team and get them here. This baby's not waiting."

Nicole began crying afraid her baby wouldn't survive being born so early.

Nora ran into the room about twenty minutes later followed by the nurse.

A team of doctors arrived who introduced themselves as from Pediatrics ICU. They did their best to reassure her that they were there to take good care of her baby. They said they were going to scrub up and would see her in the delivery room.

Nicole was wheeled into delivery with Nora in scrubs beside

her doing her best to reassure her.

The anaesthesiologist was setting things up and Nicole quickly explained she wanted to be awake for the birth.

When the next contraction came on Nicole began pushing before anyone told her to.

"Doctor," one of the nurses called out. "I think she's ready..."

Nicole's doctor quickly came over and took a seat. She took a look and said, "Oh yeah, she's ready. Go ahead and push with the next contraction."

Nora reached over and took one of Nicole's hands in her own and calmly stroked her cheek.

"You can do this love. You'll be a great mother. The baby's ready to meet you," Nora said.

Nicole pushed and pushed and nothing seemed to happen. In between contractions she cried, "William should be here."

The doctor and nurse were quietly conferring and the doctor suddenly very serious said, "With this next contraction I need you to push with everything you've got. Your baby is having a problem. Her heart rate is dropping dangerously low. We need to get her out quickly."

The contraction came and Nicole with all her strength pushed until a little head emerged. The nurse quickly suctioned the baby's nose and mouth and in an instant the rest of the baby was pushed out into the nurse's arms. The baby appeared lifeless.

Nora shouted, "It's a boy!"

Nicole realized she hadn't told Nora yet the aliens had told her she was having a boy.

"Nicole, it's a boy," Nora said looking at her as though she were saying 'How did this happen?'

That was pretty much what the aliens had said. How did this happen?

There was a lot of activity around the baby. The nurses had whisked him off to a table nearby without even taking the time to stop and show him to his mother. There were two doctors who immediately began working on the baby.

Nora had noticed there was no sound of a newborn's lusty wail. Without alerting Nicole there could be a problem she watched the nurses and two pediatrician standing over him working frantically.

"Is he all right?" Nicole asked.

The doctor motioned to the anaesthesiologist and he said to Nicole, "They're taking good care of your baby. You'll get to see him soon. I'm going to give you a little something now so you can rest while the doctor finishes up with you."

"Can I see my baby..." Nicole was saying before she was starting to feel the effects of the medication.

Nora walked over to see how the baby was doing. They had whisked him off so quickly she hardly had a chance to see him.

Nora started to cry when she saw him.

He was so tiny. He looked as though he were fighting for each breath while the doctors worked frantically on him. He was pale and limp and she wondered if he was even alive.

She looked back at her friend and wondered how she was going to take the news.

Nora wasn't sure the baby would survive. He seemed so frail. He hadn't been ready to come into this world. Would he be strong enough to make it?

Nora noticed the doctor and nurses by Nicole were suddenly very animated.

"Bring her back," the doctor told the anaesthesiologist.

The anaesthesiologist adjusted some dials and kept a careful eye on Nicole and how she was responding.

Nicole seemed to come out of it but was a bit lethargic.

"You have another baby hiding in there. It's twins. We need you to push and help us get this baby out," the doctor said.

"Twins?" Nicole said not sure she'd heard correctly.

No one had said anything about twins. Not her doctor....not even the aliens. How had they all missed it?

Nora dashed to Nicole's side and took her hand in hers. "Come on Nicole. Bring this baby into the world. You can do this."

"Push..." the doctor said. After seeing the shape the other baby was in the doctor was wanting to get this baby the care it may need as soon as possible.

One of the nurses walked over with a heated blanket ready to grab the baby once it was born.

Nicole gave what she had left finding strength she didn't know she had in her.

A loud wail filled the delivery room. A sound that had been sorely missing with the arrival of the first child.

"It's a girl," the doctor said.

This time the nurse brought the baby around for Nicole to see.

"She's good sized for a premie," the nurse said smiling at Nicole. "They're as different as night and day. Your son has dark hair and your daughter's hair is as light as her mothers."

Nora smiled. It was obvious this baby was healthy. She was a little small for a newborn she thought checking her over but considering how early she was and that she was a twin she looked to be in good shape.

"She looks just like her mother," the anaesthesiologist said. "Blonde and a beauty."

The nurse said they needed to take her and tend to her a bit and she'd bring her back soon. No mention was made of bringing her son to her.

Nicole was in shock. *Twins!* How had no one caught on that she was carrying twins. No wonder she was so big.

The ICU team whisked Baby Boy Halloway to ICU where he would receive excellent care. Even so it was clear to the entire medical team he may not survive.

71

The doctor stood by as William was preparing to leave. He was all smiles.

"I don't know what happened," the doctor said. "All I can figure is they mixed up your chart with someone elses. Either that or I'm going to start believing in miracles. You sure don't see many of those around here."

There was always a change of doctors and staff so the ones who had initially treated his burns weren't here to tell how bad of shape he had been in when he arrived.

The nurse came in with his discharge papers.

"Were you able to reach my wife? She'll want to know I'm coming home," William said to the nurse.

"I'm sorry. I've tried calling four or five times and there's no answer," she said. "I'll keep trying if you'd like."

"That's all right. She's a doctor and works long hours. I'll call her myself when I get to the states and surprise her."

Once William was discharged and left the floor the nurse wadded up the paper with Nicole's phone number on it and threw it out.

The number had been in his chart from when Nicole had called to check on her husband. Unfortunately, the nurse was the only one who had Nicole's current contact information.

The phone number now laying in the trash was a number William was unfamiliar with. With her concern for him and revealing to him they were having a baby she had completely failed to mention she had moved to Gainesville and a few weeks after the baby was born would be moving again to Cape Canaveral to work at NASA.

72

William was flying across the Atlantic heading back to the states. He was as happy as he could ever remember being.

He laughed to himself and thought that everytime he was with Nicole or going to be with her he thought the very same thing. They only seemed to be truly happy when they were together.

He imagined the reunion he and Nicole would share and thought he would make it back in time to be there for the birth of their first child. Thanks to the healing powers of his wife, via the aliens, he was heading home in good health.

Little did he know that as he day dreamed of a reunion and looking forward to becoming a father that not only a daughter had been born but a son who was at this very moment fighting for his life.

Nicole looked at her beautiful daughter in her arms. She was quite a beauty and seemed to be strong and healthy though smaller than most newborns.

How could one twin be so strong while the other was barely alive she wondered.

She'd been in the hospital for over a week now, maybe even two. She had completely lost track of time. She just knew that every day that passed increased the odds of her son surviving.

The nurse poked her head in the door and said, "She's the most beautiful baby in the nursery. It seems everybody who comes by stops and looks at her."

Nicole smiled half-heartedly. "It's a shame her brother isn't as strong as she is. They should be together in the nursery."

The nurse took the baby from her arms and wrapped her in a

swaddling cloth and placed her in the bassinette nearby.

"It isn't unusual for one twin to be strong while the other seems to struggle. They were born very early. She's still small. It's fortunate she's as strong as she is."

Nicole asked, "How's my son doing?"

The nurse wouldn't look at her as she answered. "The doctor is in with him now. He had a bit of a rough morning."

"Can you take me to see him?" Nicole asked.

When the nurse hesitated she pleaded, "Please."

When the nurse pretended to be busy with her daughter Nicole spoke up and said, "If I have to I'll walk there myself. He needs his mother. He needs to know he's loved."

"Give me a minute. I'll let them know you're coming," the nurse said as she wheeled her baby daughter in her bassinette out of the room.

Nicole struggled to get up and put on a robe and slippers. She was exhausted just from this little bit of movement.

A nurse came in with a wheelchair and said, "Let's go see your son. The doctor is waiting there to speak with you."

Nicole nodded her head. The way she said the doctor was waiting she thought didn't sound good.

Before they wheeled her in they made her scrub up and put a gown and mask on.

The nurse brought her in and the pediatric specialist who she recognized just from working at the hospital took over and pushed her wheelchair up to the incubator.

She teared up when she saw all the wires attached to her tiny infant son. He was so tiny and frail.

"Have you been able to get in contact with your husband?" the doctor asked.

"My friend has been trying to call. She found out he's been released and sent to a hospital in the states. They said they weren't able to give her the information of where he was sent but said they would do their best to pass on the information to him."

"I hope your friend stressed how vital it is that we reach him," the doctor said. "We may have some decisions to make here."

"Decisions? What kind of decisions?" Nicole asked.

The doctor pulled up a chair and said, "You're a doctor yourself. I'm not going to lie to you. Your son is in grave condition. I'm not sure if he's strong enough to survive."

Nicole told herself to hold it together. She needed to get whatever information she could.

"What are his chances?" Nicole asked.

The doctor looked at her son for a long moment.

"He was born premature and that would have been a fight enough itself. Being a twin made it even more difficult. It appears his twin has all the strength that he's lacking."

"His chances?" Nicole asked again.

"Maybe a twenty percent chance on the high end," the doctor answered. "Realistically a ten to fifteen percent chance at best. Each day he survives increases his odds. I have to be honest. It's not looking good. We seem to be losing the fight."

"Can I hold him?" Nicole asked.

"Not at this time. I'm sorry. If we want to increase his odds we need to keep him as germ free as possible. I'm sure you understand," the doctor said.

"But the nurses come in and change him and care for him. I won't do anything to add to his risk," she begged.

He hesitated.

"Please. I just want to hold my son. He needs to feel that he's loved. Give him something to fight for," Nicole said.

He finally relented and allowed her to reach in and hold his little hand. As she touched him she spoke quietly to her son telling him how much he was loved and how he had to be a fighter like his father and pull through.

Then it hit her. If she could heal William, surely she could heal her own son.

73

William had been released from the VA hospital in Baltimore weeks ago. He had been desperately searching for his wife. She seemed to have just vanished without a trace.

The last address he had for her was in Atlanta, Georgia. He contacted the university she had graduated from, some of her professors, the hospital, yet no one seemed to have her current address.

He called Daniel's wife who was glad to hear from him but when asked about how to contact his wife she also didn't have any contact information. She told him the last time she'd talked to her that Nicole had called her. After receiving the news about William she never thought to mention where she was and Rhiannon hadn't thought to ask.

He called his mother who spent more time in Iowa with family these days than in Florida. She told him Elke and Klaus had moved to Orlando to be closer to where Klaus worked but kept the house in St. Augustine. She had their phone number in Orlando but she told him they were currently vacationing in Germany.

When he hung up he threw the phone across the room.

"Where is my wife?" he yelled to an empty room.

He paced his hotel room thinking that she was alone and close to time of giving birth. He had no way to reach her to let her know he was completely healed and back in the states.

He threw his things in his bags and decided to head to St. Augustine. Perhaps she was staying at the house there. He was at a loss of where else to look.

How could she just disappear like this?

Nicole begged the medical staff each day to let her hold her son. So far she had only been allowed to reach her hand in and stroke his little body. It was a difficult ordeal with all the wires that were attached to him.

Nicole pumped her breast milk so they could feed him but when she saw the little bit of nourishment he took in she thought he would never grow strong enough to survive.

She felt defeated. She knew she could heal him if given the chance. She was desperate and knew she would do whatever she had to do to make it happen.

She had tried to heal him when she reached in and took his little hand in hers but it wasn't enough to be effective. Regardless she kept trying every day.

Nora was in her room when she came back.

"Nicole, I'm so sorry. This should be such a joyous time for you."

"Have you been able to locate William?" Nicole asked despondently.

Nora simply shook her head. "The government is a pain in the ass to try to work with. I've explained how important it is. They just promise they'll notify him if they can locate him and pass on any messages."

The nurse brought in her daughter and placed her in her arms. "You have a very hungry little girl here."

Nicole opened her gown and put her daughter to her breast.

The nurse looked at her and said, "She'll be able to go home soon. She's just under five pounds now. Once she hits five pounds they'll release her to go home. You'll be released then too."

"And my son?" Nicole asked.

"I'm afraid he's nowhere near ready to go home," the nurse said.

"I'm not going without him. He needs me," Nicole said.

"So does your daughter," the nurse said.

Before the nurse left the room she said, "The babies are almost three weeks old now. They need names."

After the nurse left the room Nora said, "She's right. They need names so they aren't just Baby Girl Halloway and Baby Boy Halloway. You need to not neglect your daughter because she's strong and your son isn't. They both need their mother, Nicole."

"I know," Nicole said. "This is so hard to do without William. Where could he possibly be?"

She thought just possibly he'd gone back to their home on the beach in St. Augustine. She tried the number there but the phone just rang and rang. Nobody answered and the answer machine didn't come on.

74

William was just unloading the car after the long drive from Atlanta when he heard the phone ringing in the cottage.

It certainly can't be for me he thought. He ignored the phone and took his time getting his bags out of the car. By the time he got the door unlocked the phone had stopped ringing.

He took a last look over at the house where Nicole had grown up. It was empty.

The ICU pediatrician came into Nicole's room.

She sat right up. "Is my son all right?"

He didn't answer and pulled up a chair. "Have you been able to locate your husband?"

"No," she answered. "All I get is the run around from the government. No one seems to know where he is."

"Would you like to hold your son?" the doctor asked.

"More than anything," she answered.

The doctor said, "We don't believe your son will survive through the night. We're going to allow you to hold him. They're removing most of the tubes and wires from him as we speak. He's breathing on his own but.... You can hold him. It's not going to make a difference at this point."

"Take me to him...right now," she insisted. "Then I want everyone to leave us alone. Just let me be alone with him."

"You realize he may expire while you have him..." the doctor was saying.

"Then allow us time alone. Let him go in his mother's arms feeling loved if that's to be his fate," she insisted.

The doctor pushed Nicole in a wheelchair down to the ICU and a nurse was there to help her scrub up and put a clean gown on.

When they rolled her wheelchair in the nurse reached in and took her son out of the incubator and placed him in his mother's arms.

He still had a few wires attached to him that allowed the doctors to keep track of his vitals but other than that they had all been removed.

"He may not have long," the doctor warned her.

"Please leave. Everyone leave us alone. I need to be alone with my son," she insisted.

When someone started to argue the doctor nodded his head and said, "Give her some time."

"We'll be right outside if you need us," he said and turned and walked out with the nurse reluctantly following behind him.

She touched her son's tiny little face and told him, "Mommy's here. I'm right here. I'm going to make you better now. We're going to prove them wrong. You have to fight with me. Show them how strong are. Fight for your life my little one. Between the two of us we can do this," she said the tears flowing.

She unwrapped the front of his blanket and laid his tiny body up against her own and took his tiny little hands in hers.

She concentrated hard. She knew this was a matter of life and death and time was running out.

After a few moments she could feel the healing begin. At first the feeling was very faint and she wondered if it was going to work. Then she felt it flowing through her body.

She felt her son stir beneath her or did she imagine it? Yes, there it was again. It was even stronger this time.

She saw a nurse peer in but stayed out of the room. She could see the nurse and the doctor watching the monitor that was still tracking the vitals of her son.

Her son began making a mewling noise, a faint little desperate cry.

By the time she felt the healing process leave her body she saw a couple nurses and doctors animated looking at the monitor.

She felt her son push against her with his little foot.

He began to cry. This time it wasn't a faint cry but stronger.

The sound of a baby crying had never sounded so good.

The medical team rushed in and the doctor explained, "We need to check him."

Nicole reluctantly handed him over to the nurse. He wasn't the lethargic baby that the nurse had initially handed over. He was kicking and crying.

His cries grew stronger as the team checked him over.

The doctor after examining her son looked over at her and smiled. A genuine, ecstatic smile.

"We should have brought you in before. He's made a miraculous turn. His chances have just improved exponentially. I believe he just may prove us all wrong."

"Not all...I've always had faith he would make it," she said.

The baby began to cry and with his cry her milk began to flow.

"May I try to feed him?" she asked.

"We can give it a try. Let's see how he does," the doctor said.

The doctor motioned for the nurse to give her the baby.

Her son moved his head back and forth looking for his food source. She pulled her gown down on one side and guided his mouth to her breast. He initially had a hard time latching on but with his mother's help he seemed to catch on and greedily nursed.

The nurse and doctor stared amazed. Twenty minutes ago they had believed his time on this earth was up. Now here he was off the tubes and wires he'd been connected to since birth and thriving while nursing at his mother's breast.

Nicole knew with all her heart at this moment her son would survive.

75

Nora sat on the end of Nicole's bed as she changed her daughter's diaper. She would call out different names and Nicole would either make a face, say write that one down, or say maybe.

It was time these babies had a name.

Now that Nicole was confident her son would survive she was finally able to enjoy being a mother.

After she finished changing her daughter she placed her in a bassinette situated next to her brother. He was out of ICU and thriving. The twins were finally together as they belonged.

The hospital had let Nicole remain in the hospital until her son was strong enough to be released. He was almost ready.

The nurse had reminded her yet again that the babies couldn't leave until they had a name. She reminded her that there were birth certificates that needed filling out and Baby Girl and Baby Boy Halloway wouldn't pass muster.

Nora had brought Nicole's list from home that she had previously made of girl names. She said, "Let's find a boy's name to go with the girl names and then choose which pair of names you like."

Nicole looked at her son and reached over and covered his foot where he had kicked off his blanket.

"Look how strong he is now. He's a little fighter," she said with pride.

Nora said, "Let's get down to business here. To be three months old and not have a name is just wrong."

"I know. It was just hard to think of naming them when we didn't know if he would live. That's all I could think about at the time. O.K., let's go over the list."

Nora called out baby boy names from a baby name book. She called out name after name and would look up at Nicole for her reaction after each name. Getting no positive result she finally just handed the baby name book to Nicole.

Nora dug through her purse and pulled out the list that had the baby girl's names on it that Nicole had previously picked out.

"Let's start with the names on the list of girl's names and find a boy's name to go with what I already picked," Nicole said.

"You liked Edward for a boy after William's father. Did you have a girl's name you liked that starts with an E?" Nora asked not seeing any girl names beginning with an E on the list.

"Emma," Nicole said.

"O.K. I'll put that down to go with Edward. The next name you had on the list was Madison," Nora said.

Nicole skimmed through her baby book name and said, "What do you think of Mason?"

"It doesn't matter if I like it," Nora said. "Well yeah, it kinda does since I'm going to be their godmother and nanny."

They finally had the names narrowed down to the last four on the list. Nicole got up and looked the twins over when she went over each name.

Looking at her son she asked, "Do you look like a Pierce or a Roman?" Then looking at her daughter said, "That would make you a Piper or a Renae."

She looked back at her son and said, "Or are you Edward or Roman?"

She turned to her daughter and said, "And are you Emma or Riley?"

"I don't care for Roman. It sounds so fierce for such a little guy. It sounds like a warrior or something," Nora said.

"But isn't that the point? To remind him that he's a fighter who fought for his life? Maybe you're right. What other boy name starts with an R that you like?"

While she was looking up names Nicole was looking back and

forth at the babies trying to decide which name fit them the most.

"How about Ron?" the ICU pediatrician said who had walked in during their conversation. "You can name him after me."

"I never knew it would be so hard to name a baby...make that two babies," she said.

"I think Ron is a perfect name for him," the doctor said while examining the little boy who was the subject of their conversation.

"We'll add that to our list," Nora said only pretending to write it down. They were trying to narrow the list down, not add to it.

"I wish we knew where their daddy was. He ought to be here to have a say in naming them," Nicole said.

The doctor looked up and said, "They still haven't been able to locate him?"

"No," Nicole said. "You better believe when I get out of here I'm going to find him myself."

"I have good news for you then. Little Ron just reached his milestone and I've signed his discharge papers. Once you name these two babies you can all go home."

"That's incentive," Nicole said smiling.

The doctor said, "I'm certainly thankful things turned out so well. He sure gave us all a terrible scare. He seems to be suffering no after effects. He's small but perfectly healthy now."

After the doctor left Nicole said, "Give me that list. I need to make a decision."

She looked the list over without saying a word while occasionally looking up at the twins then back at the list.

She finally looked up and set the list aside and looked once again at the twins and nodded her head and smiled.

"Nora, meet your godchildren Madison Emma Halloway and Mason Edward Halloway. Now everybody, let's go home and find your daddy."

76

Before he had been discharged from the Maryland hospital William had filled out the paperwork to apply for a position as an astronaut with NASA. This morning in the mail he had found a letter requesting him to come to the Johnson Space Center in Houston to interview for the position.

He knew potential astronaut candidates undergo one of the world's most competitive selection processes and that there were over a thousand other applicants who he assumed were as equally qualified as he was. Keeping that in mind he wasn't so sure how excited he should be but it was one step closer to his goal.

There was one thing he had to do before he headed to Houston. He stopped in at the downtown area where he had an appointment with a private detective. He had given up of finding his wife on his own and was seeking professional help.

Nicole was dressed and putting little booties on her son getting the twins ready for their first outing in the outside world. They were finally going home.

She had decided to go back to her childhood home in St. Augustine until it was time for her job at NASA to begin. Nora had offered to go to Cape Canaveral to find them a place to live once they were settled in at the beach house.

Mariah walked in carrying a baby car seat in each hand. "I brought you a belated gift. I spoke to Nora to see what you needed and she said you were in need of car seats."

"How thoughtful of you. Thank you," Nicole said.

Mariah came over and peered in the bassinettes at the babies.

"They're as different as night and day. He's so dark and her hair and complexion are as light as your own. Aren't they precious?"

"Mason looks just like his daddy and everyone tells me Madison looks like me," Nicole said with motherly pride.

Nora came in the room and said, "We're all ready to go."

She spotted the car seats and said, "Perfect. I was wondering how we were going to manage the twins in the car."

Nicole looked at the car seats and said, "You know two babies need a lot of things. I think since we became such a large family so quickly that we've outgrown my little car."

Mariah seemed to be thinking for a few minutes and then said, "Want to trade? I have a big SUV that's too much for a single woman and I'll save gas money with your little Toyota."

"Seriously?" Nicole asked.

"Dead serious. I've always loved your little Toyota and wished I had bought something similar," Mariah answered.

They exchanged keys and Mariah said she'd take care of exchanging the names on the titles and mail Nicole the title to the SUV to her home in St. Augustine.

Mariah took a few minutes to hold and cuddle each baby while Nicole signed off on the papers before leaving the hospital.

Even though she was recovered after a stint of three months hospial policy required Nicole to ride down to the exit in a wheelchair. She held a baby in each arm and received lots of ooh's and aah's on her way out.

Nora had everything packed and ready to load up in the new SUV.

Nora was driving and Nicole sat in the middle seat between the car seats on their way to St. Augustine.

The road to the cottage on the beach was pretty private and so Nora was surprised to see a car leaving the area when she pulled down their street. She couldn't see the driver as it was dark out and Nicole was bent over tending to one of the babies so she didn't see anything.

Little did either driver know who the other was.

William had just pulled out and driven right by his wife and children. He too had wondered who was driving down their private road but he didn't recognize the SUV and kept on driving. He was on his way to Houston.

William was in Houston for two weeks. He had been accepted as one of NASA's future astronauts.

In the time he had been in Houston he had undergone a strenuous physical exam to make sure he was fit to travel in space. He silently thanked his wife for her healing power or he knew he never would have been able to pass the physical part of the exam. He was so exhausted at the end of each day that it helped keep him from being depressed over the circumstances of his missing wife.

"Congratulations, Mr. Halloway. How does it feel to be an astronaut?"

"It feels pretty good I have to admit. This is something I've worked towards for a very long time," he said shaking the man's hand who was one of NASA's officials.

"You'll need to report in at the Cape in Florida in a week for orientation and to begin your training. You'll go through intensive training before you'll begin your specialized mission training. After you complete that you'll become eligible for a flight assignment. From what I've seen these last two weeks I know I'll be seeing you one day soon going into space. Pretty exciting, isn't it?"

"Yes sir," William said.

Walking to his car he thought back to that night when a little six year old girl told him he would be flying to the moon one day.

That little girl, now his wife, meant more to him than any trip to the moon. He'd trade that opportunity in a minute just to find her and be with her right now.

As William was leaving Houston he thought he'd go back to the beach house and stay one or two more nights and then drive to the Cape. That would give him time to check with the private detective and see if he'd come up with anything on his search for Nicole.

Nora and Nicole stood out on the back deck looking out at the beach that evening once they got the babies to sleep.

"It's as though I feel his presence. I know he's not near here but I keep looking over at his house and thinking he's been there," Nicole said.

"Perhaps it's wishful thinking," Nora said.

"I just don't understand. He was so happy to hear he was going to be a father. Even if he's still hospitalized you'd think he'd find some way of contacting me," Nicole said.

She stared out watching the ocean waves. She was deep in thought as to why her husband hadn't contacted her after being in the states all this time.

Nicole looked up with a started look on her face. "I just remembered something. When I got in contact with Rhiannon she said no one knew where I was. What if he's been looking for me and can't find me?"

"Wouldn't your mom or dad give him your information? Surely he'd think to contact them," Nora said.

"But they were leaving for Germany just a day or two after they came to visit us at the hospital. As far as he knew they were still living here. What if all this time..."

A baby started crying and ended the conversation but didn't stop Nicole from thinking about it.

After she fed and changed Madison and carried her back to her bassinette she whispered to her, "We're going to find your daddy. I promise you."

No sooner had she put Madison back to bed and little Mason began stirring. She knew as tiny as he was he needed to be fed more often and went ahead and picked him up and fed him too.

"What time are you leaving in the morning?" Nicole asked.

"I'm leaving about 7:00. I need to rent a car and I have an appointment with a realtor in Cape Canaveral early tomorrow afternoon to go look at a couple of places," Nora answered.

"I'll just have to take the twins with me then," Nicole said.

"Take them where?" Nora asked.

"I'm going to hire a private detective to find William. They're better at that type of thing and maybe they can cut through all the government bullshit bureacracy. I have to find him Nora. He needs to know his babies have arrived. He doesn't even know he has a daughter let alone a son."

77

As soon as the private detective's office opened that morning she called to make an appointment.

"I'm sorry but he's in Atlanta right now. We expect him back in the office in two days. Would you like me to set up an appointment for the day he returns?"

Nicole was deeply disappointed that she couldn't get in to see him that day but knew she had no other choice.

She had already made up her mind that after her appointment with the private detective she was going to go ahead and make the move to Cape Canaveral. It was too painful being here and seeing reminders of William everywhere she looked.

That night when the twins were down and she knew they would sleep for at least two hours she took a leisure walk along the beach.

She loved listening to the ocean waves breaking on the shore. She sat in the sand and looked out remembering the day William had first been taken by the aliens.

How many other guys would accept the fact that aliens were a part of your life? And that their girlfriend, now wife she thought, carried genes of aliens herself.

She knew it wouldn't be long before the aliens paid another visit. Surely they must be aware by now that she had given birth and that another baby had hidden herself from everyone while still in her womb.

So the next generation of daughters of destiny had arrived. She knew it would only be a matter of time before she discovered what powers and "gifts" her own daughter carried.

And Mason? She supposed he was just a normal little boy. A special gift is how she looked at her son.

What a blessing these two beautiful children were.

If only their father were here to share the joy.

She got up and brushed herself off and walked a little further down the beach to the area where they had first made love. She was glad to see a real estate developer hadn't come in and put up a huge new hotel on the spot.

She headed back towards home recalling the night they had met during the night and went skinny dipping and made love in the ocean.

She had such wonderful memories. She wondered if he remembered these special times in their lives too.

As she passed his house she couldn't stop herself. She walked up on his back deck and sat for awhile just to feel his energy. She knew for a fact that he had been here at some point in time since he had returned home. If only he had stayed a little longer they would have been reunited.

"Please William. Come back to me," she said.

She headed back home knowing the twins would soon be demanding to be fed again.

That night the babies were restless and she didn't get much sleep. If she had been awake and delayed her walk on the beach a little later she may have seen William return home.

He came in shortly after midnight.

William was wide awake, unable to sleep. He went out on his deck and flashed his flashlight towards Nicole's bedroom window and gave their old childhood message. He flashed the light once, then four times, and then three times meaning I love you.

78

When Nicole got up to tend to one of the babies she saw a light flash on her bedroom window three times. She thought it must be a boat coming in and the boat rocking on the waves only made the light appear to be flashing. It reminded her of the days when she and William had messaged each other. It made her sad to think about.

Early that morning at daybreak before the rest of the world was scurrying about William decided to take a last walk along the beach before he left for Cape Canaveral.

He too came upon the place where they had first made love. He turned around and headed home.

He started to walk up his deck and he thought he heard a baby crying. He stopped in his tracks. It appeared to come from the direction of Nicole's house.

Overhead flew some sea gulls and he supposed that it was the cry of the gulls he had heard.

Wishful thinking, he told himself as he walked inside and prepared to leave.

He noticed a SUV in the driveway at the Newhouse home but it wasn't a vehicle he recognized. Perhaps they had rented the place out since they weren't using it.

He threw his bags in his car and locked the house up. As he drove by Nicole's home he stopped long enough to write down the tag number of the SUV parked in front of the house.

He thought he'd pass it on to the detective and see if it was someone who might know the Newhouse family who could tell him where she was.

It was a long shot he knew, but he didn't want to miss any opportunity of finding her.

Nicole got a phone call the morning of her appointment with the detective. It was the detective's secretary saying they would have to delay the appointment until the following morning as he was still out of town.

Nicole agreed and said she would be leaving the area after her appointment so she hoped there would be no more delays.

Nora had called to let her know she had found a perfect place large enough for the twins and for when William returned. It had a little cottage in the back where she could live so Nicole and William would have their privacy once he returned.

"I'm beginning to wonder if that will ever happen at this point," Nicole said sounding depressed to her friend.

"It will. You have to have faith. The two of you belong together. You'll find each other," Nora reassured her.

Nicole assured Nora that she could make the drive herself with the twins and that would give Nora time to get groceries and get the place set up for their arrival.

"I have an appointment this afternoon with the detective. I'll leave from there," she said.

Nicole walked in the detective's office with the twins and took a seat. The man sitting behind the desk looked like a kind man. She assumed he had heard many heartbreaking stories. She found him very easy to talk to.

Midway through her explanation of looking for her husband he sat up on the edge of his seat and said, "What did you say your name was?"

"Nicole Halloway," she answered.

He ran his hand through his hair and sat there a minute. "This is a first for me. I don't believe I'm breaking any confidentialities in revealing this to you, but your husband hired me to find you."

"What! William was here? William is looking for me?" she asked suddenly animated.

"That's where I've been the last few days. Trying to track you down. He called me while I was still in Atlanta searching for you and gave me a license plate number for a woman by the name of Dr. Mariah Archer."

"Mariah's license plate number? Why?" she asked.

He said he drove by your old house and saw an SUV there that didn't belong there and thought maybe it was a friend of the family who would know how to locate you or your parents," the detective explained.

"He drove by the house? That was me there," she said.

She began crying real tears of joy. "We were so close. Why didn't he knock on the door and ask himself?"

"He said it was too early in the morning or he would have," the detective explained.

"Should I call him and tell him I found you? Or you found me?" the detective asked.

"Where is he?" she asked.

"He's in Cape Canaveral. He got a job at NASA."

She laughed and quickly related how she too had a job at NASA and was heading there as soon as she left his office.

The detective wrote down William's address where he was staying and handed it to her.

"What do I owe you?" she asked before leaving.

"Not a thing. This was the best case solved I ever had. The joy of knowing the two of you will be reunited is payment enough," he said. "I wish all my cases had happy endings like yours."

She saw the detective look at the twins and say, "He certainly has a surprise coming. He thinks there's a possibly you're still pregnant or recently gave birth to a baby girl. I see you've got quite a surprise for him."

"Indeed, I do. If he calls whatever you do please don't tell him about any of this. I want to surprise him," she pleaded.

"I wouldn't dream of spoiling your surprise," the detective said as he walked her to the door.

He helped her get the twins settled in the SUV and wished them well.

79

Nicole was barely in the door of their new place in Cape Canaveral when she was spilling the story to Nora who stood there listening with her mouth hanging open in amazement.

"Go, go find him. Leave the babies with me," Nora insisted.

Nicole's wheels were spinning as to how to best pull this off. The detective had let her know he had already begun working at NASA and she thought that was the best place to find him this time of day. She didn't want to have to wait till this evening. She'd waited long enough.

She put on work clothes with her doctor's coat and ran out kissing the babies as she was ready to leave.

"Wish me luck," she called out to Nora.

Nicole parked in the employee parking at NASA.

She was about to be reunited with the love of her life. She was giddy with excitement. Her heart was pounding thinking of how close they were.

She went into her new office and quickly pulled out the files on the astronauts that were in training.

She called down to where the astronauts trained and explained that while she wasn't scheduled to begin work for a few weeks yet she thought she'd come in to meet the astronauts one on one. She planned to meet with just one of them today she explained.

She asked the woman to send William Halloway to her office.

Now all she had to do is wait....Her husband would walk through that door. Oh, how she had waited for this day.

She paced the floor waiting for her husband. Wasn't he going to be surprised?

She heard footsteps coming down the hall. It was him. It took all the inner strength she had not to run down the hall and throw herself into his arms.

She felt his presence. William was just steps away.

She stepped back behind the screen so he wouldn't see her until he was all the way in the room.

She heard the door to her office open. She heard footsteps, the door being closed behind him, then silence.

Her heart was beating so loud she was sure he could hear it.

She stepped from behind the screen. His back was to her.

"William," she said softly.

He spun around so fast he looked like a ballerina doing a pirouette.

His mouth dropped open and he walked over and took her in his arms hugging her so tight she could hardly breathe.

He pulled back and ran his hands over her face, her hair, all over, kissing her on top of her head, her cheeks, then dropped his eyes to look at her stomach.

"Where have you been? I've been looking everywhere for you?" he asked hugging her.

She was laughing and hugging him back holding him just as tightly.

"I've been looking for you everywhere," she said.

"We found each other now and I'm never letting you out of my sight again," he said.

"But I hear you're going to the moon. You can hardly take me with you," she said.

"I'll hide you in the spacecraft and take you with me. Oh Nicole, I love you so much. I thought I'd never find you. I hired a private detective to find you after I'd given up. How did you find me? You had the baby?" his words tumbled out.

They had so much catching up to do.

"I hired the same private detective. That was my SUV in the driveway at the beach house," she said. "And yes, I'm obviously not pregnant anymore. I have so much to tell you."

"You were there? You were at the beach house? I thought I heard a baby crying. Was that our baby?" he asked.

"I suppose it was," she answered.

"Please...tell me about our baby. I want to know everything. Don't leave anything out," he said.

He took her by the hand and he sat on her chair behind the desk and pulled her on his lap.

"I better lock the door honey. You don't want the other men to think this is how I treat my patients," she said while laughing.

"You're the new doctor everyone's been talking about? You're working here too?" he asked.

"Yes, but officially I don't start for another few weeks. I'm off on family leave," she said.

They sat down and she told him everything that happened from the time she returned to Germany.

"Twins? We have twins?" he said in amazement.

"We do indeed. Our son looks just like you and our little girl favors me. They're so precious William. I can't wait for you to see them," she said.

"Please, take me to see them. I want to see my babies. I can't believe I'm a father. And twins," he grinned from ear to ear.

"I know. I still can't believe it myself and I've had almost four months to get used to the idea of there being two of them," she laughed.

"Most important I have my wife back by my side," he said taking her in his arms and kissing his wife passionately showing her how much he'd missed her.

80

William stared down in awe at his sleeping twins. Every day when he watched them sleep, held them in his arms, or quieted them during the night he was amazed at his good fortune. He could hardly believe he was so blessed to be father to these two beautiful children. He couldn't stop himself. He reached down in the crib to pick up his son.

Nicole stood in the doorway with her arms folded and said, "I knew you wouldn't be able to just let them sleep peacefully. Now they'll be up and ready for the day and the sun isn't even up yet."

William turned around with a guilty look on his face.

"I just wanted to get in a little cuddle time before I'm off to work."

He reached in with his other arm and scooped up his sleeping daughter.

He changed the babies diapers and rocked them while Nicole got ready for work. When she was dressed and ready she came in and nursed the twins while he got his shower.

NASA had been very understanding when they heard their story and gave both Nicole and William six weeks off. William knew even that amount of time was generous considering they were in training for their mission to the moon. But that time had come to an end and they had returned to work a week ago.

Nora knocked on the door ready to take over caring for the twins while their parents went to work. No matter the time of day or night Nora was full of energy. She was a perfect caretaker for the twins.

Madison not quite crawling yet scooted on her belly towards the door happy to greet her godmother while Mason lay on his blanket squealing in delight.

Mom and Dad gave lots of kisses to the babies and were out the door.

Nicole was content to close her eyes and snatch a few extra moments of rest on their way to work. She hadn't had a full night's sleep since the arrival of the twins. She knew she would have a busy day with the astronauts beginning their training in land and water survival.

She would be on site while the men began scuba diving lessons. The future astronauts were monitored before and after their strenuous physical exercises and training.

She was enjoying her work immensely. It gave her a chance to be by her husband's side and share these experiences with him. By the end of each day both of them were anxious to be home and spend time with the twins.

"Don't you think it's odd that the aliens have been absent since the birth?" William asked as he turned into the gate at NASA.

Nicole opened her eyes and said, "Actually I'm very surprised. I expected to at least have them come and see Madison after her birth."

"Do you think they don't know about her? You said when they visited before the birth that they felt Mason's presence and were upset that you were expecting a boy. Maybe they don't even know you also had a girl," he said.

"I hardly think that's the case," she said.

"I remember you told me they visited your mother just a few days after you were born. I would have thought as anxious as they had been for you to have the next daughter of destiny that they would have visited before now," he said as he pulled into a parking space.

Nicole reached in the backseat and grabbed her lab coat and put it on.

"I do admit the same thought has occurred to me more than

once. I've even thought perhaps Madison isn't the one. Maybe she isn't the next in line to be a daughter of destiny since she's a twin. I'm not sure how that works."

"She'd have to be wouldn't she?" he asked. "Isn't that how it works...the first daughter and all?"

"Before the twins were born when the aliens thought I was only carrying a son they made me promise once our son was born I wouldn't wait and would give birth soon after to a girl that would be the next daughter of destiny. I just assumed when Madison was born that she would be the one but maybe not."

He thought about what she had said and asked, "You actually promised you'd have another baby?"

"I did," she said.

He grinned thinking he'd be perfectly content having lots of children with his beautiful wife and he said as much.

"In the book of Psalms in the Bible it says a man is blessed whose quiver is full...meaning children," she said laughing at the look on her husband's face.

"I'm willing," he said. "Want to help me fill my quiver?"

"Glad you asked," she said. "Because I took a pregnancy test this morning and it was positive."

He stopped in his tracks.

"Are you serious? But the twins are still babies. They're not even six months old. How did that happen?" he asked.

"It happened the same way it happened the first time," she said laughing at his response.

81

While the astronauts were in classroom training the director came in to go over the records of the men with Nicole.

"I'm afraid we've a problem with one of the men," the director said.

"Let me guess. Curtiss Shepard," Nicole said who had been counseling the men.

"That's correct. As you know he's been training in the simulator which prepares the astronauts for rendezvous and payload operations training. He himself came to me and said he doesn't think he's cut out for this. When he asked to be excused from the program we agreed to let him go," Aitor said.

"How are you going to replace him with someone since the men have been training for so long? It'll be hard to bring someone up to speed at this point," Nicole said concerned for what this could mean for the other men training for their mission.

Aitor pushed five folders towards her and said, "I'm curious. Which of these men would you recommend? They've already been in training in Houston so time wise it won't set us back."

He picked up the photo of the twins from her desk while she read over the men's charts. There were no names on the charts or any personal information, only their qualifications and training to this point.

After a time she pushed one of the folders his way and said, "This one would be my recommendation."

He set the photo of the twins down and flipped to the back of the chart which had a cover over the back page. He removed the cover and showed her the name of the man she had chosen for the replacement.

"Daniel Kraft," she said shocked. "Seriously?"

"He's been training in Houston. He's our new replacement. I understand you're familiar with him," Aitor said.

"Yes. He went to the Air Force Academy with William and pilot's training school. They were together in Vietnam. They're very good friends and his wife and I were roommates in college," Nicole said. She wanted to be sure there was no conflict and wanted the director to be aware there were personal ties here.

"I'd say he'd be a good replacement then," Aitor stood to leave as Nora walked in the door pushing the babies in their stroller.

"I'm sorry. I didn't mean to interrupt," Nora said seeing that Nicole wasn't alone.

"Please come in," Aitor said holding the door for her.

When Nora came in he watched her not taking his eyes off her.

"Introduce me," Aitor said to Nicole.

"I'm sorry," Nicole said forgetting her manners. "This is my best friend and nanny of our children Nora."

"And godmother of these beautiful babes," Nora added.

She smiled a smile at Aitor that lit up her face.

Aitor appeared to be quite captivated by her friend Nicole noticed. She sat back quietly and watched the two of them interact.

That night as they were preparing the babies for bed Nicole and William were discussing the events of the day and what a coincidence it was that Daniel or "Cheese" would be flying with him yet again, this time in a spacecraft.

"My parents and Nora's mother are planning to come this weekend to see the babies," she said.

"My mother was just here last week. Are you up for more visitors?" William asked concerned his wife stretched herself too thin especially now that she was pregnant again.

"They'll be a great help. I'm looking forward to their visit, besides Shannon said she had something she had to give me," Nicole said.

"Did she say what? I don't think we could fit another baby toy or accessory in here. I think we're outgrowing this place as it is," he said.

"She didn't say but I have a pretty good idea of what it is," she said.

"You sound mysterious," he said quietly jiggling little Mason trying to get him to sleep.

"I believe it's the diary," she said.

William knew instantly what she meant. "The daughters of destiny diaries. I have to admit I'm rather anxious to see it."

"Me too," Nicole said.

82

"I'm sorry I'm so late in getting this to you. I had it stored away in a safe place and it wasn't easy to get to. It's been put away for years," Shannon said as she held with reverance a package wrapped in oilskin cloth and several layers of protective covering.

Nicole looked at the package and said, "I've heard about this book for most of my life. I'm anxious to read the stories."

"Wait until we're all gone and you have time to read it in private. You're to write your own story of the new generation of daughters of destiny. Once that's complete you're to put it in the hands of someone you trust implicitly who will keep it in their care until Madison herself gives birth to the next generation of daughters of destiny. Now my role is complete," Shannon said handing the package to Nicole.

"Thank you Shannon for caring for this and for me all these years. You've been someone very special in my life. I suppose you know it will be placed in your daughter's care after I write my own story," Nicole said.

"I'm sure she'll be as honored as I've been to be a keeper of the diary," Shannon said.

The following day their guests left early and Nicole asked Nora if she would mind taking the babies for a walk in the park to give her and William some time to go through the diary.

As they were speaking Aitor the director at NASA drove up coming to visit Nora.

Nicole looked at her friend as though asking what this was

about.

"We've been talking on the phone every day since the day we met in your office. We've gone out a couple of times too."

"Aren't you full of surprises," Nicole said. "Never mind taking the babies then. Go have a good time."

"Nope, this will be a great way to test to see if he can cut the mustard. You know us Irish girls want big families, lots of babies. This will be a way to see if he can handle them. See if I'm wasting my time with him or go for it," she said and with a wink she walked up to Aitor and asked if he minded going with her to take the babies for a walk in the park.

He at least appeared to be delighted with the idea.

Nicole laughed. Her friend was a piece of work. She hoped things worked out between the two of them.

Nicole gently unwrapped the book taking care knowing the book was very old. From what she remembered she believed her mother told her the stories went back as far as the sixteeenth century.

She was anxious to read the stories of those who came before her who were also a part of the alien's lives. Through no choice of their own these women's lives had also been entwined with the aliens. She knew the stories throughout different eras of history would be interesting to read.

William stood over her watching.

She gently ran her hand over the cover of the book. It felt as though it jumped to life. Images ran through her head as she placed her palm on the book.

She opened the book and stared.

It was blank. There was nothing written in the book. She flipped through the pages. They were all empty.

"It's empty," William said. "I thought you said other people wrote their stories in this book."

Nicole looked confused. "I don't understand."

She looked again and nothing.

She held the open book up against her stomach tenderly while thinking back if her mother had said anything about having any problem reading the book when it was in her possession.

She had to wonder again why the aliens hadn't come to see Madison and if that had anything to do with the pages not revealing the stories of the past. She would wrap the book up and pack it away until she had an opportunity to ask the aliens about it. She set the book on the table.

"Do you suppose this means that Madison isn't the next generation of daughters of destiny?" she asked her husband.

She looked down ready to close the book and put it away until she could figure out what to do with it.

Faintly she could see writing begin to appear. Mesmerized she watched the page and watched as the writing became clear.

"What is it? What are you looking at?" William asked.

"Don't you see? Writing of some sort is beginning to appear. She flipped through the book, quickly at first as she watched the pages fill up with text, then more slowly as she tried to identify the different languages she was seeing on the pages.

"I don't see anything," he said in frustration.

"Perhaps it's not for your eyes to see as you aren't one of the daughters of destiny. I'll read it to you," she said.

83

"What does it say?" William asked standing over her shoulder trying to see what she was reading.

He walked around and pulled up a chair at the table realizing no matter how hard he looked he wasn't going to see what she saw in the book.

Nicole stared intently at the book as images came into focus.

"It looks like symbols....like hieroglyphics, maybe."

She turned to another page and was delighted to see a written language although it was in a foreign language. "This looks like some type of Egyptian language. She kept turning the pages and recognized the French language and even German, there was a story written in Spanish and another in Greek. These stories were from events that occurred from different parts of the world.

She began to understand the text. Even though they were written in foreign languages she was unfamiliar with she was stunned to realize she could read it. She tried different pages, different languages and found she was able to read them all.

"William, these are written in languages from different parts of Europe and from other parts of the world," she said.

"I wonder what they say," he said.

"That's what's so amazing. I can actually read each and every one of them," she said.

He stared at his wife in amazement trying to comprehend what she was saying.

"Are you saying you can speak these languages?" he asked.

"No, probably not. But I can clearly read them from the diary. These are all stories written by women who had visitations from aliens. They tell the story of how the aliens were a part of their lives," she said.

William was speechless at her revelation.

"These stories are all from different eras in history. One speaks of her time with a man who was a French sculptor who was her father. He was the designer of a statue. The woman who wrote this writes that he was making the statue as a gift to America. As she's describing it I realize she's talking about the Statue of Liberty. She's the daughter of Frédéric-Auguste Bartholdi."

"This one further towards the back was written by a woman from Egypt. The story was told by her but as she was illiterate it was written by a scribe. She speaks of the tombs of the pharoahs."

"That's incredible," William said getting up and looking again hoping to see writing in the book himself.

"This story took place during the Spanish Civil War. This woman worked for Franco but she was actually a spy. These stories are amazing. They all include a piece of history of the times that they lived."

"What history will you include in your story?" William asked her.

Nicole thought a moment and said, "Perhaps about the Vietnam War and of my husband going to the moon. Yes, the Space Age definitely needs to be a part of my story."

William looked at the book. Frustrated he was unable to see any of this for himself he asked, "What about your mother? Have you seen what she wrote yet?"

Nicole flipped a little ways through the book gently, taking care due to the age of the book. While searching for her mother's story she came across that of one a little earlier that caught her eye. She stopped to read it.

"My grandmother's story is here. It makes me feel like I actually knew her. She was a well-known artist. And here's my mother's story. I feel as though I'm intruding in her life reading something so intimate. One day my own daughter will read my story that I'll write," she said.

"What's the date of the earliest story written?" he asked.

She flipped to the back of the book as she had noticed the most recent stories, those of her mother and grandmother were in the front. She looked for a date or for a time in history to give a time frame.

"The stories seem to have started sometime in the 1500's," she said in awe. "Though some in the very back aren't dated and appear to be much older. There's a frontispiece that I believe was written by the aliens themselves explaining what the book is."

"What language did the aliens write in?" he asked his wife.

"To tell the truth I don't know what it is but I can read it. It speaks of the story of how they searched for generations for a lineage worthy to be the ones to carry the chosen one. They speak of how the line will begin....how they will....oh, this is describing me and what they did to my mother....the beginning of the daughters of destiny. This tells of the great honor of the ones chosen to carry this mission out and how important they will be to the outcome of the world. It actually says the fate of the world lies in our hands. That we are the chosen ones."

She looked at her husband and said, "That certainly puts quite a load on my shoulders. I don't know whether to be honored or horrified."

"Do you realize the importance of this book? That book belongs in a museum," he said.

She laughed. "Can you imagine what sort of reaction you'd get from the curators of a museum if you told them you had a book dating back to the 1500's about visitations of aliens? Besides the aliens would never allow this book to fall in the hands of ...."

"You are correct. It is not meant for other's eyes. These are for our records and for those who are a part of us," an alien communicated to the two of them.

Neither Nicole or William had noticed the three aliens standing off to the side of the room until now.

84

William and Nicole were so intent on studying the contents of the diary that neither had noticed the arrival of the aliens.

"I expected you would have come long before now. It seems we were all surprised. You told me I was having a man-child but you failed to notice I was also carrying a girl," Nicole said to the three aliens.

"The girl child was very good at cloaking herself. She was indeed quite a surprise," one of the aliens communicated.

"So you have your daughter of destiny. I suppose you're happy then?" Nicole said.

"The daughter of destiny....the next in line....yes, we are happy."

"I imagine you want to see her but she isn't here right now," Nicole said.

"We are aware of that. We will see her when the time is right," the alien stated.

"The gateway has remained open. I see you are carrying life yet again just as you promised. You have kept your word," the alien closest to her said telepathically.

"You are a woman of your word and you are to be honored."

"Evidently I didn't need to keep my word as far as having another child since I've already given birth to a daughter. I won't say this baby was planned but this child will be loved and we look forward to his or her arrival," Nicole said.

"We too look forward to her arrival," one of the aliens communicated.

One of the aliens stepped forward and placed his hand on her belly not yet showing with child.

"I thought all you cared about was the daughter of destiny, but thank you," Nicole said.

"You are correct. The daughter of destiny is our only concern," the alien responded.

"Wait a minute. You said *her* a few moments ago. It's a girl? The baby I'm carrying is a girl?" Nicole asked.

"Of course. Is that not what you promised us? To bring forth a girl child soon after the last birth."

"Well yes, I did promise that. I made that promise going by what you told me, that I was carrying a man child. I mean a boy. I also gave birth to the girl child you long awaited for."

"You did give life to a girl child also. We are aware."

"You're sure this time that it's a girl?" Nicole asked.

"There is no question. You are carrying...," one alien began before he was interrupted by another.

"In the past this has never been allowed. A woman in the lineage of the daughters of destiny was allowed one child. It was meant to be that way until the arrival of the chosen one. There is a reason you have been given this gift of additional life," the alien said.

"I imagine my husband and my love for one another had something to do with it," she said sarcastically.

"Aah, but you and your loved one had many years of loving one another without bringing forth life. Do you not ask yourself why another so soon after the other two you bore?"

"We made up for lost time," William said not caring for the alien's provocative tone.

"Actually I thought nursing the twins would have kept me from getting pregnant so soon, but regardless we're very happy to add another child to our family," Nicole said.

"Your womb was filled with child or children as it turned out because it was your role in life. Your mission as a daughter of destiny is to bring forth life to the next daughter of destiny."

"Whether you see it as my mission in life we see it as our

desire to have children because of our love for one another. I don't know why you're being antagonistic. The next daughter of destiny that you so desired is...."

"You have done well. You have respected your end of the bargain. We will take our leave. We will be watching over you," the alien said in parting.

That night William held Nicole and said, "I'm so thankful this time I'll be here to share in the joy of this pregnancy and be here for the birth."

"Me too. This time I hope I'll give birth a little late. She's due just days after the *Apollo* mission should be completed. Knowing my luck she'll come while you're on the moon," she said.

"We'll just tell her to hold on a little so daddy can be the first one to greet her with a kiss," he said.

As Nicole slept he pondered carefully the words the aliens had passed on to them.

The aliens had seemed to speak in riddles. What were they trying to say or imply?

Before he could give it too much thought one of the babies started crying.

As he rocked his daughter back to sleep he thought again about what the aliens could have meant. The thought crossed his mind that perhaps Madison wasn't the long awaited for daughter of destiny after all. Perhaps it was the new life his wife now carried that would be the one. They did say it was a girl.

He quietly got up and put Madison back in her crib and covered her.

No use in fretting about it, he thought. We'll find out one day. Either the aliens will reveal it to us or our daughter will when she reveals her own gifts she inherited from the aliens.

85

Nicole didn't know why but she was unsettled after the aliens left. She couldn't figure out why they were being so argumentive. You would have thought they would have been thrilled they finally got their wish and the next daughter of destiny had arrived. But then they weren't ones to show emotion of any kind so perhaps this was normal to them.

She decided she wasn't going to let them bother her and get on with life and enjoy her loved ones.

She had already made up her mind that her children would all be raised the same. She wouldn't put any special emphasis on the next generation daughter of destiny. Her children would all be loved and treated equally.

As a matter of fact she and William had discussed it for quite some time and decided not to pursue her daughter's "gifts" from the aliens once they became evident.

She wasn't even sure she would tell her daughter about what the aliens claimed would be her role in life. Let her live a normal life not worrying about being accepted by others or worrying about being different. She thought her daughter would find much more happiness that way.

Becoming an astronaut is a high risk job that is mentally, emotionally, and physically demanding. She could see that each of the astronauts gave it their all but were feeling the stress.

Nicole's job was in screening the astronauts during their training both medically to be sure they were in top shape and coping well with their training along with psychiatric screening.

She was right there with them as they trained in different equipment and only had some downtime while they were in the classrooms.

She would go over different scenarios with each of the men that they may encounter on their time in space and on the moon. She monitored their stress levels and wrote evaluations giving her medical opinion on how well prepared and how she thought each of them would cope while in space and on their time on the moon.

It was fascinating work and while she loved her work she was very pregnant and the hard work and long hours were taking it's toll. With another two children who had just celebrated their first birthday she had quite a few demands on her time and energy. Frankly, she was exhausted.

She was in her third trimester as the days were ticked off on the calendar counting down to the days the men would climb in the spacecraft and be shot off into space heading to the moon.

In a few more days the men would go into isolation in order to be kept from any germs before the mission.

It was really happening. Her husband was going to the moon.

She was anxious for him to have this experience but frankly she would be happy when it was all behind them.

Days after his return from the mission their baby was due. Hopefully this time she wouldn't go into labor until her husband was there by her side.

She had agreed to work until the end of this mission working even once the men were in space via radio contact as needed. She would be there to evaluate what they were experiencing and also evaluate their stress levels in their voice and their body language and the monitors.

Once the men returned to earth after their mission she was calling it quits and going to be a full time stay-at-home mom. She looked forward to those days.

Her due date was exactly one week after the astronauts returned home. She felt her unborn child restless, never still for a moment. Once this one was born she would have three children in diapers all under the age of a year and a half.

"I'm the one that needs a psychiatrist," she said to Aitor who was at the moment her sounding board.

"What? Twins weren't enough? You and William couldn't have waited awhile to add to the family?" he asked in jest.

"Obviously not," she said rubbing her very large pregnant belly.

"I imagine Nora will want to keep up with you. She wants a houseful of kids. I never thought I wanted kids before or even a wife with the demands of my job, but now I find myself looking forward to it."

"Are you saying what I think you're saying?" Nicole asked.

He said, "I want to show you something."

She had her feet up on a chair resting trying to give her back and legs a rest.

She started to get up.

"No, stay just as you are," he said.

"What did you want to show me?" she asked.

He pulled a box out of his pocket and opened it smiling like a little boy who'd just done something he was proud of. He showed her a diamond engagement ring.

"I'm going to ask Nora to marry me tonight. Do you think she'll say yes?" he asked.

"You're taking my babies' nanny away from me?" she joked.

She admired the ring and thought to herself that she was really happy her best friend had found someone special to spend her life with.

"She'll say yes. I'm sure of it," Nicole said.

He put the ring back in his pocket.

"Please, just promise me you won't get married before the end of this mission and after this baby is born. I don't know what I'd do without her," Nicole said.

"Promise," he said with a big grin on his face as he got up to leave.

He poked his head back in the door but said, "Once that baby is born though I've upheld my end of the bargain. I'm hoping I can talk her into eloping and I'm taking her to Ireland for an entire month for our honeymoon if she'll have me."

She thought to herself that it was a good thing she was quitting her job as it looked like Nora would be married soon herself. If she knew Nora she wouldn't waste anytime before she herself was expecting.

Nicole looked at her watch and sighed knowing the men would be finished with their classwork in about ten minutes. After that it would be back to work for them and for her.

She walked down the hall with a smile on her face happy for her best friend.

86

It was the day of liftoff.

As William suited up he thought back to a night long ago when he was seven years old. It was the night he had met his wife who was six years old at the time.

He recalled looking through the telescope on the back deck of her home and Nicole showing him the moon. He recalled her exact words. She had said, 'One day you'll go there. You're going to be an astronaut and travel to that very moon that you're looking at.'

How he remembered her exact words all these years later he didn't know, but she had said it in such a matter-of-fact way that it had stuck with him and peaked his interest.

He recalled he and his family had flown into St. Augustine that very day and he had just decided he wanted to become a pilot when he grew up.

Nicole had much loftier plans for his future than a mere pilot and soon her words left such an impact on him even at the age of seven that he too longed one day to become an astronaut.

And here he was on this very day preparing to fly to the moon.

The families of the astronauts had gathered together to watch their husbands and fathers being launched into space. It would be each of their first launching experience.

William would be at the helm. He was the crew's pilot. Each of the men were former Air Force. All three were aviators and worked well together.

Rhiannon came and stood by Nicole's side. As she walked up

with her infant son in a stroller Nicole noticed the baby she was carrying suddenly became very active. She wondered if the child was feeling her own nervousness waiting in anticipation of her husband being shot into space.

"I'm so nervous. I don't know how I'll ever make it through this day," Rhiannon said.

She held up her hands and showed Nicole how her hands were shaking.

Nicole took Rhiannon's hands and held them in her own calming her friend.

"Hush now. You'll scare the children. Everything is going to be fine," Nicole reassured her.

Rhiannon nodded her head that she understood. She had her son with her that was just a few months old.

Nicole had the twins with her and another child ready to be born any minute.

Skip's wife stood off to one side not being as familiar with the other wives having only met them recently. She also had her four children in attendance.

Nicole said to Rhiannon, "I imagine to the public the astronaut's wives look like baby factories."

Rachel's youngest son was running about with a toy space craft pretending to blast off. Her other son had a Superman figure he was playing with. The two girls stood quietly. They were in awe of the huge spacecraft sitting on the tarmac.

One of the men who were there to help answer any questions the families had and take them to where they needed to be at specific times walked up to Ethan, Skip's son who was holding the Superman figure.

The man squatted down to his level and said, "Do you know what's faster than a speeding bullet?"

Ethan grinned from ear to ear, "Faster than a speeding bullet and more powerful than a locomotive, it's Superman."

The man laughed and said, "You're right but do you know that spacecraft your father is going to travel to space in is faster than a speeding bullet too."

"Really?" Ethan asked.

"I bet you didn't know that Superman came to Earth on a spacecraft?" the man asked him.

"I didn't know that," Ethan said.

After he thought about that he said, "Will my daddy have super powers when he comes home from the moon?"

"Don't you think he has super powers now? He's going to the moon. How many people do you know who have ever done that? Not even Superman."

Ethan's eyes lit up and he said, "My dad's even better than Superman."

Nicole said to Rhiannon, "Come on."

She walked over to Rachel and the three wives talked amongst themselves.

The representative who was there to take the families where they were to go to have a moment to say good-bye, albeit from a distance, informed the families their husbands and fathers would be arriving to say good-bye before they boarded *Apollo*. He reminded each of them not to cross the line.

In order to keep germs at bay and not to risk any damage to their space suits the best they could do was give air hugs and throw kisses and have a few final words from a distance.

William's last words to Nicole before the astronauts were escorted to the spacecraft was, "Don't have that baby without me."

It had been stressed by NASA to the wives that they too were representatives to the outside world and people would be closely watching them. They weren't to show nervousness or fear before liftoff. The media would have their eye on them as would the rest of the world.

A contract had been made with a major magazine who would follow the families during the days the men were in space and write of their personal lives.

Nicole, not only a wife but the astronaut's doctor and

psychologist, was of special interest to the editors of the magazine. That and the fact that it was very possible she would give birth while her husband was in space.

William's mother was there to watch her son make history. She would also be there in case Nicole went into labor, a very real possibility. The plan was that if that happened she could watch the children and Nora would go into the delivery room with her.

As the men were strapped into the spacecraft they discussed among themselves that the weather that day was beautiful. Blue skies and no threat of rain or strong winds.

"I believe today will be the day. I can't foresee any reason why this mission will be delayed," one of the crew who was aiding the astronauts into position said. "Good luck and God bless" he said as he left the shuttle.

The shuttle door was closed and sealed.

Daniel said, "I do believe my heart rate just skyrocketed. We're about to be shot off into space in a tin can."

Moments later the countdown began.

It was a moving moment for those on the ground. Especially for the families that watched as their husbands, fathers, and sons were hurtled into space.

Nicole reached for her mother-in-law's hand and gave it a squeeze. Liz had Mason on her lap while Nicole had Madison sitting on what lap she had left.

The crowds on the ground that had gathered to watch cheered as *Apollo* was launched.

87

Their years of training were over. This was the real thing.

They heard, "We have a Go for main engine start … "

With less than a minute before liftoff the ground launch sequencer handed over control of the countdown to the spacecraft's computers.

The anxious crowd waiting to witness this historic event cheered when they heard over the loud speakers, " … seven, six, five … We have main engine start …"

The spacecraft came to life. The astronauts felt the vibrations of *Apollo* like a racehorse waiting for the gates to be lowered to begin the race.

The countdown was completed.

"….And we have liftoff!" came from over the loud speakers.

Nicole silently wished her husband a momentous, safe journey. As *Apollo* lifted off she felt the child in her womb make her presence known.

After lift off Liz took the twins and headed back to the house.

Nicole had work to do. She would be sitting in with the communications between *Apollo* and Mission Control.

As *Apollo* left Earth's orbit the men gazed down at the planet they lived on floating in space. It was a sobering sight. It was like glimpsing a blue marble with white swirls through it laid out on a black velvet backdrop.

At one point they could visually see almost an entire hemisphere. They saw coastlines, deserts, rainforests and entire continents simultaneously.

They felt like they had a handle on how early explorers in history must have felt as they first laid their eyes on lands previously unknown to man.

They saw the curvature of Earth. That wasn't all they saw...

Daniel motioned to William, "Do you see what I see?"

William already had his eyes on them.

The spacecraft's speed was being matched by a convoy of UFO's who appeared to be escorting the crew.

"If I hadn't seen them before in 'Nam I would be *really* freaked out right now," Daniel said.

Once William and Daniel had finished their stints in Vietnam and were back in the states they had discussed what Daniel had seen when they were attempting to rescue William after he had been shot down over the jungles of Vietnam. When Daniel told him what he had witnessed William too admitted to having had similar experiences though he didn't go into great detail.

The UFO's made no threatening maneuvers. All the same the astronauts kept their eye on them. They had heard rumors of other astronauts in the past also seeing UFO's on their missions.

None of these observations were ever reported to the public. In fact, Mission Control had specifically warned the men to watch what they said when they were making radio transmissions if they did see something extraterrestrial. That announcement was as good as verifying that NASA knew of their existence.

William told Nicole that if he saw or experienced any UFO or alien sightings he would try to get a message to her.

She tried to talk him out of it telling him, "We already know they're out there. What's your point? Let things be. You can tell me if you see anything *after* you return home."

William was stubborn.

"Mission Control this is Major Halloway," William called out over the air waves.

"This is Mission Control. We read you."

"Is my wife Doc Halloway there as we speak?" William asked.

Perry Ward, Mission Control's ground controller looked about the crowded room and spotted Nicole seated in the back of the room. She waved to make sure he spotted her.

"Doctor Halloway is in attendance as we speak," Ward answered.

"I'd like to play our favorite song in celebration of this special day. I'm sure the world out there listening will approve," William said.

Ward looked over at Aitor director of this mission. Aitor nodded his head in approval.

Over the airwaves came the song, *'Starman'* by David Bowie.

Nicole couldn't believe he'd done it. She wasn't surprised they had seen evidence of the aliens but she couldn't believe he had the audacity to do this.

Aitor looked at her and gave her a dirty look as though this was something she and William had planned together.

Many listeners caught on to the message. It would later result in a conspiracy theory that NASA was none too happy about.

The rumors really exploded when the public put two and two together and realized that it was his father that had been in charge of Project Blue Book and had written a book on UFOs.

When interviewed after the astronauts returned home William would be asked over and over if indeed the song was meant as a message that they had seen UFO's while in orbit or on the moon. He had stirred up a hornet's nest.

She had received her husband's message loud and clear. The astronauts weren't alone. The aliens were there and had been sighted by the astronauts.

As William was preparing to step on the moon Nicole was being prepped for the birth of their daughter.

Nicole said to Nora, "It's a good thing you've stuck with me.

William for one reason or another always seems to miss out on these momentous occasions."

Nora said, "From what I'm hearing on the radio he's about to embark on a momentous occasion of his own. He's getting ready to walk on the moon."

Nicole smiled. The medical staff whisked her into delivery as this baby was not going to wait.

At the sound of a lusty wail from the newborn who was announcing her arrival one of the nurses called out, "They just announced it. Your husband is on the moon. He stepped on the moon at the same time that your daughter took her first breath."

They brought the baby over for Nicole to see. She had a headful of wispy, white hair and a fair complexion. She was much larger than the twins had been at birth arriving five days before her due date.

"You'll have to call her some space or moon name in reminder of where her dad was during her birth," her doctor said.

At the next transmission Mission Control had an announcement to make.

"Major Halloway, congratulations. Your wife has given birth. Your daughter has arrived," Ward said.

William laughed and said, "Of course she couldn't wait till I came home. Is all well with my wife and the baby?"

"Well and anxious for you to come home," Ward answered.

Aitor walked over and handed Ward a note.

Ward read the note and said, "Your wife wants to know what you want to name the baby. She said this one's on you."

William replied, "Luna. Her name is Luna."

William had one more job to do on the moon. This was his third and final time on the moon and then they would be headed home.

Before he boarded *Apollo* for the final time in the moondust he scratched out in large letters, *To The Moon And Back*.

He had Skip take a photograph of what he had written to show his wife and family back home. The public when they saw the photo thought he was saying that the United States had been here and left. Nicole understood it's true meaning. The message was for her.

The photograph was shared across the world. It was one of the most famous photos of the mission..

88

As William and Nicole rocked the children to sleep, William with a twin on each side of him and Nicole with Luna in her arms, they quietly talked.

"I don't understand how this works. Since all three children carry your DNA wouldn't all three of them carry the alien gene?"

"You would think so, but no. The alien gene isn't passed on to the male offspring."

"Then would both the girls be considered a daughter of destiny?" he asked while quietly getting up and putting the twins in their crib.

After covering the twins up and making sure they would stay asleep he came and took the sleeping Luna from Nicole's arms and put her in her crib.

Luna squirmed about for a time, a restless baby, but finally settled down and William came over and gave Nicole a hand up.

They continued the conversation as they climbed into bed hoping for a couple hours of sleep before Luna needed to be fed.

"The way I was made to understand it, from the aliens themselves mind you, a daughter of destiny which in this case would be me would have one child...a daughter. That daughter would become the next daughter of destiny," Nicole tried to explain it.

"I guess their plan got messed up when you had twins," William laughed.

"I still find it amazing that they didn't foresee that. They appeared quite shocked the night they arrived to check on their next generation only to discover I was carrying a boy, or man-child as they called him. After that I don't think they knew what to do," Nicole said.

"Is the daughter of destiny an automatic thing when the first daughter arrives? This is very confusing to me how this works. Now that we have two daughters I wonder which one it is or is it both?" William asked.

"No, it won't be both. There is only one per generation. From what I understand that keeps the strain strong and powerful. I have to wonder since Madison was a twin if she will be bypassed and Luna will be the chosen one. Or is it Madison? I really don't know and I don't feel anything as far as which one it will be. My foresight on this subject is completely blocked," Nicole said as she snuggled under the covers.

"I suppose one day we'll find out," William said.

"You know. I'm not sure how this will be passed on to one of the girls. As far as it went with me it was something they implanted within me while I was yet within the womb. I'm not sure if they will implant something within the next generation or if it is something automatically passed on through DNA."

Long after Nicole had fallen asleep William dwelled on this in his mind. He fell asleep in the middle of the night and neither he nor Nicole heard the aliens arrive and remove both girls from their cribs.

"Which one will be the next generation?" one of the aliens asked as they traveled with the daughters both sleeping.

"It is not our decision to make," the one alien answered the other.

The aliens arrived to a room where there were others awaiting their arrival. Both girls were examined. One was chosen, one rejected.

Without being detected both daughters were returned to their home and to their cribs.

The following morning Nicole said, "What time is it?"

William looked at the bedside clock and said, "6:00. I was so tired I didn't even hear you get up during the night to feed Luna."

"I didn't," Nicole said jumping out of bed to go check on the baby.

She came back in the bedroom with Luna in her arms.

"That's the first time any of them slept through the night. She slept through two feedings but it sure was nice having a full night's sleep," Nicole said.

William reached down and kissed his daughter while her mother was changing her diaper.

"What's that?" William asked seeing a red mark below her navel. He lightly touched the area. The mark was warm to the touch.

Nicole looked at it carefully and said, "It looks like she's been stuck with something. You didn't stick her with a diaper pin when you changed her last night, did you?" Nicole said while examining the mark.

"No, she would have screamed bloody murder if I had."

"Well, it doesn't seem to be bothering her. I'll keep an eye on it," Nicole said. She finished changing Luna and propped herself up in bed and nursed her while William took his shower.

Later that day when she thought to check it again the mark was gone.

"It must not have been anything too bad. The mark is already gone," she told William.

After that they never gave it another thought.

89

About six weeks after the birth of Luna the aliens made another appearance, the first one Nicole and William were aware of. Nicole and William appeared to be the only ones aware of their presence as the twins played together quietly in the room as Luna slept in her mother's arms.

"Have you come to see the daughter of destiny or our new addition?" Nicole asked the aliens quietly so as not to wake the baby.

It was a loaded question, one she thought just may give her the answer she was looking for.

"We have come to check on our daughters of destiny," one of the aliens communicated to her.

"Yes, I seem to forget that I too am one of them," Nicole responded.

"You are indeed," the alien said telepathically. "The arrival of the next generation doesn't change that."

Nicole moved the baby off her shoulder and held her in her lap so the aliens could see her.

The baby woke and opened her eyes. She appeared to look right at the aliens.

Nicole feared she would cry seeing such strange looking creatures but she merely closed her eyes and went back to sleep.

The aliens however didn't step forward to look at her. They remained where they were.

Nicole had thought she would have her question answered as to which of her daughters was the next generation daughter in destiny by watching to see which of the girls had the attention of the aliens. They made no obvious gesture revealing that answer.

"Even when you are unaware of our presence we watch over our own," the second alien said.

"Our own. I don't like the sound of that," Nicole said.

"Regardless of whether you like it or not it is so," the alien said telepathically.

"Which of the girls will be the next daughter of destiny?" Nicole asked, her curiosity getting the best of her.

"Not will be...is," seemed to be all the alien was willing to say about the matter.

"Regardless of which one it is we'll take good care of her. Nicole's a remarkable mother," William said tenderly placing his hand on his wife's shoulder.

"As will we," the alien said so both parents could "hear" his thoughts and then they were gone.

"They left as fast as they came. I wanted to find out if it's Madison or Luna who would be the next daughter of destiny," Nicole said.

"Does it really matter? We agreed to treat them all the same," William said.

"You're right of course. But it would be nice to know all the same," Nicole said as she handed the baby to William to put in her crib.

As William left the room she thought, I imagine one of these days she will reveal herself to be the one when her gifts are revealed.

Epilogue

Being premies the twins were a bit smaller than average. At three years of age Luna had caught up to them in size. She was identical in looks and mannerisms to Madison. People constantly confused them to be the twins or thought they were triplets. Mason had his own unique looks but as far as the girls went only Nicole and William could tell them apart....most of the time anyway.

Elke had come for the weekend to have some grandma time with the kids and spoil them. She couldn't tell the girls apart either and constantly confused them.

Nicole and Elke were sitting out on the beach with the children nearby building sand castles and having a wonderful time.

"The girls are so fair skinned you might want to put some sunscreen on them," Elke said to Nicole.

Nicole got up and was looking through her bag for their hats and the sunscreen when she heard a terrifying sound.

A large German Shepherd being walked on the beach by it's owner spotted the children and began barking ferociously. The owner tried to pull the dog back but in doing so the dog pulled out of it's collar and ran with teeth bared towards the children.

The owner of the dog was screaming at the dog to stop but it ran directly for the children growling viciously.

Elke jumped up and before Nicole could stand up and turn around to see anything the dog stopped dead in it's tracks, tucked it's tail between it's legs, and began whimpering and ran towards it's owner cowering.

The owner looked in amazement at his dog not knowing what to think of his dog's complete change of mannerism. He was just thankful a terrible tragedy had been avoided.

"I'm sorry," the owner yelled and took his dog and left in a hurry.

"Mom? What just happened?" Nicole asked.

Mason was crying scared of the recent events but the girls put their heads down and began playing again as though nothing had happened.

"I think....I'm pretty sure....I believe....one of the girls just stopped that dog from attacking," Elke answered still shaking from this near tragedy.

"How? What did she do?" Nicole asked.

"I think one of the gifts of the daughter of destiny has just revealed itself," she said quietly for Nicole's ears only.

Mason ran over crying throwing himself into his mother's arms.

Nicole picked him up to comfort him.

"Which one was it? Which of the girls stopped the dog from attacking?" Nicole asked.

The girls looked over at her and both smiled. They called Mason over to help them with their sand castle.

He too seemed to put the event behind him and joined his sisters.

"Which one was it? Madison or Luna?" Nicole asked thinking she would now know which of her daughters was the next daughter of destiny.

Elke answered, "I have no idea."

www.ingramcontent.com/pod-product-compliance
Lightning Source LLC
Chambersburg PA
CBHW071209250626
47159CB00001B/262